Land Shadows

by

R.J. Striegel

To all the J's in my life. You know who you are. - R.J.

Copyright Statement

Published by Open Instructional Narratives LLC
Farmington, New Mexico

978-0-9904141-6-2 Paperback ISBN
978-0-9904141-7-9 Hardback ISBN
978-0-9904141-8-6 EBook ISBN

Suggested Library of Congress Subject Headings:
Potawatomi children
Potawatomi literature
Maxwell Land Grant (N.M. and Colo.)
City and town life--New York (State)--New York--Fiction
Orphans--Fiction
Fraud--United States
Legal stories

Suggested LCC Classification and Cutter Number:
PS3569.T742 L36 2025
Suggested DDC Cutter Number:
813.6 St84L36 2025

Cover Illustration by Othmane Zidane.
Maps by Nadia Ikram and Norm Karim.
Treasure Map by Khayyam Akhtar.

Author's Note & Disclaimer

This is a work of historical fiction. While Land Shadows is based on real historical events and includes references to actual historical figures, the narrative, dialogue, and characterizations are products of the author's imagination. Any portrayals of historical figures are speculative and should not be taken as factual representations of their actions, words, or personalities.

Additionally, many characters, locations, and events in this book are entirely fictional or have been adapted for storytelling purposes. Any similarities to real persons, living or dead, outside of the well-documented historical figures, are purely coincidental.

This novel is not intended as a historical record but as a dramatized interpretation of past events. Readers interested in the historical background of this time period are encouraged to consult scholarly sources for factual information. http://www.landshadows.com contains an extensive list of the sources used in reference for this work.

Acknowledgements

Writing this book would have been impossible without the guidance of my editor and writing coach, Jennifer Goodland, who has so much expertise in so many areas this book required. Her sound experience in research methodology acquired by years of work as a college librarian and her ability to teach me these skills has made the facts in this book at most unassailable and at least defensible.

Her coaching and guidance in the mechanics of writing come from years of teaching creative writing at the college level. Her ability to suggest changes while preserving the author's voice is a unique skill as is her ability to insist with clarity and reason that the author defend passages and wording that she challenged. As a historian and a librarian specializing in misinformation, she insists on historical accuracy in the book. Hence the bibliography on the book's website contains over 400 different references.

My research took me to the Kit Carson Museum just outside of Cimarron, New Mexico. I was fortunate to meet Jesus Abreu, a guide who gave me a personal tour of the Lucien Maxwell Home. This lent an immersive experience to my description of the area and the architecture of the McNeil Ranch.

Lastly, my sister Jana Striegel was an author in her own right. She was taken much too soon by breast cancer. She remains a significant influence on my desire to write.

Contents

Chapter I: The Clearances

Saturday, August 9th, 1851
Near Castlebay
Isle of Barra, Scotland

"...That sheep would scatter the warrior and turn their homes into a wilderness"
Angus Mac Mhuirich

The plan and all the necessary steps to carry it out had been set-there was no changing it. My neighbors and friends were blinded with a glimmer of hope that things would remain as they had been. We paid our rent, the landlords raised it, we managed somehow, and we paid our rent. My friends said Colonel Gordon was not that great monster, Patrick Sellar. Their words swirled in my mind like a scythe cutting a swath into my sleep.

I bleed grief and sorrow because I knew what was to come. Mary breathes softly in her sleep. Her warm body beside me is usually a comfort, but tonight, it is a cold blade of reality. The signs are everywhere, but nobody wants to see them. They are blind. I will be forced from my home. My home is the only one my family has known since the 1600s. We are being forced out to make room for Gordon's sheep. Sheep! For God's sake! We've been here on this land since the MacDonalds and the McNeils were at each other's throats, centuries ago and when they made their peace centuries ago – and now, sheep!

I have a proud family name. McNeil, a distant relative of the McNeils who owned the Isle of Barra with Ranald George MacDonald as the chief of the clans, whose excesses and debt led him to sell out to Gordon of Cluny. Gordon is allied with Patrick Sellar, that bastard, who enacted clearances all over northern Scotland. Sellar led his army of paid-for constables and estate agents that rounded up crofters and forced them onto ships bound for God knows where. Gordon has done the same in Barra.

I've got to wake Mary up; she needs to be a part of this now. I kiss the back of her neck and run my hands over her back. She sighs pleasantly.

"James McNeil, it's too early for that."

"Mary, there's something we need to talk about, my dear. I'm sorry. We have to be quiet; we mustn't wake Murdoch and Elizabeth," I whisper.

Her brown eyes flutter open, showing a depth of concern that she hides so well during the day. Mary is a petite woman, with auburn hair that, when not braided, is tied into a simple bun held in place with a hand-sewn piece of linen. Her skin is weathered from years of hard work, but beautiful. She has a strength that never fades.

"The meeting at Castlebay with Gordon's agents? That's about the rents, yes?" she asked.

"Yes, and more. There's a meeting at Uist, too, and I don't think there's going to be much talk. Three years back, do you remember, Gordon had over a hundred crofters rounded up for passage to Nova Scotia? And he just had them dumped on the streets of Glasgow. Just left them there with nothing.... We have to leave. I will go to the meeting at Castlebay, but you, Murdoch, and Elizabeth —"

"No, James." Her voice rose a bit. "You know the fine if we don't present ourselves and our children. Two pounds sterling! We've finally caught up with the rents and the cost of the food Gordon gave us, and you want to put us back into debt?"

"Gordon means to force us onto steamers bound for some unknown place with only the clothes on our backs."

"They will not finish with us until we are all out and every croft is burned to the ground!" I had a difficulty keeping my voice down, but Elizabeth and Murdoch didn't stir.

"James, what if you're wrong? What if the meeting really is about rents? No one has been talking about being thrown onto a ship. Do you think they'd do that? What if we're to get aid from Britain? If you're wrong, we will have lost our home for nothing!"

I ignore her worry. "After I send Elizabeth and Murdoch to your sister's, we'll pack only what we can carry. After the children are asleep, I'll take our bundles to John Crawford's Arran boat. He's agreed to take us to Glasgow. Monday morning, I'll go to the meeting, and you take the children to Crawford's boat. He'll be waiting. We can always come home if they don't try to force us to board a ship. Either way, we will be safe." I pray I'm not just telling her what she wants to hear.

"After Glasgow, then? Do we settle there somehow?"

"There's nothing for us there. We go to New York. In America."

Mary shed a tear. "This is all we have, what we can see around us. Your grandfather built the furniture. I bore your two children upon this very bed. Your ancestors built this whole croft, and you have all added to it. This is where I came to when we married."

I am silent. Mary is not saying anything I haven't repeated to myself over and over again, as first we were squeezed out with the rents, and now we are at the precipice of being forced to leave. We will be rounded up like cattle and thrown on board an immigrant steamer with no care as to what awaits us at the other end.

Mary laid her head on my chest, and I held her close. "What do we take, what do we decide is most important to us? My mother's quilts, the silver set we hide from the landlord, your ceilidh fiddle…"

I've lifted the *clach cuid fir*, the manhood stones until they seemed light as anything. But her tears were heavier than all the clach cuid fir borne all at once. Her face nuzzled in my chest and then she knew.

"You sold the silver."

I was ashamed, but I did what I must. "Anything of value. It will all be taken from us anyway. Sellar, Gordon, the landlords, the English, they are one and the same, part of the system. You know how they look down on the Gaels. Our language, our customs, and even our clothing are vilified. I hear America treats their own native people this way, too. These people, they mean to get rid of us all, the people of the land. And not just because of the sheep, but because they can."

Mary's tone soured as she does when I stand up in church. "I've heard this one before, James McNeil, and you've not convinced anyone at the church or any of your friends at the public house. The wives talk, and they talk to me of their husbands' opinions. They say you're dangerous. That you will bring the wrath of God himself down onto Barra."

"If God comes in the form of Gordon of Cluny, that's as may be. But I suspect he is more of the devil himself!"

"The Reverend Beatson refused our invitation to supper –"

"Your invitation." She knows how I feel about the false prophets.

"–our invitation to supper. He says the church is against you talking so about Gordon."

"And this is from God? Gordon is in the Holy Book? Beatson's church follows the laws of man and those who would lord over their fellows, not the Lord of Heaven. They preach that we deserve what they're doing, because then we will accept it. I say that no righteous God would punish the lamb to feed the wolf."

"And I thought you were polishing the silver set to surprise me," she whispers. "Did you really think I wouldn't miss it?"

"There is no other way. We can choose our destination or let Gordon choose it for us."

She sighs. "I know, James. I know you're right. I just wish you weren't. I wish that..." And her shoulders begin to shake. She sobs from a depth that I cannot reach. I can only hold her close as the dawn approaches. Our last dawn in the croft. I think of the brutality of all this. Would Gordon and Sellar be so cold as to witness the heartache that their policies cause? What is within a man who can allow the evisceration of home and land for profit?

Mary's sobbing lessens. "Kathryn admires my quilts. I can see what else we might sell."

"I think I've sold off what I can without arousing suspicion. It's enough for our passage from Glasgow to New York."

"I know I can't go on like this, wondering when our turn will come to be cleared like so many thistles. I can't keep wondering if we'll have another week or another month. But, James, we are crofters. What will we tell Murdoch and Elizabeth? Of why we lost our home and why we had to leave? We're tied to this land."

"We cannot be tied to what we can never own. Not really."

Mary seals it off in her mind. "Then it's to be New York."

The fog is rolling in now. A light drizzle starts just when it's light enough to see. Mary gets out of bed without a word and adds more peat to the fire. I can hear the clank of the kettle as she readies the tea. I hear our milk cows moo on the other end of our blackhouse, and our chickens cluck contentedly; they are separated from us by wood and stone rail, and they begin with their demands the second they hear us moving about in the morning. I hear running feet mixed with laughter and murmured conversation, and I smell oatmeal porridge. I must remember to tell Mary to make some barley cakes for the boat. I don't feel hungry, but I pull myself out of bed and dress, then step into the main room of our little stone blackhouse.

"Papa!" cried Murdoch and Elizabeth in one voice.

Murdoch, nine, and Elizabeth, eight could be twins and act as such. Sometimes I think they talk to each other without speaking. They favor their mother, thankfully, both having auburn hair and round faces with a few freckles. The only difference one can see at first glance is their eyes. Murdoch eyes are a riveting blue. That blue no painter could paint. Elizabeth has the same warm brown eyes as her mother. Those eyes a father looks at and knows she will get her way.

"Good morning, my wee bairns. Hungry this morning, I see. Well, get your breakfast and then do your chores."

"James, do you want eggs this morning?"

"No, just tea."

"You'll have some porridge too, James; you have to eat something."

I don't argue. After breakfast Murdoch and Elizabeth feed the chickens and milk the cows. We are better off than most of our neighbors, and we help them when we can by giving them eggs, and a bit of beef when we have it, and vegetables from our garden. I try not to judge them as they accept our help, even as they complain that I'm stirring up trouble by being against Gordon's plans.

I whisper as quietly as possible and as far away from the children as possible. "Mary, we should send Murdoch and Elizabeth to your sister for the day. We can start to bundle our things."

Mary's fingers fidget restlessly. "James, two of Gordon's agents were here yesterday. You got home so late..."

"What? Who? And what did they want?"

"They said they were auditing our rent for the meeting on Monday. One of them was McBride. I didn't know the other."

"An audit? But our rent is caught up."

"They said they wanted to compare Gordon's records with our receipts. I showed them the receipts for last year. James, they snatched them from my hand and would not give them back. They said they needed them for the audit. Then they left." Mary's voice trembles as she bites her lip, her worry etched across her face.

"They'll accuse us of not paying, and we won't have proof," James worried aloud.

"I couldn't do anything to stop them."

I take a deep breath and think this is not Mary's fault. It's just another transgression by Gordon's agents, a ruse to accuse us of not paying rent so they can evict us.

"Mary, it doesn't matter. Gordon will have us off the land, with receipts or not. They'll evict us, with receipts or not."

Murdoch bounded back from the livestock area. "The cows and the chickens are fed!"

I let the matter of the rent drop. "Murdoch, you and your sister are to go to your Aunt Kathryn's to help with their harvest. They'll be expecting you. Your cousins will be glad to have you over! Be home as the sun sets."

Mary and I spend the day sifting through our lives, deciding what to take and what to abandon. I've dreaded this moment since the day I understood that there was no other path for us. But when did I truly grasp that we had to leave our home? Was it a year ago, when they began driving out our neighbors like cattle? I denied it for as long as I could, even as a gnawing sickness took hold. Not unease – a deep, gut-wrenching nausea brought on by the relentless march of grief and terror that has swept through Barra. Nauseated by the knowledge that no matter what I do, I cannot alter this grim fate.

It is as if I am looking out to sea at a ship, and she's in trouble and I can't help her. Not one that sails off never to return, but one that is just far enough away that I can't swim to it, yet close enough that I can hear the wails and see the crying, pleading faces of the men on deck. They cry to God to save them and the ship sinks beneath the cold, dark water. Close enough I can hear her timbers crack and break like bones. And on shore, I hear voices saying, "The water was calm! There's no reason the ship should sink!"

Yet it does sink.

That is Barra.

I watch Mary pack. Our home is now different somehow. Every item, every bit of furniture, every timber holding the thatch in place, and every stone in the walls is seen in crystalline sharpness. Even Mary's demeanor has changed. There is no anger in her, no resignation, just stalwart determination to see this through. More than an anchor, she defines hope.

My grandfather made this furniture. I am abandoning it. Each mark in the wood and each scratch was put there by me, my ancestors, or by Murdoch and Elizabeth. Scratches that will never be there, because they should have been left by Murdoch's and Elizabeth's children and grandchildren. I feel like I've grown up in this house, and I haven't seen it until now.

"I know this is hard," Mary said, taking a break to embrace me amid my sorrow.

I take a deep breath and look at her with resignation.

She is leaving her home too, and still, she takes the time to comfort me. "We've our memories, James, and not even Sellar or Gordon can take those from us."

"Our memories, no; they can't steal those. But they've stolen our way of life."

Mary pulls a bundle tight, leaving rope loops for us to hoist our things when the time comes. We finish packing without speaking and exchanging sympathetic glances. We have no disagreements about what to take and what to leave. We place the bundles in our bedroom and think of what to say to each other. All I can think of is to tell her that I love her.

"Mr. McNeil, shall we pick up our activities from this morning?" She knows what we both need in this moment. We hold each other.

We let ourselves get lost in each other's eyes, and we begin our gentle, experienced caresses. I want to touch her, taste her, and I move slowly down her body as though it may be my last such moment.

She grabs my shoulders and pulls me down with her legs. She grips me and moves me on my back, then moves on top of me, controlling the action, and showing her strength.

She kisses me passionately in perfect concert with her body's movements. We tremble together as one, and her soft face falls to my chest, both of us breathing deeply, slowly.

"James," she whispers, her face still nuzzling in my chest.

"Yes."

"The stone walls and the thatch roof. All of our things. They don't make us a family. We don't need them to be a family."

"True," I agreed.

Mary raised herself up and began her motions again.

"James, I do believe you are still..."

"Yes."

"Well, then," she continued, "we are to leave this bed, and let's leave it a wreck."

***

Murdoch and Elizabeth arrive home that Saturday just as the August sun sets. The evening came and went. Our familiar routines of chores, dinner, and nighttime storytelling followed its usual course. I was torn between going to church on Sunday and not going to church. Once again we would hear Reverend Beatson, the supposed emissary to God, preach about the hell that has befallen us. He'd tell us again that we'd brought it on ourselves by our sins, and that when we have our land seized and our people are oppressed, it is our lot to be patient with our oppressors. I didn't want to go. I was finished with arguing.

If we stayed at home, there would be questions. They would come to our home to check on us. We wanted to avoid suspicion, so Mary and I agreed to present ourselves to church one last time.

Sunday morning, we allowed ourselves a large breakfast. Mary had made as many barley cakes as possible before church. Murdoch and Elizabeth asked why she was making so many, but Mary explained to their satisfaction that she meant to distribute them to our needy neighbors. At church we sat in our regular pew and listened to Beatson lecture us on our sins. Familiar faces were strained with worry, and nobody listened to the Reverend's droning. We were all preoccupied with Monday's meeting, so preoccupied that none dared speak of it. As we made our way out of church, one of Mary's friends detained us.

"Mary, Mary!"

"Hello, Ellen. Please forgive me, but we don't have the time to speak right now. We've got to…"

"Elizabeth says you made barley cakes for everyone. The crops have been so poor this year on the island. It's wonderful what you're doing. I'll drop by later to lend a hand."

"No, Ellen, that won't be necessary. I've finished baking them."

"Oh, you can always use a few more."

Mary liked Ellen, but she had a way of testing her patience with her enthusiasm. "It's not a good time to come, Ellen, I'm sorry," she said in a commanding tone. "James, Murdoch, Elizabeth, we must go." We turned sharply and left Ellen, jaw dropped in confusion, standing at the church entrance.

If we meant to project normalcy as a family, I fear that we did not, but I could also see that it may not have mattered much, if at all. We made our way home, and we had the children resume their usual routines. They couldn't know of our plan in advance, and even if we did tell them, they wouldn't understand. It was hard enough for me to understand why we had to leave. For the children, it was a normal Sunday, but for me, the day would drag on until darkness came, and I could haul our bundles to the Arran boat.

Mary set to cook her Sunday roast, and she'd adopted a cheerful mood that I usually saw around the holidays. Her meal was matched, elaborate, and rich. A last meal.

"Mint sauce? Stuffing? Quite a feast, my love!" I said.

"We might as well; I can't pack all of this on the boat."

"Careful, the children might hear."

She'd just set the last of the dinner on the table when I heard the sound of knocking at the door. I opened the door, and to my anger and dismay, it was Reverend Beatson.

Reverend Beatson was a petty little man with a pinched face and narrow eyes that seemed to miss nothing. He had a way of looking down his nose at everyone, seeing himself as the expert interpreter of the Holy Bible, which he wielded as more of a weapon than a book of comfort and knowledge. Though his frame was slight and frail, his presence was overbearing, as if he were constantly measuring the worth of those around him against his own inflated self.

"Reverend," I said, my voice hard and flat.

"James." He pushed past me into our home. "Mary, this smells so grand! I tried to catch up to you at church this morning, but you seemed to be in such a hurry. I wanted to let you know I'd be able to dine with you after all. I hope you don't mind; even men of God make mistakes. It was so unchristian of me to refuse your invitation earlier. Do you forgive me?"

Mary glanced at me and barely shook her head as if to warn me not to arouse suspicion. On a day of lasts – last chores, last lovemaking on the bed, last dinner – it would have been wonderful to take advantage of my last forced interaction with Beatson.

"Of course, Reverend Beatson, there is nothing to forgive. We are delighted and blessed that you're here," she lied. "I'll get another place setting."

I was still measuring my words as Beatson strode to the head of the table, to my place, pulled out my chair, and seated himself. I rearranged the settings while Mary grabbed another chair. I sat.

"Well, James, I trust you and your family will be at the meeting tomorrow morning."

I swallowed hard. It was not a question. "Of course." I didn't know what he wanted, but I was certain that his purpose here was not to eat dinner. Beatson wasn't a man of God as much as he was a man of the landowners.

Beatson said grace. We passed the food and ate our meal. Mary had a better sense of social politics than I did, and she kept Beatson occupied with talking about the congregation's smaller affairs. Murdoch and Elizabeth asked Beatson questions about Jesus that he answered curtly and with annoyance.

Mary spared Murdoch and Elizabeth Beatson's impatience. "I think you've asked enough questions of the Reverend for now, Murdoch."

Reverend Beatson wiped his hands on his napkin, "Yes, well, Mary, that was an excellent meal. I'm surprised that you were able to come by such excellent roast beef. James, I thought you'd lost all your cattle. How was it they were lost, again?"

I was incredulous. "You know what happened to them."

Benson smirked. "You failed to keep them on your land."

"Gordon's men let them out in the middle of the night, just as they did our neighbor's cattle, and their neighbors, going from croft to croft. Then they rounded them up, claiming property by way of trespass, and any that would not be penned up, they drove off the cliff and into the sea." I'd lost the ability to measure my words as carefully as I might have liked, especially as the children were not used to seeing adults argue.

"James. I would counsel you to choose your words carefully. You have no proof. The Lord does not favor those who bear false witness against his neighbor. Do not seek to place blame when your trouble reflects your own sins! Micah, chapter 2, verse 3, remember: You crofters may make accusations against good men like Gordon, but in the eyes of God, you are stealing their property, and you place your own necks in the nooses of your sins."

I was seething at the audacity of using God for such a profane purpose. I felt Mary's pleading stare. I tried to calm my voice. "Yes, well, please kindly forgive me, Reverend Beatson. Mary, do we have any more tea for our guest?"

"Oh, no, no, I am quite full. That was a wonderful meal, Mary. James, these are evil times as the Bible says, and the Lord forgives easily. Look within yourself and admit your sins, ask His forgiveness, accept the fate the Lord has laid out for you, and encourage your neighbors to do likewise." Beatson pushed his chair back. "See me to the door, James; we must speak outside for a moment. Mary, thank you again for dinner, and may the Lord bless you."

Once we were out of the blackhouse, I didn't assault him only because I knew that this time tomorrow, my family and I would be on board John Crawford's Arran boat bound for Glasgow. This servant of Gordon claimed again to be the servant of God, and instead of holiness, he embodied all that was evil about the clearances.

"I know you see me as your enemy, James. Sometimes, the church needs to protect its existence. I'm warning you that tomorrow at the meeting, you will be accused of being delinquent on your rent. Gordon's agents will claim that your rent audit shows a deficit, and they'll demand your receipts, but since they have possession of those receipts, not all of them will be counted in your favor. They mean to send you to debtor's prison, James. Gordon grows weary of your slander and thinks emigration is too lenient, though they may expel Mary and the children. They'll be cleared from the land without you."

"Why are you telling me this?"

"I'm hoping you and your family will all come with me now to the church. I can offer you protection there. I hear rumors that you plan to leave Barra on your own. Is that true?"

I didn't trust his offer. "Your concern for my family has been noted, Reverend, but a McNeil has never turned away from an honest fight, and I'll not be the first. I will see you at the meeting tomorrow. Good night, Reverend."

"But, James —"

"Good evening, Reverend."

I stepped back into our blackhouse and closed the door. Smoke and the wonderful lingering smells from our hearth hung in the air as Mary put Murdoch and Elizabeth to bed. I stood on the stone floor and stretched up to touch the thatched roof. I remembered as I grew, stretching my fingertips, trying to touch the new thatch as my parents replaced it year after year. Then finally, I was tall enough to touch it. How proud I was! We'd use the old thatch to fertilize our fields. This year we would not be here to replace the old thatch. I wondered what the farmhouses looked like in New York.

I followed Mary to tuck in the children, and then I sat at the table waiting for Mary to finish her own nighttime rituals: rubbing unfinished sheep's fleece in her hands to make them soft. Putting up her favorite woolen shawl for the night with a bit of bog myrtle flowers folded in so the midges would keep away whenever she wore it.

"What did the Reverend want to talk to you about?" Mary asked as she sat across from me.

"Trying to persuade me to be calm at the meeting tomorrow and not incite the other crofters." I decided not to tell Mary the details, or else she'd not want me to go. I was determined to have my say and let the other crofters know that Gordon's accusations against me were false.

"I think the children are well asleep now, James."

"I'll take our bundles to the boat. I'll take the cart. I won't be long," I said.

"Cover the bundles with peat. If someone sees you, you can say you ran out and needed to gather more for the night."

I nodded and loaded what suddenly seemed like very few possessions into the cart. I headed to the little cove where John Crawford would be waiting with his sixteen-foot Arran boat. The night air was cool, and the cloudy weather only accented the darkness. I pulled back the night with a small lantern, just enough light to pass safely through the path to the cove.

I had arranged with Crawford to come on board the craft weeks before. He was somewhat short and stout, but tough and loyal, a friend to the McNeil name which still held some sway despite my distant ancestry from the original McNeils, who once owned the island. I soon saw the boat's outline as she moored in the hidden cove. John stood on the bow, peering into the darkness. He spotted my light and stepped ashore. His voice was roughened by years of enjoying the island's Scotch whiskey.

"Did anyone see you, James? Anyone follow you?"

"No, not that I could see or hear."

"Good. Come aboard then, and we can store your things in the deck compartments. They'll be well-hidden."

John had been a good friend to Barra and me, as were some of the other Arran boat skippers. They all made a fair living moving goods about the islands while avoiding the King's taxes. John was a master at many things, but he was most adept at cloaking his movements and avoiding revenue cutters. He knew the tides, the caves, and the coves that could keep him hidden throughout the Hebrides.

Arran boats were designed for this purpose. They were named after the Isle of Arran, whose resourceful folk built them with a shallow keel yet packed with hidden compartments to store goods out of sight. The keel could skip along rocky coves and be easily pulled ashore on hidden beaches. They could be fast as well. John was known to lead revenue cutters on a merry chase through the numerous straits in the Hebrides. Some captains allowed their egos to overcome their seafaring knowledge and, trying to pursue John's boat a little too close to the shore, wrecked the cutters on the sharp rocks. No one knows just how many revenue cutters were sent to the bottom of some Hebridean channel at the end of a fox-and-hound chase at John's urging, but every time we heard of his victories, we'd drink a toast to him.

"Mary, Murdoch, and Elizabeth will be here tomorrow morning. I'll be along after the meeting."

"James, I don't think going to the meeting is a good idea. You should come here with the family instead. Gordon's men might arrest you or hold you."

"I mean to have my say, John. I'll not run from Barra like the criminal they'll make me out to be. Everyone there needs to know how Gordon has fixed the rent audits." I told John about Beatson's visit and how Gordon's agents had seized our rent receipts. "But I allow they might try to run us down across the open water between Castlebay and Gunna Sound," I worried aloud.

"By the time they get a cutter after us, we'll be at the Sound, and it'll be getting dark. There's many a hideout along the coast, and they won't be able to find us," he said with confidence.

"Right, then." He knew his business.

"Bit of scotch to warm you on your way home?"

"Thanks, but no. I must be off. You've been such a good friend all these years, and I thank you for doing this for us. If I'm not here by

11:00 a.m. tomorrow morning, please see Mary and the children make it on board the City of Glasgow steamer."

"Heart of a lion, skills of a smuggler, that's me! You're welcome, James. Day after tomorrow, we'll have you all safely on board the steamer."

The moon was almost full, and it peeked out from behind a cloud. It provided just enough light to follow the path home without risking relighting the lantern. I should have been filled with dread for the morrow, but I was not. I had already mourned the loss of our home, our land, and the McNeil legacy. It was time to let go of the sorrow and move on. I made my way along the rocky moonlit path to our home and stepped inside, where Mary sat quietly at the table.

"Mary, my dear," I said, keeping my voice low, "John will expect you and the children early in the morning. You'll need to leave before the sun is up." I gave her careful directions to the cove where John's boat was moored. She knew each place and each cove on the isle, but I wanted to be sure there was no possibility that she might be unable to find him quickly. We went to bed and held each other, and there was nothing left to say. We fell asleep easily.

***

Mary nudged me awake. "James, it's time."

I had slept well without worry or burden, as if the past years of troubles dissolved like salt in brine.

"I'll tell Murdoch and Elizabeth that John asked them to fish with him this morning. They'll be excited," I said.

"What do I tell them when we get to the boat?"

"The truth. The meeting is at 9:00, and I suspect I'll say my words quickly. You'll need to take our money with you. Mary, in case..."

"In case what?"

For a moment I thought of warning her that Gordon's men may plan to have me arrested, but I thought better of it.

"Anything can happen. Once you and the children are on the boat with John, he will get you to Glasgow and on the ship for New York.

Take the money and hide it well on your person. If I'm not there by 11:00 a.m., I've told John to push off without me. No arguments. I'll do everything I can, but you must know what to do if I run into any trouble at the meeting."

"And if the meeting is only about the rent?" she said with a faint glimmer of hope.

"It won't be."

I finished dressing and picked up two barley cakes from the small crock on the table. I kissed Mary on the cheek and went in to awaken Murdoch and Elizabeth. The last such time I would do so in this house, though I tried not to think of it.

"Wake up, my bairns. I'm off to Castlebay. You must go with your mother this morning to meet John Crawford. He's taking you both fishing in his little Arran boat!" I tried to make it sound like an adventure. Mary came in to help me with the children and she slipped her hand in mine. We squeezed each other's palms.

"James. Be there." I nodded and kissed her cheek again before heading out the door.

As I crested the steep hills, the short growths of bright green grass seemed to battle the rocky outcroppings for a chance to warm the landscape. At the bottom of the hills and at the water's edge lay Castlebay. The Kismule Castle, which had given the town its name, was built on a small island nearer to the water's edge, and it had been abandoned for thirteen years ever since the Isle of Barra had been sold to Gordon of Cluny.

The sight of Castlebay was familiar to me, but this time as I crested the last of the hills, I was startled out of my fast paced hike. I sat on a rock, squinted, and stared at an immigrant steamer moored in the harbor. Freighters bringing supplies among the islands of the Hebrides were a common enough sight, but the steamers carried passengers to and from Glasgow, not the smaller isles. I'd hoped that perhaps she'd limped into Castlebay needing repairs, but I suspected better.

I quickened my pace, jogged down the steep hill to the church, and arrived early. The old stone church had walls darkly streaked from centuries of rainfall. The assault of the water on the stone gave the church the appearance that it was weeping. The door was open for early visitors, and I walked inside to greet my friends. We'd all gathered to wait for Gordon's men to arrive and begin their accusations, and without any other purpose we milled about the pews like worker ants who had lost their queen. A few talked in murmurs. A few acknowledged my presence.

"How much do you think they'll raise our rents?" asked one.

"We're barely making it now," complained another.

"What's the steamer doing in the harbor?" I heard.

The church's stained-glass windows were small, just twenty small panes held in place by metal frames in each of the four walls. They let but little light into the sanctuary, and it was difficult to see. The cloudy weather further refused us the light from outside, but I could see well enough to know that Beatson was nowhere to be found.

I stepped up to the altar.

"I must say my words to you all."

The murmurs quieted for a moment, and then a voice boomed out from the back of the church, near the open doors.

"We need not hear any of your talk, James McNeil. Your name gives you no right to assault our ears! We've heard enough from you in your cups at the pub!"

"Aye, that!" someone else called out.

"I'm finished trying to convince you that we're to be cleared from our homes, but you need to know you'll be hearing a lie about me from Gordon himself. I want you to know the truth before you hear the lies."

"What's the lie, then?"

"Gordon's men were at my home on Friday last, telling Mary that they needed my rent receipts for an audit. I've been warned they will alter those receipts and accuse me of being in arrears. They'll use this as an excuse to arrest me and send me to debtor's prison."

I stared into the faces of my friends. I heard horses and wagons drawing up to the church. The sharp, menacing baying of hounds came with them. Children, instantly put ill at ease, clutched at their parents.

"Gordon's agents are out front!" someone yelled. "There must be thirty of them! They've got ropes and shackles to hand – they mean to bind us like sheep trussed to market!"

Men with their wives and children lagging behind surged out of the church, some through the front door and some through the back. Gordon's men and their dogs covered both entrances; some rushed through the front of the church and began striking the parishioners as they attempted to flee. I was frozen at the pulpit; not with fear but trying to decide which way to run.

"You can either get into the wagons by choice, or we will tie you and throw you in!" the agents yelled out.

"James was right! They mean to throw us on the steamer!" cried a crofter.

The women screamed, the children cried, the men cursed. Gordon's men were ruthless. They clubbed the crofters with truncheons where they huddled in the church. Man, woman, or child; all were treated brutally. They bound and shackled the hands and feet of whomever they caught, dragging them out and tossing them in cages. The children in their path were shoved to the ground or picked up and carried to one of the cages. No one was spared. Anyone attempting to run off had to contend with the dogs. Wives who had not yet been captured remained, attempting to give aid to the wounded, only to become seized themselves.

In God's name I did not think this moment would be so horrific.

I heard a group of Gordon's men yelling my name. "There's McNeil, by the pulpit! Gordon doesn't want him in the ship, but in prison! Grab him!"

I wanted to save everyone, but that chance had been long lost before this day. I ran to the back door of the church. Though Gordon's men were thick, and ready to attack, I set to charge them nonetheless. I kicked at a hound and it howled. Still the men smiled with dark, dead eyes and bared teeth.

"They want McNeil, lads!" yelled someone from the crowd. "Don't let these bastards have him!" It was one of my neighbors. Then another, and another, and then they crowded around me fighting off Gordon's men and pushing me through the rear door. "McNeil, we'll get you out of here – now make a run for it!"

Those who had been so vocal in their criticisms now saved my life for the sheer pleasure of denying our oppressors one single thing. I was not out of danger, but I was outside. Blood was everywhere. Skulls split open, the screams of women and children, the wails and curses of families bound in cages and ready to be hauled off in carts. The noise filled the August air.

I ran. I glanced over my shoulder to see the thugs held back by everyone remaining standing. The sounds of this tragedy faded behind me as I ran along the coast to where my family awaited me in John's Arran boat. Two of the thugs, hired policemen, had broken from the crowd and were close behind me wielding their clubs and ropes in hand. A hound closed at my heels, and I grabbed a sharp rock. I hurled it at the animal's front leg, and it went down with a shriek. I thought for a moment I should head in another direction and lead them away from my family, but I reasoned John and I stood a good chance of fighting them off.

I topped the small hill leading down to a hidden cove and spotted the Arran boat and John and Mary on her deck. I jumped in as Gordon's men reached the water's edge. One of them grabbed the mooring line and started to board the boat.

John brought down the body of a hand spike onto the thug's hand. The man howled in pain. "You broke my hand, you goddamned bastard!"

John glared at the men who backed off to the shore. He pointed the sharp end of the bloody spike at them. "You touch this boat again, and I swear on all that is holy that I'll split both your heads open and feed your godless bodies to the sharks!"

The men looked at John and each other trying to decide what to do, but John did not allow them any choice. He hopped out of his boat raising the hand spike high above his head and screamed, "Now is when I'd be running!" They fell over one another making their escape. The injured man cradled his broken hand, turned, and shouted, "We'll be burning your home to the ground, McNeil! All you damned crofters! To the ground!" And they disappeared over the hill.

"Release the mooring line, James, and cast us off! We'll be lucky to make the Gunna Sound before we lose the light!"

I tossed the line into the boat and jumped aboard, grabbed the oar, and joined John in pushing her off. We reached a rhythm to the sea of Hebrides, the two of us rowing while Mary manned the rudder with the experience of many a Barra seagoing lass. John called to Murdoch and Elizabeth, "Push the panels away now, and come out of your places!" Our little stowaways did as they asked, and they were soon on deck, their faces dirty and streaked with tears. They seated themselves close to Mary as John and I put our backs into the oars through the calm sea waters.

I thought of the turmoil that my neighbors and friends were experiencing at the very moment of our escape. The sun came out, and for us the seas were quiet but my mind wasn't. As if to spoil any attempt at feeling the safety that our little Arran Boat afforded us, dark rolling plumes of smoke began to dance from the Isle of Barra to the blue morning sky. My mouth was dry, I felt sick, and I thought that the chase had merely paused.

"Papa, what's that smoke doing?" Murdoch asked.

I looked at Mary whose tears glistened on her cheeks in the sunshine. She held Murdoch and Elizabeth tightly, then said, "That's our home saying its goodbye to us, and wishing us a safe and wonderful journey to our new home in America."

I nodded, and John said simply, "Aye." He pulled his oar with ferocity and anger.

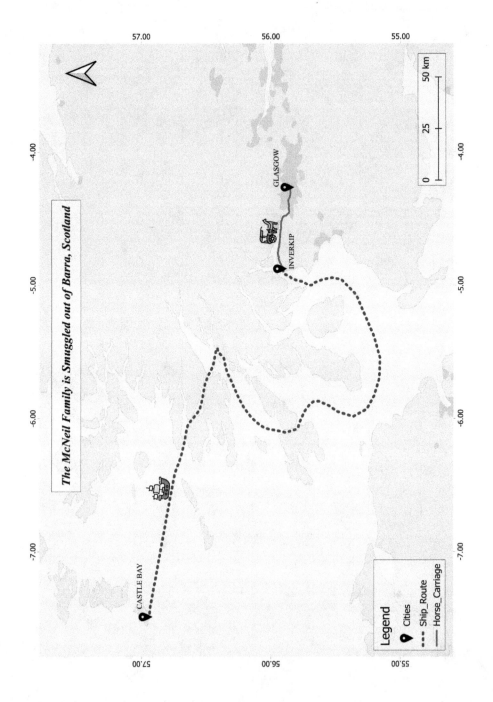

The McNeil Family is Smuggled out of Barra, Scotland

Chapter II: H.M.S. Badger

Monday, August 11, 1851
Sea of Hebrides

"Sometimes one side wins, sometimes the other, but there is nearly always a splendidly exciting tussle before either party can claim victory."
Edward Keble Chatterton, Kings Cutters and Smugglers 1700-1855, 1912

We pulled the Arran boat's oars through the blue calm waters of the Sea of Hebrides. I saw the smoke rising from Barra. The smoke came from our homes, the fire set by Gordon's men. Our lives went up into the air and streaked the sky. A light easterly wind kept the black smoke well in our sights even as the Isle of Barra disappeared over the horizon.

We were making for Gunna Sound, with any luck. Gunna Sound was a narrow rocky strait between the Isle of Tiree and the Isle of Gunna. Like many of the waters around the Hebrides and the Scotland coast, Gunna Sound was dangerous to navigate except by one who knew it. How John could slip through these waters even in the darkest, foggiest night was like its own magic to me. He'd won this skill through years of experience smuggling tea, rum, and everything else he might wish to avoid the King's Tax.

We had to make more haste than I liked. The confrontation with Gordon's men cost us time and likely our hope of making it through the strait before darkness. But even as the darkness closed in on us, and we cut through these waters, we were safe, a lot safer than the others.

Murdoch and Elizabeth huddled under their blankets. John and I rowed. Mary manned the tiller, using it to hold the boat on a straight course. She'd passed out barley cakes and encouraged the children to eat, but they did not, and they fell asleep clutching their cakes in their hands. We saw a few boats, mostly fishing boats from the surrounding islands. John swept his trained eyes along the horizon and peered over his shoulders regularly. I kept a sharp watch, too. John had told me to look out for the revenue cutters, which could easily overtake us, board us, and arrest us. Thankfully, none were in sight.

"Looks like no one is trying to chase us down," I said in a low voice.

John looked cautiously triumphant. "Gordon's probably furious that you all escaped. They're busy dealing with the rest of Barra, loading everyone onto the steamers. They won't send a cutter after a single crofter." Aside from this bit of optimism, we rowed the Arran boat in silence for miles through the open water.

Murdoch and Elizabeth awoke, their half-open eyes full of questions. Very little had been said to their mother or me, but Murdoch and Elizabeth occasionally whispered to each other. They had started the day thinking they were going fishing with John, only to be told when they reached his boat that they were leaving their home, never to return. What could I have said to the children? Mary looked at me, then at them, then back at me, pleading for some comfort.

"Murdoch, Elizabeth, you are being very brave right now. You've been brave all day, and I need you to be brave a little longer. Your mother and I love you very much, and we are so proud of you." I paused. "Someday in the future, I can explain everything to you, but right now, you might not be able to understand it."

I don't really understand it either, I thought.

"Did they put everyone on the ships?" asked Murdoch.

"Aye," I answered.

"Even Aunt Kathryn and our cousins?" asked Elizabeth.

"Aye."

"I'm afraid so," said Mary.

John and I kept rowing. Murdoch was upset. "I don't understand why we had to go!" he blurted out. "I want to go home!"

Someday might have to be now. "Even though our family worked real hard on our land, and we were there for longer than anyone living can remember, we did not own anything. Gordon of Cluny owns everything. He gets to decide who can stay and who cannot stay on his land. It isn't fair, but it happened."

Murdoch, ever trying to work out the angle, asked, "Papa, can we own the land where we are going?"

"I hope so. Murdoch, land is everything. Do whatever you have to in this life to acquire it, and do whatever you have to in this life to keep it. Do you understand?"

"Everything I have to do to get it, and to keep it. I understand, Papa," he answered.

Finally, Murdoch and Elizabeth ate their barley cakes and asked Mary for another. Then, bellies full, they settled into the gentle rocking motion of the Arran boat. They fell asleep on each other's shoulders. I grew weary as well, and Mary took a turn at the oars. I sat at the tiller guiding the rudder. The clear day had turned into twilight, and the evening clouds returned as usual. Fog rolled in across the ocean.

The Isle of Tiree and the Isle of Gunna came into sight on the horizon, but the fog cast a film over them and made them unclear. The temperature dropped. I gave John a break at his oar, and he took over at the tiller. Murdoch and Elizabeth pulled their blankets in closer. John seemed more intense, peering out into the fog, which grew ever thicker until we could not see Tiree, or Gunna, or even twenty feet in front of us. How quickly the fog closed in around us!

John held a hand up, signaling us to be quiet. The sound of something, I could not tell what, splashed on the water.

"Hear that?" I whispered.

"Papa…" Elizabeth sleepily called out. Mary held her finger up to her lips.

It was a ship. It was close in the water. We could not see it, but we had heard it; we heard the bow breaking the water as she moved through. The sound in the fog seemed to have no direction, as if a ghost ship moved out there. Then, suddenly, she appeared in front of us, passing in a northwestern direction at an angle to our southeasterly course. She passed within a few yards, and I saw her nameplate: The *H.M.S. Badger*. We were lucky she didn't cut us in two.

John switched with Mary; he was at the oar, and she was back at the tiller. We heard yelling come from the deck of the cutter.

"There! Off the aft and to the port side! Arran boat a few yards out!"

"Put your back into it, James!" John exclaimed. "She's too big to slip alongside! We'll make for the inlet at Gunna Sound so she can't maneuver around. Pull hard! Mary, make for a diagonal with your rudder; follow the angle of my arm!" He stretched out his arm briefly to give her guidance.

The fog became even more dense and thick, and we could now see only two or three feet out. We were moving blind, but so was the revenue cutter. I knew we were moving away from her now, and the splash of her bow was not as near. The orders on the deck cut through the stillness.

"You! On the Arran boat! By order of Captain Mercer of the *H.M.S. Badger*, heave to! Cease rowing immediately!"

"Will they fire on us, John?" asked Mary.

"No, they must show us their stripes and fire a warning shot first. They can't do that if they can't see us. Keep rowing; we're in the soup, and so are they. They're as blind as we are. Mary, take this direction now." He signaled forty-five degrees to starboard. Then forty-five degrees in the opposite direction. He guided Mary in a zig-zag course. After an hour of aggressive rowing and evasion, we were finally out of range of the revenue cutter.

"Okay, James, let's stop rowing for a moment and listen."

We could not hear a sound and we could see nothing in the dark and the fog. John knew the islands well and would be able to guide his Arran boat safely to one of the sandy coves in the sound between Gunna and Tiree.

"I don't think Cap'n Mercer will try the Sound in this fog. He'd be a fool. I had a run-in with him before, and he grounded the *Badger* once in the chase. He won't be trying it again."

We continued toward Gunna Sound then. The fog lifted partially, and the sky remained cloudy and starless. It was difficult to see over the water, but I was not worried. Smugglers like John worked at night, at home in cloudy, rainy, foggy weather, when it was difficult for the Revenue agents to see them and even harder to give chase in treacherous waters. We did not talk openly about John's smuggling on

36

Barra, but this I knew about him.

Finally, the sea grew calm and windless, but we still could not make out the shapes of Gunna and Tiree as we continued to approach the shore. Instead, we navigated by listening to the sounds of the shoreline. The ocean changed as it met the rocks and John knew their patterns as well as his own face.

"Mary, come take my oar. I'll take the rudder and guide us close. We'll follow the shoreline until we get just south of Gunna, and then we'll put ashore there until tomorrow's light. Then we will row onward."

Mary and I rowed slowly through the night, still difficult for us to see. The little boat had a shallow keel and was built for skipping close along the coasts. John could maneuver with little fear of hitting the jagged rocks. The clouds started to part, and the fog moved just enough to allow some moonlight. The full moon would not deny its light from us much longer, and then John could find the cove.

Suddenly we'd regained our visibility on the water, and at once, the *H.M.S. Badger* appeared still in pursuit as much as the becalmed waters would allow. We heard the sound of falling canvas, and the sails on the big ship fell but did not bow out with any wind. The *Badger* was too far off to drop her away boat and overtake us by rowing. Then the breeze started, and her sails began to fill. We rowed furiously.

"She must have maneuvered around and then circled back on us, then just lay still in the water waiting for us to pass into the Sound," John called out.

"Will she overtake us?" I asked.

"She can't get close enough on these rocks, or she'll wreck. Most likely she'll drop one of her boats and give us a fine chase. If we can make the cove without being seen, we should escape her."

"And if she does see us?"

"Can't we just row through the Sound?" Mary asked.

"Then we'll be playing hide and seek all night. Captain Mercer is a stubborn cuss, and he holds a grudge. He'll not give up unless he's got a reason to. If we head through the Sound, then she'll catch us for sure on the other side. That's open water."

I thought it was my nervousness at being overtaken and captured, but I believed I saw figures outlined by the moonlight scrambling aboard the deck. Maybe the creak of heavy iron rolling on timber. It wasn't my nervousness, and I heard a shot come from the *Badger*. John heard it, too. He let go of the tiller and raised his spyglass.

"By the Lord! He's raised his stripes and fired the warning shot! But he can't overtake us unless he gets more wind in his sails. He wants us to think he can sink us!"

"What's happening?" Elizabeth cried, wakened by the commotion. "I'm scared!" She began to cry. Murdoch sat still in the boat with no fear on his face. He comforted Elizabeth. Mary and I rowed with all our might.

"John," Mary asked fearfully, "should we give up? For God's sake, the children! Why shouldn't we let them board us? Maybe they won't arrest us after all?"

"You and James are my friends. I wouldn't have done this for anyone else. But I am also a smuggler, and I've got money to make. I wouldn't travel all the way to Glasgow with an empty boat. The rope – smell it."

She did so. "Tobacco!"

"Yes, old smuggler's secret. The rope is woven hemp-tobacco mix, and there's a false bottom in the boat filled with French brandy. We cannot allow them to board. They will know in an instant."

"Well then, we must make it to the cove," she said.

"Aye! We can make it. He's already too close to shore, and he knows from our last match that the bottom is too rocky for him. He'd have to stop and drop his away boat if he wants to give chase, and that takes time he doesn't have. He'll never catch us," he said with the confidence of someone used to working outside the law.

"What about the cannon?" I asked.

"He thinks we've got a load of tea and brandy, and he's half right, which means he wants his share of the prize, and so do his men. He'd rather not have his loot at the bottom of the sea. Now row as fast as you can, you two! I'll get us to safety in no time!"

Once again I heard the sound of cannon fire. It echoed across the water, but just as John said, the cannonball dropped nowhere near us. Elizabeth and Murdoch were wide-eyed, but John did not flinch.

Another shot from the ship flew well over our heads and splashed harmlessly twenty yards away.

"She'll not fire another," John predicted. "We're too small for them to waste so much shot on a few jugs of brandy."

He knew his business. He guided the Arran boat close to the shore of Gunna Sound and into a small cove beyond a ring of jagged rocks jutting out of the water. Mary had stamina beyond my comprehension, and she continued to pull the oars, though her hands blistered and her muscles ached. She was silent and angry that John had risked our lives over tobacco and liquor, but John faced choices no better than the ones we had. It would have been worse to stay on Barra.

John slipped us to shore, jumping out of the boat and into calf-deep water. I did the same, and we pulled the boat onto the beach, the ankers of brandy and gin in their barrels in their hiding places, the excess jugs bouncing off the sandy bottom beneath the boat. It was chilly on the beach, but we dared not light a fire lest the revenue cutter finds its wind and continues its pursuit. I retrieved the last of the barley cakes we'd brought with us, and John shared the bread and cheese he'd packed. He pulled a half anker of brandy from behind a concealed panel, and we each drank a small glass.

"First class fare!" he joked. "And for steerage price!" He poured himself another glass. "At sunup, we'll put out the fishing gear and bring in some breakfast. Then, we'll cross the open water between Gunna Sound and Treshnish on the Isle of Mull. From there we will follow the coast."

"Won't the customs boats be along the coasts?" asked Mary.

"No, just like us smugglers, the customs boats drop at night to search the coves and inlets. During the day, they aren't looking."

"Where are we landing?" I asked.

"We'll land at Inverkip. From there, it's a three-mile walk to Glasgow, but I have some connections there where I drop my goods. They'll take you and your things by cart to Glasgow Harbor. It's all been arranged, part of the first-class service. Murdoch, Elizabeth, you'll have quite a tale to tell your children someday!"

"It's a good night to navigate by the stars. Murdoch, Elizabeth, you can see the constellations. There's Hercules; he was very strong. And there's Aquarius, holding a jug of water as it spills at his feet." I tried to remember as many of the old tales of the stars my father taught me to look for during tough times.

"James," Mary whispered, "they're already asleep." Mary and I pulled the blankets close around us, and she soon followed them. She breathed deeply and regularly, but I was restless, expecting to hear a boat launched from the *Badger* at any minute. I glanced at John, and he was awake as well, staring out onto the sea. I dozed as much as I was able.

As daylight found our cove, John was already up and checking the boat. We loaded the children inside, and Mary steadied the oars as John and I pushed the boat off. John dropped his fishing lines using ragworms for bait. Murdoch and Elizabeth pulled in grey long-snouted dogfish and flounder, laughing at the way they flopped in the bottom of the boat. We saw Men-of-War, revenue cutters, luggers, and Arran boats like ours, but none paid any attention to our little crew. We were just one of many ships on the water, and the closer we approached to the Firth of Clyde, the more ships provided us this cover.

John landed the Arran boat outside the port of Glasgow at Inverkip and met with a group of men who unloaded his goods. Just as promised, they took us and our belongings by cart to the port of Glasgow, leaving us off at the shipping passenger office. One of the men handed me a worn copy of a pamphlet called "Out to Sea: The Immigrant Afloat" and nodded at it.

"Best read that before you buy your ticket contracts," he said. "You'll be needing some supplies you've not brought with you, if you're to make the trip successfully." He only exchanged these words and nothing more.

We went inside and rested on the office benches. Murdoch and Elizabeth were quiet, but their eyes darted about in excitement and discovery. Mary and I read through the little booklet, which was written for people with more means than we now possessed. I bit at the inside of my lower lip and wished I was able to afford better for my family.

I stepped to the ticket contract window and asked the agent for information on any available passages to New York. There were two: The *City of Glasgow*, leaving Thursday, and the *Sarah*, leaving in two hours. The agent gave the price and how long each voyage would take. I sighed and walked back to Mary.

"Ticket contracts on the are six pounds six per contract. She takes fourteen days. Single screw, steam driven."

"That's almost all we have, James," Mary worried.

"I know. Steerage contracts for you and me on the *Sarah* are three pounds and three quarters each. The children are not charged. She'll take thirty-eight days to cross. Square-rigged wooden-hulled ship. She's slow, but she'll get us there. Help me with our things. We need to give them to the agent so they can store them in the hold. Take anything you think we'll need out of the bundles. We won't be able to get at the rest until we get to New York."

Mary rummaged through the bundles for a change of clothes for each of us, along with two books, plates, tableware, cups, and bedding. We'd started teaching Elizabeth and Murdoch to read the Queen's English even before they attended the church school. Murdoch was especially fond of reading and preferred reading to us rather than the other way around.

We carried the bundles to the counter, purchased two ticket contracts in steerage, and waited to be called on board. The guidebook advised that we hurry onto the ship as soon as we were called, as the best berths were quickly spoken for. Agents soon made the boarding announcement, and a grand bustle of two hundred passengers made their way toward the ship, we four among them.

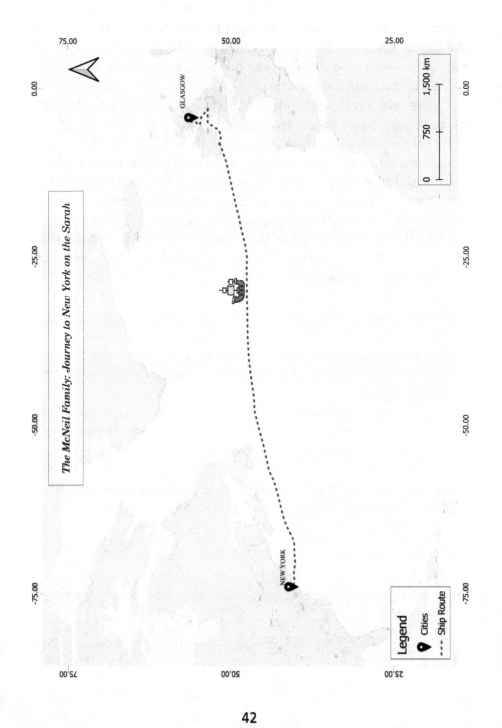

The McNeil Family: Journey to New York on the Sarah

Chapter III: Sarah

Tuesday, August 12, 1851
Onboard the Sarah
Glasgow to New York

"But since it falls into my lot,
That I should rise and you should not...."
Sir Alex Boswell, The Parting Glass, 1770s

The ticket steward barked orders into the disorganized masses. "Passengers to the left, first and second-class passengers only! To the right, steerage class! Have your ticket contracts out! Come on now! To the left, first and second class ticketed passengers! To the right, steerage!"

"Mary, hold tight of Elizabeth! I've got Murdoch!"

We hurried to the gangplank, where we ran into the wall of passengers, who were in long lines looking to board. Babies and children were crying, squealing, and screaming. The voices of over two hundred people made for an incoherent hum.

"I can't hold onto Elizabeth and the bundle at the same time! I dropped one!"

"Wait! I see it! Oh no!" I cried out. "Murdoch! Grab my belt! If you don't, you'll be lost!"

"Papa!" Murdoch yelled.

"Hold on tight!"

The young man behind Mary tripped on the package that she dropped and fell flat. I helped the man up, thinking that he'd be angry, but he was not, not even in this great teeming circus of people. He stood a head shorter than me and was very stout, his disheveled thick red hair seemed to fit the chaos that surround us but his demeanor was calm, compared to those pushing to hurry abroad.

The man picked up the package and handed it to Mary, who smiled.

"No harm done, just mind you don't lose the bairns in all the chaos. It's all a bit confusing, isn't it?" the man said.

"Yes, thank you," said Mary.

"Thank you!" added James.

"Ahh, Scottish sir? Name's Dan'l Redfall, and I know, my locks match my moniker!"

"James McNeil. Isle of Barra. My wife, Mary," I said, nodding to Mary.

"Isle of Coll, myself. Say, that business over in Barra. Heinous! Absolutely heinous! And Uist, too! Shameful!"

"What did you hear?" I asked.

"Step forward now! Tickets out! First and second class to the left, steerage to the right!" The din rose as if to prevent conversation. The crowd jostled.

"Too noisy — we are well met!" Dan'l called out.

We turned, stepped forward, and gave our ticket contracts to the steward. We were onboard, carried by the crowd along 's deck with its uneven, worn boards. We flowed like water into the open steerage hatch. We hadn't had as many in the whole of the Hebrides as was on this ship, it seemed — but islanders know to follow the flow, whether the ocean or the masses. In this way we went down the hatch, down the wide stairs, no railing, nothing except the flowing crowd to keep us upright and a member of the crew shouting to keep it all going.

"Awright, steerage passengers down through the hatch tween-deck! Come along now, don't push! Mind where you step! On down, tween-deck!"

At the bottom of the stairs, a steward directed us further. "Spinsters all the way forward to the front of the ship! Single men to the area just aft of their section! All family members, your area is to the stern!" Then, the steward started his speech over and over and over as more of us came in.

"Am I a spinster?" asked Elizabeth.

I chuckled, "No, you are not. A spinster is an unaccompanied girl."

"Oh, I'm glad I'm not that! I don't want to be without you. I'm not un-company!" Elizabeth announced. Mary chuckled and gave her little hand a squeeze. I even caught a few smiles in the near part of the crowd.

We had been on the lee side of a big burly chap, who moved in front of Mary and me. In his thick brogue, he paused at the bottom of the steps to ask the steward a question. "Say, where are –?" he tried to ask.

The steward put his hand in the middle of the Irishman's back and gave him a gentle push. "Don't have time for that now; the second mate will address you all before we shove off!"

"Say! You'll be leaving your hands off me, there!" he said, pulling away.

"Another word from you, Irish, and you'll be off this ship and not portside, either! Go on or get off this ship! Don't matter to me either way!" The Irishman did not say another word and continued to make his way with the rest of the single men to their area.

The stairs were steep and slick from moisture coming in off the harbor. We held our belongings tight to our chest with one arm and, with the other, held onto Murdoch and Elizabeth. It was a balancing act with our Irishman no longer parting the way. I caught the heel of my boot on the next to the last stair and slipped. Dan'l was close behind me, grabbed my coat, and put me back on balance. When we reached the bottom of the stairs, I turned to thank Dan'l, but he had already started to the bow of the ship after the big Irishman, so we began to move to the stern, looking for a pair of open berths among the other families.

The berths were stacked on top of each other two deep along both the port and starboard sides. They were simply constructed: hardwood upright supports and pine or cedar flat planks about six feet long, atop it a straw mattress covered with muslin. I had to crouch my own six-foot frame slightly to keep from bumping my head on the decking above. I looked for a water closet but did not see one. Slop buckets were fastened by hooks intermittently along the narrow aisle. There were no dining tables or chairs, as we were meant to eat wherever we could. Even as the hatch was open, the air smelled foul of feces, urine, and vomit. What horrors would the compartment smell like in a few days...?

There were few scuttles along the sides of the ship, and all berths that had any glimpse of fresh air were taken. Still, we found a place next to one that had a small scuttle. It was open, but its small size allowed little of the fresh sea air into the tween-deck area. I had counted the places as we walked along, and we were just shy of midway to the stern of the ship in the eighteenth row – not as close to the hatch as I had hoped, but we would make do.

"Murdoch, Elizabeth, take your bedding and fix up your berths as you'd like. You're on the bottom; Mother and I will take the top."

Mary and I tossed our bedding onto the top bunk. Our little handbook that John's associate gave me said children should be placed in the lower berths, and I could see how with their need for fresher air and lack of sea legs. I could picture Elizabeth rolling out of bed and taking a five-foot fall! The berths were only about two feet wide, and the top berth had only a foot of clearance to the top deck. It would be cramped but survivable.

I peered toward the hatch, wondering when the stream of passengers filing down the aisle would end. A young man of not more than twenty-five passed in front of us, then paused and motioned to our belongings in the upper berth.

"Ja, you are not claiming two berths?" He asked in a thick German accent. "The children should not take up a full berth, I will take the top one above you, and your children go with you."

I heard a voice through this moving mangle of people say in German, "These berths are taken anyway; they're in the family section, not the single men's section."

"Yes, okay, please excuse me," said the young German, who turned and started back up the aisle. Dan'l had once again come to our aid.

"I told him the upper berth was taken, and this was the family section. I saw our German friend in the bachelor's area, and he couldn't find a place he was happy with," Dan'l said, chuckling.

"Dan'l!" I exclaimed. "I didn't have time to thank you for helping me keep my balance. I would not know, but it seems you speak German well."

"*Ein bischen, a little,* Fairly well. My father was Scots and my mother, German. I apprenticed as a stonecutter to my grandfather in Bremen back when I was fourteen. We'll all have a meeting with the second mate, and he'll explain all the rules of the ship before we set off."

"You've been on lots of ships before, then," Mary said.

"Often enough, never to the colonies. Don't worry about the kids or your belongings; these ships don't tolerate thievery or anyone trying to bully passengers. Still, watch yourself. Cramped ships make the kind, kinder – and the mean, meaner."

Dan'l excused himself off to the single men's hold. Not long afterward, a crewman walked down the middle of the hold. "Meeting now at the hatch! Meeting now at the hatch!" he shouted.

I told Murdoch and Elizabeth to stow everything underneath the blankets and make sure our things were out of sight. We made our way to the bottom of the stairs leading up to the hatch. Already the salty sea air drifting in from above was a welcome change from the smells of too many people. We stood near Dan'l, who could no doubt answer any questions we might have better than a remote, disinterested crewman. Murdoch and Elizabeth, always helpful children, occupied some of the less patient children by making faces and crossing their eyes.

The crewman spoke from the top of the stairs. "I am second mate, Nathaniel Leonard. We have 181 passengers in steerage class for this voyage to New York. We have strict rules, and they are strictly enforced.

"Listen carefully. Water closets are located on deck to the starboard side. That's the right side from where you stand. Steerage passengers are only allowed on deck in the white chalk line area. When seas get rough, the hatch will be shut tight. If you have a berth with a scuttle, you must close the scuttle when the hatch is closed. Should the water closets be occupied, slop pails are located on the floor. Use them and empty them out as soon as possible. And make sure they are fastened tightly when not in use!"

Over the next half hour, Second Mate Leonard divided us into groups of eight adults. Each group appointed a manager responsible for drawing food, assigning the cleaning, and representing our concerns to the steerage steward. We elected a Mr. Greenly as our head man, reasoning that with all the children he had, he must know how to keep folks in line. We set up a rotating cooking schedule. The ship would provide us with water for cooking, tea, and cleaning at 8:00 in the morning and 5:00 in the afternoon. No lanterns should be lit after 10:00 in the evening or before 7:00 in the morning. Each passenger would take turns cleaning once a day, and slop buckets cleaned after each use if possible. Single men were to have additional responsibilities since many of us would have enough to do watching over our children.

As the meeting ended, Dan'l and I went to the steerage area of the deck to gulp the fresh air while we waited to strike off.

"Sounds like most of us here are Scots," I said.

"Seems so," said Dan'l as he pulled out a cigarette. "A lot of us have heard what happened at Barra and Uist."

"Aye. I went to Gordon of Cluny's meeting at Castlebay. It was to discuss rents with a two-pound fine for every man, woman, and child who didn't attend. But there'd be no reason to compel the children to come, and I thought it was a ruse to round us all up. Nobody would listen to me." From below decks, I heard Mary chatting with the women of our group, and I heard Murdoch and Elizabeth delighting the other children with their tricks and faces.

"People are incensed. I don't know what we can do about it, but we've got our anger. Did you know John McDougal? I heard Gordon's men chased down his family, caught John and his wife, bound them, and threw them on board a ship headed for Canada. His daughters were left on Barra alone."

"Aye, good friends. The girls would come to our place for ceilidh. Good singers and dancers. The older one played our fiddle. That's gone, too, burned with the rest of our croft. We could see the smoke rising as we left. Everything either burnt or stolen."

Dan'l let me know that most of our kith and kin at Barra who were still alive were forced onto a ship called the *Admiral*. I thought when we got to New York, we might see who we could track down as Canada did not look too far away from there on the map. I related our family's own escape, but as John was still an active smuggler in the Hebrides, I didn't want to jeopardize his business by naming him or his boat. Dan'l seemed to be genuine, but these were difficult times, and I'd had my share of allegiances crumbling around me of late. Any news Dan'l had, however, was most welcome. Information could only help as long as it was not exaggerated gossip.

Elizabeth scrambled onto the deck and tugged at my pants. "Papa! Papa! Look what my new friend gave me!" She held out a small doll just like the muslin-covered straw dolls I used to make for her in Barra. Her favorite, Lorna, had stitched eyes nose, and mouth. I'd forgotten to pack any of them. I tried not to think of her dolls burning along with everything else.

Mary came up on deck close behind her. As though she knew already, she said, "She asked about them. I told her not to bother you about it. She's got a new one."

"It's just that we left so much behind."

A gust of wind caught Dan'l's hat, which blew off and landed at Elizabeth's feet. She snatched it up and put it on her own head, smiling.

"I'm a sailor-man!" she hollered.

Dan'l bent down. "And what's this little sailor-man's name?"

"Elizabeth, hand Mr. Redfall's hat to him and say hello properly."

"Hello, Mr. Redfall. I'm Elizabeth, and I'm seven!" She squared her shoulders, took off his hat, and handed it back to him.

"Well, Elizabeth, this isn't a sailing cap, but it looks so when you wear it! Seven is a big age; have you started your *ceilidh* dancing?"

"Oh, yes!" she said, and she raised her arms and started the Highland Fling. The other Scots on deck surrounded us and started clapping their hands to the tempo.

Someone back of the crowd hollered, "Ceilidh! Ceilidh!" and suddenly, a fiddle erupted from below decks. Someone had saved theirs, after all.

Mary and I clapped our hands, too. Murdoch stopped playing with the group of boys he'd found, came over, and began dancing with his sister. The fiddle player started a good reel, and it seemed like the ceilidh back home, spontaneously erupting on bridges, in the middle of the road, in the kitchens. Ceilidh always pushed away my sorrows. I felt lucky to be here on the *Sarah* with my family. We were bound for

New York. I watched Elizabeth and Murdoch practice the same dance steps as my parents and their parents at a ceilidh. Mary and I danced. Dan'l found a partner among the "spinsters." A flute player appeared to argue with the fiddle, and you would think at that moment that none of us had a care in the world. This is what Elizabeth brought. She'd started the ceilidh, and I was proud of her.

After a few dances, the crew pushed through with small barrels of hot water for us to prepare our meal. We all filed tween-deck to divide into our groups and prepare a feast of biscuits and boiled meat. The music had stopped, but the laughter carried on, and more than a few passengers paused by our group to praise Elizabeth for her ceilidh.

And suddenly, the crew members on deck started shouting their orders. They cast off the mooring lines, and rowboats guided the out of the harbor. Then we were really, truly off to New York. To America.

Dan'l found us once again before we'd finished our meal. "You asked if I had more news. I did hear talk of one man who got away from Gordon with his family on a small boat. It's said that when one of Gordon's men tried to prevent their escape, the boat master broke his hand with a spike."

"Whoever it was, Gordon's men had it coming."

"Godspeed to them. I reckon they couldn't have made it through the isles with such a small boat. Maybe there is some luck left for the Gaels. Miss Elizabeth, Master Murdoch, you are both quite the dancers. Good night, all."

We bade him good evening, and he left for the single men's area. There had to be a point to him asking me about the escaped family, and I believe he did know it was us. Just in case it was only idle curiosity, I did not directly acknowledge it for fear that we would be given up by an eavesdropper.

"Rather an abrupt good night," Mary said.

"He's probably exhausted like all of us. We won't be staying up that much longer either."

The ceilidh carried on still in fits and starts, small groups playing a reel here, a jig there, and even a few strathspeys. Those who did not play or dance cleaned the dishes. This was not the task we were used to. There was only one tub of water for all three steerage areas, and each family had to clean their own. We stood in line. Mary then scraped the plates into the slop bucket and slipped the dishes in the soiled murky water.

"Next meal," she said, her nose crinkling, "we need to eat faster so we can clean sooner. Murdoch, you clean next. Elizabeth, you're after him. James, you get to clean last," she said, and chuckled. The children managed to clean their dishes without complaint, but they crinkled their noses in the same way. I think Murdoch held his breath. The poor souls aboard had to deal with a tub of dirty water, chunks of waterlogged food, the foul odors, and one poor woman who cleaned after us vomited into the wash basin. We could not be angry. Rather, we felt sorry for her. Those who hadn't gotten the chance to wash their dishes went topside to hold them over the railing of the ship and hoped that the sea spray would get them clean enough.

Despite the cramped quarters and the foul odors, our fellow passengers seemed in good spirits the first night. We walked unsteadily like new sailors who had not managed their legs yet. Murdoch and Elizabeth giggled at the loopy gait as people walked past our berths. Elizabeth had already become quite a favorite, delighting in the attention and dancing and singing with little urging. Murdoch was comforted by the large proportion of Scots on board and the way we all clung to our traditions wherever they happened to be.

Mary and I tucked the children into bed and climbed onto our own berths. The bad air and unfamiliar surroundings could not keep us from sleep. It was ages ago in memory that we'd lay in each other's arms and made love in our dear little croft, warmed by the peat fire. Two days and a lifetime in the past.

***

"Are you awake?" I whispered.

"I slept for a while, but it didn't last. I'm not used to the motion of the ship and the sounds of so many other people," Mary said.

"It smells awful. Some people are already getting seasick."

Mary let out a quiet laugh. "I miss the smell of the cows and even the sheep."

"I miss the smell of the peat fire." And all that happened near it, I didn't add. "I wish..."

"I know, James. I wish you'd have been wrong too." She brushed back a tear. "You were so right. I talked with some of the others last night as you were making friends with Dan'l. Gordon's men chased everyone down, and Reverend Beatson helped them do it. One woman said they dragged a lass from her barn by her hair and then set the dogs on her. In Uist they had a ship, and they forced everyone from the crofts on board."

"How could the people of England stand for this? How could they let it happen when so many of us Scots have fought alongside them? Now this is done in their name, and they just stand by. I don't understand."

"But we are here. So many Scots here on board with stories, and so many of them worse than our own. You can see it in their eyes."

James had indeed seen the haunted look that accompanied a tartan. "I don't know if that makes it any easier. We are all abandoned by England to our injustices."

"We'll be embraced by this new land. We're still young, and we have young children. They're only nine and seven. They're the future. Where they're going, they can own the very land they live on. I've heard that America is such a place."

I loved her optimism even in the darkest of times. "I wonder, Mary – we were foreigners on our own soil. We were a nuisance. America does this too, just not to people who are like us. They have clearances, too. They don't tolerate people with their own languages and cultures."

"We should never forget where we came from or what we are or who we are. We can't forget what's been taken from us. But we must focus on now and on the future."

I held Mary tighter, unable to tell the time of day or night. We might have been asleep for two, four, or six hours, but my bones told me that we still had a long night to go. The motion of the ship, even in moderate swell, married the creaking of the wood. Adding to the lack of harmony was the constant clinking of pots and pans, cooking utensils, and any assortment of oddities that hung by hooks to the ceiling throughout steerage. It was all in a constant, dissonant motion. The ship descended into the trough of the deep ocean waves, then back up. We would fall asleep to the rocking and wake up abruptly to the clanging.

This was only the first night. There were 181 passengers in steerage and another 80 or so passengers with better lodgings elsewhere. Someone was always in and out of their berths headed topside to use the water closet or just pacing. At any given time, one of the many infants on board shrieked with colic. Crying babies did not bother me much, but the smells of steerage made it difficult. I covered my nose with my blanket and did my best to sleep through this assault on the senses.

The night passed slowly with little sleep. Elizabeth and Murdoch awoke in the morning.

"We need to go to the bathroom!" Elizabeth cried.

"I'll take them," Mary said, "then we will trade off."

The hatch remained uncovered during the night, and daylight found its way downstairs. Mary took Murdoch and Elizabeth to the water closet, and I swung myself over the side of our berth, almost hitting my head on the overhead timbers. All the families surrounding us were Scots, so we bade each other good morning and made our talk. Mary and the children straightened up and went on deck to await breakfast. The sky was clear and the air cool, and the sea air was a relief to me.

The crew proceeded with the morning rations of food, water, and tea through the hatch and down the stairs. Each of the group's headmen collected the provisions.

"I'm hungry!" Elizabeth cried.

"What did they give us, James?" Mary said.

"Worse than last night, I'm afraid. Tea, biscuits, that's all. And damn little of that. How can they expect us to survive on this?"

"We'll make do."

"What's the brown stuff?" asked Murdoch.

"Molasses, I think. It's sweet. You dip your biscuit in it to make it taste better."

We sat in our berths, trying to eat the cold, hard, and burnt biscuits.

They were impossible to chew without dipping them into our lukewarm tea or our short molasses ration. Elizabeth and Murdoch only ate half their portion, and Mary and I did not want to encourage them to eat more. I wished Mary'd packed more barley cakes.

"I'll get in the line to wash our dishes," Mary said.

We went topside after straightening up and washing the deck in our area. I'd wished people could have been more careful with their slop pails in the middle of the night, but with the motion of the ship, it was certain that we would have spillage to deal with every morning. Today the ocean was blessedly calm, and the air seemed fresh. The children busied themselves playing the little games they'd improvised. Mary and I fell into crowds to socialize. Time passed, and I could see that life aboard a ship had its own rhythms.

"Mary, have you seen Dan'l this morning?" I'd wanted to ask him more of the rumors of Barra.

"Not since last evening when he headed off to sleep. He left the ceilidh a bit early, probably seasick." She paused. "Speaking of missing people, I've lost sight of Murdoch and Elizabeth."

"They're hard to see in this crowd. I'll look."

We split up and hunted the top deck area that had been designated for steerage passengers. I could not find the children anywhere. I headed down the stairs through the hatch, and there they were, sitting at our berths, happily peeling an orange.

"What on Earth! Where did you get that?" I was shocked. Oranges cost three shillings each, six days' wage if you could even find them. So rare that Murdoch and Elizabeth had never even seen an orange before, much less tasted one.

"A sailor man gave it to us," Elizabeth said. "He said we're not supposed to eat the outside part even if it smells good."

Mary caught up to me, her jaw dropping when she saw the bright orange peels. Even through the stench of steerage, the orange smell came through. "Is that what I think it is?" she asked.

"Yes, they've somehow gotten an orange. Elizabeth said a sailor gave it to her."

"Who?"

"I don't know."

"Well," she told the children, "eat it quickly while everyone is topside. If the rest of the passengers see it, they'll have a fit." She took the orange from Murdoch who'd been struggling to peel it, and she handed them each half.

"The crew thinks they're the darlings of the ship after last night. Probably why they got their orange," I said. "Murdoch, Elizabeth, there's a disease called scurvy and sailors use oranges to keep it away."

Mary took hold of Elizabeth's little hands and pushed them into her nose. She breathed deeply, drinking in the scent of the orange, closing her eyes. After gathering the peels, she smelled her own handful, then put them underneath her blankets in our top berth. "What a wonderful smell," she said.

"I don't ever want to wash my hands again!" exclaimed Elizabeth.

"You two, don't ever let on that someone gave you this orange," Mary warned.

"Do as your mother says. I'm going forward to see if I can find Dan'l." I walked through steerage to the single men's section, where I found only one passenger.

"Hello, name's James McNeil. I wondered if you'd seen a friend of mine. Dan'l Redfall."

"I'm James too, but I go by Jim. Jim Davidson. Not since early this morning. He was awful sick last night. The surgeon was here and later they carried him up. He was unconscious."

"Did they say what the matter was?"

"I asked, but they didn't answer."

I nodded and went back to my family's berths. Mary's face was concerned. Murdoch and Elizabeth sat together and looked afraid, not at all the expression I'd expect after they'd had such a treat.

"What's wrong?" I said.

"You said you were going to look for Dan'l, and they became very quiet and teary."

"You two, what are you thinking? Someone in the single men's quarters said Dan'l took sick last night."

"He's not here anymore!" cried Murdoch, and Elizabeth too began to cry.

"He's in the ocean!" she blubbered.

"What do you mean, he's in the ocean? Murdoch, explain what you know. And does this have to do with the orange?"

"We were playing, and I wanted to see what the front of the ship looked like, so we went up front and saw two men putting Mr. Redfall over the side of the boat. The men told us not to tell anyone what we saw and then they gave us the orange."

I turned to Mary. "It makes sense. He was very ill last night. The man I talked with said the surgeon came below to check on him and couldn't rouse him. He's died."

"Do you think what he had was contagious?" Mary asked with worry.

"I don't know. We spent little time with him really. If he were contagious, the single men's section would be in the most danger. I just don't know. I'll see if I can get any more out of the steward when I see him."

We spent the day on deck, and even with the faint hint of orange, the air in steerage was fouler and hotter in the summer heat. I was able to find the steward, but he either did not know what had happened to Dan'l, or he wouldn't say what he did know. Only a few passengers had even been aware of his existence on board the ship, and they all had problems of their own. It was as if he was never even there. I knew deaths aboard ships were not uncommon, and we'd heard nightmarish stories of packed crossings to America that were full of disease.

Still, it saddened and angered me that they would callously dump his body over the side. Then when Murdoch and Elizabeth had seen and were shocked by what they saw, they'd been sworn to silence. I did my best to explain everything to the children, but my words felt inadequate. They had, of course, seen people in our village die before, but they could not understand the coldness of it on the ship.

Still, the next few days were pleasant enough. Each night, somewhere in steerage, we held ceilidh to keep up our spirits. The music, dancing, and storytelling helped with the boredom of the crossing. I allowed Mary to coerce me into telling a few stories of my own on occasion.

One of her favorites was "Castle Urquhart and the Fugitive Lovers," and it seemed fitting, given our escape from Gordon. I thought of Mary as brave as Mary McLauchlan, who refused to give away her lover's position even with the threat of an officer's sword at her bosom. Of course, the heroine shared her given name with my wife, which I think was a reason why she so loved the story.

Mary corralled both Elizabeth and Murdoch on deck one sunny afternoon and had found an Irish lady who herself had a son and daughter about their ages. They spent all afternoon giving the four of them a bath in vinegar and combing their hair to keep away the lice and nits. It's a mystery how they were able to keep the children still long enough.

Late on our seventh night, the seas grew angry. Mary and I awoke.

"James, what's happening?" she cried.

"Papa! Papa!" Elizabeth yelled.

A crew member slammed the hatch shut, and all became black as pitch.

"We're in for quite a storm!" I said, climbing out of our top berth and back into the children's bed to calm them. Mary carefully climbed out as well, holding fast to the upright support post and climbing in beside me.

The ship dropped violently and rolled hard to starboard, then to portside. The children in steerage screamed in terror. Lightning flashed through the scuttles and was so bright and continuous that it no longer mattered that the hatch had shut out our light. All of the pots, pans, and utensils hanging on the hooks went flying and crashed into whatever lay in their path. The metal pots eerily reflected the lightning. The wind screamed, and we could hear crewmen on deck trying to secure the sails, keeping them from being torn apart. The slop buckets pulled loose and spilled their contents.

"James! Elizabeth is burning up!"

"I'm going to throw up!" she yelled.

I reached underneath the berth, hoping that a bucket was still in place, and luckily it was. She threw up in it, fell against Mary, and held on.

"Murdoch! If I put you in our berth, can you hang on and not get tossed out?"

"Yes!" he yelled. I helped him up and then pressed my hand to Elizabeth's forehead. She was on fire with fever.

"I'm so cold," she whimpered. She shook and moaned loudly as the ship rolled violently from side to side and pitched up and down.

"James, I feel so helpless! What shall I do?" Mary yelled over the din.

"All we can do is wait out the storm and hope she doesn't become any sicker. Murdoch! Are you okay? Do you feel sick?"

"No, Papa, I feel okay."

The storm continued through the night, lessening and strengthening by turns, the wind howling like a great wounded creature. Elizabeth vomited until there was nothing left in her stomach, then she heaved without ceasing. I prayed. I cursed. No more, God, please. No more. But her fever did not lessen its attack.

The storm finally subsided, and a crewmember threw open the hatch. I went topside and asked if the ship's surgeon would come to treat her, but he never showed himself. I had heard that ships sometimes did not care well for steerage passengers, and what care they did provide could be incompetent. I could do little for Elizabeth as she developed a violent, painful headache that morning. She had no appetite and felt pain everywhere. Once the coughing started she spoke but little, except through her eyes, which pleaded for some way to understand what was happening to her.

"James, I've not seen her this sick ever. I can't get any drink or food in her at all. I don't know what's wrong with her!"

"I know," I said, shaking my head. "She's so sick. People have asked if they can help, but they're afraid she might pass the sickness on to them. Nobody wants to come close to her." The Greenlys, the large family who had up until now been managing our group, offered to take charge of Murdoch, and we gratefully accepted, over his protests at leaving his sister's side.

The fever continued. Her muscles and joints pained her so much that she screamed whenever we'd lift her onto the bucket to pee. This

58

nightmare continued for the next six days, and then we knew what the disease was, and our hearts were broken. We were helpless, and there was nothing we could do but try and comfort her and each other. Our tears flowed. I was angry.

The crimson rash started on her abdomen. It spread like fire to her legs and then the rest of her body. She was consumed by some monster we could not fight. Her expression, once so sweet as she danced on decks, was now dusky.

Typhus.

"Papa, Papa!" she cried in her small voice, her eyes wide and wild. "You always know. What is wrong with me? What did I do wrong? I'm sorry, I'm sorry! What is wrong with me? Fix me! It hurts so bad and I don't understand! Tell me! Please!" She blamed herself for being sick, as though the fault lay with her. If her illness was caused by her sins, then she could perhaps repent it away if she knew what she'd done. She'd learned something from Beatson, the seeds of self-blame now reaped, planted by him and harvested through her body with the typhus.

Once the rash appeared, word spread rapidly through the ship. Our close friends quickly began avoiding our area, and we didn't blame them. The Greenlys continued to take charge of Murdoch, and we decided to keep him well away from us. No one knew how the disease spread, and we had to protect him, despite his fury with us. Fear permeated steerage.

Mary and I held each other. We cried. We became mentally strong, then broken, then strong again. I blamed God. Mary did not. I blamed Gordon and Sellar and the whole of Britain. She did not. I waited for her to blame me, but she did not. That's where my own blame finally settled. On myself.

After five more days in hell, my little girl was thrown into delirium and hallucination. She was pushed over the cliff by the pain of this heartless disease. She came into a coma and then she was gone.

News spread quickly through the ship and the ship's surgeon finally paid us attention – to tell us to bring her body up for committal to the ocean. We wrapped her in muslin and met the surgeon on deck, the crowd keeping their distance. The surgeon had seen this often, and I suppose he was numb to it. Our tears had been spent watching her suffer over two weeks. We prayed, and we let her go.

A week later, Mary became ill.

Two days after that, I was sick.

There were angels among our Highlander kin, and the other passengers helped as they could and dared. The Greenlys still helped with Murdoch. I worried over what would happen if Mary and I died, and the Greenlys assured that he would be cared for. I thought back to the pamphlet saying that should parents die in transit, the captain was responsible for arranging the care of any orphans once at our destination.

Mr. Greenly brought Murdoch close, stopping just short of our berth. He stood silently beside the boy, his presence a quiet reassurance. I met Robert's eyes, the weight of unspoken words between us. "Robert, thank you for watching over our son. We owe you more than we can say."

Robert nodded, his voice steady but low. "If you don't make it to New York, we'll see that he's cared for."

I turned to Murdoch, forcing calm into my voice. "Murdoch, your mother and I are very sick, like Elizabeth was. If we can't be with you in America, do your best to live well and be happy in your new home."

"I want you to get well," Murdoch said.

"I know, son," Mary said.

There were no other words beyond this. Our pains were unbearable, but we did not suffer long. Mary was gone in another week. They took her that morning. I went overboard three days later. Murdoch, while not by himself, was alone as the *Sarah* sailed into New York Harbor and anchored off Staten Island for inspection. Since there had been a typhus outbreak onboard, the surviving passengers were taken to the Marine Quarantine Hospital.

The first-class passengers were placed in St. Nicholas Hospital, and the steerage passengers were held in rough, crowded barracks. Those in steerage were stripped and sprayed with disinfecting hot water and given caustic lye soap.

Murdoch, cold from being sprayed down unclothed, could not

comprehend what was happening and why. He floated on a sea of confusion. He was hungry and in the primitive part of the brain that keeps humans alive beyond all reason, he existed outside any linear understanding from the past to the present. He was given clothes, dressed himself by instinct, and stood in front of a man wearing a white gown. The man put a stick into his mouth and peered inside. His sister was dead. He vaguely recalled his mother and his father, sick. He was hungry. So hungry.

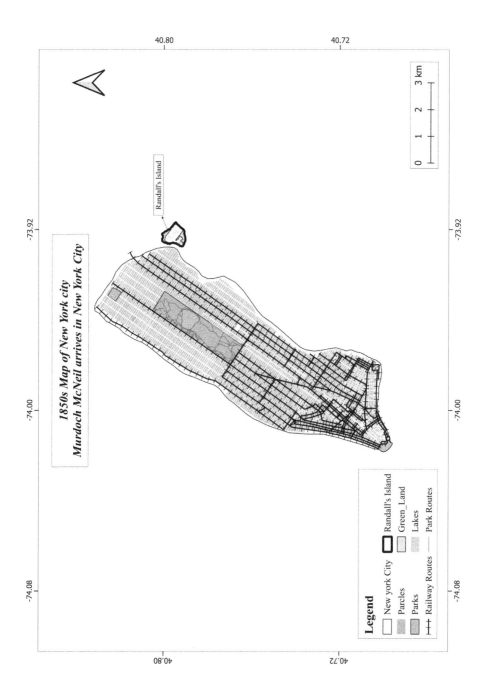

1850s Map of New York city
Murdoch McNeil arrives in New York City

Randall's Island

Legend

New york City	Randall's Island
Parcles	Green_Land
Parks	Lakes
Railway Routes	Park Routes

63

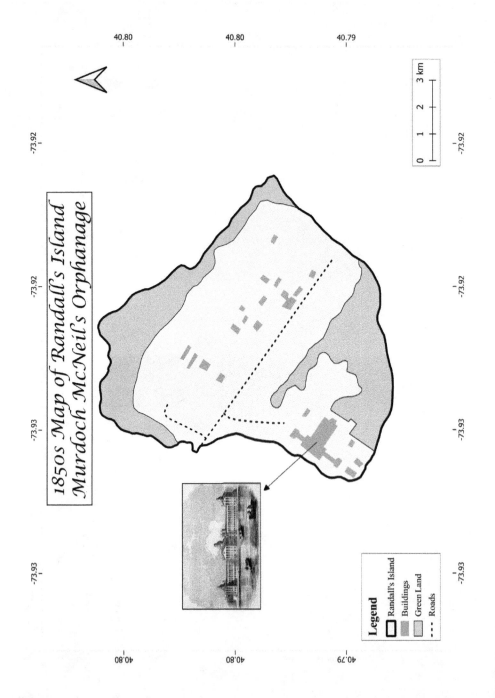

1850s Map of Randall's Island
Murdoch McNeil's Orphanage

Legend
☐ Randall's Island
▨ Buildings
▨ Green Land
--- Roads

Chapter IV: Randall's Island

Friday, September 19th,1851
Marine Quarantine Hospital
Staten Island, New York

"Sticks and stones may break my bones, but words will never hurt me."
Alexander William Kinglake, 1844

"Open your mouth," said the doctor. "Did you hear what I said? Open your mouth. I have to check your throat."

Murdoch stood in a long line of young boys in the exam area of the quarantine hospital on Staten Island. He slowly opened his mouth. The doctor, in his white gown, placed the flat wooden tongue depressor on the boy's tongue and pressed it down. Murdoch tried not to pull away. "Say Ahhh!" The doctor stuck out his tongue.

Murdoch made the noise and gagged slightly.

"Everything looks fine. No rash, your temperature is normal, you don't seem to have any pain, no cough. You're fine." He looked at his notes. "Parents and sister died of typhus aboard the *Sarah*." Murdoch, take Murdoch here; he's ready. Here's his paperwork. Next! Step up, young man! Open your mouth!"

The nurse took Murdoch to a waiting area filled with newly arrived immigrant children, all looking bewildered and lost.

"Sit right here," the nurse said. "Greenlys... do you see the Greenlys?"

"I'm Mr. Greenly, right here."

"Ah, yes, you're the family to take charge of Murdoch?"

"No, no, that's not quite right. We promised the McNeils that we'd see to it Murdoch got to New York, but we have so many children already. We can't..."

The nurse moved on from the same story she'd heard a thousand times before. "I see. Well, do you wish to say goodbye to him?"

"No, you may, I just wanted to make sure he would be looked after.

Does he have a place somewhere?"

"Randall's Island is where we send them. I have other patients, Mr. Greenly. Do you want to see him or not?"

"My wife's waiting." And he left.

The nurse turned and walked over to Murdoch. She crouched down so she was at eye level with his round face. There was a hollowness in his eyes. "Murdoch, look at me. Listen carefully."

He pulled himself out of his trance.

"You are in New York. I am sorry, but your mother, father, and sister died of typhus aboard the ship. They were buried at sea. Do you understand?"

Murdoch's voice was desperate, "Yes, I know, but what am I to do now? Why am I alive, and they're gone? It shouldn't be this way! I wish I was gone, too! I don't want to be here! I want to be back on Barra!"

He squeezed his eyes tightly shut, swallowed hard, and drew in three pained gasps. Then the tears started. He sobbed. The nurse placed her arms around him. "Cry as much as you want, Murdoch." She pulled his head to her shoulder.

"Nurse!" the doctor yelled. "I need you!"

She rose to her feet and pulled Murdoch along with her. "Come with me now." She walked him over to a room, opened the door, and spoke briefly with an attendant. "Murdoch, I have to go. You'll wait here until someone from the Randall's Island Asylum arrives to take you and the other boys there. This is Mr. Smith. He'll take charge of you for now."

Murdoch wiped away his tears and pushed himself down into the large wooden chair as if attempting to hide. He did not know what an asylum was, but he said nothing. He thought of his mother, father, and sister and wished he were home.

There were a number of other boys in the holding room at the Staten Island facility, and every so often, the nurse would add another. They were all aged between seven and fifteen, and all of them had lost their parents or relatives on their way to New York. They were all alone now. The room was eerily quiet for having been full of so many boys. Some were weeping; others, in shock, were expressionless. A few whispered to the other boys sitting near them.

New York City had an increasing number of children who were homeless. Some, like Murdoch, had lost parents aboard the immigrant ships. Others were orphaned when their parents died in the city. Still more had parents who'd abandoned them. All of them came to the same place: Randall's Island. Murdoch and the other boys were herded onto a ferry and transported to the Island, which had a place set aside for orphans and homeless children. Then, the city added children who'd run afoul of the law and were placed there by the courts. These children could be petty thieves, or they could have committed serious, violent crimes. Regardless of the reasons for their placement at Randall's Island, they were all housed together.

Once they'd arrived, the staff lined up the boys in front of the building. Murdoch had never seen anything so big until he'd come to New York: The cavernous facility had multiple stories and was made from tan, hand-chiseled blocks of stone. The roof wore a crown of spires, and to Murdoch seemed to be telling him: you are doomed here. This wasn't the only place on the island, just the biggest. Twenty more buildings lay scattered throughout the grounds like ancient forbidding tombstones.

A tall, thin woman wearing a plain dark dress with a sour expression spoke. "I'm Mrs. Abernathy, and I'm a matron here on Randall's Island. You are here because you do not have anywhere else to go. Your parents may be dead or in jail; maybe they just don't want you. Here, you will learn discipline and respect. You will be told what to do exactly once, and if you disobey, you will be punished."

She continued her severe explanations of duties and rules. An older boy stood next to Murdoch and whispered to nobody in particular, "What an old hag."

Murdoch was surprised at the boy's comment, and he couldn't stop himself from saying a bit too loudly, "You shouldn't call her an old hag! What's wrong with you?"

Murdoch thought he'd been buried by the crowd, but an attendant Murdoch would soon come to know as Mr. Schneider had been watching for any disrespect. He grabbed the boy and Murdoch by their shirt collars and hauled them to the front to face Mrs. Abernathy.

"These two were talking out of turn. They said you were an old hag."

"What are your names?" Mrs. Abernathy said with no hint of surprise or offense.

"Braden."

"Murdoch."

"Braden and Murdoch. Is this so? Did you say this?" They were silent. Braden glared at Mrs. Abernathy. Murdoch was too frightened to do much more than shake his head. Fear captured the protests his mouth would have liked to make.

"Let this stand as a lesson to the rest of you!" she shouted. "Talking out of turn and disrespecting staff will not be tolerated!"

She grabbed Braden by his red hair and pulled him forward and downward. Mr. Schneider had a wide wooden paddle at the ready. He'd drilled holes into it and fastened iron rivets into the holes.

He struck Braden on his buttocks. He hit him over and over, ten times, and with each swat, Braden whimpered and cried.

Then Mr. Schneider stepped toward Murdoch. His words finally loosened and protested to Mrs. Abernathy, "I didn't call you an old hag, I didn't!" Mrs. Abernathy grabbed him by the hair and forced him to double over.

Murdoch didn't cry; he only flinched with each strike. His anger surged, trapped with no release, and sank deep inside him. When Murdoch finished receiving his lashes, Mrs. Abernathy wrenched the boys' faces up to look at her. "Both of you owe me an apology. You should be ashamed of yourselves." Each of them mumbled as much of an apology as they could through their pain. Mr. Schneider grabbed them again by their shirt collars and dragged them roughly back to their places.

"You will all follow Mr. Schneider into the dormitory. You'll be assigned your sleeping area, then you'll be led to the dining hall for dinner. After dining, you'll be led back to your dorms. Lights are out at 7:00 p.m. You will wake up at 5:00 a.m. You will walk in silence. Is that understood?"

As if to underline the last rule, Murdoch and Braden limped painfully as Mr. Schneider led the boys up the stairs. After they'd gotten to their assigned narrow metal cots, they sat on wooden benches in front of wooden tables. The walls were bare of artwork and ornaments, and they only held unlit gas lamps placed at ineffective intervals. The windows were small and also ineffective at lighting the space. The boys were called up in rows to have their food served. Quiet talking was now allowed, and the boys murmured almost inaudibly.

Braden sat next to Murdoch and bumped his shoulder. "You got me into trouble there. I could kill that damned old bitch. Beat me, will you! It wouldn't have happened if it wasn't for you. You're gonna pay."

Murdoch ignored Braden's threats and said nothing as their table was called to be served. He was famished, and at the quarantine hospital, he'd had little to eat. The dinner here of boiled meat, potatoes, and bread was modest, but Murdoch finished it quickly and felt it was a feast. Braden saw Mr. Schneider keeping watch and said nothing more to Murdoch. The boys all marched back to the dorm and were ordered immediately to bed.

Murdoch lay down on the narrow metal cot, which was the size of his berth on the *Sarah,* covered with a single thin blanket and a small hay-filled pillow. There were no other comforts. He slept fitfully, at time not knowing where he was, or what was real.

The sounds, the narrowness, and discomfort of the cot flung him back aboard the *Sarah,* alone in is berth. He felt the relentless rocking of the ship and the overpowering stench of too many people packed into a small space, the slop buckets, and stale salt air.

"Momma! Pappa! Don't let them throw us in the water! Elizabeth!" His voice cracked with fear. He watched in horror as he and his family were thrown overboard. He screamed.

The matron and the nurse stationed in their dorm ran to Murdoch's cot and shook him awake.

"Wake up! You're all right; you're safe! Wake up!"

He was soaked in sweat. His heart pounded; fear clung to him from his nightmare. The shadowy images of his father, mother, and Elizabeth unshakably present. He could not release it. Exhaustion was substituted for sleep and he spent the rest of the night never really awake or asleep yearning for morning. An exchange of nightmares.

Life at Randall's Island proceeded harshly and with discipline. The days were structured into calculated forced segments. Four hours a day of formal education and two hours in the trades. Murdoch was put into harness and leather work, which he tolerated reasonably well, but his favorite subjects were math and reading. A bell rang loudly and sharply to signal their every movement throughout the day. Twelve hundred were juveniles awakened by the bell, going to classes by the bell, eating by the bell, sleeping by the bell. All wards and dormitories had a matron and a nurse supervising all activities.

In the night, Murdoch often thought of his parents and his sister, remembering the words they had spoken, especially those of his father that seemed to stick in his soul: *"Do anything you have to do to get land and to keep it."* He had nothing now, except the feeling that those words would haunt him until he finally regained what they had all lost. He had no idea how that could possibly happen.

He tried to think on the good memories, just to survive; the fun they had at ceilidh, his family's pride at being Highlanders, his father's stories of incredible bravery, and his mother's stories of great love. These memories comforted him in the harsh environment.

He learned that he had to fight to survive here. Although he was stout and strong for his age, Randall's Island held juvenile criminals as well as orphans, boys as old as fifteen who bullied and harassed anyone younger and weaker. Some of the younger boys whispered at night that these older boys had even beaten some children to death.

His first Christmas in America was spent with his ankles chained and his wrists handcuffed in a detention cell. He'd been fighting, in his own defense, but that seemed not to matter. Outside the cell he heard the sounds of laughter and song. New York's wealthy elite liked to visit the poor unfortunates of the Island during Christmas, bringing feasts and presents with them in exchange for a Christmas concert put on by the children. The papers wrote that it was a wonderful time of charity and giving, and praised the Randall's Island staff for their compassionate and wonderful treatment of the children. Murdoch had been in the detention cells four times already, and he did not expect to share in anything except the usual detention bread and water.

In February, he returned to his usual cell.

"Fighting again, Murdoch McNeil?" asked Duncan Ferguson, a blustery old man with a reddish face that made him look either perpetually angry or freshly intoxicated. Murdoch could almost smell the sea on him, and though he didn't want to rely on this new adult, there was something familiar about him. Ferguson was newly hired, and while Murdoch wasn't ready to speak to him, he felt it was safe enough to listen.

"I understand you're from the Isle of Barra. Crofters, I'd wager and kicked out of there. Me, I had the fortune to leave when the storm built, not after it hit." He removed Murdoch's restraints. "Braden belongs in the cell where I put him. You don't. I'm to tell you a story my father passed onto me at ceilidh. Listen carefully, then go back to your class.

Murdoch's mind snapped Mr. Ferguson into place. He reminded Murdoch of John Crawford back on Barra with his easy talk and raspy voice, and he wished he was back home.

"A boy, about your age, lived on the Isle of Barra, about where you lived. He was strong and capable, and his father had him lift the great stones even at the age of nine. His name was Balgair, which, as you know, means Fox. He was smart and cunning like a fox, too.

"The older boys in Castlebay would beat him. Sure, he'd never start a fight. He didn't want to disappoint his father, and he was taught never to start something like that, but the Castlebay boys would catch him and beat the tar out of him. So he found a thinking rock, the kind scattered all over Barra, and sat on a thinking rock over the bay, hoping that the solution would come to him.

"He couldn't ask his father for help, as he'd been taught that his battles were his own. Then Balgair saw a fox dart from his den. Foxes hunt by stealth and surprise. The fox waits in the deep heather, and when his prey walks by, he pounces. He does not chase the rabbit; he does not challenge the dog. He waits for his moment.

"So Balgair waited, and he watched. He watched the boys now as though they, and not he, were the prey. He noticed when they were alone rather than with the group. Being small, he found himself a strong rod and concealed its purpose as a walking stick. When one of the boys walked by alone, he pounced like a fox.

"Embarrassed by losing to a smaller boy, the gang could not tell their friends that Balgair had beaten them. But they never dared attack Balgair again."

"It's not a fair fight if he used the stick, is it?" asked Murdoch.

"In this life, in fights, there are only winners and losers. Nothing fair about any fight," Mr. Ferguson said. "Now let's get you out of here, and you can go to your class. I've written a note for your teacher. It's reading time right now."

They think they've won, he brooded, but they don't know what's coming. His grip tightened as he imagined the moment, each strike returning the pain they'd inflicted on him tenfold. They'll never see it coming, he told himself, not when I'm done planning. The thought of their surprise brought a bitter satisfaction. I won't let them get away with it. They'll regret every bruise, every insult. The anger that had taken root inside him now fueled his determination, each step closer to the classroom strengthening his resolve. I'll make sure of it.   H e got to his classroom and handed Mr. Ferguson's note to Miss Walker, the teacher. She saw his lower lip and shook her head. "Take your seat and see me after class. We are continuing our reading of Marco Paul's *Adventures in the Pursuit of Knowledge*. Take a book from the shelf."

"Okay, Miss Walker," he said brightly. She was one of the kinder teachers at the school and therefore, his favorite. Her face was pleasant and reassuring, but she readily used what she called her 'teacher voice' when she commanded attention or discipline. He loved to read and sometimes wished he could read all of the books in the world. He'd start with this one, so he sat down at is assigned seat, row five seat four, as he recited to himself each day as he entered class.

He held the book as if it were his most prized possession. Back on Barra, he had been given a few books, but they had likely gone up in flames with the blackhouse. Seeing so many books on Miss Walker's classroom shelves made him feel like he hadn't lost as much as he'd thought. His father always said that once you've read a book, it's yours forever.

"I will start reading where we left off last time, and then we will go around the room. Each of you will take a turn reading until I ask you to stop. 'Forester and Marco followed the runner down one of those flights of stairs, and there they found a packet-boat…'" Miss Walker read.

Murdoch closed his eyes, and in his mind he saw the very sentence in the book. Page 29, top of the page, first paragraph, he thought. He liked to play a game where he tested himself not only on the words but where they sat on the paper.

Miss Walker mistook his game for a lack of attention. "I'm sorry, Murdoch, and any others who have lost their place. We are on page 29, at the top of the page."

"Thank you, Miss Walker," he said with a smile.

She finished the paragraph and called on the first boy to read aloud. Some boys read painfully slowly and had trouble recognizing and pronouncing words. It would be quite some time before Murdoch would get his chance to read. Glancing up to make sure Miss Walker did not see him, he skipped ahead to page 94 where he'd left off his own reading the day before. As she called on the boy two seats ahead of Murdoch, he closed his eyes and listened carefully.

"'I do not know, said Marco, shaking his head. I do not know anything about it.'" Page 37, last paragraph, Murdoch thought. He flipped to the page as the boy in front of him, Logan, was called on to read. Logan was one of Braden's gang.

"'They passed throw,'" Logan read. "'…Thruff…'"

"Through," Miss Walker corrected.

"'Through the crowd and went down the steps and got a boat.'"

"Upon the boat, Logan. You're doing fine." The boy struggled through the next few lines. "That will do, Logan. Murdoch, please finish the paragraph and go on to the next one."

Murdoch finished the paragraph and read much slower than he usually did. He started the next paragraph, hesitated here and there, paused at the word "instrument", and asked Miss Walker how to pronounce it. He'd already found that reading aloud at his own pace and skill made him a target for the boys who needed help and hated it. He read through his assigned paragraph with pretended difficulty just as the bell rang.

"Close your books and place your markers on the page where we've left off and put your books back on the shelf. Line up to go to the dining hall. Murdoch, stay back at my desk, please." The boys lined up outside in the hall, and Miss Walker put some salve on Murdoch's busted lip. "It's okay to read ahead. What page are you really on?"

"Page ninety-four," he answered warily.

"What paragraph did you read last?"

"I'm not sure."

"Which paragraph?"

"The third."

"And what did it say?"

"It said, 'yes, but the engine man is their agent. They choose him and employ him and commit the engine and the life of all his passengers to his cause'."

"That's fine, Murdoch."

"There's more to it, but I stopped at the semicolon. That links one sentence that has two independent thoughts together. That's why there's a semicolon."

"You should be proud of how well you read; you don't need to cover that up, do you? Can you remember everything you read?"

"If I tell myself to. It's a game I like to play." She couldn't possibly understand, he thought, why he had to hide like this. She dismissed him to go line up with the rest of his class, and she walked them all to the dining hall for lunch. She had heard about people like Murdoch who could remember what they read, but she neither knew what to do with such a skill, nor did she know how to develop it. She had also heard from the math teacher that he was quite good at the problems, and now she knew why.

Murdoch practiced his memory not only at reading but also memorized names, events, and places. He lay in his metal bunk that night, thinking of how the violent older boys moved and what they did when they were about to target him. He was weary of hearing his Scottish accent ridiculed, but many of the other boys had accents too: German, English, Dutch, and especially Irish, the latter of which seemed to form the worst of the gangs. He reflected on Mr. Ferguson's story and realized that he'd seen each of the Irish boys alone, walking by themselves, at certain times of the day. As he tossed in his narrow bunk, he mapped out a plan in his head but it wouldn't stick. Images of his family kept interrupting his thoughts and finally took them over. He saw his sister, Mother and Father tossed into the sea yet again. Would those images ever leave? He hated his perfect memory and pounded his fists into the metal sides of his bed until he could no longer feel them. *"Do everything you have to..."* those words from his father again.

"Quiet over there!" someone yelled. The voice pulled him from his dreadful thoughts and he drifted off to sleep, tears seeping from his eyelids.

In the next few weeks, he snooped in the wood shop where the staff trained the boys in furniture repair. He found some discarded table legs about two feet long, round, made from hardwood. Maple, he guessed, as he always loved seeing the different grains and looks of wood furniture back on Barra.

Maybe someday he'd have nice wooden furniture and some land on which to build a home. At odd times, the memory of his father surfaced—handing him tools as they built a chest for his and Elizabeth's room. He could still see Elizabeth's excitement as they placed it by the window, her smile as she carefully lined it with her favorite things. That memory, tied to both his father and his sister, lingered with him, refusing to fade.

He was not about to let the boys have the upper hand, so he took the table legs and stashed them in corners and under bushes where the Irish boys sometimes passed. His ability to plan made him feel strong and capable. He may have been smaller, but he knew he was smarter: Murdoch goaded the boys and then retreated, usually closer to one of the matrons or teachers. He made them think he had given up on fighting back.

Braden would be the first to confront Murdoch the Fox. Ever since he'd gotten the both of them paddled for calling Mrs. Abernathy names, he blamed Murdoch, and his hatred only grew with time. Murdoch watched from behind a shrub as Braden walked alone toward the dormitory. Then he stepped from behind the shrub and drew out his table leg. It felt good in his hands – but not quite right. He heard his father's voice talking about Gordon's thugs and how they'd clubbed their neighbors and threw them into the carts. Was Murdoch a fox? Or a thug? What would his father think if he ran up behind Braden and clubbed him? He placed his stick back in the bushes.

"Hey!" Murdoch yelled. Braden turned, and Murdoch ran as fast as he could, then delivered a solid punch just below the belt. Braden fell to the ground in shock and pain. Murdoch straddled him and struck him over and over with his fists until his knuckles became bloody, torn by contact with Braden's teeth. Then he cocked his fist back one last time, grabbed Braden by the collar, and paused the beating.

"If you or any of your gang touch me again, I'm coming after you. Whichever one of you beats me, I'm coming after *you*." And then he let his last punch fly.

After Murdoch walked away, Braden struggled to his feet and resumed walking to the dormitory. That week Murdoch found the other four Irish boys in Braden's gang walking alone in their turn. Logan, Sean, Bran, Cian – the last two tried outrunning him, futilely. Every last one walked away with fewer teeth than they had before, and with the same warning: What your friends to do me, I will revisit upon *you*. Eventually each of them feared not only what Murdoch might to do them, but what would happen as a result of their friends' actions.

The teachers noticed an increase in bruised and bloodied faces, and they noticed that Murdoch's knuckles wore constant scars and bandages. But the boys claimed that they were merely clumsy: they fell down the stairs, or they ran into the wall, or they tripped. Mr. Ferguson drew Murdoch aside at dinner one evening.

"How is the Fox?" he asked. "Your knuckles look pretty swollen. Decided against a stick?"

"Gordon of Cluny's men beat my people with clubs. I didn't want to be like him."

Mr. Ferguson nodded. "I didn't know your father, but I think he would be proud of you. If you haven't beaten all the brains out of their skulls, they'll realize they should take your point by now." He smiled like he had a secret. "Miss Walker says you're an exceptional student, though you don't like to admit it."

Murdoch shrugged.

"Some people in the city are forming the Children's Aid Society. They want to help boys like you, who don't really belong here, by placing you somewhere better. Miss Walker and I are going to talk to them."

Murdoch had been hopeful about this, but a full month passed by. He wondered if Mr. Ferguson and Miss Walker forgot, or maybe the Children's Aid Society didn't happen after all. He'd accomplished what he wanted, which was a lack of beatings; the Irish boys didn't so much as glare at him anymore. He assumed the matter with Braden and his gang was finished.

Murdoch went to bed at 6:30 one spring evening, and read a book until the matron put the lamps out. His stomach growled uncomfortably from a dinner that had been worse than usual. It kept him up through the night and into the early morning. He thought about waking the dormitory nurse who slept in the little room by the door, but he decided his stomach didn't hurt that badly.

The dormitory doors squeaked open and then flopped shut, but quietly. His bed was halfway down the ward, and he could see three figures walking softly in his direction. They carried something in their hands. They whispered imperceptibly. They were almost at Murdoch's bed, and then one of the younger children in the ward shrieked: "My stomach hurts! Oh, Nurse Becker, please! My stomach hurts!"

The nurse leapt out of bed and lit the lamp, illuminating Braden, Sean, and Cian, who were holding the table legs Murdoch had stashed around the grounds. They ran toward the door. Mr. Ferguson, who had been up walking in the early dawn, heard the commotion and had hurried to the ward, where he found the dormitory nurse blocking their escape. Mr. Ferguson grabbed Cian and roughly tore the table leg from his hands. The other boys dropped their clubs.

"So, you weren't just wandering, I suppose, with clubs in your hands? You thought nobody would notice?" Murdoch had never seen

Mr. Ferguson so angry. "Who were you going to hurt? What are you playing at here?" The boys stared in silence, but they could not help looking right at Murdoch. "You're all going to the detention cells until one of you tells me." He carted them off.

The next day Mr. Ferguson talked with Bran and Logan, the only two members of the gang who had not been caught in the dormitory. Bran and Logan protested that they'd refused going with the other three boys. Beating Murdoch was one thing, but Braden was determined to kill him, and Sean and Cian were only too happy to follow him. By luck, they'd found the clubs hidden around the bushes, though they did not know who'd left them there. By luck, one of the younger children had cried out for the nurse which awakened her.

Mr. Ferguson saw that Braden, Sean, and Cian would spend the rest of their time at Randall's Island in another ward where they would either learn to behave or learn how to commit crimes without being caught. Either way they would not be bothering Murdoch again. Despite the Children's Aid Society, Mr. Ferguson and Miss Walker had a hard time finding an apprenticeship for Murdoch: Regardless of his gifts, most businesses and trades in the city believed Randall's Island children were nothing more than criminals, every one of them, especially the orphans. While he was disappointed, Murdoch learned to enjoy the occasional outings and make the best of them. Fall came, and he faced the second Christmas without his family, but at least he did not spend this holiday in a detention cell. He got to enjoy the feast and the presents brought by the wealthy citizens of New York, their most significant act of charity for the children they would not deign to take in themselves. This year he would get his Christmas packet with the rest of the children: candy, small trinkets, and an orange – which he enjoyed but also brought on a relentless sorrow that lasted until he could no longer smell the peels.

It was a new year, January 17, 1853. Caroline Kelly and Jane Ley were in charge of one of the wards the morning. One of the seven-year-olds, John McCaffrey, did not join the ward's lineup for breakfast. Miss Kelly went to his bed to chastise him about his laziness to find him lying beside it, bludgeoned to death in the night. Investigators and the coroner came to Randall's Island and held an inquest, and soon a reporter followed, asking questions of his own about the shocking brutality. The published the results in its City Intelligence column two days later, and Murdoch found a copy:

> JUVENILE DEPRAVITY – DEATH OF A BOY FROM CRUEL TRATMENT BY OTHERS, AT RANDALL'S ISLAND

Murdoch imagined himself in a printing office, correcting spelling errors. He continued reading:

> Coroner Gamble held an inquest, on Monday afternoon, at the hospital, Randall's Island, upon the body of a young lad, named John McCaffrey, an inmate of the institution, who died there from convulsions, superinduced by a violent beating, which he received at the hands of two boys named James Cremley and Charles Collins. The deceased and his assailants were all about the same age – seven years – and the case will be understood from the depositions given below: –

The article left off with testimony from Miss Ley. Why did the nurse claim to have heard nothing while a violent murder went on a short distance away? The paper asked from its adult perspective how seven-year-olds could murder anyone, but Murdoch reckoned that all the boys on Randall's Island knew someone who was capable, if only they had the opportunity. The paper didn't talk about how John McCaffrey saved his Christmas candy and gave pieces to the other boys in his ward. The reporter didn't even spell James Cromley's name correctly. Murdoch felt that words mattered, facts mattered. The article gave him new words: depositions. Superinduced. Depravity. He asked Miss Walker what that last word meant, but she told him it was for much older boys. He looked it up in the dictionary later, in secret, and still didn't know what the fuss was.

That same day the *Herald*'s article came out, Murdoch saw Mrs.

Abernathy approach with a man who wore an expression of self-importance. Murdoch hastily stuffed the page of the newspaper into his pocket. The two adults passed by him and went to Mr. Ferguson. "You have a visitor. A Mr. Casper Childs to see you." They went into another room away from the children.

"I hope I am not disturbing you, Mr. Ferguson," Mr. Childs said. "I would have messaged you for an appointment, but I thought the matter too urgent to wait."

"No bother at all," Mr. Ferguson said. "The children usually keep my hands full, but they are very quiet and subdued today for obvious reasons. They're all quite upset."

"That's why I'm here. I read the article in the *Herald* today and was shocked at the inquest. I immediately thought of the boy you were trying to place into an apprenticeship last year. I know these aren't the same boys involved, but still... Oh, I'm rambling. I felt that if something happened to your boy, to Murdoch, and he was placed in danger because I didn't act... He's a year older now, yes? How old?"

"He's ten now, almost eleven. Still a bit young to be a printer's devil, but once you meet him, I think you'll find he has a capacity beyond his years."

"You say he remembers all that he reads?"

"Yes, and he reads fast. He would be a good proofreader for you, and he has excellent marks in math as well. Would you like to meet him?"

"That won't be necessary." Mr. Childs checked his pocket watch. "Can you have him brought round to the print shop? 103 Nassau, tomorrow. I'll get him started. I must rush; I have ballots to print. 103 Nassau." He turned to leave and then had one last question for Mr. Ferguson. "The nurse in the ward the other night. How could she have stayed asleep through such savagery? She heard nothing?"

"That's what she said."

"I don't see how that's possible. Well, good day, Mr. Ferguson." Mr. Childs left, brushing past Murdoch with not even a cursory glance. Mr. Childs was too preoccupied with his thoughts and schemes, of the new printer's devil, maybe a newsboy to boot, and one who would present a sensational story to rival *The Herald*. He could see the headline: Orphan Survives Brutal Attack on Randall's Island. If only he could contact the nurse who slept through the murder. The *Herald* and the *Times* won't have what I've got, he thought. The Randall's Island Boy Survivor, as he'd come to call him in his own mind, would be just the thing to make the *True National Democrat* a standout paper.

In any case, the boy couldn't possibly be worse at the business than his layabout brother or his own son, who he was sure skimmed money off the top of their printing contracts. Who wouldn't want to buy a paper from a boy hero—one who was selling his own story writ large in newsprint?

Chapter V: The Hawker

January 20, 1853
Randall's Island, New York

No one has ever completed their apprenticeship.
Johann Wolfgang von Goethe

My reading class was almost over. Miss Walker had us put our books away as Mr. Ferguson walked through the door and over to Miss Walker's desk. He leaned toward her and whispered to her. Her eyes went from Mr. Ferguson to staring at me. I must be in trouble again. I had managed to stay out of fights with the Irish, and they were now avoiding me as much as I was avoiding them. In fact, I was avoiding everyone I could. I had been at Randall's Island for over a year, and I can't say that I had made any friends, nor did I care to. Mr. Ferguson and Miss Walker, I trusted – but I didn't count them as friends.

"Murdoch, please remain after class. Mr. Ferguson and I have something we need to talk to you about."

I sat at my desk, wondering what was wrong. Maybe they found out I had stolen all those chair legs hidden all over the grounds. I bet that was it, even though I had not told anyone about it. Miss walker called me to her desk.

"Murdoch," Mr. Ferguson began, "do you remember when we were looking for an apprenticeship for you last year? Well, we have secured one for you. You're leaving today to apprentice for Mr. Casper Childs. He owns a printing business, and he just started a newspaper last December. The *True National Democrat.*"

"You'll be learning the printing trade!" Miss Walker said.

I was excited. "What? Does this mean I'm leaving?"

"That's exactly what it means, Murdoch," Miss Walker said. "I'm to take you there as soon as you get your things together. You'll be living at the print shop. Mrs. Abernathy will help you pack."

"Not Mrs. Abernathy – Miss Walker, would you help me?"

"Well, I suppose that would be all right."

Mr. Ferguson explained more. "I talked with Superintendent Ripley as soon as Mr. Childs left the building. He wanted to send you out of the city on the orphan train to work on a farm, but with help from Miss Walker, we convinced him that working in Mr. Childs' print shop would be best for a boy of your talents. Everything is arranged."

I had given up on the apprenticeship, as neither Mr. Ferguson nor Miss Walker had said anything about it after they first explained they wanted to get me out of Randall's Island. I was leaving, really leaving, and I was going to learn the printing trade. I knew nothing about it except that a printer made books and newspapers. Anything with words on it had first been in the printer's hand. I knew a little about presses, but everything else I knew about how printing worked would fit in a frog's ear.

We walked to the dorm, and Miss Walker paused to talk to Mrs. Abernathy, who slammed a book on her desk and stalked off.

"Why is Mrs. Abernathy mad this time, Miss Walker?"

"She's just upset that you're leaving."

"Well, she's always mad," I said.

I stared at my bed. I'd spent the last year in that bed shivering, from the cold or shivering with fear or both. I hadn't been able to sleep well ever since those Irish came through the door with their clubs in their hands. Every creak of the floor that I heard set my heart racing.

I woke up from one nightmare that happened on the *Sarah* to another that happened here. It might be someone getting up at night, it might be a rat or even nothing. And then John, in the next ward, was murdered by two seven-year-olds. Randall's Island was made worse, and everyone was so afraid. Who knows who walked around at night and what for? What if I was the one who didn't wake up? The nurse in John's ward sure slept through the night right when it counted the most.

I got my things together. I mostly just had old clothes that didn't fit well. I kept them in the wooden crate Miss Walker had given me. Miss Walker told me to check under the bed to make sure I hadn't forgotten anything, though I had so little that forgetting anything was unlikely. I never thought I could have less than I did when I'd left Barra, but I was wrong. I only had a small handful of things, anyhow.

The few boys that were in the dormitory stared at me and I could tell they wanted to ask me what was happening, where I was going, but they only knew me well enough to have left me alone. In looking at them, looking at me, I felt I lost something that I didn't even know I lost. I had plenty of friends on Barra. Being in this place, I no longer knew how to make friends, and that didn't bother me—at all.

Miss Walker slipped two books inside my little wooden crate, and I couldn't resist looking. She didn't know it, but to me she filled up that crate with just those two books.

"For me?"

"Yes, for you."

One was Marco Paul's *Adventures* in *Pursuit of Knowledge*, which we'd been enjoying in class. The other was *A Christmas Carol*.

"Oh, thank you, Miss Walker!" I gave her a hug and didn't want to let go.

I put on my old, oversized coat and carried the crate down the stairs and through the front door. We took the ferry across the Hudson River for a short trip into the city. A carriage awaited us with Mr. Schneider at the reins. He was the same person who'd brought me to Randall's Island. He looked a lot older, and not in the least bit scary.

"*Gibface zonderkite*," I whispered.

"What was that?" asked Miss Walker.

"Nothing, Miss Walker."

She smiled. "Your vocabulary's expanded, Murdoch. Careful how you use words. They are like bullets from a pistol: Very difficult to call back."

We traveled east five miles or so on West Washington Market Street with the background noise of the horse trotting along with its clip-clop-clip sound on the macadam surface. We crossed south on Liberty Street and then back west on Nassau Street. I'd already memorized most of the city map during one of our outings to the city library, so I knew these directions. Gibface, I mean Mr. Schneider, missed the turn on Liberty, but I didn't say anything.

We arrived at 103 Nassau Street, which housed Childs' printing and newspaper business, at about 12:30 p.m. that Thursday. It was a cold January day in the city, the 20th. I climbed out of the carriage, and Miss Walker handed me my crate, then she stepped out.

"I'll be right back, Mr. Schneider," she said.

Mr. Schneider grunted his reply.

We entered the building, and a man stood up from his desk to greet us. There were several people in the shop, most of them hunched over tables with slanted tops, taking something out of large, sectioned cases on top of the desks. They'd look down at a piece of paper, then grab something small from the case, put it into a holder, and repeat.

"Hello, Miss Walker, and hello, young Master Murdoch," the man said, extending his hands. "I'm Mr. Childs, Casper Childs." He took my hand, squeezed it too tight, and gave it a rugged downward pump. He was a pleasant enough older man, large-bellied and missing most of his hair, which he had made up for with a substantial greying beard. Not quite in the Santa Claus league, but close. His puffy eyes, supported by dark circles beneath them, made him look perpetually sleepy. He smelled of strong pipe tobacco, which reminded me of my father's pipe, and I instantly missed him and wondered if the sadness would ever go away.

"Did Mr. Ferguson tell you about his abilities? They are quite remarkable," said Miss Walker.

I could feel my face turning red. I always get embarrassed when she talks about me. I sometimes wish I didn't have my ability. It made me feel like I wasn't normal somehow, but at the same time, I'm not against using it to my advantage. Mr. Childs didn't notice my discomfort, or he didn't care about it, and he asked me about my reading.

Miss Walker left me with him. "Mr. Childs, please contact us if there is any issue. Thank you for giving him this opportunity. Murdoch, you are to do exactly as Mr. Childs tells you; is that understood? If everything works out, you won't have to come back to Randall's Island, and it's up to you to make sure of that. Goodbye, Mr. Childs. Goodbye, Murdoch." The horses neighed as she stepped into the carriage, and she was gone.

Mr. Childs stared at me and made me nervous. Then he spoke.

"Murdoch, how would you like to help me write a story for the City Intelligence piece in the newspaper?"

"Sure, I guess so."

"Good, good. Bring that chair over here and come sit next to my desk. I'm going to ask you some questions about Randall's Island."

I found it odd that he wanted to ask me questions instead of telling me to clean or teaching me about cleaning. "What do you want to know?"

He took a notepad and a curved briar pipe out of his desk. He spent a minute loading and lighting it, took a long pull, exhaled, and seemed satisfied. "Tell me about the time those three Irish boys attacked you with clubs while you were sleeping."

"I wasn't attacked with clubs, but I had to fight them from the first day I got to Randall's Island. I thought that fighting back would make them leave me alone, and I guess they did for a while, but at night, they came into the ward I slept in. The staff caught them before they could hurt me."

Mr. Childs wrote notes on his pad, which were a lot more words than I said. But maybe this was how writing worked.

Mr. Childs look up from his notepad, "How many times did they strike you with their clubs?"

"They never hit me with them," I thought I said. "One of the younger children had a stomachache, and he called out to the nurse, which woke her up, and then they started to run, and Mr. Ferguson caught them."

"They meant to club you to death, is that right?"

"I think so." He seemed to like that.

"I have all I need for right now. I'll write it up on page two for tomorrow's paper. It will be short, but it will lead into the other story about the boy who was killed. What was his name?"

"John, but I don't know his last name."

"Were you friends?"

"He was a lot younger than me. We talked sometimes, but I didn't know him that well."

"Okay, take the broom over there and get to work sweeping the floor."

Mr. Childs stayed busy writing the news story with his pen. When he finished, he walked over to a table with a slanted top. He set his written page down, walked to a cabinet, and pulled out a tray divided into different sections. Each section held a metal letter.

Now I could see what the other men had been doing: they were setting type. I had never seen that before. I finished sweeping the floor around the other workers and then watched Mr. Childs as he placed the small metal letters from left to right and upside down in a holder.

Of course! I thought, they must be positioned so that the printing comes out right side up. He didn't seem to mind me standing beside him, so I read the story he was building from his handwritten copy. It did not take long for me to learn how to read upside down, and this story was not at all what happened to me on Randall's Island..

"I see you're watching closely," Mr. Childs said. "That's a good thing. Do you understand why I place the slugs upside-down in the composing stick?"

"Yes, so the print will come out right side up."

"That's right. Once you finish a sentence, you place it on the tow board. This story is complete, so I'll lock it up, and we'll take it into the back room for printing."

He led me into the back room where he kept the press. An older man with a limp entered the room, and Mr. Childs introduced him as his brother Charles. If Casper Childs was Santa looking, Charles looked like an injured and cranky elf that could have been in a sword fight. He had a deep reddened scar on his left cheek that supported my theory, and I was keen to find out if my imagination was getting the better of me or if I was right. I was too afraid of him to ask.

Charles didn't say anything to me or even acknowledge me as he moved us both back from the press with a wave of his hand. He seemed equally annoyed with both of us. He applied ink to the press with a roller, and the distinct smell of printing ink filled the room. I had never smelled anything like it. It smelled oily and like varnish at the same time. It was so strong that I swore I could taste soot, and I didn't like it.

Mr. Childs didn't seem to mind his brother's rudeness and explained how the printing press worked. When he finished, he lifted the frame that held the paper in place, and then he removed the paper.

"Okay," Mr. Childs said. "Murdoch, you can proofread it first, and then I'll check it. We'll see if you can read as well as Miss Walker says."

"I already read it," I said.

"How? When?" Mr. Childs asked.

"When you were putting the letters in the composing stick and putting them into the chase bed. I read it then. There's only one mistake: You mixed up the letters in the word 'as.' It's halfway through the story. Also, it didn't happen like you wrote."

"Well, suppose you read it aloud to me."

"The whole thing?" I asked. And I started from memory.

CITY INTELLIGENCE

Boy Survives Randall's Island Attack – a boy at Randall's Island is lucky to be alive after Irish hoodlum inmates broke into the ward where the boy was sleeping and attacked him with clubs. The boy, Murdoch McNeil, 10, feared for his life such that two of the orphan's teachers, Miss Walker, and Mr. Ferguson, implored the TRUE DEMOCRAT newspaper's owner, Mr. Casper Childs, to take the youngster in as an apprentice. Seeing the protection of young Murdoch as his civic duty, Mr. Childs has given the boy a place at the prestigious newspaper, thus removing him from the danger of living on Randall's Island. sA has been reported in other newspapers, a six-year-old child was beaten to death by two young boys while the nurse in charge slept in the same ward, deaf to the boy's loud cries for help. We wonder if this 'nurse' who was charged to protect these poor orphans was even at her appointed post. We will continue to investigate and keep our readers informed.

Mr. Childs followed along, reading the proof, his brother looking over his shoulder. After I finished, I waited for them to say something. They said nothing, so I said something. "You see where the mistake is? About halfway down, right there."

Charles glared. "Well, you think you're some pumpkins, don't you, kid? With your parlor tricks. Casper, I say you send him back. We don't need a printer's devil here, we just don't. He's some Mick guttersnipe. We've got the Tammany Hall printer's contract now. I don't know why you think we need a damned newspaper. It's just going to cause more work for me."

"You tell me you like cleaning the ink off the type when all you do is complain? This is my business. Maybe you can go back into the Navy – or maybe you can't. How did the Revenue Cutter Service work out? We've had these words before, and I'll not have them again. I'm fixing the error, and we're running it in tomorrow's edition. Murdoch, come with me."

Charles continued his menacing stare. I wanted to tell him I'm not a Mick, I'm a Scot, but it didn't matter. Their family was from England, and to some of them, all the Gaels and Celts might as well be Irish. It didn't seem worth it to arguing with someone like Charles. I followed Mr. Childs out to the front office, and he handed me a folded paper.

"That was some impressive reading. You'll be a first-rate printer, but just because you can read like that doesn't mean you can skip to setting print. You have to work your way up. This is the address of the print supply shop, Davis & Black. They have an order for me, ink and ammonia to clean type. They're at 112 John Street. Do you know where that is, or do you need directions?"

"I can find it."

"I'll just bet you can. Tell him who you are and who you work for, get the order, bring it back, and no stops anywhere else. Just to the print supply and back. Got it?"

"Okay."

John Street was only six blocks away, west on Nassau, then it would be the southwest corner of Nassau and John. I made it a point to watch the newsboys hawking their evening papers on the corners as I went. At this time of day, they barked their pitches less enthusiastically, and their customers also lagged in their energy. I soon reached Davis & Black, where an elderly man was finishing his sweeping.

"What can I do for you, young fella?"

"I'm to pick up an order for Mr. Childs." I handed him the paper. "I'm his new apprentice, Murdoch McNeil."

He leaned the broom against the counter and seemed to balance with it himself as he did. "So Childs has himself a new printer's devil, eh? Interesting. Never thought he'd take an apprentice. Your father must be someone over at Tammany Hall then."

"Begging your pardon, I don't have any parents."

"Oh, I see. Well, I'm Mr. Davis. I'll get your order." He brought out a tightly wrapped box. "Order ticket is in there; take care you don't drop it on your way back. It won't do to have black ink all over Nassau Street."

"Mr. Davis, what's a printer's devil?" I asked.

"Fair question. Well, it's you, an apprentice printer. Some say it's because the art of printing used to be considered a sort of black magic. Some say it's because the apprentices mix the ink and clean the presses, and their skin stains black like a devil. And others say that print shops are all haunted, and there's a ghost, called a printer's devil, causing mischief with the presses."

"What kind of mischief?"

"Oh, messing with the print, mixing up letters and ruining type, spilling ink, things like that."

"I'd never mix up the letters or anything!"

"Easier for the journeyman printer to blame things on the apprentice, I think, instead of owning up to his mistakes. If the apprentice argues, then he's getting the short end of the horn for sure."

He seemed kind, good-natured, and a good source of information, so I continued my questioning. "Why did you think my father must be in Tammany Hall? I heard Mr. Childs' brother mention it, too."

"Tammany Hall, well, that's a powerful political organization. Your boss, Mr. Childs, is their official printer, so usually, Tammany Hall would be the one to say if he needed an apprentice and who that should be. Don't mention to Casper that I said that. I talk too much sometimes."

I put my finger to my lips.

"Fair enough. You're smart like a steel trap, aren't you?"

I shrugged. He bade me good day, and I walked back to the print shop. I still didn't really understand what Tammany Hall was, other than it seemed to have power and some people seemed to be afraid of it, but that was enough for me to want to avoid it. When I arrived back at the shop, Mr. Childs was there, but his angry brother Charles was not. The others were gone as well.

"Ah, there you are. Did Mr. Davis talk your ear off? What's he think of me having an apprentice?"

"He talked a little, but he didn't say anything about me being your apprentice. He just said not to drop the package on the way back."

"Strange, he usually has a lot to say about everything. Well, we've printed five hundred copies of tomorrow's paper. There'll be some newsboys by to pick them up. My foreman is Mr. Baptiste, and he'll be in by five to open up. Don't open the shop to the newsboys before he gets here; they'd steal every paper if they could. You don't even need to be talking to them; they'll try to con you six ways before breakfast, or they'll just bully you. Mr. Baptiste makes sure that all the bundles are paid for before they get out the door and that nobody gets hurt. Understand?"

I nodded.

"I won't have time to show you how to set type, but you'll learn eventually, and I'll bet you can learn it fast. Tomorrow, after you finish selling the newspapers, Mr. Baptiste will show you how to clean the ink off the letters. You'll get your hands dirty!"

"When I see the boys selling the papers, they're always yelling something. Sometimes I can't understand them. What should I yell?"

"You're the boy who survived a severe attack by a gang of hoodlums on Randall's Island. You use that. Here, like this." He picked up a newspaper and started yelling, "Get your paper here! Another boy attacked on Randall's Island! Lucky to be alive! Exclusive story from the lad himself! *True Democrat* hires Randall's Island attack victim! Exclusive!" He put it down. "You see? You yell something to get the people's attention so they don't pass by you, they stop and buy."

"But it's not true."

"Truth doesn't sell newspapers, Murdoch. Your young innocent face will. You say anything to get our newspaper into the customer's hands. Understand?"

"Do anything I have to do to sell the paper and anything I have to say to make them come back."

"Yes, exactly! Mrs. Childs, that's my wife, Sophronia; she came by and fixed up the back room for you. She'll bring in a basket of food for you every day. A place to sleep, and food for your apprenticeship. We will see what you can sell, and if you do well, you can keep some of the money; how's that? I made up a contract for seven years and sent it on to your supervisor at Randall's Island, and after that, you'll be a journeyman. A good trade, it is."

"Thank you, Mr. Childs."

He finished at his desk, tidied a bit, and then left, locking the door behind him. Other than spending a few nights locked in the detention cell at Randall's Island, I never had a whole room to myself, and I liked the feeling. I sat on my bed in the little room as it grew dark outside. I lit the lantern and opened up the basket. So much food! I could have eaten it all, but then I remembered that Mrs. Childs meant for this to be spread over three meals.

I took a copy of the newspaper from tomorrow's bundle. I dared to sit at Mr. Childs' desk, ate my dinner, and read the paper. Friday, January 21st, 1853. "Mayor intends to appoint Francis W. Edmonds of Merchants' Bank chamberlain of the city." Not interesting to me. Female telegraph operators approved. A man named Stinson had his home robbed. Then, my story on page two. Marine law a failure, The *Times* prints lies... it seemed to me everyone did, anyway. Whatever has to be said to sell papers.

I finished my dinner, and I could not stop myself from finishing tomorrow's breakfast and lunch. At Randall's Island, we had to eat what was available when we could, and I told myself that I'd worry about tomorrow's food tomorrow. I cleared off Mr. Childs' desk and made sure there was not a crumb left. He probably wouldn't have liked me eating my food there or even sitting there, but he wasn't around anyhow.

I went to my sleeping room, which was obviously the printer's storeroom. The printing supplies had been moved about to make room for a small wood-framed bed and a little nightstand with a small kerosene lamp. The bed was adorned with a brightly patterned patchwork quilt of greens and blues. Mrs. Childs's touch was evident.

A wash basin was placed on the floor. I thought I wouldn't be using it anyway, so I pushed it underneath the bed with my foot. The room was cramped but seemed big enough to me. I remember how small our sleeping area was on the *Sarah* and shuddered. I crawled into my bed, so warm even in the thick of winter. I wasn't cold, but I put my hands close to the lamp anyway, just to feel the warmth. I had my first job and I knew my dad would be proud of me, and my mom would worry. I felt safer here than at Randall's Island, but not safe enough to not worry about the sounds in the street. I tried to fall asleep through those new sounds.

***

Five a.m. did not seem to come any later here than it did at Randall's Island, but here I slept without waking up constantly through the night with fear, cold, or hunger. I went to the water closet, washed up, dressed, and went to the front of the shop. Out the large window that faced Nassau Street, I saw several boys gathered around outside. They motioned for me to come and unlock the door. I was curious about these newsboys, and I wanted to speak with them despite Mr. Childs' insistence that I should not, but I didn't have a key to the door. Mr. Baptiste arrived at 5:30 and let the boys stream in, chattering away.

"Hey, Mr. Baptiste, who's this then?"

"Boys, this is Murdoch McNeil, our new apprentice. He's been on Randall's Island for the last year, so you know he can take care of himself well enough. You're not to meddle with him."

"I've been on since September of 1851," I corrected.

"Was you attacked by that gang?" one of them asked. "What do you know about those kids beat cold as a wagon tire?" "What about

94

the inmates what killed him?" They peppered me with questions. "Did you kill anyone? We heard all about them murders." "Careful, Tommy, he's probably savage as a meat axe!"

One of them asked Mr. Baptiste, "What's with making him an apprentice? How does he rate?"

He brushed them all off. "You're wasting time. Plank down your coin and pick up your papers. And if any of you want to tell Mr. Childs how he should run his business, I'll be glad to let him know. He'll be in directly."

The boys clammed up. "Hey, we were just having fun with him. No harm meant."

"Mr. Childs wants Murdoch to hawk the paper in front of the shop, so that's his territory. Brian, I think that's been your spot. Better give it over and smile about it and find somewhere else."

Brian shrugged his shoulder and said "Okay, I can hawk anything to anyone anywhere." I didn't want a corner that had been taken from someone and handed to me. I could find my own corner even if I had to fight for it. If someone were to ask the most important thing I'd learned on Randall's Island, it wouldn't be whatever the rich folks thought they saw when they paid their yearly charity visit. What I had really learned, the lesson I would take with me always, was to fight and survive. To me, newsboys could be no different than Braden's gang. If I had to fight to sell Mr. Childs' newspapers as he'd asked me to do, I was ready for it.

The newsboys all grabbed their papers and headed out. I grabbed my stack as well. Mr. Baptiste told me to be back by 4:00 in the afternoon and he would show me how to clean the type. I nodded and then left to catch up with the boy who'd been pushed off his corner.

"Brian!" I called out.

He turned and frowned.

"I'm not taking your corner. I can find my own."

"What about Childs?"

"If I sell my papers, he won't say anything about it." Brian walked back in front of the print shop and started his pitch. I went to 170 Nassau Street, on the corner close to City Hall. A few newsboys stood there shivering and blowing on their hands to keep the chill from freezing their fingers. They struggled to untie their bundles through a haze of sleep and morning chill. The corner in front of City Hall was unoccupied, which was a prime location. I started my pitch prepared to defend my turf.

"I survived Randall's Island! Read my story here! Irish gang attack on Randall's Island! Orphan lucky to be alive! Two child murderers on Randall's Island! Inmates attack orphan on Randall's Island! Read the exclusive here in the *True National Democrat*! *True National Democrat* takes in Randall's Island attack survivor!"

Mr. Childs was right, this pitch worked. People crowded around buying their newspapers from the orphan hero of Randall's Island, and most of them paid me more than I charged for the paper. I can't say that I'd told any more truth on the street corner than what was in the paper, but the pitch sold. After the first busy hour, an older boy approached.

"You there, Scot, this is my corner," he said through a thick Irish brogue.

"Maybe it was, but it's not now," I said, dropping my papers and balling up my fists.

The boy walked cautiously toward me, and then another boy the same age joined us. "You're Murdoch, aren't you?"

"Who wants to know?"

"Danny's my name. Half the boys in this neighborhood work for me, selling the papers."

We stared at each other. Miss Walker wouldn't be around to patch up my face. No matter.

"I need this corner."

"Did you really beat up all those kids on Randall's Island?" Danny asked. "One by one? Is that true?"

"Yeah, fair and square, one at a time. How did you know?"

Danny kicked at some loose rocks on the ground, took out cigarette papers and a bag of tobacco tied with yellow string, rolled one, put it in his mouth, and lit it. The acrid sulfur puff from the match stung my eyes, but I refused to show that it bothered me. Danny blew the smoke away from me and spit out a crumb of tobacco stuck on his tongue from the end of his smoke, then brushed off another crumb from his tongue with the back of his hand.

"Word gets out. Some of those guys—they're on Randall's Island because they stole money from us and started fights. Some of them used clubs. You kicked them to Hoboken and back." Danny smiled with approval.

"I just want to sell my papers, is all."

"All right, Scot, nobody will bother you," Danny said as he pulled from his cigarette and left.

I sold everything by 1:00 p.m., the coins bulging out of my pockets. By the time I made it back to the print shop, I felt frozen. It seemed colder to hawk papers outside than to be in one of those detention cells back at Randall's Island, but at least I didn't have to wear handcuffs.

I saw Mr. Childs engaged in a heated conversation with his brother. I started to walk past them, but Charles grabbed me roughly by the shoulders.

"Put up your fiddle already? You can't make any money by coming back early."

"Leave him be, Charles. We're nearly finished with tomorrow's run," Charles said. "I want Anthony to show him how to clean the type."

"You dumped the unsold papers in the streets, I'll bet," Charles chided.

I dug my hands into my pockets and pulled out as many coins as would fit in my hands, dropping a few of them to clatter on the floor. My handfuls crashed on top of the desk. I then turned out my pockets, letting the rest of the coins spill out.

"I sold all the papers."

Charles looked at the coins, then at me, then at Mr. Childs. "This discussion is not over, Casper," he said, and he stormed out.

"Great work, Murdoch. Where did you set up?"

"I didn't want to take a corner from a boy like that, so I took the corner of Nassau and Spruce Street right across from City Hall."

"I'm surprised one of the other newsboys hadn't taken it already. Great spot to sell."

"We worked it out." I didn't want him to write another article about me.

"Count out the money, write out the amount on this pay slip, then put it in my desk. I noticed you had a good appetite last night. Sophronia brought you some more food. Have something for lunch, then find me. Mr. Baptiste will train you on cleaning the press and the type."

I told him that quite a few people paid me more than what the papers cost because of the pitch, and several of them stayed to ask me questions about the Island, or about John's death, or about me fighting off the gang.

"We'll have another story in the news tomorrow about it. Say, that nurse who slept through the whole thing, did she ever smell like liquor? Were the nurses ever absent when you went to bed at night?"

I'd wanted to put Randall's Island behind me completely, and I would be glad when everyone stopped talking about it. But I wanted to be truthful with Mr. Childs, and I'd observed that the story held plenty of advantages for me. As a matter of fact, I had heard the nurse in John's ward was gone quite a lot, and the boys would say she 'wobbled by habit.' But I didn't want to testify or point fingers. So, I remained silent.

He could see in my face that I was reluctant. "I respect your right to plead the Fifth," Mr. Childs said. I would have to look up what that meant later.

In my room, I counted my pay total in my head, and I had brought in one dollar and thirty-five cents. I opened my food basket. Sophronia Childs was determined to keep me well fed. I had never felt richer, or more full. After my lunch I went to look for Mr. Baptiste, but Mr. Childs called me over first.

"This is what hard work does for a boy," he said. He handed me an envelope with some coins in it, and on the envelope, he'd written my name and 85 cents. "I give you the standard 50% wholesale price for the newspapers, and that's 100 papers, so you made fifty cents in sales plus thirty-five cents in tips. Most newsboys make about thirty cents a day, so you've done very well! You may want to put some money away, save it."

I finished out the day cleaning the type on Mr. Childs' prized Columbian printing press. The cleaning fluid smelled awful, and using it made my hands burn. Mr. Baptiste said it was ammonia, bought from a merchant who also sold the supply to make gunpowder and detergents. I knew exactly what this kind of ammonia was: On Barra, we were made to relieve ourselves in buckets, and then the contents were sold to the tanner. The older, the better, he'd say. Whenever the tanner came to church, he'd sit alone in the very last pew. Mr. Baptiste said that when he was the printer's devil, he had to save his own urine to clean off the type. I was glad for some progress.

As I went to bed that night, I couldn't help but feel lucky. For the first time since leaving Barra, fear did not steal my sleep or gnaw at my chest. Even on the ship, when my family was still alive, I carried some implacable anxiety. But now, I had money in my pocket, my stomach was full, and I did not feel the need to eat everything I could, lest I not get another meal. I had a room and bed to myself. It was January 21st, my birthday, and I just turned eleven.

The days came one right after the other, but I always knew what date it was, hawking my papers, reading the *True National Democrat*, every word, and looking up whatever I didn't understand in the print shop's large dictionary. Not long into my apprenticeship I bought a dictionary for myself and placed it with my little growing collection. Saving was not easy for me when there were so many good books to buy.

Then I found the library.

On Barra, we barely had any books, and on Randall's Island our books were locked up in the classrooms. Here on the corner of Broadway and Leonard Street was the New York Society Library. I could not borrow books there because I was not a subscriber, but the librarians allowed me to wander through the shelves and page through what I wanted. The print shop kept me occupied from 5:30 a.m. to 7:00 p.m. every day except Sunday, but on days when I sold my papers early, I headed to the library. I made sure that I sold my papers early almost every single day.

I became something of a fixture at the library, or maybe just a squatter. At least the librarians seemed to tolerate me. Miss Thompson was the head librarian in charge.

She reminded me of my mother on Barra, and I don't know why, because she didn't look anything like her, but every time I saw her, my mother's memory would hijack my day. She had very short black hair in tight curls, was very skinny and seemed to glide instead of walk. I quickly grew very fond of her and felt safe around her.

One day, she told me she could hold books for me so I wouldn't have to keep replacing them on the shelf before I was finished. It was nice not having a subscriber take home something I'd been reading.

The spring rains started and the smells of the city changed with the season. A mixture of wet horse dung, horses blowing their winter coat and the perfume of spring flowers permeated the air. People began to open their windows, and In the evening, a kaleidoscope of cooking food aromas reminded me of how lucky I was to be eating on a regular basis.

Before I knew it, we hurtled into summer and the pleasant smells of the foliage were more intense as were the other, unpleasant smells. Summers in New York could get hot, but I preferred heat to winter cold. Mr. Childs gave me a key to the back door, and Miss Thompson began letting me take a book home with me in the evenings as long as I told her which one I had. She would always ask me how I liked the book and what page I was on. I think she was merely trying to ensure I wouldn't forget that I had the book, but I knew there was no chance of that.

Then it turned into fall. The leaves became proud with color, and all talk now centered on the upcoming election on November 8th. I had no interest in politics and felt that the election would not have much impact on the fate of an eleven-year-old boy.

I was wrong.

One afternoon day, right after the election, I'd made sixty-five cents for myself by selling the papers. I had just finished cleaning the front office when a man entered the shop. I recognized him, but by appearance rather than by name. He introduced himself and asked to see Mr. Childs.

"Mr. Childs, there's a man out front asking for you. He says his name is Cummings Tucker," I said taking care to pronounce his name correctly.

"Tell him I'll be right out. Before you start cleaning the press, I have an order stacked on the shelf. Box it up, and make sure your hands are clean. I've got to deliver the order today."

I went to pick up the print job and glanced at the top sheet as I always do. This was an election ballot to be delivered to a Mr. Holmes. But the election was yesterday, and this didn't seem right. On the very top of the stack was the order form with the example of what the customer wanted. This, too, was odd. Next to the word "Alderman," where voters should select their candidate, was the name of the man at the counter: Cummings H. Tucker. There was a line drawn through the name, and underneath was printed just "C. Tucker." I knew from the voting instructions in the papers that it was important to write the candidate's name only one way, so this seemed like an error. How would the vote counters in Tammany Hall know what was meant by this?

I'd already boxed up the orders of election tickets a week before voting, so what were these tickets doing here, and why would they be delivered to someone else while the man on the ballot stood right here in the shop? This had to be a mistake. I picked up a sample ticket and the order form and brought them to Mr. Childs.

"Excuse me, sir, these election tickets are for yesterday," I said. "Are you sure you want these delivered to Mr. Holmes?"

The man who introduced himself as Cummings Tucker, the man who was supposed to be on the ballot, looked at me like I had corn growing out of my ears. "Let me see that, young man."

Mr. Childs snatched the papers from my hand before I could give them to Mr. Tucker, and said "Get back to work, Murdoch, and box the order up like I told you to."

Mr. Tucker frowned. "Casper, you've got to let me have a look at that ballot. Don't make me take it from you."

"I don't know anything about it, Cummings. It's just another print order," Mr. Childs said as he handed him the papers.

"My name appears on the ballot here, but crossed out? And C. Tucker in its place? Who ordered these? Why are they marked for delivery now, and to Holmes, as though they've been cast?"

"I've nothing to do with it. It says right there Holmes ordered them. What he does with them is his business."

"But he's the Clerk of the Polls. You're playing dumb about this, then, Casper?" Mr. Tucker grew furious, though I still didn't understand what this was all about, only that it was wrong somehow.

Mr. Childs stammered, "I know nothing about it. I'm just the printer."

"Well then, be the printer if you must. You're going to deliver these fraudulent ballots to Holmes just as instructed. They will be counted against me just as Holmes intended. Then I will bring charges against Holmes and the Board of Inspectors for election fraud, and if you don't want to join them in jail, you'll testify that Holmes ordered the thing done!"

Mr. Tucker stormed out. I'd heard everything from the back room. When I looked into the front office, Mr. Childs stared out the window frowning, his index finger and his middle finger drumming rapidly on his desk. He was upset. I was the only person who heard Mr. Tucker's angry accusations, and I had a feeling that somehow, I was to blame. I walked up to Mr. Childs so I could get my punishment over with.

"Sir? Did I do something wrong?"

"Are all those ballots boxed up?"

"Yes, sir."

"I'm going to deliver them to Mr. Holmes. I won't be back until tomorrow morning. Lock up at the usual time. Find something to do, and Murdoch? Don't say a single word to anyone about what just happened. It's none of your business, and it isn't anyone else's business, either. Got it?"

"Yes, sir." I locked up at 7:00, went to the library, and started reading. I'd hoped to find something on election law, but I found I could not concentrate. I started over on the same page five times and finally gave up. Miss Thompson asked me what was wrong, but I told her everything was fine. The library closed at 9:00, and I headed back to the shop.

In the front, where the typesetters work, a light was on, and I saw Mr. Childs' brother Charles sitting at the editor's desk. I briefly thought of not going in, maybe even sleeping on the street as cold as it was, but I decided to sneak in through the back and head straight to my room. It was not enough to escape notice, and a minute later, Charles burst through the door. He reeked of bad liquor, and the front of his trousers was stained with something that smelled even worse.

"Don't you know what you've done, you little bastard!" he yelled. He blocked the door, and I had nowhere to go, so I tried retreating to the corner of my room. He lunged at me, but he tripped and fell on his bum leg, then, before I could blink, he was up on his feet again. He grabbed my shirt collar, then backhanded me across my face with such force that he knocked me against the wall.

"You've ruined us! Everyone is going to know now! You God-damned bastard!"

I heard the front door open. "Charles! Are you in here?" Mr. Childs yelled.

"Mr. Childs! Help me! He's back here!" I cried.

Charles hit me again and then Mr. Childs appeared. He grabbed his brother, spun him around, and hit him hard in his jaw, on the left where Charles had sported that terrible-looking scar. "Charles! Get out of here, or I'll make sure you have to limp on your other leg too! Get the hell out!"

"Casper! Your damned printer's devil has ruined us!" he cried. But he stumbled out of my room and out the front door.

I sat on my bed, shaking. Mr. Childs stood over me.

"Murdoch, I am sorry. I don't know what to say. He's, well, he's, my brother. You've got to get out of here. I can't take a chance on what else he might do. He's like that when he drinks."

It seemed to me he was like that when he didn't drink, but I held my tongue. "I don't know where to go, sir." I was crying for the first time since I heard my parents' bodies splash on the ocean.

"Find somewhere tonight. The street, even. He might be back, and I might not be here to restrain him. Maybe tomorrow I can have you sent back to Randall's Island."

I did not know which would be worse.

Chapter VI: Counselor

November 8th, 1853
New York City

"They are exposed to such wretched influences, sleeping in bad cellars – often under drinking cellars or in brothels-or in the streets."
Charles Loring Brace, September 19th, 1853

Mr. Childs said he'd find a way to get my belongings to me. This was of little help at 9:30 on a cold November evening. I knew that other boys slept in boxes, door stoops, basements, and some seedy places that I had rather not heard about in the first place. I'd already had cigarettes thrust into my face. I tried a puff and got sick and wondered why in blazes anyone would smoke them, though most boys did. The same went for liquor. I tried a drink, but it burned my mouth and throat.

I don't even remember walking the streets when I left Mr. Childs's print shop. New York City was becoming windy. Colder. The dim lights from the gas and oil lamps in building windows made the streetlights seem brighter. They glowed with an apologetic false heat that made me feel like any warmth of the city had been snatched up and held captive. I walked up to the front doorsteps of the library, hoping that the doorframe had not been claimed by another kid, and it was not a cop's place to check for us guttersnipes.

I started to wedge myself into the protected well of the doorframe when the door handle rattled. The door opened, and I toppled through the entrance. Miss Thompson was looking down at me.

"Murdoch, is that you? It is you! What are you doing here? Why aren't you at the Childs's? Come inside, you must be freezing!" Her astonishment tumbled out of her at once.

She led me over to a metal radiator, spreading its warmth to the building. I held my hands out to it, trying to turn my bruised and bloody face away from her, but she saw. She gently placed her hand on my shoulder and turned my face toward hers with her other hand. She looked concerned.

"Who did this to you? Did Casper do this?" Her tone grew in anger.

"No. His brother, Charles."

"I might have known. Was he drunk?"

"Yes."

"Is that why he hit you?"

"I'm not supposed to say. I can't say. I told Mr. Childs I wouldn't say, and he said it was none of my business and I had to leave. He wants me back at Randall's Island."

"Murdoch, that's not going to happen. I won't allow it. Find a book to keep you company and sit at the table behind the bookshelf. Don't leave. I'll be back in half an hour."

Miss Thompson left me to my reading. I sat at the large, dark, square table and stared at the rows of books. Somehow, even in the dim building with the singular lamp Miss Thompson had lit, I felt as though the books surrounding me were some sort of magic that shielded me from the coldness and anger of the outside. They protected me somehow from all of Mr. Childses, Mr. Schneiders, and Mrs. Abernathys, who appeared as monsters in my nightmares even more than they'd appeared in real life.

The books on the shelves in front of where I sat were stacked so high that, in the dim light, they seemed to disappear into a dark, starless sky. The scent of these books was different in this part of the library, and it made me curious. The books pulled, gnawed and scolded me for feeling sorry for myself until I finally stood up and walked over to the massive shelf. I hadn't been in this area of the library before.

The books looked much the same, with brownish red leather bindings and gold lettering which proclaimed *Johnson's Reports Cases Argued and Determined in the Supreme Court of New York.* I pulled out Volume 10, placed my thumbs on the closed pages in the center of the thick book, and opened it. I took a deep breath, getting to know the book by smell first. The rough linen pages reminded me of the earth, the peat that burned so familiar in my home on Barra. This book brought me home, and this was where I belonged.

I could read the words, of course, and I could memorize pages and pages if I had any reason to, but I couldn't tell you the meaning of the story. The writing was different. Different in a way that I couldn't yet explain to myself, and I couldn't yet understand. It seemed to be a book full of stories about people who argued with each other, but in a way that was very polite and followed a lot of rules. The stories and arguments made little sense to me, and it was unlike any reading I had ever done. Still, it was a story. Instead of closing the book in frustration, disregarding the words I couldn't understand and putting the book back on its shelf, I told myself that I would figure out this kind of story.

Usually, I could just use the dictionary to look up a word I didn't understand. I'd learn what the word meant and then continue on with my reading. But this book was different. I would need help to understand this kind of story, which disappointed and excited me. I should have been tired, but this book seemed to reach all the way to me from 1814, thirty-two years ago, still bright in its bindings as if I was the first to handle it. My mind raced with questions rather than thoughts of sleep. I saw other bindings that looked new but old at the same time. Did they all have this kind of story in it? The same complicated words? I put Volume 10 back and started to pull out its neighbor, when I heard the front door open. I feared discovery for a moment, but I heard the click of Miss Thompson's heels. My new adventure could wait.

"Murdoch?"

"I'm here by the back shelves," I answered.

"I have some food and bedding for you. You can sleep in the basement; let's make a place for you." She picked up the lamp and led the way down the stairs and to a small room in the back corner of the basement. "This will do for tonight. I wish you could come to the boarding house with me, but I only have the one room and the landlady won't allow it. She would notify the orphan asylum right away."

I still wanted to know about those books, and Miss Thompson seemed to know something about all of them whenever I'd had questions before. "Those books on the shelf where I'd been sitting. I pulled one of them down and looked through it."

"They're law books; they talk about decisions the courts made about different cases. They're for lawyers to check their references, so they don't leave the building. I can't imagine they'd be interesting to you." She spread the blankets and cushions onto the floor.

"I could read the words, but the stories didn't make sense."

Miss Thompson laughed. "They don't make sense to me either! You have to be a lawyer to understand it, and even then, I don't know."

"But the stories seemed..."

"Let's talk about your law career tomorrow, Murdoch. It's late, and you still need to have some dinner before you go to bed! And so do I. I don't know what I'm going to do with you, but for tonight you're safe." Miss Thompson stayed with me a while longer, and I ate the chicken she'd brought. We didn't talk much, and I could tell she was worried. Then she left, and I was alone, my oil lamp shining on the floor by my bed. I was tempted to go back upstairs and grab one of those curious law books, but sleep came too quickly for that.

***

I felt my feet being gently wiggled back and forth. I drifted in that hazy place between deep sleep and waking. I was back in my bed at home in Barra, and my mother was wiggling my feet to wake me up, just as she'd do every morning.

"Mom?" I called out without opening my eyes. "Elizabeth can milk the cows; I want to sleep."

"Murdoch, it's Miss Thompson. It's time to get up, and we've got a lot to do today! No cows to milk though. Get yourself together and come upstairs and we'll talk." She smiled and went back upstairs.

I was both embarrassed and sorrowful. I missed Barra. I missed my sister, my mother, and my father. It all seemed too much, and I pounded my fists into my pillow, screamed as quietly as I could, and cried. "Why, why didn't I die too?" Staying so busy that there was no room for memories was the only way for me to survive. Maybe I should go back to Randall's Island, I thought. At least there, I was so afraid that the fear buried the horrible memories deep. I shook off the sorrow and anger.

Miss Thompson had left a basin and a cloth next to my bed. I splashed the cold water on my face and drank a handful. She'd set a brick of lye soap next to the basin as well, but I felt that just the smell of the lye cleaned me well enough.

Miss Thompson was at her desk in the front of the library, and the other library staff smiled at me quietly as I passed.

"Have a seat, Murdoch," Miss Thompson said. Her director's office wasn't large, especially with the clutter of books on carts, the floor, and every other available space. She moved a stack of books off a chair, and I sat. My clothes and my own small collection of books, which I'd left at Mr. Childs, were in a box. "Did you sleep well?"

I nodded.

"I can fix that room up downstairs and bring in a real bed for you. I had a talk with Mr. Childs this morning."

"What did he say?"

"He told me what his brother did. He was very upset and wanted me to tell you he was very, very sorry for what happened. He didn't say why his brother acted that way other than he was drunk. It's not against the law to hit children. It should be, but it's not."

"Am I going back to Randall's Island?"

"Absolutely not. Mr. Childs also said you have a good memory, that you seem to remember every word you read. Is that true?"

My face felt hot. "Yes, but it's hard to talk about. I don't like for people to think I'm a freak, that I belong in the circus."

"You're not a freak; it's a gift. It's your gift. How you use it will be up to you. You could use it to take advantage of people, or you can use it to help people."

"How would my reading help people?"

"When the time comes, I think you will know. You have two choices in front of you now. One, you can ask for another apprenticeship. Mr. Childs said he can put a word in for you at the *Sun* newspaper. Two, you can work here, delivering books, trimming the new books, cleaning, that sort of thing. Did you like being Mr. Childs' apprentice?"

"Yes, at first. But setting type is the same thing over and over. I didn't like my hands being inky."

"What did you like best about it?"

"I liked hawking newspapers. I was good at it."

"You can sell the *Sun* morning edition and then do chores here at the library in the afternoons. Mr. Childs can talk with Mr. Day. He's the editor of *The Sun*, and I'm sure he'll be glad to have you. You can stay here until we find a proper place for you."

I didn't know what she meant by "a proper place" for me. Living in the library was the best thing that could have happened to me. Books had always been my teachers and my friends. With my time divided between making money selling papers and the money I'd make here, I felt I would do pretty well for myself. I could even afford to invest in a stack of *New York Times* on occasion and sell that paper, too. My mind rolled with the possibilities of the business of words.

Miss Thompson had me trimming the new books that morning. It was new to me, but I got to use my pocketknife, the first thing I'd ever bought with my own money from selling Mr. Childs' newspapers. A newsboy had to have one anyway to cut the string holding the bundles of paper together. I'd never had a brand-new book for myself, so I didn't know the pages had to be trimmed at the open ends before they could be opened. When I'd explored the library, I'd run across a page that seemed stuck to another page, not like it was glued, but like the two pages were printed that way on one sheet. I had thought it was a mistake. I'd asked Mr. Childs about it, but he wouldn't take the time to explain, and he brushed me off.

I learned that morning that all books were printed that way. The pages were printed many to a sheet, then folded the right way and bound. The buyer knew the books were brand new if the pages had to be released from their folds. That was trimming a book. I finished a whole cart of new books, then set to my deliveries, cleaned, and ended the day by sweeping the library.

Miss Thompson gave me some final directions before she went back to her boarding house. "Murdoch, you can pick up a bundle of *The Sun* newspapers and start that business in the morning tomorrow. Mr. Day knows you'll be working for him. After you've finished with that, I'll have more work for you here. We all fixed up your room downstairs.

Draw some water, get cleaned up, and soap won't kill you if you use it."

My life moved into a comfortable routine again, but this time I was not anxious and walking on pins and needles like at Mr. Childs. The people at the library, especially Miss Thompson, treated me very kindly. I knew they meant well, but it still took time to trust that I could safely get used to being treated well by adults. I enjoyed the quiet, and the only yelling I heard came from me as I hawked the newspapers.

Just before Thanksgiving, November 22, I picked up an extra bundle of the *New York Times*. I read that the ballot fraud that kicked up such a ruckus at Mr. Childs' print shop had been investigated. That man, Holmes, who ordered the ballots that caused the fuss, was arrested for election fraud along with the board of inspectors, William Murray, Hugh Mooney, and William Turner. Mr. Childs had not been charged or investigated, and I thought it curious that he was not in any trouble given that he had to have known that the ballots were ordered to rig the election. I even looked in the law books to find any cases of similar fraud, but all those volumes were just too much for me to get through.

Miss Thompson's landlady was kind enough to allow her to invite me to a Thanksgiving dinner. I was the only child there, and everyone was polite, asking questions about what it was like to be a newsie. I disliked the way the old ladies pinched my cheeks and called me cute, but I felt that was a fair price for the dinner.

In December, the weather grew quite a bit colder than it usually did. Between *The Sun* and *The Times*, I had never seen so much money coming my way. I grew taller and stronger. Miss Thompson said it was a growth spurt because I was finally eating well. I tried to pay her for it, but she said room and board was part of my library salary.

Toward Christmas, everyone at the library tacked decorations onto everything that didn't move. We had the most spectacular Christmas tree. The library's ceiling was so high that it almost didn't feel like it was there, but the tree nearly brushed it. Since I was the only person who could be hoisted that high, I got to place the star on top.

The library Christmas party attracted people from all over the city. It was the first Christmas I had money to buy presents, so I bought Miss Thompson a nice silver-plate brush for her hair. Under the tree I saw a wrapped parcel with my name on it. It was heavy as a brick and shaped like one, too! I opened it and traced the gilt words on the spine: A *New Law Dictionary and Glossary* by Alexander M. Burrill, published in 1850, and in two volumes!

I'd gotten into a routine of sitting at the desk in front of the law books whenever I had spare time. After the library closed, I'd take up this post again. I had learned enough to piece out some of the cases, each of them involving real people, and with this dictionary, I would understand a lot more. I devoured the law: When I'd sold the bulk of my papers every day, I'd page through the legal notices in *The Times*. Most of them were simple summonses but interesting nonetheless, and I always found a word or two I still did not know.

These words sometimes helped me hawk the papers. On January 20, every newsie in town hollered "Fire in City Hall!" But I had another term. "Fire in City Hall! Unknown Arsonist!" Two words can completely change a pitch, and I sold out of *The Sun* and *The Times* by 10:00 a.m. I tried to suppress a grin as I walked back to the library past newsies still standing among their bundles.

That day I entered the library early to find Miss Walker from Randall's Island meeting with Miss Thompson. The library staff stared at me as I walked by, and I worried that I would be sent back. I nearly bolted out when Miss Thompson called me into her office.

"Hello, Murdoch!" Miss Walker greeted me. "I'm so glad to see you! I've been hearing great things about you from Miss Thompson."

"I'm not going back! I'll run away; I can live on the streets. I can be with the newsies!"

"Whoa, calm down, Murdoch," Miss Thompson said. "No one is sending you back to Randall's Island."

"What, then?" I asked, rubbing my wrist nervously. I swore I could feel the handcuffs from detention.

"First," Miss Walker continued, "I want to say how sorry I am for what happened at Mr. Childs' print shop. Mr. Ferguson and I felt awful, and he went to see Charles. I'm not sure what he said or did to him, but Charles will never bother you again, I'm certain."

Miss Thompson had a plan. "There are people here at the library and even at Randall's Island who care a great deal about you, Murdoch. We've spoken about that group looking to take care of orphans right here in the city, and they've formed the Children's Aid Society. A Mr. Charles Brace is opening the News Boys Lodging House in the top floor of the *Sun* building, and it opens in March."

"It's another asylum, isn't it?" I asked.

"No, nothing like that," Miss Walker reassured me. "You pay for your bed, six cents a night. They have running water, good lighting, fresh air, and it's safe. You can come and go as you please, curfew is at 10:00 p.m., and no drinking is allowed."

"You can still work here at the library," Miss Thompson added. "We all want what's best for you, and we like you being here at the library. However, you do need to be around other children, boys your age. You need classes, not just what you can read about in these books. The adults there will look after you, too."

"You know Jerry, the Oysterman? And Mr. Glendinning at the coffee salon?" asked Miss Walker.

"They help out the newsies all the time, but I always pay my way," I said proudly.

"They know Mr. Brace, and they know Charles Tracy, who will be the superintendent of the house. You'll have until March to think about it," Miss Thompson said. She had been pressured by the Library's Board of Trustees to send me back to Randall's Island, as they didn't approve of me living in the library. But if she told them I was going to the lodging house in March, they might leave me alone for now. I agreed to the deal, said my farewells to Miss Walker, and then went back to my usual errands.

As it happened, my pickup and delivery list took me past Jerry the Oysterman. He said the boarding house was a "glowing capital idea – where else can a man get a bed and a wash for six cents?" He joked that I'd have to clean up if I was to be of any use to a young lady. I vowed that I would continue my distrustful relationship with soap, but I could stand water as long as it was plenty cold. I went into the coffee salon as well, and Mr. Glendinning said the newsies would do well to know where they'd sleep at night instead of wandering about. I didn't have many problems with the other newsboys and had earned the reputation of a scrapper, and that was fine with me. I'd get along with the other newsies all right. I supposed my choice was clear, and I told Miss Thompson that I'd sign up for the lodging home.

With all of this change coming my way, it wasn't until I went to bed that night that I realized the next day would be my birthday. I would be twelve. I tried to remember what my mother's voice sounded like, or my father's or my sister's. I can remember so much; why not this? Why could I recall nothing but the sight of bodies thrown overboard and the hollow splash they made when they hit the water?

I cried.

***

As I promised Miss Thompson and Miss Walker, on March 18, I climbed the stairs to the second floor of the *Sun* Building and registered at the News Boys Lodging House. I paid a week's stay in advance and met with Mr. Tracy. He asked me a few questions: My parents' names, what happened to them, if I answered to anyone.

"Is Murdoch your real name? Your Christian name?" he asked.

"What other name would I have?"

"Most of the newsies have a nickname. You know, what the other boys call you."

A boy waiting in line behind me said, "We call him 'Counselor,' but not to his face. He's always looking something up in some law book or reading the legal notices in the back of the paper."

I ignored him. "Murdoch McNeil is my name and the only name I use."

"That's just fine," said Mr. Tracy.

I picked out a bed in the dormitory and took one of the top bunks. It was less comfortable than my cozy room at the library, but better than Randall's Island's mean metal cots. I would make the best of it. I was surprised that living at this boarding house was just as Miss Walker and Miss Thompson said it would be. I came and went as I liked. The beds were always clean and comfortable. I even started enjoying a bath with soap every now and then. Mr. Tracy took our money for us overnight so it wouldn't be stolen. I attended the evening classes in reading and math, though I already knew most of the lessons and often skipped out. There were no beatings, no whippings, no handcuffs, no detention cells. Our only punishment was to be denied a bed for showing up drunk or after 10:00 p.m.

The *New York Times* on May 17 ran a story about the ballot fraud. In the ensuing days this scandal took up a great number of column inches with stories and court testimonies reprinted for all to see. Mr. Childs was mentioned, and he testified that he printed the false ballots, but I could not understand why he was not charged. It seemed to me that getting away with fraud was pretty easy to do.

One fine day in June, I finished my library chores early, so I headed for my usual table near the law books. I carried my prized possessions, my two law dictionaries, in my arms. I could have a terrible day, and the very smell of the law books would bring me a sense of peace. Even a good day was made better by the smell of horsehair bindings and strong animal glue .I didn't know it at that moment, but the law books were about to bring me the best day I would ever have, and not because of the smell.

A tall, well-dressed man with a kind face came into the library, "Hello, Miss Thompson. How are you today?" He had a commanding presence that made people pay attention, and I found myself staring.

"I am just fine, Mr. Townsend. How is little Anne?" she asked.

Mr. Townsend leaned against the counter in a relaxed manner, "Oh, she's giggling up a storm now. Curious about everything!"

Miss Thompson smiled, "Good to hear! Can I help you with something?"

"No, I'm just here for some case law out of Johnson's Reports. But I was curious about the youngster I always see at the table, surrounded by law books." He glanced in my direction. "I've seen him selling the *Times*, but a newsboy studying law? Isn't there a more appropriate book, maybe something safer for him to handle?"

I continued my reading and looked away but couldn't help wanting to hear what he was saying. It was the way the man talked that made you listen to him, even if you didn't want to.

"That's Murdoch McNeil. He works part-time for us and delivers the books all over the city. He's probably been to your office a time or two. He's quite careful with the books. He remembers everything he reads. He likes reading about the law and learning about all the complicated words and cases. He loves the law so much that the staff here bought him a new law dictionary last Christmas so he could make notes in the margins." I liked hearing Miss Thompson's voice when she was proud of me.

"I'm afraid my time as a solicitor has tainted my ability to believe in absence of proof," Mr. Townsend chuckled. "But I must yield to your opinion as the librarian and protector of books."

When Mr. Townsend headed my way, I felt I needed to be guarded. I'd thought to just put the law books back, but then I thought that I had as much a right to be looking at the case law as anyone else. Besides, he could find some other law book on the shelf. At first that's what he did: He stood at the volumes of *Johnson's Reports,* and ran his fingers along the spines looking for the one he needed. Then he let out a sigh of exasperation. He turned and looked at me.

"Murdoch? That's your name, yes?"

"Yes, sir," I answered politely.

"Is that, by any chance, Volume 10?"

"Yes, sir."

"May I have a look at that for a while? I need to prepare a case for next week and the precedent happens to be in volume 10."

"Which case?"

I couldn't tell if Mr. Townsend was smirking or smiling, but he answered. "Whitmarsh against Cutting."

This one, I had made it stick in my mind. The case was simple, and the outcome seemed to be common sense. "Page 360. The judgment was reversed," I said. "What kind of fool would plant crops if his lease would expire before the crops came to harvest?" I handed him the book.

He thumbed through it to page 360 and read the case from the chair next to me. He took a long time with it, occasionally letting out a

"Hmmm" and "Interesting." He made notes on his pad, closed the book, and handed it back to me. "Miss Thompson says you're interested in the law. Do you want to become a lawyer?"

"Yes, I would like that, but I don't have any idea how to go about it, what kind of schooling I need, or who would help me with it."

"Do you know what an apprentice is?"

"Yes, sir. I was a printer's devil for Mr. Childs before all the ballot problems. Do you know Mr. Childs?"

"Yes, he's well-known in the city. You were his apprentice?"

"Yes, sir, but I'm not supposed to talk about the ballot fraud. I promised Mr. Childs."

"It's not important that we talk about that right now. Perhaps later. Law offices have apprentices too, and we call them law clerks. You're younger than most clerks, but Miss Thompson says you can read and remember things very well. I imagine you could be a very good law clerk for me, if you wish to try. Once you finish your apprenticeship, you can sit for your exams in front of a judge. Then you become a solicitor. It's hard work, but it's worth it." Mr. Townsend wrote an address on a piece of paper in his notebook and tore it out for me, but I already knew where his firm was. "Think about it. If the offer suits you, drop by this address tomorrow, and we can work out the details."

Mr. Townsend held out his hand, and I shook it. I was not sure what had just happened, but it seemed to me that I was to become a lawyer after all. I watched as Mr. Townsend exited the library, stopping to chat with Miss Thompson for ten or fifteen long minutes. Then Miss Thompson came over to my table.

"Mr. Townsend said he offered you a position as a law clerk! And at your age!" She beamed. "You'd make a fine solicitor, Murdoch. You are going to accept, aren't you? I gave him a little more background about your life and how you came to be here, what happened to your parents. I hope you don't mind." I knew she only had my interests at heart, and being seen as a smart orphan seemed a better way to start an apprenticeship than being seen as a heroic fighting orphan.

I could barely sleep all night. It seemed like I was just settling into my work selling newspapers, and working at the library, and now there was this new possibility, which meant another change. It was one thing to think, and dream about something, but I gave little thought how I'd feel if it really happened. Doubt had set in. What if I didn't like studying law?

The darkness seemed to last forever. Every creak, cough, and snore in the boarding house was suddenly three times louder than normal. When morning finally came, I picked up the newspapers with bleary eyes. Time stood still until I'd sold my papers. I got to Mr. Townsend's office at noon, and I stammered a greeting to the secretary.

"Hello, Mr. ... Mr. Townsend, he asked that I come by at noon," I said thinking that I'd lost the ability to speak English. "I'm Murdoch McNeil."

"Oh, yes, he said you'd be coming by. He's with his family, but he'll be with you in a minute."

I sat down by the closed office door and listened to a muffled conversation punctuated by a little girl's giggling voice. The door opened, and the giggler came careening out of his office. She noticed me and stopped to look me right in the eye.

"Hi! I'm Anne. Who are you?"

I didn't have time to answer before Mrs. Townsend emerged from the office, followed by Mr. Townsend.

"Dear, this is Murdoch McNeil, the young man I told you about. He reads very quickly, and he remembers what he reads, so I'm asking him to be my law clerk. Since he's here, I hope that means he accepts."

I felt my face getting warm.

"Daddy! He's turning red! Look!" shrieked Anne with delight.

"That's not polite, Anne," admonished Mrs. Townsend. "It is very nice to meet you. Please excuse our daughter. She says whatever comes into her mind. I'm afraid we don't have much time to visit right now, so I must say it's been good to meet you, Murdoch." And the two left the office, Anne rushing ahead.

"Come into my office, Murdoch, and we'll talk."

Mr. Townsend outlined the duties of a law clerk, handed me an apprentice agreement, and made sure that I understood it. I knew from my readings that I ought to be careful about what I signed, and I felt I should make a little show out of carefully reading the contract. Mr.

Townsend explained the details of the work. He pointed out that the contract said I'd be eligible to become a solicitor after seven years of satisfactory progress. I told Mr. Townsend about the News Boys Lodging Home, and he said that would be the best place for me to stay until I was old enough to afford a room of my own at a boarding house. With what he would be paying me, I thought that would take but little time. I laid down my signature, he did so with his, we shook hands, and my life changed again.

I headed back to the boarding house, my head down staring at the bugs crawling around on the walkway as I moved along. I know I should have been excited and grateful that I'd been chosen to study law, but I wasn't. The people who mattered most to me, those whom I really yearned to tell and celebrate this were not here, and they never would be. I'd been in this county now for two years, but it seemed much, much longer. I'd never felt more alone.

Miss Thompson would be happy for me, but it wasn't the same as my father and mother being proud of me, although I knew that they somehow must know. Elizabeth would have teased me about it, and wondered if I would get to wear one of those wigs that the solicitors wore. I smiled at the thought. This new opportunity did take me one step closer to the one thing my father wanted for me. His word echoed in my head: *Do anything you have to, to get land and to keep it.* Mr. Townsend would have the knowledge to teach me how.

Chapter VII: Central Park

Saturday, April 4th, 1868
New York City

"The making of the far-famed New York Central Park was opposed by even good men, with misguided pluck, perseverance, and ingenuity, but straight right won its way, and now that park is appreciated."
John Muir

"Henry P. Townsend, you close that law book and come with me to Central Park. The servants are waiting to hook up the carriage. It's Saturday afternoon, and court isn't even in session today, for goodness sakes," scolded Ada.

Henry pulled his watch from its vest pocket and sighed, realizing it was almost 4:00 p.m. The days do get away from me, he thought.

Ada placed her arms around his neck and kissed him on the cheek. "You did promise me a ride through the park and a walk on the mall. The flowers are in full bloom!"

"Yes, I did promise that, didn't I?"

"You certainly did, Counselor," Ada said, taking the legal dictionary off the shelf in Henry's study and leafing through it. "Ah, here it is, 'breach of promise. The act of breaching a sworn assurance to do something.' I believe I have a case, and I know just the handsome young attorney to represent me, and I bet he is out this moment spending his time courting a young lady instead of a law book," she said, slamming the dictionary shut. "A worthy expenditure of time, in my opinion."

"I plead *nolo contendere*, my dear. And Murdoch usually spends Saturdays at the office preparing for the next week, so I have some free time."

"That's what he tells you. "You've trained your young clerk tolerably well and made him into a work-obsessed, successful attorney just like his mentor," she laughed.

"Very well, I'll bring the carriage 'round front. We'll have dinner at Del's, if this is an acceptable settlement for my breach of promise. Is Anne coming?"

"She said she was shopping at A.T. Stewart with some friends. Besides, hasn't it been a while since we had a nice romantic dinner? Just the two of us... I'm holding you to that settlement offer, which will be restricted to the party of the first part and the party of the second part. No mediators required."

Ada settled into the carriage next to Henry, slipping her arm through his and laying her head on his shoulder. He had some stubble on his usually clean-shaven face, but she didn't mind. The team trotted easily pulling the little Brewster coupé at a steady pace. Henry guided the carriage onto the 5th Avenue entrance leading to the crowded tree-lined parkway in Central Park.

Henry still had his thoughts on Monday's cases and idly glanced at the ornate benches scattered around the small plaza. There, on one of those benches, sat Murdoch, obviously not in the law offices but certainly putting up a good argument for something with a young lady. He was whispering into the young lady's ear and holding her hands with a relaxed familiarity. Henry was startled to see that the young lady herself had not gone shopping at A.T. Stewart as she'd told her parents. And from the look of things, she was putting up an equally good argument for something with Murdoch.

At the sight, Henry pulled the reins back out of reflex, stood up in the carriage, and shouted, "Murdoch! What do you think you're doing with our daughter?"

Ada's eyes widened as she, too, saw Murdoch and Anne. The horses, startled by the sudden movements and the yelling, whinnied and shook their heads. They reared up, their powerful bodies in a panic, and bolted. Henry was slammed back into his seat. He fought to control the team, now at a full gallop. Ada could do nothing but grip the seat, white-knuckled, too frightened to scream.

The road curved to the left. The team scrambled to make the turn and failed. The Brewster coupé struck a large elm. The force of the crash exploded the carriage into splinters, sending Henry and Ada flying through the air, striking branches as they came down. The horses, bound by their harness and critically injured, struggled and screamed. Their cries of pain and fright echoed down the pathway. Quickly, the passers-by ran to their aid. Henry and Ada lay motionless and pale in the springtime sunlight. Two shots rang out, and the horses screamed no more.

The crowd gathered around Henry and Ada, some trying to give aid. Henry bled from a head wound and did not come to. Ada started to rouse but could not move her arm well. It bent at a bad angle. Murdoch and Anne ran as fast as they could and were shocked by the horrific scene. Anne covered her mouth and began to cry.

"My God, Murdoch, what have we done?" she cried out as she ran to her father's side.

A policeman arrived. "All right, everyone, move back," he said. "Let's get these folks to a hospital. Bring a wagon. Careful, now."

Whispers from the crowd did nothing to comfort Murdoch and Anne. "Are they alive?"

Another bystander called out, "I don't know."

"He won't survive that. I was in the war, and I know," called another.

"Even if they survive, they'll be maimed for life," remarked another.

The police placed Henry and Ada into a wagon as gently as they could and headed out of the park. The wagon went to St. Luke's Hospital; Anne and Murdoch followed close behind, and neither spoke.

Anne and Murdoch shared a strong mutual attraction. When Anne was nineteen, Murdoch fell in love with the outgoing and precocious young woman. He was acutely aware of the class system that pervaded New York City's elite, knowing he simply did not fit in. Anne had long auburn hair and snowflake soft skin dotted with a few freckles as if placed by a skilled artist. She had a demeanor that was anything but soft. She insisted that he confront her father, his employer, challenging him in her romantic tone to fight for her if he deemed himself worthy. He could not say no to her.

He approached Henry and Ada and asked for formal permission to begin courting Anne. Henry refused to grant that permission, despite

Anne pleading with her parents to change their minds. The Townsends looked at Murdoch as though he were a big brother to Anne, not a potential matrimonial prospect. He was an immigrant crofter with no living parents and no estate to speak of. Anne was expected to marry within her parents' class, which Henry had fought to achieve, and Ada fiercely protected. Murdoch and Anne were forbidden to court, but their attraction for each other was far too strong for obedience.

The two arrived at the four-story gothic-style hospital, where Henry was carried on a stretcher, still unconscious, to an exam room. They carried in Ada, too, who was conscious but moaning insensibly in pain. Murdoch and Anne were told to wait in the reception area while a flurry of physicians, nurses, and attendants moved quickly into the exam rooms.

They sat in silence, each of their thoughts independent yet the same, each blaming themselves for the accident. Anne knew she had the power to end their relationship, but she wouldn't; her love for Murdoch was too strong. Ada would throw society men at her as if they were breeding stallions, and she refused them all. She kept thinking her parents would come around, and she would have her way. She would tell them both that if she were not allowed to be with Murdoch, she'd never marry.

For Murdoch's part, his guilt was an enormous burden. He felt that he had committed an unpardonable sin against the person who had taken him from being a street newsie to one of the finest attorneys in the city. He could never forgive himself, though his guilt was mixed with a substantial serving of anger — anger at the New York elite and the rules imposed on Anne and him.

"Oh, Anne, I am so sorry. This is all my fault. I should have respected your father's wishes."

Anne wiped her tears. "It doesn't matter now. With what's happened, we can never marry. Mother and Daddy are the only important people right now. It simply must be over between us."

Henry's and Ada's exam rooms opened from time to time, and a physician or a nurse in a crisp white uniform would scurry out. They gave the couple no information and had no expressions Anne and Murdoch might read. Murdoch rose, stretched, paced, and occasionally leaned against a wall, resting his head against his forearm. Anne and Murdoch continued their silence. The exam room doors opened again, and two serious-looking men approached them.

"Are you friends or relatives?" one asked.

Murdoch spoke for the couple. "I am Murdoch McNeil, Mr. Townsend's law partner. This is Miss Anne Townsend, their daughter."

"I'm the chief orthopedic surgeon here. Dr. Newton Shatter. This is Dr. Abbe, attending physician. Please follow us and we can speak privately." They led Murdoch and Anne to an office across the hall, where they sat around a small conference table.

"Mrs. Townsend," Dr. Shatter started. "She has fractured bones in her arms, some bruising and superficial cuts, but nothing life-threatening. She'll be in the room next to where she's had her exam."

Dr. Abbe had been treating Henry. "Unfortunately," he said addressing Anne, "your father's injury is very serious. He has had an injury to his head. He's a sturdy fellow in good health, so we aren't concerned about his scrapes and bruises. The head injury is serious enough on its own. It seems when he was thrown from the carriage, he struck his head on a thick tree branch."

Dr. Shatter continued: "During the war, we learned a great deal about head injuries, but we are limited in what we can do with present staff. I'd like to bring in a few specialists. The first of these is Dr. Stephen Smith, professor of surgery at Bellevue Hospital."

"Dr. Shatter, brain surgery is such a serious undertaking. Please," she pleaded, "is he going to live or die?"

"I'll be straightforward with you: we don't know. I think we will have to do surgery, yes. We don't know a lot about head injuries except that they are all serious. I'm sorry that I can't give you a more hopeful answer, but perhaps we'll know more after Dr. Smith examines him," Dr. Abbe said.

"May we see them?" Murdoch asked.

"Mrs. Townsend can have visitors, but we'd prefer you wait to see Henry until after Dr. Smith has seen him, and we can transfer him to his room," Dr. Shatter said.

Murdoch and Anne went in to see her mother. Ada's left arm was encased in a plaster cast elevated upwards on a board, with a rope attaching the hand to a pulley at the end of the bed. Ada's eyes were closed, but they flickered open at the sound of Anne's voice.

"Mother, Mother, it's Anne."

"Your father... Is he okay?"

"He'll be fine," she reassured Ada. "He's just two rooms away. You need to rest."

Ada's eyes closed, the morphine keeping her drowsy. Anne pulled up the chair next to the bed while Murdoch stood at the window watching the light fade. His concern for the Townsends weighed heavy on his mind, along with concern for Townsend's clients and practice. Too many thoughts whirled around. Anne said it was over between them, and it felt like his own life was ending. He demanded that his mind think, overcome emotion, and use reason. Don't try to control the uncontrollable, he thought. He could not cure Henry or Ada. He could not fulfill his dream of marrying Anne. But he could do what he was best at, and practice law. He decided to focus on his work and see how his life would unfold.

A nurse entered the room. "Mr. McNeil, Miss Townsend, Dr. Smith needs to see you in the conference room."

"I'm Dr. Smith," the man said, motioning for them to sit down. "I believe that Mr. Townsend has a concussion and a surface contusion from striking the tree branch. There's a great deal of swelling, and I believe ice and keeping his head elevated in bed is the appropriate approach. I fear if we resort to trepanning the skull to relieve the pressure on his brain, it could do more harm than good. We don't know for sure if there is any swelling or injury directly to the brain, so surgery would be a last resort."

"What do Dr. Abbe and Dr. Shatter think?" Murdoch asked.

"Well, we call it the 'art of medicine' because it's not an exact science. They think he may have a compression injury due to the force with which his head struck the branch, potentially injuring his brain. However, I disagree, as he would exhibit a slow, bounding pulse and noisy, snoring-like breathing. He doesn't have those symptoms, so I don't believe surgery is necessary and could even be harmful. The best course is to wait, but I'd like to consult Dr. Spencer, a surgeon with extensive experience in such injuries. During the war, he served as a medical director and saved many lives at the Battle of Williamsburg."

"Yes," Anne said, "please, bring in the very best physicians that you can. When can I see him?"

"Now, but only for a few minutes. Then you should go home and get some rest. If anything changes, we will send for you."

Murdoch and Anne looked in on Mr. Townsend. He lay in bed with his head elevated, the ice pack applied to a large swelling the size of Anne's handprint. He had cuts and bruises about his face and arms, but he appeared to be resting without pain.

The Townsends' valet had been sent for and waited patiently in front of the hospital. He took Anne to the Townsend brownstone, where the household staff waited anxiously for any news. Murdoch requested instead to be taken to the law offices. Sleep would not visit him any time soon, and he got to work assessing Mr. Townsend's client files. He prioritized those cases which required a stay, and he drafted client letters explaining that Mr. Townsend's cases would be handled by the junior partner for the time being, but that Mr. Townsend would soon be well. Finally, at 3:00 a.m., he lay down on the couch in Henry's office and allowed sleep to take him.

At 7:00 a.m. he awoke again and walked to his boarding house to wash up and put on fresh clothing. On the way he walked past the library where he'd stayed as a boy and where he'd read his first lawbook so long ago.

He paused and sat wearily on a bench in front. His status as a mere crofter orphan seemed to stick to him like the wretched smell of a drunk. He could change clothes all he wished, he could bathe, he could take education, but he would always be an orphan from Scotland with no connections. He would never have the kind of esteem in New York society that would allow him to court the one woman who mattered to him the most.

Well, he thought, if that's the way things are and will always be, then I will use the law to take what's mine and look out for myself.

Nobody else is going to do it.

* * *

Frank Angel stood before the door of the Townsends' brownstone and gently let the knocker fall against the metal. The streets were still quiet at 9:00 a.m. on a Sunday, and he was hesitant to present himself so early. He waited with the *New York Herald* tucked under his arm. He tapped shyly once again and was just about to step away from the door when it opened.

"Good morning, Mr. Angel, how may I assist you?" the parlor maid, Heidi, asked.

"I'm here to see Miss Townsend."

"I'll check, but Mr. and Mrs. Townsend were in an awful accident yesterday afternoon and are in the hospital. I don't believe Miss Townsend is receiving guests at this time."

Anne's voice came from the hall. "It's all right, Heidi, you may show him in."

"Anne, forgive me for being so bold, but I've just seen the morning *Herald*," he said and he held the paper out to her.

Anne took it and it was already folded to page six. The headline "Frightful Accident in Central Park" led to the story of the Townsends' mishap. It seemed mostly accurate when quoting the eyewitnesses, but at the end of the story an unnamed attending doctor said that Mr. Townsend was not expected to survive.

Anne protested, shocked. "Murdoch and I talked with the doctors last night. They said nothing like, 'he is not expected to live'! It even says here that Mother was seriously, 'if not fatally injured'! She has a broken arm, and she'll be just fine! Oh, what is going on?" she cried.

Frank tried to calm her. "The newspapers always exaggerate things. It's not right, but it happens all the time. Do you want me to take you to St. Luke's? My carriage is right outside."

Anne dabbed her eye with her handkerchief. "Yes, thank you, that's very kind."

"If I can help with Mr. Townsend's cases or the firm, it would be my pleasure. I'm only a year away from being admitted to the bar. I'm sure Mr. Harding would lend me to Mr. Townsend as his clerk as long as is needed."

"Murdoch went straight to the office last night after the hospital," Anne explained. "I wouldn't be surprised if he'd been working the entire night getting the cases ready for Monday."

"That would be like him," Frank said as he urged the horses forward. "Anne?"

"Yes?"

Courage, Frank, he thought. "I know it might not be right to ask, especially just now, but I don't think I'll get another chance to be alone with you for some time. I must ask. Your father granted me permission to court you. Are you still so resolute that you won't? Perhaps all of this means we're meant to be together."

Anne exploded. "Perhaps. No! I mean, I don't know! I can't even think of courting right now, not anyone. There is too much for me to do. I just want Daddy and Mother to be okay. I don't care about fancy parties or plays or balls or dinners, even when I don't have any worries. It's all so superficial, the games everyone plays in our set, the socialites, as if there's no suffering going on in New York at all!"

Her face hot, she blinked back tears but only barely. Frank had played his hand and lost. Anne was upset at him for trying to take advantage of the situation, she was angry at the situation itself, she was upset at the reporter who wrote the story, and she was mad at herself most of all for practically insisting that she and Murdoch see each other despite her parent's objections. She was fond of Frank, but she could never be in love with him. Not that love mattered much in their New York society, where marriage was more of a financial and social contract, but she would never allow herself to be stock to be traded on some exchange. Daddy and Mother approved of Frank's family, well established among the elites of the city. He was going to have a successful career in law just like his father. But she did not love him.

Frank loved her, and he sincerely apologized. "I'm sorry, I didn't mean to upset you. You're right; take some time. I'll see you to the entrance of the hospital, and then I'll see if I can find Murdoch at the firm. I can at least offer to write some briefs and research the cases. I should have given you more time at the beginning. I'm sorry." He turned his face away from her and left her to check on her parents.

Anne sat by her father's side. Henry was still unconscious with the ice packs and the head of his bed elevated. Dr. Smith was due shortly, and then she would know more. She kissed her father on his cheek, and swore that his eyelids fluttered. Then she went into her mother's room and was pleased to see Ada awake.

"Mother!" Anne kissed her warmly on the cheek and Ada brightened.

"Anne! No one will talk to me about your father! Not knowing is torture. Do you know anything?"

"I suppose they didn't want to alarm you unnecessarily."

Ada brought her fist down forcefully on the bed. "I need to know what's happening! Please, just tell me!"

Ann tried to speak as calmly as she could. "He hasn't woken up since the accident, but I was just in to see him and he looks better than he did yesterday. He has a whole boat full of doctors! There's a Dr. Smith from Bellevue who specializes in head injuries and surgery, and he says Daddy just has a bad concussion and needs time. He doesn't want to operate. Dr. Smith is bringing in a Dr. Spencer who used to treat head wounds in the war, and everyone says he is the very best."

"That hard head of his finally met its match! Oh, I shouldn't joke. Standing up and shouting like that, scaring the horses. I love him, but oh! He can sometimes..." she said, exasperated. "Oh, no, I remember a shot! The poor horses!"

Anne took her mother's uninjured hand. "Mother, I'm so sorry, I..."

Ada knew what she wanted to say. "Not another word. Your father and I are to blame, not you. And certainly not Murdoch. If Henry can't see the truth in his own house as well as he can in the courthouse, at least I can. God knows I love him, but he's almost killed us!"

A nurse called from the hallway. "Miss Townsend, your father is awake and asking for you. And someone named Murdoch."

"Thank goodness!" Ada said. "Go check on your father."

Anne bolted to Henry's room. Dr. Abbe unwrapped the dressing on Henry's forehead and examined the wound. The swelling had gone down, and Henry's color improved.

"Mr. Townsend, you will need to be patient with a head injury like this. It can take some time to recover, and recovery has to be a careful process. How are you feeling right now?"

"Awful. My head hurts, and I..." He stopped speaking, then his right hand twitched uncontrollably. His eyes rolled, and he shook and convulsed.

"What's happening to him?" Anne cried.

The nurse grabbed Anne's arm and led her out of the room. "Come with me, dear, we will take care of him."

The seizure disappeared quickly. Dr. Abbe shook Henry's shoulder. "Mr. Townsend, can you hear me? Mr. Townsend!"

His eyes opened again and focused. He coughed and took a deep breath. "What happened?"

"You've had a seizure, Mr. Townsend. Can you tell me what day it is?" Dr. Abbe looked into his eyes to check his pupils.

"Sunday, 5th of April, I think."

"Who was in here before, visiting you?"

"My daughter."

"And what is her name?"

"Anne, for Christ's sakes, Anne!"

Dr. Abbe seemed satisfied with these responses.

Murdoch had made his way to the hospital, stopping at his boarding house for a change of clothes. Anne greeted him in the hallway outside Henry's room and told him about the seizure. Dr. Abbe helped her explain about head injuries and the importance of rest. Dr. Smith arrived with another man following close behind.

"Thomas! I'm glad you're here!" Murdoch cried at seeing his friend, Dr. Spencer. "How did you ever hear of Henry's accident?"

"Dr. Smith called me in to consult yesterday, as a matter of fact. We'll talk after I examine Henry." The three physicians went into the room.

"How do you know him?" Anne asked.

"He's a fine doctor, but he has a hand in real estate as well. Before he got called up in the war, he worked as a receiver in the U.S. Land

131

Office over in Bayfield on Long Island. The Union had him stop all that and put him in as a medical director, and now that the war's over, he still maintains his interest in land deals. The firm helps him with his filings."

"Speaking of the firm, Frank came by the house this morning and said he might find you at the office. Wanted to know if you needed the help of a clerk." She omitted the rest of their conversation.

"No, I left at about 7:00. Must have missed him. I should get back soon, though, and it would be nice to have a clerk prepped for Monday. I'll send for him."

Anne felt hope in her heart. "When Daddy came to this morning, he asked for you."

Murdoch's surprise paused as the physicians left Henry's room. "How is he, Thomas?"

"Two opinions, and either could be correct. Shatter and Abbe think he has a compression fracture of the skull. We'd have to operate to relieve the pressure in that case. Dr. Smith here thinks the symptoms strongly fit a concussion rather than fracture."

"Doesn't the seizure give us a sign one way or the other?" Anne asked.

"Seizures can happen with either diagnosis. I saw a lot of these cases at the Battle of Williamsburg. Brain injuries are hard to diagnose, hard to get right, and hard to treat. But I agree with Dr. Smith: opening up the skull should be a last resort. Operations opening the skull to the air seem to invite infection. If the swelling keeps going down, then we can find out for sure by feeling for the fracture from the outside."

"What does Daddy think? What does he want to do?" asked Anne.

"He has a brain injury, so we aren't sure if he is capable of making his own decisions about his treatment," Dr. Abbe replied.

"Daddy's awake, he's talking in complete sentences, therefore, from where I stand he can make his own damn decision. Did you ask him directly?" Anne demanded.

Murdoch placed his hand on her shoulder. "Thomas, you know Henry well enough. He's a smart man. Did he tell you which course of action he wanted?"

Dr. Abbe frowned. "It's normally the doctor's decision, not the patient's."

"Not what I asked," said Anne shaking her head.

"He wants to wait and see if the swelling goes down." Dr. Spencer knew better than to challenge a Townsend when they had their mind made up.

"Then that's what you'll all do. You'll wait. So will we," Anne stated. "Murdoch, we need to go in together and see what Daddy wanted to see you about, I think."

"In a moment, I want to speak with Dr. Spencer about something." The other physicians left, knowing when they could no longer argue their case against a pair of New York attorneys and a free-spirited young woman. "First, thank you for seeing Mr. Townsend. I trust your instincts. It's good to see you're still practicing medicine after your experience in the Union Army."

"Only consulting, really. Williamsburg still haunts me. I'm hoping for an appointment as Surveyor General in the New Mexico Territory, and then I expect I'll leave medicine. But when Dr. Smith told me who his patient was, I, of course, came right down to see him."

"A difficult decision, I'm sure. I appreciated your help in getting me my exemption. The firm had so many draft law cases—Henry would have drowned in work otherwise. I can't imagine what you must have seen and been through." Murdoch often measured himself against the scarred men and women who'd seen and done too much. He'd already had his share of violence and death, and the law did not relent. As for the war, it only intensified.

"It's intriguing that you're pushing for the Surveyor General position in New Mexico, Spencer," Murdoch said, leaning forward with a glint of curiosity in his eyes. "The papers are buzzing with stories about the Maxwell Land Grant. Rumor has it that no one even knows its true boundaries or rightful owners. You've always had a keen eye for the land business. What's really going on out there? Are there opportunities to be had, or is it all just smoke and mirrors?"

Spencer shrugged, a faint smile playing at his lips. "New Mexico is as tangled as a lasso in a dust devil," he said. "Whether it's the land or the culture, nothing's ever straightforward. The Maxwell Land Grant is supposedly between 1.7 and 2 million acres, sprawling across northern New Mexico and southern Colorado. Lucien Maxwell has been rumored to be selling it off to a British firm, but even he doesn't know the exact boundaries of what he's selling. His memory is hazy, and the paperwork's worse. But where there's confusion, there's opportunity. And in New Mexico, there's plenty of both."

Spencer placed a hand on Murdoch's shoulder and continued, "And I'm glad to have run into you, though I wish it had been under better circumstances. If I get that appointment, I'll need attorneys here in New York who understand real estate but aren't too caught up in the Tammany Hall or the Boss Tweed fiasco. The Townsend firm has kept its reputation intact, and I expect that the Maxwell Land Grant will involve years, maybe decades, of litigation. The New Mexico Governor and the Territorial Supreme Court are already gearing up for a fight, or at least their part of it. The squatters, claim-seekers, and practically the entire population will be tangled up in courts and claims for the foreseeable future."

Murdoch confidently agreed to have the Townsend firm pursue the Maxwell Land Grant litigation, or as much of it as they could handle. He'd hoped his mentor would come back to full health with his practice as busy and thriving as it ever was.

"If the sale to the British happens, I'm sure we'd find a way to enter the market. Mr. Townsend has made noise about entering the freight business out West; it's the spirit of the '49er in him as he likes to say. He's talked about a little town called Cimarron as a sort of hub."

"I better not let them poke a hole in his head, then. He will need to have his wits about him if he's to get in line with the rest of the fortune-seekers. Every politician from here to Santa Fe is ripe to make themselves a pile of money and tell themselves it's all for the public good." They agreed not to burden Mr. Townsend with the land grant deal until he'd suitably recovered, and they parted ways.

Back in Henry's room, Murdoch saw Anne seated by her father's bedside, her hands clasping his. He dozed lightly, and upon hearing Murdoch enter, he opened his eyes.

"Murdoch."

"Mr. Townsend, I am so very sorry. I knew that you and Mrs. Townsend did not approve of us courting. We won't be seeing each other any longer." He wanted to fight for Anne, but he cared deeply about Henry as well.

Henry silenced him. "Anne has been in love with you ever since she made you turn red as a beet. Ever since the first time she ever laid eyes on you when you were twelve. Ada and I both should have known Anne and you better than to bar you from courting. We put social status above Anne's happiness, and this is the reward we've gotten. I feel so awfully stupid."

"I don't know what to say, Mr. Townsend."

"You can tell Ada that it's time to start planning a wedding. And I'd go do it before Anne changes her mind."

136

Chapter VIII: Payback

Monday April 6[th,] 1868
Home of Diego & Consuela Gonzales
On the Cimarroncito, New Mexico

"The fraudster's greatest liability is the certainty that the fraud is too clever to be detected."
Louis J. Freeh

April, especially at the beginning of the month, and especially south and west of Cimarron, New Mexico, was predictably unpredictable. The hills at seven-thousand-foot elevation did not respect the spring. The European calendar's attempt at imposing seasons was a dismal failure here, and the first call of the nighthawk, the true signal of impending spring, had not yet been heard.

Few of the remaining parties of Jicarilla Apache dared go hunting at this time of year, depending instead on their enforced reliance of Lucien Maxwell's food and blankets. Maxwell enjoyed the power of being the deedholder and the *Patrón* of 1.7 million acres. On this land, Diego and Consuela Gonzalez farmed, maintained an herb garden and raised a few sheep. Diego's ancestors had settled where the small, steady Cimarroncito bubbled out of the ground just south and west of the new town of Cimarron. The Gonzalez's sheep grazed the abundant grassland to the east.

Like many of the other Mexican families in the area, the Gonzalez's worked and lived in harmony with the land and its Patrón. This was a centuries-old tradition: their land had no boundaries or fences, no written obligation to rent, and yet everyone fully understood and respected their responsibilities and duties. Then Diego returned one day from doing business in Taos on the other side of the mountains and had news: Lucien Maxwell was selling his land.

A new Patrón was sure to come. The Anglos were saying that the land would be sold to the English. The English were like the Americans. They did not trust themselves, so they built fences to keep others honest. They claimed exclusive use of their lands and removed anyone whose name was not on the deed. Some Mexican families like Diego's had been on the land so long, they knew no other; they'd developed it, they'd improved it, and they were more than lodgers.

Then the war came in the 1840s, and who owned the land on paper became a looming conversation. The Anglo ranchers came after the war, built fences, continuing the displacement of the Indigenous, the Mexicans, and now fretted over whether they would be caught short by their own system. Diego found it ironic.

For now, Diego and Consuela felt safe wrapped in the security blanket of winter snows, protected from the outside by the thick adobe walls of their home, warmed by the burning piñon in the kiva fireplace. Diego thought of what he would miss the most if his family were forced off the land. He decided he would miss the familiar rhythms, how the land seemed to behave erratically to anyone who did not respect it.

Some cultures describe winter as the dead months, but Diego experienced winter as pre-life—a time of silence to reflect on the past year and plan for the year to come. Even the snow in this part of New Mexico had a different smell than what one might find in Santa Fe, Taos, or Albuquerque. Here at the Cimarroncito, the snow mingled with the scent of sage, mountain cedar, piñon, and even the dirt. These were the spices of winter.

Spring brought new water rushing down the east-facing mountain slopes, swelling the Cimarroncito but never as a surprise. The Cimarron River to the north would swell and flood the town, but the Cimarroncito only joined the river to the east of town and never overflowed its banks.

The people might label the water as good or bad depending on its effect, frequency, and volume, but Diego knew it was neither. It just was. Predictable chaos existed on the ground in the river, and in the sky as the storm. The Gonzaleses knew to stay inside during spring storms, avoiding the hail and the lightning that could kill a man and his stock seemingly out of nowhere. Diego enjoyed winter, for it was in the spring that the animals, the land, the weather, and the men all became more active and destructive.

In the summers Diego and Consuela made adobe bricks from the earth and straw. Building new things was a sign of hope that what was built would last. The bricks were always heavier than they looked. Diego would miss building with adobe if his family were forced off. He would mourn the loss of the summer smells: The new crops just picked, the mud after a summer rainstorm, the smell of his wife as they worked in her herb garden together, the fish freshly caught from the Cimarron River. Even the smell of death was stronger in the summer, and when it happened, that smell overpowered everything else.

Should the Gonzaleses not be displaced until after the fall, Diego resolved to fix this season, too, in his memory to the smallest detail. The way the aspens turned to gold commanded one last look. The sticky sap that he'd complained about for so many years, covered his hands when he chopped the piñon trees for firewood. He'd gather the piñon nuts then, too, before the early snow. He would miss the *Padre* at their church. He would miss their friends, for they would be displaced too. He and Consuela had planned to be buried on this land like Diego's parents and their parents before them. He couldn't think of where they would possibly go, but he decided to live by the Apache proverb: *It is better to have less thunder in the mouth and more lightning in the hand.* He did not know where the lightning would come from.

***

Monday, April 6th, 1868
New York City

I can't get back our land on Barra, but I can surely take my piece of the Maxwell Land Grant out from under the damned British and they will never know, Murdoch thought. They owe me that much. Dr. Spencer had just told him that the Maxwell was likely to be sold to a British investment firm. Murdoch was surprised by the visceral reaction this information brought to his gut, but he immediately resolved to use

139

this information for his own benefit. He crafted a plan like an artist mixes his paints, and shortly he'd conceived the whole scheme from beginning to end. A portrait of revenge. Spencer would just have to get his appointment in New Mexico.

Murdoch was pleased that Henry and Ada had finally realized he and Anne belonged together, and he should have felt vindicated— ecstatic at their blessing and permission to marry. But what gnawed at his very soul was how quickly Anne had given up on their love, on their relationship. Right after the accident, while they waited at the hospital, she said they were through. The accident was serious, of course. But had she been so close to giving up on him already that the accident pushed her to renounce their relationship? Right now, he wasn't sure if he was still in love with her or just in love with the idea of acquiring a great deal of land, which wouldn't happen without her. In this moment, he thought, that's why he'd marry her.

He hadn't changed. He was still the crofter turned attorney, and marrying Anne wouldn't change that. He resolved to use his legal prowess to claim what was his. Anne's quick abandonment of their relationship only intensified his lust for land. And he would have it. Out west, land was power, he thought. No one would care if he was a crofter. He would be Mr. McNeil, rancher and owner of vast stretches of land. It didn't matter to him how he got it. "Murdoch, I dropped by yesterday, but you'd already left. How is Henry? Have you seen him this morning?" Frank Angel asked as he walked into the office.

"Good to see you. Yes, he seems to be doing a bit better. He's talking anyhow. Anne is with him. She said you'd dropped by yesterday. Is your offer to clerk still valid? I could use you."

"It would be my pleasure, and Mr. Harding's approved lending me to the firm. Mr. Harding should be along later this afternoon, and he would like to know a good time to pay his respects to Henry." They resolved to go to the hospital around lunch, and they worked solidly through the rest of the morning. Murdoch gave Frank the case files that needed a stay, but most of the cases were routine: land title defense, nonpayment of rents, and title transfers. Murdoch was grateful for Frank's assistance, and despite their quiet rivalry for Anne's affections, they had a strong friendship and mutual respect.

At noon they went to meet Anne at the hospital, where she alternated between Henry's and Ada's rooms. She was with Henry when they arrived, and Henry looked much more alert than he had in the morning.

"Frank! It's good to see you. I understand Mr. Harding is lending you out," he said.

"That's right," Frank said, "and we've got a good start on the cases."

"Oh, I wish they'd let me go home already! I feel fine except for the bump on my head."

"Daddy, you will stay as long as the doctors tell you," Anne scolded. "I'll go and visit with Mother, and you boys can all talk business. Murdoch, Mother is not thrilled with the date you've chosen for the wedding, and Daddy's just no help at all."

Frank looked like he'd swallowed a frog. "What did I miss?"

"We haven't announced yet," Anne said, "But we plan to send the notice to the *Times* and the *Herald* today. Just as soon as Murdoch compromises on the date."

"Mr. Townsend, sir, how often do you see me compromise on a case I truly believe in?" Murdoch asked.

"I will not be drawn into this conflict," Henry stated.

"But May 1 of all days!" Anne cried.

"It's Beltane. It's important to the Gaels. It means the renewal of spring and the promise of life to come. And not a little drinking and celebration." Murdoch remembered one year, long ago, when his father would wobble home, and then his mother would kick him out of the blackhouse. Nine months later he had a baby sister.

"Moving Day?" Frank had regained his composure. "What fun! It's so horrid and crowded and smelly. A wedding will be just the thing to take the sting out of such a busy, chaotic time! Bravo!"

"Frank, you're no help at all." Anne gave no indication of their earlier conversation. Frank guessed correctly that she had kept it between themselves. "Who would come to a wedding on Moving Day?"

"I would! It's the only chance I'll ever have to kiss you now that I've lost the war. Now I understand why you refused me. Murdoch, I am slightly jealous, I am eternally envious, and I am hysterically happy for both of you!"

"I think you're all awful!" she joked. "May 1, 1869 it is. If no one shows up for our wedding, I'm not responsible. Daddy, you and my fiancé will just have to deal with Mother. I'll let her know that you have formed a confederacy against us, and you will not budge." She headed off to Ada's room to deliver the news.

The impromptu firm of Townsend, McNeil, & Angel got down to business. "We've been talking about establishing a freighting business in New Mexico Territory, perhaps headquartered in the little town of Cimarron. Have you given more thought to the matter?" Murdoch asked.

Henry nodded his head. "Yes, now I want you to proceed with all due haste. I've felt close to death, my young associates, and I find I have a new clarity. Opportunities come before you, Murdoch, Frank. If you allow your chances to languish before your eyes, the reaper himself will come along and snatch them. We can move around the deceptions of other men and their politics, but that reaper stays in the shadows always, silent and stalking." Mr. Townsend seemed a man possessed with a new, decisive resolve.

"Then I will look into the land purchase and a freighting center located in Cimarron. That's close enough to Fort Union along the Santa Fe Trail." And I'll finally get mine, Murdoch thought.

"How are my cases coming?"

"Frank has filed for what stays were needed, and I'll be arguing the Murphy case this afternoon."

"It sounds as though everything is in order. Frank, thank you for clerking. Keep me updated, and I'll try to convince Dr. Spencer that I'm fine to rest at home."

***

Ada remained in the hospital for two weeks, recovering from her injuries, and she fretted over wedding plans the entire time. Dr. Spencer determined that Henry's brain injury was a severe concussion, but he'd avoided a compression fracture. Henry recovered slowly due to his age and he experienced some additional seizures. Dr. Spencer finally approved his discharge on June 15, but Frank and Murdoch continued running the firm until fall, when he once again felt able to vigorously argue before the courts. "Good!" Ada joked, "I'm tired of having to cite precedent about the right temperature of his morning coffee!"

Through this summer and fall, Murdoch used the chance to talk with Dr. Spencer and learn all he could about the Maxwell Land Grant and the territory of New Mexico. As Henry had trained him, he knew a good real estate deal started with maps: which surveys were accurate, where the boundary disputes might be, and the advantages and disadvantages of natural borders like rivers and creeks. The most important thing Murdoch found out was that nobody, not even Lucien Maxwell or the government in New Mexico, knew how big the grant was or where its borders might lie. The only constant was dispute, and in dispute, Murdoch knew he could find opportunity.

He was in his office and it was late. He drew a rectangle on the map from the origin of a creek called Cimarroncito. He drew thirty miles east, six miles south, thirty miles west, and six miles north. This meant 57,600 acres on the far western edge of the grant. The size of his rectangle looked insignificant compared to the total size of what was currently asserted by potential investors. One little speck in a sea of high desert, quietly placed where it would not be noticed or missed. He drew up the contract-dated January 21st, 1869.'On January 21st, 1869, Henry Townsend, represented by his legal agent Murdoch McNeil, agreed to purchase the land from Lucien Maxwell.'

A birthday present, he thought, one that is deserved. One I am entitled to. His right hand held the pen in hand but couldn't sign. At first. Then it all came back to him—his family's stolen land back in Scotland, the treacherous journey to America that killed them, and his survival of the orphan asylum on Randall's Island. And Anne, her father's initial refusal to approve their courtship forever hanging in his mind.

He dipped his pen in the ink pot and placed it firmly on the document, his hand slightly trembling, the clock chiming the late hour matching the rapid beat of his pulse. It was wrong; it would change his future forever, but, filled with both elation and fear, he signed his name anyway. Then he signed for Lucien Maxwell. Who would know? Now all he had to do was file at the right moment.

Dr. Spencer took his land office appointment in New Mexico as he'd hoped. He stopped by the Townsend office in April, "Maxwell is selling to Jerome Chaffee, George Chilcott, and Charles Holly," he said.

Murdoch was perplexed, "They're legislators! What's their angle?"

"They're not buying it themselves; they're brokers. They're going to sell the Maxwell to an English firm called the Maxwell Land Grant and Railroad Company. It's all foreign money, and a lot of it."

"But that won't work – it's against New Mexico Territorial law to sell to a foreign interest, even through a straw purchase!"

Spencer was resolute and confident, "All it takes is for Governor Pile, Chief Justice Watts, and the newly appointed Surveyor General of New Mexico to turn the other way and let the sale go through. Since the Surveyor General happens to be me, I can state with confidence that we need not worry about statute." Dr. Spencer grinned. "I'll be filing the land patent as my first act of office."

Murdoch saw his opportunity. "If you might make room for some other business once you get there, I have a real estate contract for some land in New Mexico that I'd like for you to survey, and then file with the General Land Office." He took the contract from his desk drawer and handed it to Dr. Spencer.

"This looks fine, Murdoch. I'll add the survey and the legal description. I'm glad to see Henry taking advantage of the chance offered in the Maxwell Land Grant. Are you sure the acreage is adequate? We can always adjust it."

"Yes, perfectly fine, Thomas."

"Since Henry acquired his own piece of the Maxwell before the English had their chance, I may as well have your firm contract for whatever work needs doing back here in New York. I'll need you and Henry both."

"That's fair."

"Good, we understand each other." Dr. Spencer folded the contract into thirds, put it in the envelope, and sealed it with his own wax emblem.

"I won't be leaving until after your wedding, and thank you for the invitation. I'd just as well spend my last day in New York on Moving Day at your joyous event. Right after, I'll be heading out to New Mexico. Once you get out there, I'll see what I can do to help along your freight business. That little ranch should be a good size for raising beef cattle. Governor Pile will be happy to meet you, too, and talk about providing beef for the Army, maybe even the Natives if they aren't all gone by then."

Murdoch disliked Dr. Spencer's glibness about displaced Natives, for reasons he couldn't quite explain to himself. Still, it was worth it to know he had his own piece of the grant. Lucien Maxwell would never know; it was just one deal among many, some valid, some not, with nobody caring either way. The English wouldn't miss it among their 1.7 million acres; as Dr. Spencer had said, it was a small plot. Once Dr. Spencer filed it, the claim would be as valid as any other in the territory.

Anne and Murdoch were wed in the late afternoon on May 1. To Mrs. Townsend's surprise and delight, every invited guest attended, many of them remarking that they found it amusing to come to a wedding on Moving Day of all days. The Townsends and the McNeils promised that they would hold an anniversary party on Moving Day every year.

Murdoch and Anne decided that they should begin their married life in the Townsend brownstone. Henry suffered from occasional dizzy spells and did most of his legal work from home. Ada now complained that her arm ached with every change in the weather. Anne wanted to help her parents continue their recovery, and Murdoch sat with Henry planning out their new freighting and cattle businesses.

Murdoch arranged for a ranch house to be built for the sake of appearing legitimate and Dr. Spencer filed the survey and the patent as promised. He felt some vindication for what the English had done to his family on Barra. All they'd wanted was their little blackhouse and their little garden. Now, he'd taken 57,000 acres from the English.

Finally, after six months with no seizures, Henry asked Dr. Smith, who'd been checking his recovery, if he might go to New Mexico to meet with his old friend, Dick Wootton. Once approved he and Ada took the train to Trinidad, Colorado, and then by wagon to the bottom of Raton Pass where Wootton operated a toll pass road into New Mexico for freighters. He and Henry had met during the gold rush days in California, and he had extensive experience in the freighting business. Henry believed in consulting the best authorities available. That meant exposing Ada to Wootton's colorful language and even more colorful stories. If the carriage wreck slowed Henry down, he didn't show it.

In the years to come, Murdoch made his way down to Cimarron as well. On his first visit to what he'd come to think of as the McNeil Ranch, he found that the Gonzales family already lived on the property. Legally, he knew these were squatters, but they had been living on the land before it came under the control of the United States.

Murdoch chose not to explain this to Henry, who tended to believe in more absolute terms about what was proper under the law. He refused to have these people removed simply because their names weren't on a piece of paper.

He researched the traditional Patrón relationships that the Mexicans, and later Maxwell, had with the well-established families living on their land, and it sounded quite similar to how people used to live on Barra. He would be no Gordon of Cluny, no Patrick Sellar.

In June of 1871, Murdoch prepared to go back out to Cimarron, but instead, he found himself cradling twin boys. He had plenty of legal work to do back in New York with the Maxwell Land Grant. The disputes had only intensified once the residents of New Mexico learned that an English firm had bought 1.7 million acres.

As an added complication, the United States government had opened some of the Maxwell grant to homesteading and the public domain before the sale, back when the boundaries of the grant were assumed to be much smaller. "Biggest fraud of all time," gossiped the residents of Cimarron. "We'll fight," said the homesteaders. But it was not clear who they could fight except each other.

On Murdoch's latest trip in 1872, Dr. Spencer worried to him that the people were right, that the fraud was too great, and the entire Maxwell Land Grant would not stand up to any legal scrutiny. The English company seemed not to have any concerns and forged ahead with removing anyone they felt was encroaching on their land, regardless of how long they'd lived there or where they were in their land disputes.

Homesteader, Mexican, Anglo, rancher, Scot, Irish – all were put on notice that they were considered trespassers on land they'd been told was their own. Spencer had faced demands to quell the increasing number of violent incidents. His face looked gray; he had obviously not been sleeping well. His dream appointment had turned into a nightmare.

"If I'd known, I would have never taken this position," he said. He died in the next month.

Mr. Townsend had his own worries about the land. "Murdoch, I've made a decision. People are getting killed over this Maxwell Land Grant. There's fraud every way we look at it, and all the roads to this fraud lead straight back to New York. Our firm looks like it's a proxy buyer. Since the people there are attacking land agents, this puts us in danger. I dislike the appearance of impropriety as much as impropriety itself."

"Do you want to sell?"

"Tough decision. I know we can't continue to manage the business from New York, but right now the freight is in good shape. If we do sell, we had better do it before the railroad gets to Santa Fe."

"And what about the hacienda, the ranch, and the land?" Murdoch felt it all slipping away. He did not care to live there himself, but he felt as though he were still escaping Gordon of Cluny somehow. He had the land, now just as his father said, he needed to do what was necessary to keep it.

"Your name is on the contract, Murdoch. You're the buyer's agent. That may spell some trouble for us." In 1871 the Secretary of the Interior had tried to nullify the entire grant save for 99,000 acres. While the attempt didn't stick, Murdoch knew that Henry was right about the problem with the borders: If no party anywhere in the grant could come to an agreement about just how much the grant was and where it was located, all land deals in any venue were likely to be relitigated. Murdoch felt the blood drain from his face, and sweat ran down his neck. He knew if all this were brought back for reconsideration, the

Maxwell land grant sales would be scrutinized, and his fraud would be discovered.

"But, Murdoch, I suspect that the prevailing opinion in the end is going to go to the highest bidder. That's what Chaffee, Holly, and Chilcot are there to do: make sure that wealth has its own back. Senator Bayard's in on it, too, and he's been paid $5,000 to make sure the English sale stands. And that's why we can't run the business and the ranch from New York: Dick Wootton advises me that when the last hope of putting the land into the public domain is extinguished, the squatters and the homesteaders will violently retaliate against anyone who might be proxy buyers for the English. Murdoch, you look pale."

"I think my lunch hasn't agreed with me. I'll be fine," he said. But he felt he was about to be trussed, cuffed, and thrown onto a freight wagon.

"Well, I don't like to give up. I think we have a good future in New Mexico and in the cattle and freight business. We've both put a lot of work into securing our contracts, and I feel it has to be a mutual decision with the two of us."

Murdoch didn't want to sell, not just because he wanted to keep land as his father said, but because a sale would reveal that he'd never had a contract with the Maxwells. Lucien Maxwell was aged, and rumor had it that he would pass any day, but he likely still remembered whom he'd sold to and whom he hadn't. Murdoch would just have to wait him out, and persuade Henry to hold onto everything for the time being. He swallowed.

"I love New York City, you know that. I love my life here and my life here with Anne. I wouldn't have any of this if it were not for you. I want to build something for my sons, your grandchildren. I feel as you do that there is a future in New Mexico. No, I don't want to sell," he said.

He had made his decision; he couldn't give up yet. So he would hold on with all his might. He decided this then and there, but even as determined as he was, there was a part of this he also knew wasn't right. Despite those gnawing doubts, he pushed ahead, feeling a snare tightened around his soul just like a snare traps an animal that used to run free.

148

Chapter IX: Anniversary

Tuesday, May 1, 1877
New York City

"What are you laughing at? To the victor belong the spoils."
Thomas Nast, Harper's Magazine, 1871

It was Moving Day in New York! This was the day when the usually practical and officious city residents – well, at least those who rented their abodes, be they quaint or humble or opulent – this was the day when they all went temporarily insane. Bloomingdale Asylum probably achieved its peak annual census on Moving Day.

Moving Day is May 1 in New York. It was also the day that Murdoch McNeil and Anne Townsend decided to marry. That was nine years ago. Murdoch had insisted on the date: May 1 was an important day for the remaining Celtic traditions he held dear. May 1 was Beltane, the beginning of summer. Murdoch wanted to celebrate the summer he felt in his heart. So it was.

The Townsends, especially Mrs. Ada Townsend, briefly objected to the choice of Moving Day to add to the chaos in the streets. In New York City, every rental lease expired on the same day by law and custom. Some stayed put, but in the growing city, most people wanted new neighborhoods. Mrs. Townsend feared that the wedding would be sparsely attended and that everyone who wasn't moving might not be able to make their way through the crowds.

Murdoch had been clerking and then serving as an attorney in Mr. Henry Townsend's law firm for quite a few years, and he raised his counter-argument. After guests finished moving, they could enjoy a lovely wedding dinner. The festivities would last the whole day and they could go back and forth between supervising the servants as they moved from house to house and the lively dancing and socializing sure to take place.

For his part, Mr. Townsend barely even filed an amicus brief on the matter. He had no conviction either way. He did tell Ada that he'd heard Murdoch argue too many cases to challenge him when he was in full rhetoric.

Murdoch was right. The wedding was well-attended. Anyone who secured an invitation dared not disrespect the Townsends. After that, Anne and Murdoch's anniversary came to be celebrated on May 1 each year, becoming a part of Moving Day, and it was considered lucky to be invited to the celebration.

This day in particular was their ninth such anniversary. Murdoch had arrived that very afternoon from Cimarron, New Mexico, where Mr. Townsend's freighting business was headquartered. Murdoch was two days late. Usually, the travel was smooth and uneventful from the ranch in Cimarron to Trinidad in the new state of Colorado by carriage, then to Cheyenne, Wyoming and eventually to New York by rail. His travel was delayed first on the toll road over Raton Pass to Trinidad. A wagon carrying freight goods overturned, blocking all access, and at Chicago, the train needed to be switched due to mechanical issues.

That left Murdoch to try to make his way through Manhattan on the worst possible day. The streets were practically impassable. He checked his baggage at the train station and walked the short distance to the family residence. No valet would be there to pick him up by carriage, but he could send one after his luggage the next day

Mr. Townsend and Murdoch had hoped to meet before the anniversary party to discuss something important with Anne. Two days earlier would have been better, but this was a pressing matter and Anne was already waiting in the parlor with her father when Murdoch arrived.

"I don't want to leave New York, Murdoch, and I can't believe that Dad supports this. You're announcing our move after dinner tonight? So soon?" Anne said indignantly.

"Yes, Dad supports this decision, and if you want to talk around me, I will just step out," Henry Townsend stated bluntly.

"No, Dad, that's not what I meant. I just can't believe you're agreeing to this. The boys, your grandsons, they're everything to you. And Mom,

152

what does she say about this?"

"What you're saying, but in a more respectful tone."

Anne flushed and let out a sharp breath, crossed her arms, and tightened her jaw.

"New Mexico? New Mexico?! That's not even a God-damned state, Daddy!"

Murdoch ran his hand back and forth over his mouth and chin as if checking the stubble of his whiskers, but he was covering a grin. He coughed to suppress his laughter.

"You're right, Anne, it's not. Probably not any time soon, either," Murdoch said. "But it's a business decision. The chance to own and control land, lots of land. The freight business is fantastic, but I have to be out there to protect our, and your father's business interests."

Anne surveyed the beautiful Victorian parlor in the fine brownstone three-story home, its windows looking out onto Madison Avenue. She loved this room. The large white marble fireplace with gray filigree accenting the stonework always seemed warm and inviting, even in the summer. Her father had Italian artisans create the mahogany woodwork throughout the home. All of her memories were here. Every important decision she'd made here, including her decision to marry Murdoch. She'd spent hours tracing the lead in her favorite stained-glass window, a multicolored glass with a white daisy in the center. Murdoch and Anne had lived in this home ever since they married, and the boys had spent their entire five years of life here. And here she was, being told to go to New Mexico and she wanted to know why.

"Daddy, Murdoch, listen to yourselves! You're asking me to leave this brownstone, Madison Avenue, a fashionable address within walking distance of Central Park, to live in a mud hut in the middle of nowhere? And for what reason?"

"Adobe," Murdoch said.

"What?"

"I said it's adobe, not mud."

"And what is adobe made of?" Anne huffed.

"Dirt and straw."

Anne's father let loose a whistle. "Anne, I love you and I adore the twins, but this is a business matter that supports the law firm. Like any partner, Murdoch must serve the needs of the firm. I need his expertise in New Mexico. Like any partner, if he doesn't care to support the firm the way I need him to, he can always resign and find another position – but there is no reputable firm in New York that would hire a man, allowing his wife's preferences to dictate his career. I know this sounds harsh to you, but you must allow that you have had more of a say in Murdoch's career and general happiness than most wives. That has to be the end of the discussion." He moved to kiss her on her forehead, but she stamped her foot, which to Murdoch, only made her look more adorable.

The sliding door to the parlor came open, and Ada stepped through. She saw Henry trying to comfort Anne, Anne glaring at the room in general, and Murdoch suppressing a grin. All of them had fallen silent. "Your father always said that I am so becoming I can stop a conversation just by entering a room. I suppose he's still right! Anne, our guests will be here in an hour, so we need to finish some things at the last minute."

Murdoch and Anne looked at each other and then at Henry. Murdoch started to leave with Anne, and Henry asked him to stay for a minute. "I want to ask you about a case."

Anne was angry, "Murdoch, this is not finished; we need to talk."

Anne and Ada left the parlor and slid the door shut behind them. "Mother, can't you please talk to Daddy?"

"My darling, I have tried. I know your father well enough, and you must know Murdoch nearly as well. We both know that once they have landed on a decision they believe is sound, there's no getting them away from it. How many times have we heard 'it's business'?"

Anne's normally blue eyes turned a sharp grey whenever she was angry. She'd inherited her mother's will and her father's temper. According to her father, she had somehow acquired the changeable eyes of a cat. "Cat eyes," Henry would call them. He'd tease her when she was mad, knowing she disliked cats.

"Mother, that's just not a good enough reason to upend our family and move out of the country into a wild territory. We're doing so well here. Murdoch just arranged a loan to buy a brownstone right here in the neighborhood. Do we cancel that plan too? It just isn't right, Mother! What if I just refuse?"

"I quit trying to tell you what to do when you went to Bellevue to be a nurse during the war. Anne, I don't know why it's good for the firm for Murdoch to move all of you out to New Mexico, but your father does know his business. He and Murdoch have built a profitable freight operation out there, and I think they've both earned enough of your trust to give the idea a chance."

Anne and her mother stood under the stained-glass archway at the bottom of the staircase. These stairs were the site of her first adventures as a child: when she was punished she'd grip the spindles and pretend to be in jail. When she was happy, she would climb each stair as though it were a portal to some exotic land. She'd certainly never traveled to New Mexico in her staircase imagination. She started up the staircase and paused at the fifth stair, where, when her parents were out and she'd sent the servants on errands, she, and Murdoch –

Ada caught her daughter's smile returning. "What are you thinking about?"

"Oh, that we'll not have a staircase as grand as this one in that house in New Mexico. Maybe it's silly, but I'll miss it."

"You talk like you're leaving here forever! It's not as though you and the twins won't come back to visit, or perhaps we'll travel out there. You can go all the way from New York to San Francisco in a little more than six days now. Murdoch says it takes a little more time to get down to the ranch since you have to take a wagon over Raton Pass."

They paused again once they reached the top of the stairs. "Did Father give you his forty-niner speech?" Ada asked.

"No, thankfully."

"Well, after the brandy starts to flow tonight after dinner, I imagine you'll get to hear it again along with our guests."

"And then the Cuban cigar smoke takes over the air." Anne laughed, opening the door to her bedroom.

***

Mr. Townsend slid the parlor door back open. Murdoch paused and turned as he left the room. "Yes, Henry, I'm sure. All the work we did for Tweed on his real estate holdings was all above board. All the Ts crossed, and all the Is dotted. Billable hours are recorded accurately. Our internal audits will pass the closest scrutiny."

"We must be certain. Tweed's been convicted along with his ring, but with his escape and capture in Spain, everyone is talking about him again. There is renewed talk about his finances and holdings in New York. Anyone with a grudge against our firm for any reason will try to link his corruption to us. We've both worked hard to stay out of the Tammany Hall corruption. We have to keep it that way."

"I'm thankful we didn't partner with him on any of the backroom deals," Murdoch stated.

"That one fiasco was enough to make me cautious of even taking him on as a real estate client, but he was a powerful man with powerful friends back then, and I felt we didn't have a choice. But John Kelly's the Grand Sachem of Tammany Hall now. He's a good man. He and his wife will probably be here for the anniversary celebration. I doubt Tweed will come up in conversation, but if it does, I'll manage it. You concentrate on keeping Anne happy."

"Agreed."

"You've been married nine years now, and if it weren't for the carriage wreck, you might have bought a home and moved some time ago. Anne and the boys being here have made all the difference for both of us. Anne has such a sense of adventure, you know that. Once she sees the Rocky Mountains and northern New Mexico, I'm sure she'll forget all about the city. I need to go to the office for a bit but tell Ada I'll be back by six. And Murdoch?"

"Yes?"

"Happy anniversary. I envy you moving to the ranch, truly. Sometimes I wish I'd never come back from California. If I could, I would be going to New Mexico in your place."

"I appreciate that, sir. Thank you for all you've done for me."

"I don't think Anne will be happy with either of us for some time," Murdoch said with a smile. "I'll go and speak with her. She'll be fine;

she's just afraid of the unknown."

Henry scoffed, "I don't believe that for a minute, and I'm sure you don't either. She's never been afraid of anything, though I wish she were at times. Reckless, always been that way and you know it, Murdoch. Whatever is causing her concern, it's best addressed now. I don't like interfering, but I can talk with her."

Murdoch quickly climbed the stairs and entered their room. Anne was sitting on the edge of the bed and didn't turn toward him when he sat next to her. He nuzzled her neck. She forcefully pulled away from him and stood, hands clenched at her side.

She turned to face him. "Alright, what's the real reason? What are you not telling me?" she demanded.

Murdoch pleaded, "Anne, please lower your voice and calm down."

Her voice was resolute, insistent, and piercing, "I will not. Not until you come clean with me, and don't you push dad's 'this is business' bullshit. This should have been brought up and discussed weeks ago. We should just cancel this damn anniversary party, Murdoch!"

Murdoch let out a resigned sigh, looked down, and shook his head, "Alright, Anne. Yes, there's more, but you have to keep what I'm going to tell you to yourself. You know how much your dad has wanted to be a part of the West. Ever since he met Dick Wootton in California and got to know him, he wanted to be like him. Wootton convinced him to get into the freighting business, and start a ranch. You've no idea the kind of money that it takes, Anne, so I-" he paused trying to find the words that she'd understand.

"Look, your dad's done so much for me, it's the only way I could even start to repay him." And get a little something for myself and my family, too, he thought to himself.

Anne pleaded, "Murdoch?"

"Okay, I was able to get the ranch without having to use any of the firm's money, your dad's money. It's just a legal technique that everyone who's interested in acquiring land in the West uses. I just worked the paperwork with Dr. Spencer's help so that the land didn't...well, the firm has the land now, and that's what counts, Anne."

Anne slowly turned red, her breathing quickening, "Murdoch, you don't just 'get' land; you buy land. Don't you dare treat me like I'm some stupid schoolgirl!"

"Anne, please, your voice."

"Damn you, Murdoch, does that legal technique have a legal name? Fraud?"

Ada, tapped on the door. "Anne, Murdoch? I don't want to interfere, but you sound like alley cats fighting over scraps of food, and everyone in the house can hear you. If your father were here, he'd have words with both of you!"

Anne, her voice still at a high pitch, "Mother, please! This is between Murdoch and me."

Murdoch's voice rose, and he grabbed her shoulder. "That's why we have to go to New Mexico! We have to protect what's ours! We have to make sure that the ranch looks absolutely legitimate! We can't do that from New York City. Do anything you have to, to get land and to keep it! The God-damned Brits owe that to me, to us!"

"So that's what this is really about? What happened to you as a child on Barra? For Christ's sake, Murdoch!"

There was another tap at the door. "Anne? Murdoch? The guests will start arriving in just a few minutes."

Their voices quieted. "Anne, your father mustn't know. He can't know."

"You need to go, step out. You men make us wear all of these ridiculous layers. I need to get ready for the party."

"Anne, I love you."

"I know you do, I just, I can't think about it right now. I love you too; now get out."

Ada was halfway down the stairs when Murdoch came out of the room, she stopped and glanced at him, then quickly continued down the stairs without saying another word.

In the nine years they had been married, Murdoch had never put a hand on her in anger. He had grabbed her shoulder in anger, and Anne choked back a tear. She refused to let Murdoch see her cry and had begun to think of all she must do just to get ready for such a complicated move. Even with all of the help she would have, how was she to manage? What about her friends that she'd known since she was a child? How would she do all of this? Murdoch and her father had no idea what they were asking of her. They were oblivious. And the land? That just complicated her feelings for him. She imagined a knight on a horse, a silly and trite feeling, but he was that to her. Not now. Maybe not ever again. He would never know that their relationship just changed.

The guests began arriving at 306 Madison at 7:00 p.m. while the mid-spring sun still threw its light on the chaotic streets. Carts were still scattered throughout, stacked haphazardly with furniture and household items tied with rope, twine, and whatever string was available. Any attempts to secure these loads this late in the day were taken as mere decoration. These bits of string did nothing to prevent the streets from being littered with broken mirrors and shattered sticks of furniture.

"It's madness out there!" exclaimed Frank Angel, handing his light coat and his wife's wrap to Johanna, the Townsend's parlor maid. Frank had been admitted to the New York bar about three years after Murdoch in 1869 and had assisted the Townsend firm after the accident in Central Park. They were similar in age and temperament and were often in court together, either on separate cases or as rivals. Frank and Sarah Angel had been longtime friends with Murdoch and Anne, and they had been at the McNeil's anniversary parties together for the last few years. Their little daughter, Clara, already headstrong, was barely one year old. Anne had delighted in taking charge of Clara when she had the chance, saying she was the sort of daughter she'd want for herself someday. Henry and Ada were also fond of Frank, and Henry had tried to recruit him to work in his firm.

"I appreciate the offer, Mr. Townsend, but I prefer solo practice," Frank had said.

Anne laughed at the Moving Day chaos outside. "I've been watching a bit out the windows," she replied.

"The cartmen are charging as much as they dare, too. It's more stressful than a hung jury!" said Frank.

"Sarah, how is your little girl?"

"I think she just said the word 'no,' so she's doing well! How are the boys?"

"They're boys," Anne laughed. "I believe Murdoch is attempting Manhattans and whiskey sours in the parlor, Frank. That should help you brush off the streets a bit. Johanna, please show them the way."

"Oh, we will follow our spirits. We know the way. We will see how Murdoch's skill as a mixologist is coming."

Anne and Ada continued to greet their guests, and by 8:00 p.m., everyone was called to dinner. Anne did not look forward to the announcement of their move, and she knew the questions and gossip would follow. She resolved to outwardly support her father and Murdoch on their decision and let go of her arguments for the remaining time in New York. Their arguments were few, but always intense and Murdoch had a habit of displaying how much he hated the barrier between who he was and the class he longed for in pronounced ways. Yet, asking her to keep anything from her parents was against her nature.

The dinner topics flowed with the usual course, given that many of the guests were in the legal profession. The Tweed scandal was brought up, but thankfully only briefly as Grand Sachem John Kelly said he preferred the city should look to the future. The other guests took the hint and moved on.

As dessert came to the table, Mr. Townsend tapped his water glass with his teaspoon and rose from his chair.

"Thank you for joining us this evening as we celebrate Murdoch and Anne's ninth anniversary. Please join me in a toast of congratulations!"

The guests applauded and raised their glasses as Mr. Townsend continued.

"I have one more announcement to make – no, I am not retiring!" he teased as he winked at John Kelly. "Those of you familiar with this law firm already know the direction we've been taking our business. We've established our freighting operations in New Mexico and the new state of Colorado. At present we are pursuing southern routes in Colorado and northern New Mexico. The Scots have invested heavily in the cattle industry there, pulling their profits out to Europe. America, even the world, is hungry for beef, and I mean to have our share.

"In 1868, we bought fifty-seven thousand acres of the Maxwell Land Grant from Lucien Maxwell himself before he sold the remainder of the Grant to the English investment firm Maxwell Land Grant and Railway Company. This allowed us a foothold for our freighting company, and now we can establish a modest cattle ranch to diversify our holdings. We can provide beef to the United States government, not just for the military operations in the West, but also for the Indian reservations the government is responsible for."

Anne's eyes met Murdoch's, and he quickly looked away.

Townsend was proud of his ranch and continued: "What I'm coming to is to run the day-to-day operations and provide sound business management, I've asked Murdoch to oversee freight and cattle in New Mexico Territory. As most of you know, he's been traveling regularly to smooth out our operations there, and now he's agreed to move with his family to our ranch just outside the town of Cimarron.

"Please raise your glasses to his success!"

Glasses clinked once again, and the guests rose from their seats and congratulated Murdoch. Ada Townsend leaned in close to Anne. "Henry is the only person I know who can make anyone in the room want to move to a ranch in the middle of nowhere. Every man here wishes they were Murdoch right now, and every woman wishes she was you."

"Well, every woman except one," Anne corrected.

The men retired to the library, where Mr. Townsend and Murdoch served brandy, handed out Cuban cigars, and spread out the latest Rand McNally Railroad Map where he'd marked out the ranch's territory. He traced the route they would take to get there and answered everyone's questions.

"Are you naming the ranch after the firm?" John Kelly asked.

"No, I've named it the McNeil Ranch and registered the brand. I thought we'd let the Scots know just who they're dealing with!" Mr. Townsend took a piece of paper and a pen and drew the cattle brand for everyone to see. "It's based on the McNeil coat of arms, Murdoch. I think your father would be very proud."

"Yes, he would. He used to tell me that land is everything," Murdoch said.

"I would have gotten along well with him," Henry said. "Let's raise a glass to his memory. Murdoch, will you do the honors?"

"All right, then," he said, raising his glass. "To James McNeil, who once told me, 'Do what you have to do to acquire land and do what you have to do to keep it.' Cheers!"

Everyone drank the toast. "Gentlemen!" Henry said, "don't throw the snifters into the fireplace! Last time, Ada complained about it for a week! Save me some anguish!"

"Even the boss of Tammany Hall?" John Kelly chuckled.

"If you must!" replied Henry.

"I will hold in favor of Sachem, Mrs. Ada Townsend," he laughed.

"Murdoch! I shall miss you augmenting my meager solicitor's income with our poker games! As to whether I shall also miss your Manhattans, the jury is out," laughed Frank.

"Speaking of meager incomes, Frank," John Kelly said, "what will it take for you to allow me to help you with your legal career? We can move your business address close to Henry's over on Chambers Street."

"I've been trying that gambit for years, John! If you corral him, I shall not only be jealous for eternity – I might even sue!" joked Henry. But Frank allowed that he was hoping to move his practice closer to Washington D.C. and wished to avoid any regional entanglements.

"Spoken like a true politician!" Kelly said. "I could help you with that, too..." With that, the subject was dropped, and the gentlemen finished their cigars. They retired to the parlor, where the guests had dropped their anniversary gifts. Murdoch and Anne opened them together and saved what they'd bought for each other for last.

"Our anniversary party will be quite a bit smaller next year, I think. I will miss all of you!" Anne said, holding back a tear.

"Wait until you see some of the celebrations the vaqueros throw! That's what the Mexicans call cowboys. They can get pretty wild. We can invite them all, and we certainly won't be lonely!"

John Kelly raised his concerns. "Speaking of wild, we've all read the newspaper accounts. And, though we may not wish to admit it, a lot of us have read those dime novels about the Wild West. Lots of talk about the Indian Wars. Do you think this is a threat to the business, Henry? After all, if you lose a few freight wagons to the savages, that can be quite a loss in investment."

"Not at all," Henry said. "We've owned the land since before the army ended the Red River War in 1874, and we waited until then to bring in the cattle and build the hacienda – the ranch house. I suppose there might be a raid or two, but it would be unusual if the Indians wanted to make trouble and leave the reservations. Here, I'll point it out on the map. Johanna!" he called to his housekeeper. "Please bring the map on my desk, will you?"

She brought the map into the parlor and spread it out among the anniversary gifts. The guests all crowded around, and while earlier they had been following his stories of the freight maps and routes, now they envisioned the Indian attacks and tense gunfights in dime novels written by people who'd never set foot in the West.

"Look, here on the map. This, if you remember, is where the ranch is. And here again is Fort Union, not far at all. I mentioned that the army does escorts, and they accompany our Mexican teamsters and anyone else we employ to haul the freight. Safe as kittens, really."

Murdoch chimed in with his firsthand experiences: "Those dime novels, and even the newspapers in the West, love to sell hype and cause panic. I'm afraid we've solved the Indian problem and pushed them onto tightly controlled reservations."

"You don't seem too enthusiastic," Frank said.

"Let's just say I have sympathies for those who have been forcibly pushed off of their ancestral homelands. It's never pretty, but it's business. There are winners and losers, and I know what side I like to be on."

"Anne, what about you and the children?" Sarah Angel said. "Aren't you just a bit afraid of moving to the West? Sure, the stories might be exaggerated, but there's no question that the settlers have been attacked. And the savagery toward women is unthinkable!"

"Dear, this is a celebration..." Frank implored.

Anne's mind was not preoccupied with Murdoch's fraud. That was nine years ago, not yesterday, and her anger quieted with anticipation.

The anticipation of a new direction in her life--one without the drama of class and society, but one of adventure.

She gave careful thought to Sarah's question, "That's fine, Frank, I'm sure the question is on many of our minds. It's a natural thing to wonder. And I will worry about savagery when and if it occurs – but I will not worry about words on paper when we have so much violence and wildness going on in the streets of New York. The Orange Riots, the political machine, the draft riots, the war. We don't need to look for the savages in the West. They're just out the window."

"Well said, Anne!" Henry exclaimed. "She obviously inherited my forty-niner spirit! Now, who needs a nightcap for those savage streets ahead?"

The guests finished their drinks, said their goodnights, and made their way through the New York streets, finally free of wagons and frantic people. Murdoch and Anne bade Henry and Ada goodnight. Neither Henry nor Murdoch were surprised that Anne had so fiercely and candidly defended New Mexico.

Murdoch stood at the foot of the stairs with Anne and slipped his arm around her. She tightened her arms around him and leaned into his embrace. Through years of minor squabbles and deeply passionate arguments, both had learned when the time for fighting had passed and nothing more needed to be said. However, she wasn't sure if this last fight fell into that category. The rules had changed. She wondered if the dime novels had any truth to them and if their relationship, built on trust and honesty, would stand.

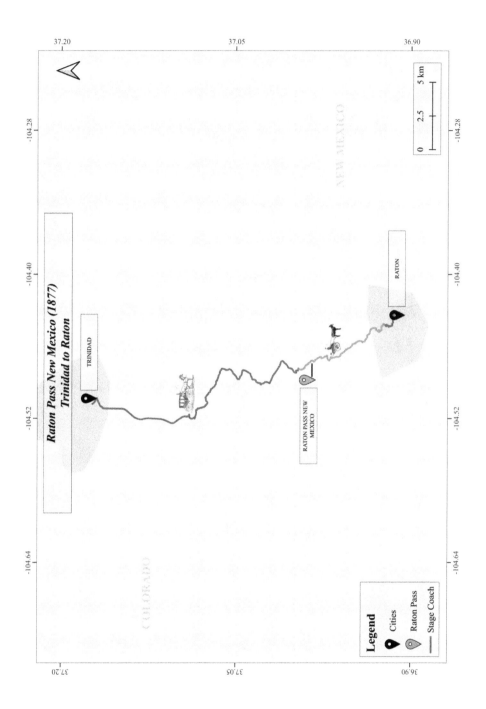

Raton Pass New Mexico (1877)
Trinidad to Raton

TRINIDAD

RATON PASS NEW MEXICO

RATON

NEW MEXICO

COLORADO

Legend
Cities
Raton Pass
Stage Coach

0   2.5   5 km

165

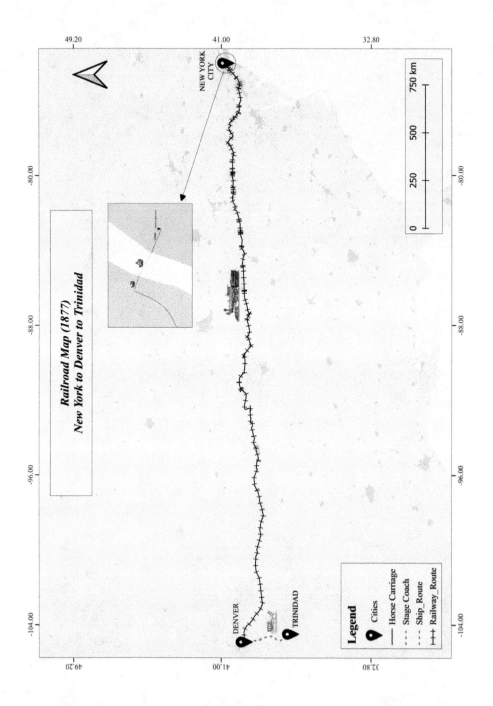

Railroad Map (1877)
New York to Denver to Trinidad

Legend

Cities

—— Horse Carriage

- - - Stage Coach

- - - Ship_Route

+++ Railway_Route

NEW YORK CITY

DENVER

TRINIDAD

0 250 500 750 km

166

Chapter X: The Ranch

Tuesday, May 15th, 1877
Grand Central Station
New York City

All calculations based on experience elsewhere, fail in New Mexico.
Lew Wallace, 1881

"All aboard!" the conductor yelled.

Murdoch held Wallace's hand securely. His six-year-old legs did double time to keep up with Murdoch's purposeful stride. Wallace occasionally let go a cheerful laugh as they moved along. Anne was not so fortunate. She had charge of William, who was screaming and crying. Anne's parents were there to see them off and try to console William.

Henry Townsend whispered to his daughter out of Murdoch's earshot. "Anne, you have the envelope I gave you?"

"Right in my bag, Daddy. Does Murdoch know that we talked?"

His voice was emphatic, "He does not, nor do I want him to know. Consider it none of your business. You take care of Murdoch and my grandchildren. Ada will see you off; I've a telegram to send to Dick Wooton." He kissed her on the cheek, rubbed Wallace's sandy blond hair, and walked briskly away.

Murdoch eyed Henry as he left the train platform. It was unlike him to depart without a word, but Murdoch understood how a busy mind could make one's actions appear abrupt. The argument with Anne played in his mind, and he wondered if Henry knew about the fraud. The thought started to gnaw at him, but he quickly dismissed it and tried to file his worry away. Murdoch handed the conductor their tickets. The conductor punched them. "These are First Class, yes?" he asked.

"Yes sir, First Class," the conductor answered.

Ada tried not to cry and was on the verge of failing the attempt. "You take good care of our daughter and grandchildren out there."

The family boarded quickly. They found their drawing room compartment on the Pullman railcar about halfway down the long train. Murdoch slid the door open and placed Wallace in one of the overstuffed cushioned seats near the window. He sat down on one of the matching wing chairs, each ornately carved, much like the furniture back at his New York practice. Anne entered close behind and sat a still-fussing William down. Anne sat next to Murdoch.

"It's about a day and a half to Chicago, then two days to Cheyenne, a quick connection, then the Denver-to-Trinidad train; that'll probably take two days. Then Raton Pass. That's always an adventure!" Murdoch said as he wondered how well Anne would tolerate the trip over the pass. She's used to such luxury, he thought. "Then again, so am I," he finished out loud.

Anne cocked her head, "Did you say something, darling?" Anne said.

"I was just musing that we're so used to the finer things. Nothing wrong with that. I was hoping that after we get to Trinidad, the trip down to the ranch won't be too disappointing to you, having to go by carriage for three days."

"I'll be fine. I'm enjoying this part quite a bit. This is even more beautiful than I remember, Murdoch!" she exclaimed at the drawing room's accommodations.

They kissed but were jolted apart by the train lurching forward. The boys had fallen asleep on the floor's plush carpeting. Anne pulled a book from her bag, sat down, and started to read. Murdoch was lost in his thoughts, looked out the window at the passing scenery, and worried over the ranch and Anne.

He had taken this trip many times to oversee Mr. Townsend's freighting business. His success was partly due to the advice and help he received from Richens Wootton, whom Mr. Townsend had met during his days in California. Richens, or "Uncle Dick" as everyone called him, was able to build a toll road over the treacherous Raton Pass because he enjoyed a close relationship with the Ute Indians and their Chief,

Connaich. Uncle Dick had said that only the Ute could have built it, and in fact, when he'd tried to recruit workers from Trinidad and Raton, none would take on the dangerous and strenuous work. The McNeils would stay with the Wootton's at their stage stop and inn at the base of the pass.

The first time Murdoch had traveled by train to New Mexico, he had accidently boarded a third-class railcar. Water closets were clearly inadequate on these cars. The smells, the dirty faces of the passengers, and the general state of filth inside the railcar instantly brought him back to the immigrant ship he'd sailed on as a boy of nine. The *Sarah* had been like this in steerage class. It seemed to him then that the railroads were no different, and this surprised and disappointed him. His experience on the *Sarah* haunted him, and he could never know when a ghost would invade his thoughts.

That first trip to Cimarron was clouded by these powerful and unrelenting memories. He couldn't set them aside, but eventually, he put them back into their box. By the time he returned to New York, this box was tightly shut. Still, every time he boarded a train, he subconsciously made extra effort to check with the conductor that he should board first class.

With its deep carpeting and rich appointments, this Pullman car was indeed first class.

The train moved along at twenty miles per hour, the familiar soothing symphony of sounds floating through the railcars. The sounds were the same, no matter the class. He glanced at Anne, steeped in her reading, and saw the twins still fast asleep, enveloped in the soft carpet.

"Anne, I'm going to the smoking car. I need to work through some accounts."

She smiled and nodded.

The trip to Cheyenne went quickly, and they reached the small city on the afternoon of May 19. They changed trains and traveled in a compartment not nearly as luxurious as the Pullmans available from the East but still comfortable. They would spend three hundred miles in this car until they reached Trinidad, Colorado. Soon after reaching the Colorado state border, Anne saw the Rocky Mountains for the first time, and though it was late May, the peaks were still draped in snow. She pressed her face against the railcar window.

"Murdoch! Come and see! My God, look how big they are! They look so close as if you could just reach out and touch them! I just want to get out of this train and walk right up to them. I've never seen snow so white and the sky so blue. I've read descriptions and seen a few pictures, but oh! I had no idea!" She told the boys to get to the window. "See, William, Wallace, it's the Rocky Mountains!"

Her glee was childlike, and Murdoch had not expected such an emotional and enthusiastic expression. The Rockies pulled different emotions from everyone, and in Murdoch's experience, no two people saw the range and the West in the same way. The dime novels were indeed inadequate to describe the view. The more poetic the attempt, the less accurate. For him, the contrast between the great plains and the snow-capped peaks made him uncomfortable that first time. His chest tightened, and he had never felt so far away from New York. He'd been filled with dread, not joy. He enjoyed Anne's enthusiasm, and he set his cheek to hers and pressed his face to the glass of the train window.

"It's beautiful, darling. So vast, and so much opportunity!"

"Will our train go up that way?"

"No, but the mountains will be in view all the way to Trinidad. It is spectacular over Raton Pass! I wish I could remember the names of all the mountains, but there are so many!" He pointed out Longs Peak as they neared Denver, where the train stopped to pick up more passengers. Anne beamed at the hustle of the Denver station, and they decided to stroll a bit as the train paused. "That's Mount Rosalie. It's over 14,000 feet high." Murdoch pointed at a mountain towering over Denver.

"Someone must have loved her very much to name a mountain after her," she said.

"I think we can find Mount Anne somewhere on our 57,000 acres."

"What did you say?"

Murdoch, proud of his acquisition of the ranch, stated, "I said I'd

170

name a mountain after you on the ranch."

"But the number you said – how many acres?" she asked in surprise.

"About 57,000, give or take. That's about 90 square miles. It would take more than half a day on a good horse running at a canter just to cross it."

"You said we have cattle on the ranch?"

"Yes, about three thousand head or so, and of course, it's okay to tell you, but one of the unwritten social rules there is that one can ask the size of a man's spread but not how many cattle he has. The acres are a point of pride, but asking about the cattle is like asking how much money he has in his wallet."

"What's that huge mountain there?" she asked, pointing.

"Pikes Peak."

"Oh, of course! I've heard of that one before. I read about that wonderful hotel in Colorado Springs, The Antlers. I'd love to stay there sometime. Not now, of course; I'm excited to get to the ranch. I really want to see what a mud house looks like."

He smiled, glad that she was teasing him and that the fight over the land acquisition seemed to be to rest. He laughed, "It's called adobe."

"I know, darling, just like to get a rise out of you. So easy to tease! Speaking of that, what did Frank say about your Manhattans last time?"

"Something about John Kelly needing to get a really specific prohibition law passed." He smiled. "I'm sure we can't get sweet vermouth out there; I'm sure we're safe."

Anne eventually allowed herself the luxury of sleep. The boys, too, allowed the rhythm and motion of the train car to put them to sleep, and soon Murdoch followed them despite his busy thoughts.

***

"Next stop, Trinidad! Next stop, Trinidad, Colorado!" the conductor yelled.

The train pulled into the small Trinidad station in the late afternoon on May 22. The whistle blew, the steam hissed, and the metal rails screeched as the train came to a stop. The McNeils, with sleep still in their eyes, slid open their compartment door and made their way down the walkway and off the train.

"Mr. McNeil! Mr. McNeil! Over here!" a voice called from the crowd.

"Joseph! Good to see you!" Murdoch exclaimed. "This is my wife, Anne, and these are our boys, William and Wallace."

"Such strong-looking young lads! Good to meet you, Mrs. McNeil."

"Joseph Lujan is the teamster," Murdoch explained. "We have four freighters in the business headed south on this trip. One to Cimarron, two to Fort Union, one to Santa Fe."

"Good to meet you all! I'll have the men collect your things, and we'll load them all onto the wagon. We have a carriage for you and the family; it should be more comfortable. I'll be your driver so you can watch your boys and the scenery and enjoy the ride. We'll be heading up the pass, and at Uncle Dick's place, we'll settle in. He's expecting you all. We'll then leave in the morning for Cimarron."

"Did Maria have the chance to make those things for Mrs. McNeil?" Murdoch asked.

"Yes, I've not seen them, but she sure can sew."

"Well, we won't have much of a surprise for Anne…"

"Oh Murdoch, tell me, please?" Anne pleaded.

"Well, I think you will just have to wait to preserve the rest of the surprise. I'm not sure what she's made for you, but some outfits will be more suited for the country and your daily rides. Your New York dresses likely won't be suitable for much other than entertaining."

"Oh, I can't wait to see them! I hope you've found me a sound horse too!" Anne dearly loved riding, though she was more used to the kind of livery one had in Central Park.

Joseph let Anne know that he'd found a wonderful animal among the wild herd at the base of the Sangre de Cristos, near the little town of San Luis. "He is 14.3 hands, his shoulder should be just under eye length with you. The wild horses he comes from are descendants of the Spanish horses the conquistadors brought over in the 1600s. They are very sturdy and surefooted, and they know their minds. Skip is well trained by our vaqueros, though he needs a firm hand."

The wagon was loaded with the large trunks the McNeils had

packed full of household essentials and a few items they wanted from New York. Added to this were goods destined for the freight office in Cimarron. Each wagon could carry over three tons of goods and held sturdy oak flooring with an iron undercarriage. Thick off-white canvas covered the loads to protect shipments from the weather. The rear wagon wheels were the height of a man and also made of oak and iron, while the front wheels were a little smaller.

The carriage, on the other hand, was rugged but elegant. Joseph drove the McNeils in their carriage all the way up Raton Pass, and the freight wagon followed. Three more wagons were in their party and had already departed; they would meet the entire group at Wootton's Stop, where they would spend the night and then travel on the next morning. Raton Pass was a rutted, bumpy, rocky, and winding toll road.

Murdoch was surprised to see the twins handling the rough ride so well. Anne remained engrossed in the scenery, excited to be in the rough, jagged mesa and craggy cliffs that lined the pass. She asked Joseph questions about the animals she saw, the pronghorns and the hawks, so unlike what she'd seen in New York. She and Joseph chatted about what life was like as a teamster and, with a fair amount of ribbing, what her husband was like as a long-distance boss. While most teamsters in Murdoch's experience were silent types, he'd asked Joseph to take their carriage because of his talkative nature.

Murdoch thought about Anne's potential reaction to Wootton's place. One could not really call it a hotel. A stage stop and saloon that happened to have sleeping rooms was the better description. The farther south they got along the route from Trinidad to Cimarron, the rougher the accommodations generally became – if not in architecture, then in spirit. This land and its people gripped the senses and could demand attention quite suddenly. Murdoch had made this trip numerous times in the past six years, but it still shocked him to come from New York's luxury and it's manageable chaos, in the decadence of Pullman travel to the basic services at Wootton's. As they continued their journey south, they wouldn't even have that and would sleep under the stars.

He got the feeling that Anne would love it after all.

***

The sun busied itself setting in the cloudless sky, and the springtime air became chilled as Joseph pulled the carriage in front of Wootton's Inn and Stage Stop. The two-story adobe inn sat in the midst of scrub oak, just leafing out with their dark green leaves. Later in the fall, they would turn deep shades of oranges and reds. The inn extended out on the sides with porches on the first and second stories. Lamplight showed through the large windows in the front. The boys jumped out of the carriage and raced up the steep hill to the door.

Anne was instantly taken by the place. "I love the smell of the air here!" she exclaimed as she stepped from the carriage.

"It'll be colder up the pass," Murdoch said, handing her a fur wrap. "Even though it's late spring, we can still get some bad snowstorms." He followed her up the steps.

Joseph agreed. "You don't want to get caught in a bad one either, up there on the pass or south of Raton on the plains." He moved to bring in their bags, and the door opened. Dick Wootton and his wife Maria warmly greeted the party.

"Good to see you again, Murdoch! How is Henry getting along these days?" Wootton extended his hand and enthusiastically slapped him on the back. "And who is this lovely lady?"

"Henry is just fine; he sends his greetings. Dick, this is Anne, my wife. Those two balls of fire are our boys, William and Wallace."

"They'll be cowboying in no time! Anne, this is Maria, my wife."

Maria Wootton clasped Anne's hand. "You're just as your husband described! Once you get settled in your room, I will bring up the clothes Mr. McNeil ordered for you. They won't need any alterations. He's done a good job remembering the sizing."

Murdoch filled out the guest register, paid for the rooms, and settled up the toll bill for the entire party. Even though it was Sunday, the Inn and Stage Stop were full of travelers. The twins loved the activity. The McNeils went to their room and soon after, Maria and another young woman came up with their arms full of dresses, shawls, blouses, skirts, belts, and hats. Anne ushered in the women.

174

"Murdoch, I think now would be a good time for you to head to the saloon. I've got to try on these clothes."

Maria called for one of her helpers. "Rosa, please teach the children how to make gourd rattles.

"This is Anita, my seamstress. She helped me sew the outfits. They're basic, but they're pretty, and they are meant for the ranch life. I do hope you like them."

Anne had seen Western dress before, but she was surprised at the simple beauty of the heavy cotton skirts and blouses. "Such a good style! And the colors are so vivid, like these greens and yellows!""

"Do you ride a lot?"

"Yes, I love to ride. I had a thoroughbred horse in New York, and I'm used to large horses. Joseph said he had a horse trained for me."

"Do you ride side saddle?"

"Yes, all the women in New York do."

"I thought as much. I made you a split riding skirt and chaparajos, chaps. You have cattle, yes? Then you'll be riding around the cholla and will want to be astride. You must pay attention to the ground on both sides of the horse and a fall onto the cholla would be painful, and riding side saddle wouldn't allow you to be balanced."

"I've ridden astride before, but I have a lot to learn. I think we'll be great friends, and you can teach me about what it is to live here!" Anne opened her trunk and pulled out a beaded purple evening gown. She held it out to Maria. "It may need a little alteration and hemming, but we're about the same size. This is the newest fashion in New York. I'd like you to have it."

Maria beamed. "We have dances here at the inn every Saturday night. This will be perfect!" As Anita arranged the new clothes in Anne's trunk, Maria and Anne spent the next hour chatting about life in the Southwest and how quickly the railroad was bringing change all the way out to Raton Pass. Maria's outfits fit Anne well, just as she promised, and Anne chose a wide sombrero and scarf to protect her skin from the harsh sun she'd encounter over the rest of her journey.

Murdoch returned to the room just after Maria and Anita left. Anne had her trunk open still and stared at her new wardrobe. "Do you like them?" he asked.

"Oh, I love them! They're so practical and comfortable compared to all the layers and things we must wear in New York to show ourselves off. Thank you for having Maria make them. I might not ever wear an evening gown again! And she said I should start riding astride rather than sidesaddle. She made me split riding skirts." She held one up. "See? It'll look like I'm riding sidesaddle, but I won't fall into the cactus this way."

"You will look as beautiful as ever! Next, you'll be wanting to learn how to handle a rifle and a six-shooter. You'll be a cowboy before our boys get the chance," he said and laughed.

"And what's so funny about that? Of course, I must learn to shoot. Maria can probably teach me how to do that, too!" She closed her trunk. "It's an exciting time for us, Dock. I can't wait to see the hacienda you've built. You've told me many times about your father, and this land must mean a great deal to you."

Murdoch looked away. "Anne, we've talked about this. It's not really mine, or even ours. It all belongs to your father, and you know that's the reason I did what I did. It's the only way that I could possibly repay him for all he's done for me. I hope you understand that."

Anne took his hand. "I was going to wait until we got to the ranch." She reached into her traveling bag and pulled out the envelope that Henry had given her before they'd boarded the train.

"What is this?" he asked.

Anne was curious, "I'm not sure; Daddy gave it to me before we left for the station. He said to give the envelope to you once we had left. I don't know why he didn't give it to you himself. He seemed to be in a hurry."

May 1, 1877

Dear Son,
You have worked and sacrificed much since I first met you selling newspapers on the street corner, devouring books in the library. I started this law firm, but you have

176

helped it grow and become prosperous. I have enclosed a
quit claim deed to the fifty-seven thousand acres of land
purchased by the firm, and the deed to the hacienda.
All of this is transferred as property in your name as an
anniversary gift to you and Anne.

We will continue our business arrangement for the
freighting and cattle concerns with the caveat that the
firm will lease your acreage for the purpose of raising
cattle. The term allows you the sum of one dollar ($1)
per year and a bottle of scotch whiskey to be renewed
on May 1st.

I hope this softens the blow of having to leave New York.
Sincerely,

Henry Perrine Townsend

Anne looked expectedly at Murdoch and smiled, "Well? Just business, or are you going to let me in on this mystery? I swear, Daddy can be so dramatic. And you men think we ladies create all the drama."

Murdoch shook his head, and handed the letter that accompanied the deed to the ranch to Anne.

She quickly read the letter, "Murdoch, this is wonderful! This is what you wanted, isn't it? Now it's ours!"

She read his expression. "What's wrong? You look like you've seen a ghost or worse. Is it how you...?"

Murdoch refused to open the issue of land fraud with Anne again. She had accepted it and managed to push it out of her mind—at least that's what he thought. He knew full well what this anniversary present from Henry meant. Having the ranch solely in his name removed any legal protection he had hoped to maintain by having the ranch in the firm's name.

"Yes, Anne, it's exactly what I wanted. It's perfect. It's a perfect anniversary gift. I'm very happy and grateful to your father. Yes, let's go collect the boys and get some dinner."

Anne tried not to guess his thoughts, but she sensed that something was not right. She'd thought he would be ecstatic at owning the land and fulfilling his own father's wishes, but the shadow of how he acquired the land would always be there. It wouldn't ever go away. Was that it? Had he guessed that she had told her father about how the land was actually acquired? Her father had told her to mind her own business. She wanted no part of all of this and refused the temptation to be drawn into it.

Their dinner tasted as good as anything they could get in New York. They had roast elk and vegetables grown in Maria Wootton's gardens. After dinner they put the children to bed and came down to the large living area, where a modestly sized fireplace was alive with the sweet smell of piñon wood that crackled and popped as it burned. Bright red embers bounced off the inside of the fire screen.

***

The McNeils awoke early the next morning and enjoyed their breakfast in Wootton's dining area. Uncle Dick was already outside directing the teamsters and the carriages as the drivers prepared their horses and mules. The McNeils were underway negotiating the narrow winding road just as the sun peeked over the top of the canyon walls, painting them in shades of pinks and purples. By 10:00 o'clock, their carriage passed into the New Mexico side high up on the pass, though they could not see the path too far to the south with the steep canyon walls blocking the view. The route could be treacherous, and Anne started to understand why Wootton's toll road was such an achievement. He had to keep peace on the road as the canyon's blocked views made her think of Indian ambushes in the dime novels. The sun warmed the rocks on the cliffs during the days, and the chill froze the rocks at night. Any loose boulders could come tumbling down onto the path and block the road. Twice, Murdoch and Joseph had to pause their party to remove small rockslides.

And then they rounded a curve, and it seemed to Anne that the entire world opened up. She could see south for miles through the crisp air. Joseph halted the carriage and the freight wagons paused behind him.

Joseph stretched out his arm and pointed to the distance, "See that mountain on the horizon, the one with the smooth curve on it? That's Mount Capulin. It's an extinct volcano. The lava used to run everywhere, and it turned into the flat mesas on the prairie floor."

Anne's more poetic soul drank in the view. "The colors, Dock! The way the clouds paint their shadows upon the plains looks more colorful than real, like a fairy tale with only pictures, not words. I've never seen so many shades of green before! Even the rocks have colors, pink and tans! And the different shapes of those little mountains in the distance. Some have flat tops, and others don't. That shade of blue the sky has just seems to hold everything on the ground together somehow. Oh, Dock, why didn't you tell me it looked like this?"

"The words to describe it are clearly your department. It changes constantly. See, just now, the clouds changed, and their shadows throw a different pattern on the ground. Even the color of Mount Capulin has changed from pink to dark blue since we stopped. Those flat mountains you see are called mesas. So many shapes that just seem to fit." He smiled to see her so happy in their new land.

Joseph cued the horses to move along. Anne could not take her eyes off the panorama, and she and Murdoch were silent with their wonder the rest of the way down the canyon and into the little town of Raton. By sundown, they were still a day and a half from the McNeil Ranch. The group paused at an arroyo under a large cottonwood tree.

"The cottonwoods know where there's water," Joseph said. Sure enough there was a water catchment full of melted mountain snow. Joseph made a campfire, and Anne learned how to make a bedroll. William and Wallace insisted on bedding down under the wagons. The chill came again with the night, and Anne was surprised by how quickly the temperatures dropped. She was glad for the campfire.

Maria Wootton had packed a basket with cooked elk meat, vegetables, and bread. While it was cold, traveling had given them an appetite better than any aroma wafting from a New York restaurant. After dinner, they bedded down, the McNeils a short distance away from the rest of the group, the teamsters giving the family – especially Murdoch and Anne – space to explore the starry night sky.

A falling star shot across the sky, "I've never seen the stars so brilliant, or so many! The Milky Way looks like silver dust spilled across the sky."

"It's magical, Anne. It gives me perspective on my thoughts. I've been a bit preoccupied since you told me about the ranch—our ranch. I guess I'll always have some of the crofter in me. Owning land was my father's dream, and it seems to be every homesteader's dream as well. But my father, along with my entire family, was cheated out of our home and land, and everyone but me lost their lives. I can never get that back."

Murdoch crumbled white yarrow flowers in his hands to keep away the mosquitos. "Seems a man spends the first half of his life getting something to hang onto and the second half of his life trying to keep it."

"Maybe someday we'll pass the ranch to our sons."

"And our daughters, too, someday." She pulled the buffalo hide around her shoulders. "Why haven't I ever slept under a buffalo hide before? It doesn't seem that cold here under this blanket. It's surprising, though, that we didn't see any buffalo on the whole trip."

"There aren't any left, really. They've been hunted out to keep the tribes starving. Good business for us, since we send beef to the reservations. I suppose it's worthwhile."

Anne fell asleep before the next shooting star pelted its way across the sky. "Life can be gone that quickly," Murdoch said to himself before he joined her in sleep.

***

Joseph and the rest of the teamsters rose before the McNeils and prepared their bacon, eggs, and hot coffee. The smell woke them up, and the party huddled close to the renewed campfire to ward off the early morning chill. The horses and mules drank their fill from the water catchment, and once hitched, they all moved on south towards Cimarron.

By noon the next day, they'd all reached the outskirts of the village and then they crossed the Cimarron River into town.

Anne stretched her hand downward, letting the river water splash onto it as the carriage crossed the stream. "The Cimarron looks tame right now. Dock, you said you built the hacienda away from the creek. The water is so low—not at all like the grand rivers we have out east. It's hard to believe the town can flood so quickly, as you say."

"When nature gets up to a summer storm, or we get an early snowmelt in the spring, the water comes rushing down the mountains," Joseph said. "The freight company is up by the St. James Hotel on the high ground, too, well away from the river."

The hacienda lay ten miles south of Cimarron. Anne thought that the closer they got, the farther away they seemed to be and the longer it seemed to take to get there. The carriage came to another hill, and when they crested the top, she could see the McNeil hacienda and the smoke billowing from the chimney.

"What day is it, Dock? I've lost any sense of time here, just as you've said."

"May 26. Saturday, I think," he replied.

The carriage entered the hacienda's land under an archway built of adobe, topped with stout pine timbers. Hanging from the center of the archway was a large wrought-iron sign proclaiming this to be the McNeil Ranch. A winding road led a half-mile from the archway through a protected canyon, with the Cimarroncito running alongside the road. Tall ponderosa pine trees were everywhere. The carriage emerged from the canyon and arrived at the hacienda. She could understand why Murdoch was so adamant about acquiring the land. The hacienda solidified her understanding, but conflict arose in her as she admired the land and the hacienda. *Was it ours?* she wondered. The spring wind began to sing through the pines and the piñon, and she could almost hear voices beckoning her to this land. Right now, at this moment, she believed Murdoch's father was right. She felt herself falling into New Mexico. And she loved it.

"Oh, Murdoch, look at it! The hacienda is more magnificent than I ever imagined. The adobe walls catch the glow of the setting sun and hold onto it! It just seems to soften the rugged landscape somehow."

Joseph smiled at Anne's excitement and hopped from the carriage. "I'll see what hands are close by and get your things unloaded and put inside." He headed to the bunkhouse.

A trim woman with a warm, bronzed complexion, a wide, friendly face, and long black hair moved gracefully and met the family at the door. "Señora McNeil, I'm Consuela. I'm here to help you with the house. And the children! Such fine boys!" She took them by their hands, while with their other hands, they gripped the gourd rattles they'd made at Wootton's. "Come, *mijos*, you have such a big room to explore!" She led them upstairs, with William hollering that he would get the best bed in the room for himself, and Wallace happily trotting along.

Murdoch halted Anne as she was about to cross into the door. He lifted her into his arms and carried her across the threshold. "You're such a romantic, my dear!"

Consuela descended the staircase after she knew the boys would be safely occupied, marking out their territories in their room. Murdoch explained that Consuela and her husband, Diego Gonzales, managed the day-to-day operations at the ranch and cooked for both the hands and the family. Consuela also kept a garden and served as something of a nurse. The Gonzaleses lived in their own small adobe home on a corner of the ranch, and Diego's family had been there for many generations. He hoped the women would become fast friends.

Anne met several of the vaqueros as they brought in the crates and trunks. Most of the vaqueros were Mexican, a few were white, and some of them were former Buffalo Soldiers who'd become accustomed to life out west. Anne found them all to be polite, not at all rough as she expected. Each of them addressed her with "Yes Ma'am" and "No Ma'am" even after she asked them to call her Anne. Murdoch led Anne through the hacienda and explained how it was made so differently from the houses in New York and why adobe suited the climate better than wood or stone.

"Most of the furniture is from Mexico or Spain, brought over to be sold in Taos. Some of the pieces were made for us by craftsmen here. I don't know if you like this style but it's sturdy and practical. Consuela picked out everything really, and if there's anything you don't like, we can always replace it," Murdoch said.

He needn't have worried; Anne and Consuela moved through the house with Anne requesting only small changes here and there. "The furniture you've picked is so beautiful, and it suits the house well! The ceiling is tall and open, not close like in the New York houses. I can see why the style is simple."

"We call the style Spanish colonial. Most of the haciendas here, the big ranch houses, have furniture like this. We use oak and a lot of pinewood. I thought Señor McNeil would want you to have a house suitable for a lady of New Mexico rather than New York."

Murdoch sat on a carved dark oak couch in front of the grand fireplace in the living room. He sank into its tan cushions, his head framed by dark diamond insets in the oak trim. Anne came down to join him.

"I feel so at home here already. The stillness here has a sound all its own. I didn't know what to expect, but this house and New Mexico, I feel such freedom. Finally, our own home."

Murdoch struggled to understand. "But didn't you have plenty of freedom in New York? Everything you could want?"

"We didn't own anything; we lived in my parents' house. I know everyone does that in New York, but now that I'm here, I don't feel trapped. You can't imagine what it's like to have your whole life planned out for you. I've never felt this before, and I have to say that I like it. Murdoch, *I don't feel trapped here*. Can't you understand that?"

"Yes, I think I do. Like me being trapped as a crofter. Maybe we were both trapped in our own way." Unlike Anne, he felt like he still was. "I do wonder, if I'll ever feel what you do, anywhere in the world. Uncle Dick is like that too, and we've spoken around the campfires about what it means to feel like home is just around the next corner. Searching to belong more than anything."

"You belong with me." She snuggled close.

"I know, and that's not nothing. You know, Dick Wootton has been married four times? His last three wives died in childbirth. I don't know how a man survives that. Maybe because of that, he says his home is wherever he is. I wish I felt that way, but I do feel at home with you, Anne. You can lend your peace to me, and it will have to do for both of us."

"I know what I can do to help you feel more at home here, in our first night in our first real house." She stood up. "Let's go upstairs."

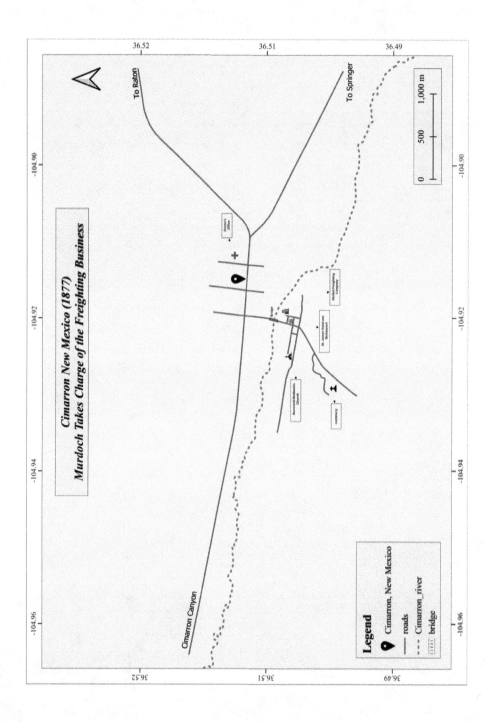

Cimarron New Mexico (1877)
Murdoch Takes Charge of the Freighting Business

To Raton

To Springer

0   500   1,000 m

Doctor's Office

Mutual Freighting Company

St. James Hotel and Restaurant

Reverend McMasters Church

Cemetery

Cimarron Canyon

Legend

● Cimarron, New Mexico

— roads

Cimarron_river

bridge

Chapter XI: Another Preacher

May 27, 1877
McNeil Ranch
New Mexico Territory

"When you want a piece of land, you find a way to seize it. When you want someone's house, you take it by fraud and violence. You cheat a man of his property, stealing his family's inheritance."
Micah 2:2

Murdoch awoke to the smells of bacon, coffee, and New Mexico. The sage stick—she called it smudging—that Consuela habitually lit when she arrived each morning competed with the tangled, pleasant scents of dawn. It had rained in the early morning, which released the pungent scent of sage, mountain cedar, and piñon. Anne stirred. "Coffee…" she said, stretching her arms and legs outward. She clasped her arms around his neck and kissed him.

He stroked her cheek with the back of his hand. "How was your first night's sleep in our new hacienda?"

"Wonderful! It smells like Consuela has made breakfast. What is that other smell? That sweet smell?"

Murdoch chuckled. "Consuela calls it smudging. She lights a bundle of dried sage. She says it's cleansing."

"Well, I love it. I could wake up to that smell every morning! How ever did you find her and Diego?"

"I didn't find them; they were already here."

Anne found that curious. "What do you mean?"

"When our hired men looked for a suitable building site for the hacienda, they found Diego and Consuela living about a mile from here. Just near the start of the Cimarroncito."

"How long have they been living here?"

"Diego's third generation, at least. His grandparents built the house

187

under their *Patrón,* which is like a Spanish way of saying boss. It was Spain then, and Diego was born here when it was still México."

Anne went to the basin and washed her face, starting her morning dressing routine much the same as she had in New York. "They were already here? Does that mean they sold it to Daddy?"

"Land works differently out here than it does back home. When it was México or Spain, it was the Patrón's job to help the people."

"Does Daddy even know?"

"No, he doesn't. I figured they're crofters like back in Barra, just using different words. That was how I grew up, too, and how I was supposed to live."

"I thought you were told that this was desolate and uninhabited."

"I found out quickly that it was only uninhabited in the way we're used to thinking about it back east. Farmers and ranchers have been living out here for generations. Most of them are Mexicans, but there's Indians too. And Anglos who thought they had homestead rights out here. Everyone's getting word that their land is now owned by a Dutch company. It's harder to sell land if the buyer knows that it's full of what they would call squatters, and nobody here really has a legal claim, plus the Utes and the Jicarilla Apache who don't settle in one place, and then the Tewa who have their own city."

Anne's anger over the way Murdoch acquired the land flared up again. "Couldn't that mean us? Could the Dutch decide we're squatters and kick us off?"

He could see the worry on her face and hear the sharpness in her voice. "Not really. The way that the purchase was structured, it looks like your Dad bought the land directly from Lucien Maxwell, so we're not affected by the land grant that's causing all the trouble.

She tucked her lower lip, and looked away. She had resolved to put his dishonesty at rest, and she justified it in her mind when she crossed the threshold to the ranch and first saw the hacienda. She wanted it to be theirs. She kept silent.

"I did ask Diego about it because he's seen it change hands so many times, but he said he doesn't put stock to gossip, and he just pays attention to his sheep."

188

"So… mind your own business is what he says, and that's the way it's been out here a long time, just like it was in Barra. I worry, though – the British and the Dutch have been doing just as the English did against my people, forcing people off their lands no matter how many generations of work they've put into it. I hope Diego and Consuela never have to face that."

***

Murdoch saddled one of the ranch horses and rode into Cimarron. At the freight warehouse he met with his teamsters, then walked the short distance over to Lambert's, the local inn and eatery, for lunch and whatever social business might greet him there.

That social business started right away. He'd barely sat down when a man walked up to greet him. "You're Mr. McNeil, if I am not mistaken," the stranger said. "I'm James McDaniel. Jim. I have the ranch over at Rayado Creek, which makes us neighbors."

McDaniel was a large man, both in height and build. He was one of those men who didn't have to speak to know that he was locked into a serious confrontation with either himself or someone around him. For some reason, he reminded Murdoch of one of the men that tried to board John Crawford's Aaron boat on Bara. The man that felt the sting of his spike.

Murdoch shook his hand. "Yes, that's right. Care to join me for lunch?"

"I have just a few minutes, but thank you. You're a hard man to track down, but I've run into some of your hands on the range, and of course, I know Diego fairly well."

"I used to run the ranch from New York and come out here only sometimes on contracts, but I just moved my family out here for good. That would be my wife, Anne, and our two boys, William and Wallace. Twins. I should be easier to find from now on."

"We're a little rough for someone from the East, but if you can ignore the politics, it's a decent place to live."

"I'm not sure that I follow."

189

McDaniels was explicit, "The politics of the Maxwell Land Grant. Out here, most are either settlers who are defending their land against the Maxwell Land and Railway Company or who work for them."

Murdoch understood, "I'm not involved in any of it. I tend to my own business."

McDaniel was expressionless, "I've got to go arrange for some winter seed, but it was good to meet you, Mr. McNeil." McDaniel stood and made his exit. While Murdoch thought this was abrupt, this was also another custom of the West that took some getting used to: men here did not waste their words with puffery and decoration. Had they met on the range, it might have been a tip of the hat at a distance.

Murdoch planned to spend most of his first week of his permanent installation at the Townsend Freighting office working on contracts and sending telegrams to customers. Being calving season he'd check beef prices daily from Kansas City and Chicago, and he'd send plenty of communiqués back to Henry keeping him apprised of the health of the business. With any luck he would spend as little time as possible on the range or on horseback. He hired a foreman to take care of those details. The only in-person interaction he wanted with any livestock was in the form of the steak lunch he'd just eaten.

***

When Murdoch returned to the McNeil hacienda, he handed the reins of the horse to one of the ranchhands and briefed Diego on his progress with the teamsters. Then he walked to the house to see how Anne was getting on.

"Our neighbor dropped by with an apple pie! How friendly people are here," Anne said. "Her name is Emma. Emma McDaniel."

"I met her husband, James, down at Lambert's just now."

"They're coming for supper this Saturday — I hope that's alright." Anne was used to having a wide social circle in New York, and anything he could do to ease the transition out here, he felt she deserved.

"If we were back home, you'd have guests for supper every night."

"We are home. And if I wanted to be a socialite, I'd have married

Frank. That's what I told him when he asked to court."

Murdoch felt a tinge of jealousy, "Glad you said no."

Even without her usual expansive social circle, Anne stayed busy. She and Consuela planted an enormous garden to complement Consuela's patch of herbs. They gave the twins little shovels to keep them occupied with digging. Consuela also taught Anne the Three Sisters planting method, which was tradition passed down from her mother.

Consuela had another surprise for Anne. "Our *casa* has lilacs, and I brought some to plant. Good aroma. Do you know lilac?"

"One of my favorites! We can plant these at the front entrance, so we'll smell them as we're coming and going."

The greens of Consuela's garden stood in contrast to the surrounding area.

"We're fortunate to have the Cimarroncito to make this valley rich, but it's still a desert. If you go a half mile from the river, the ground is dry. It can only hold the sage, rabbit brush, buffalo grass, and cholla."

The skill handed down through Consuela's family, along with Diego's careful management of the river's water, carved out an oasis of herbal smells and tastes.

Saturday afternoon, Emma, Jim McDaniels, and their two daughters came for supper. Consuela's garden harvest added complex flavor to the roast lamb, carrots, and potatoes. Emma guessed correctly that the apple pie she'd brought wouldn't last until Saturday, so she'd brought a cobbler she made from the last of the peaches she got all the way from Española on the other side of the mountains. She promised to teach Anne to can as good as fresh.

The McDaniels' two girls, Sarah and Alice, were at five and three, right around the age of the McNeil twins. They seemed to have a way even with William, who was cranky and prone to tantrums but delighted in Sarah's gift at making faces. As the children occupied each other after supper, Murdoch and Jim retired to the imposing bench on the front porch. Jim pulled out a briar pipe and a pouch of tobacco.

"We must have filed our land patents about the same time," Jim said, tamping down his tobacco.

Murdoch knew from his legal practice and from the veiled way people often spoke in the West that Jim was asking about more than the date of a patent. Jim wouldn't have been asking directly about information he could get easier out of the land office – and likely already had. But neither was Jim intending to deceive, judging by his body language and facial expressions. Instead, Murdoch believed Jim sought to test whether his new neighbor would be straight with him.

"Mr. Townsend is my father-in-law, but he's also the lead partner at my legal firm. He decided to get into freighting in '69. Back when he went out to California before the war, he'd met Dick Wootton, who taught him the real money was in freight rather than prospecting. So when Mr. Townsend got established in law, he got some friends in the business of supplying beef contracts to the government, and he bought some land to go in on the deal." A lot of information, and it was true enough for his purposes.

"Sixty-nine is about when I filed for the patent on my place, and I bought out some of the neighbors on the other side. Heard anything about how the Maxwell land grant is coming out? They keep changing the survey."

"My place isn't a part of that, luckily." At least it wasn't once Murdoch got his hands on a sales invoice and a blank land patent. "We're just beyond the edge of it and glad of it. Nasty part of the business, really." Jim didn't know just how nasty.

"Agreed, awful business between the settlers and the Maxwell agents," Jim said.

"Diego says to just ignore it and mind the sheep, which in my case means the cattle. So I won't be mixed up in all that."

"With your law learning and your business, there'll be plenty trying to draw you into taking sides. They'll want you to have influence one way or the other."

"If there's one thing I've learned in my sixteen years as a lawyer, it's that you can't force someone into something they don't want to do." Murdoch's current situation in New Mexico and recent exile from New York contradicted this belief, but it sounded convincing. He knew how to use the law to remove himself from unwanted situations. So, when it came to his own affairs, he believed in it.

"Maybe in New York. But here, I've seen men do things contrary to their judgments and natures. It's this place. It's New Mexico," Jim said and punctuated it with a puff of his sweet tobacco.

The sun was setting over the western mountain ridge. A piñon jaybird issued a staccato call to the waning light of day, like an old stuck door complaining about being wedged back open. The silhouette of a coyote emerged from behind a bush, glanced at the hacienda, and smugly trotted off to its nightly business.

"That's what anyone wants here," said Jim as the coyote disappeared. "To be left to their own business like the coyote. I run a few head on my place. There's no fences here. I don't want any, either. It's calving season, and we'll trade strays here and there, but we don't need to get fired up about it."

"I understand, Jim. Any problems with any of my boys, come to me first and we'll take care of it."

A peal of laughter burst from inside the hacienda. "You'd think there was a party going on in there. We should join them, or they'll think we mean to ignore them."

Murdoch laughed. "You're probably right."

The June evening settled in. A few of the hands had gone into Lambert's in town. Most of the ranch hands were reasonable in their habits, but one or two always had to trust their horses' instincts to get them home. Murdoch believed his presence on the ranch generally discouraged any recklessness and ill behavior, and his ranch foreman, Lawrence, was quick to discharge any troublemakers among his crew. Lawrence had an eye for good cowhands and prevented most issues from ever occurring.

It was a quiet evening. A few cowboys straggled back from town to the bunkhouse early as the McDaniels said their goodbyes. Jim, Emma, little Sarah, and little Alice headed home in their buggy. Murdoch could tell that Anne got on well with Emma, and he was glad to have someone to help her adjust to a very different life than what she'd had in New York. Jim was reserved with Murdoch, sure, but people seemed that way in New Mexico in general, harder to crack open than a walnut with a wet sponge.

"Murdoch, Emma asked if we're joining them at church tomorrow. I know how you feel about religion, and I know why. I told her that I didn't know, but that we'd talk about it."

"What church?" Most of the churches in New Mexico were Catholic and had services only in Spanish. With the influx of Scots into the cattle business, other sects had been setting up shop.

"Methodist."

"Remember a couple years back, the story in the *New York Sun* about Reverend Tolby?"

Anne grimaced. "Awful business, I know."

"Are you sure you want to go to that church? It won't be making us a target, you don't think?"

"Emma and Jim go; they haven't had any troubles. I think it's more of a social call."

"Okay," Murdoch said quietly. He would go to make Anne happy, and perhaps there would be some business benefit to belonging to a church, but he could not help but think of his childhood on Barra and the church's active role in destroying his family and his people. Reverend Tolby had involved himself in the land squabbles around Cimarron, and from what he'd read in the *Sun*, Murdoch cautiously respected him. Tolby complained to the New York papers that the Maxwell Land Grant's owners treated the settlers on the land with brutality and fraud. He blamed the violence and ill feelings on a conspiracy of politicians and lawyers known as the "Santa Fe Ring."

Murdoch had spoken to Mr. Townsend, keeping him notified of anything that may affect their freighting and land interests. The fraudulent activity and influence-peddling were the reasons Townsend had started sending Murdoch to the ranch to represent the firm in person.

In September of 1875, Tolby was found in Cimarron Canyon, murdered. Local rumor blamed the Dutch owners of the Maxwell Land Grant. New York was still at least partially run by Dutch influence, and Murdoch wondered if Tolby's church was in fact the Methodist church in Cimarron. He believed it was. And if it was, did the McDaniels' attendance at this church risk embroiling them in the land grant business after all? Or did attending the Methodist church indicate a more complicated set of allegiances than Jim had represented?

I guess I'll find out tomorrow, he thought.

The next morning, the ride into Cimarron seemed to drag on. Murdoch was silent most of the way, which Anne attributed to his conflicted feelings about organized religion. The twins settled into the motion of the carriage, and when the McNeils pulled up to the church, they were fast asleep. The little wooden church was humble and fit the general feeling of Cimarron. A small plaque on the side proclaimed Reverend McMannis as the leader of the church. Murdoch could not help but think of the church on Barra, also small and humble, but no less deceitful, due to Reverend Beatson's corruption.

The McDaniels had arrived before the McNeils. Jim and Murdoch briefly greeted each other. Anne and Emma quickly fell into conversation. The two families sat at the pews to the rear in case their small children became fussy and noisy, and William and Wallace delighted in just how many small children took up those last pews. The morning started cool and pleasant, but as more people arrived to fill the church, the air turned hot and stuffy.

Reverend McMannis appeared behind the pulpit, its top just meeting the height of his broad chest. He was an angry-looking man with huge hands and thick fingers resembling railroad spikes. He gripped the pulpit tightly and finished his opening prayer:

"Let us not forget the founder of our church, Reverend Franklin Tolby, who was taken from us by an assassin's bullet fired by evil men. Tolby became a martyr to the cause of righteous men everywhere with the right and destiny to live on one's own land, free, Lord, to do Your work. Amen."

"Amen," the congregation repeated with enthusiasm.

"Our reading today is Micah, chapter 2, verses 1-5. 'Woe to them that devise iniquity, and work evil upon their beds! When the morning is light, they practice it, because it is in the power of their hand.'"

Murdoch sat in his pew with his arms crossed. McMannis clearly spoke against the Dutch owners of the Maxwell, and maybe the English who sold it to them, too. He had seen so much iniquity and heard this exact verse used to get the people to go along with it. Here, McMannis seemed to interpret the verse for the contrary purpose.

"And they covet fields, and take them by violence; and houses, and take them away: so they oppress a man and his house, even a man and his heritage.'"

Murdoch remembered the smoke rising from his family's croft as they fled. He remembered how his family boarded a ship to their deaths. The waves of the dune grasses as they followed the winds. The blue and green tartan. The smell of Elizabeth's orange. It all mixed together, good and bad, in his memory.

"'Therefore, thus saith the Lord; Behold, against this family I do devise an evil, from which ye shall not remove your necks; neither shall ye go haughtily: for this time is evil.'"

Sarah McDaniel fidgeted in her seat. She was about Elizabeth's age. Murdoch tried and failed to assuage his guilt. This time is evil, and as he saw it, it was common practice to do evil. Families just got in the way, that's all. It was his own family's turn once.

"'In that day shall one take up a parable against you, and lament with a doleful lamentation, and say, We be utterly spoiled: he hath changed the portion of my people: how hath he removed it from me! Turning away he hath divided our fields. Therefore, thou shalt have none that shall cast a cord by lot in the congregation of the Lord.' My friends, foreign invaders have come to steal your land..." McMannis took aim at the Maxwell's owners, but Murdoch shifted in his seat and grew hot.

"You see, then, how we cry out that the Lord has taken our lands and split their boundaries among our enemies! Verse 4! And verse 3, how can such people who do these things walk around with any sense of pride and accomplishment over what they have done? They have made money for themselves, and for us they have made an enemy! They have taken our boundaries and substituted evil feeding upon evil!" Just there, the Reverend quieted his voice. "But be patient, good friends, I say to you, be patient..."

This seemed more familiar, the shepherd telling his flock to wait a

196

little while longer for the wolf to tire of killing the sheep. McMannis drew lessons of fortitude rather than true resistance. Just like the law, the Bible was bent and molded to whatever meaning suited those with power. The Bible is a law text, he thought.

After the Reverend had the church's new visitors introduce themselves to the congregation, the service ended, and the parishioners began filing out of the entrance. Most of them paused a few seconds to chat with McMannis. Murdoch and Anne followed Jim and Emma so that Jim could introduce the McNeils personally. William and Wallace, having no patience for the line, darted outside to roughhouse with a few of the other boys.

Meeting McMannis was like meeting a stage actor who played the villain. The stern preacher, when not behind the pulpit was friendly, courteous, and welcoming.

"It's good to meet you both," the Reverend began. "I heard that you were finally moving into your ranch house. I'm glad to have you in our little community. Will you be practicing here? Cimarron could use a good attorney."

"Unfortunately, the freighting and ranching businesses will keep me too busy to practice law," Murdoch replied.

"Well, that's a shame. I was hoping we could talk more at length sometime, perhaps over a meal?"

Anne spoke before Murdoch could object. "That would be lovely! Why don't you plan on Sunday evening dinner next week after service? Around four o'clock if that suits."

Murdoch shot a glance at Anne, but she did not catch it, and he resigned himself to the social call. "Yes, Reverend, next Sunday, if you have no plans yet."

McMannis said that would be just fine.

"Well, the reverend caught you off guard," Jim said and chuckled when they were a short distance away from the church. Anne and Emma had gone to a group of women on the church lawn.

"Yes, well, Anne is quite outgoing. I must admit it, Jim, when I heard Reverend Tolby's name mentioned, I was surprised that you and Emma attended here. We read his letters to the *New York Sun* talking about the politicians in Santa Fe, this so-called *Santa Fe Ring*, and the land grab. And then he was murdered."

"Yes, Reverend McMannis, much like Reverend Tolby, speaks against the land fraud out here. Some people like, well, your Diego have been living on this land for generations, and now these foreigners are coming in and taking it all away. Present company excepted, of course, you're as American as anyone. Two years this September, Tolby's been murdered, and nobody's been charged. Nobody will, either. There's been so much death since then. I fear there's more to come, but I've managed to stay out of it and the reverend has never pushed me to take a side."

Murdoch wanted nothing to do with choosing sides in this war, and Jim said he felt the same. As young as he was when his family had been forced from the Isle of Barra, he remembered how fighting against the landowners destroyed his mother and father. Though they were buried at sea along with his sister, Murdoch thought, it was really the land that killed them, and now he was deep into it himself. He wondered if the Maxwell Land Grant would kill him too. He wondered what his father would think about the irony of it all.

The following Sunday, Anne was nervous. She was unaccustomed to preparing meals and greeting visitors in the New Mexico style, though she was learning a lot from Consuela. She'd rather Consuela would have prepared supper for the Reverend's visit, but Sunday was reserved for Consuela and Diego to attend their own church. Why did I suggest Sunday? she thought.

Murdoch's mind fixed on the last time he had a Reverend over for dinner. He'd been nine, and it was back on Barra. Reverend Beatson, who his father seemed to dislike, had come for dinner. He remembered the tension in the blackhouse when Father answered the door and Reverend Beatson pushed rudely past him. He'd been so angry with both Beatson and his father then: Beatson for forcing his way in and his father for allowing it. He recalled Beatson chastising his father and quoting the same scripture McMannis used for his sermon.

Unlike Beatson, Reverend McMannis at least when he was not behind the pulpit, was a quiet, pleasant, and welcoming man. The talk at the table revolved around the day-to-day events at the church. He had not asked Murdoch any questions about the Maxwell Land Grant, nor did Murdoch offer his opinion on the subject.

"Mrs. McNeil, you've served a magnificent dinner. It's as though you'd been living here your whole life! The *machaca*, the *elote*, the *frijoles negres* – all of it wonderful!"

"Consuela has been a good and patient teacher!"

"The Gonzalezes are good people. I get along well with our Catholic brothers and sisters. Many of them have lived and worked on this land since well before the war, and the war before that. Mr. McNeil, you can suspect my stance on this land issue."

"Yes, and I hope you understand that my stance is much like Jim McDaniels'."

McMannis skirted the truth, "Good to hear. He thinks with a clear mind and is a valuable member of the church, but New Mexico has a way of changing people. A person may not want to become involved, but this place will draw you to one side or the other. If you try and track the middle road, you can get hit from both directions. I hope to see you all next Sunday, and we're about to lose the sunlight. I prefer not to travel when it's so dark, so I will take my leave."

Chapter XII: A Friend Indeed

Tuesday, April 4, 1878
Telegraph Office
Cimarron, New Mexico Territory

"The challenge for capitalism is that the things that breed trust also breed the environment for fraud."
James Surowiecki

Murdoch collected the stack of telegrams that had been sent to him in the last two days. His business flew swiftly across the lines, and not checking the telegraph office every day could cost him. He'd expected his business to be slower paced in the West, as was commonly thought in the East, but the West was for sale, and the word was out. He wasn't the only freighting company seeking to do business along the old Santa Fe Trail, and plenty of other outfits bid on beef contracts. A missed message was a missed opportunity.

He sorted the telegrams into status updates, immediate response required, and social calls. One in the stack was from Frank Angel. The two friends hadn't seen each other for almost a year, ever since Murdoch and Anne's anniversary party back in New York. It was close to Moving Day again, and he found he missed the chaos and excitement unique to Manhattan. The flowers would be blooming in Central Park. Frank would chide him about his bartending abilities. Alas, not this year.

With his pen knife, he cut the seal of the envelope and pulled out the yellowish paper.

APPOINTED SPECIAL INVESTIGATOR DEPTS INTERIOR JUSTICE BY WASHINGTON. INVESTIGATING LAND GRANT FRAUD COLFAX COUNTY VIOLENCE LINCOLN COUNTY. YOUR ASSISTANCE APPRECIATED. ARRIVE CIMARRON APRIL 22 BRINGING SWEET VERMOUTH. STOP

Murdoch stared as if he'd need to read it more than once, though it was already seared into his mind. He'd known that Frank was lobbying for a Washington appointment where he could use his legal education. Frank was admitted to the bar in 1869 and had the reputation of being pointedly honest. He'd been a tenacious adversary in the courtroom. Townsend never gave up trying to recruit Frank to his practice and had even held a celebration at the family home when Frank was admitted to the bar, but otherwise, his old friend refused any assistance from anyone associated with Tammany Hall, no matter how remote. And now, the irony of the situation sank in – Frank unknowingly asked for help in his new investigation for the Hayes Administration and from someone embroiled in it.

Murdoch felt the seeds of panic. His mind presented a litany of "what if" scenarios. What will I say when he asks about the McNeil Ranch? What if he rides out to Fort Sumner to look through Lucien Maxwell's records for a bill of sale? Will he check the land patent office? Will he check the survey?

Damnit, Murdoch, calm down, use your mind, he thought. For a moment he regretted his decision to take the land. He hated that he would be lying to a friend, a good friend. He shook his head. No, that land is mine. It's my boys' land. It's the land that was stolen from me. It's my heritage.

Frank is waiting for a reply, he thought. If I don't reply soon, he will think something is wrong.

"Mr. McNeil is everything okay?" asked the telegraph operator from behind the counter. "I don't mean to intrude."

"Oh, yes, I was lost in thought for a second. I need to reply to this telegram right away." He addressed the message paper and wrote

WILL MEET YOU AT CIMARRON STAGE STOP MI CASA ES
SU CASA STOP ANNE DELIGHTED WILL HELP ANY WAY
WE CAN STOP.

He handed the reply to the telegraph operator and walked down

202

the street to his freighting warehouse, the telegram still fixed in his mind. He entered his windowless office, left word that he wasn't to be disturbed, and shut the door. He sat at his desk, pulled Frank's telegram from the stack, and spread it out in front of him, his hands framing the message. He tapped his index finger on Frank's name.

Okay, he thought to himself, act like an attorney. This is no more than a fact pattern. A legal problem to be solved before he arrives. Analyze it like you are your own client. His breathing became slower and more relaxed. Townsend taught him to find the issue, apply the rule, consider the application, and reach your conclusion.

What was the issue? A client falsified a real estate contract. What would Frank need to prove it? He would need to see a copy of the bill of sale, plus proof that Murdoch had forged Maxwell's signature. Frank would first have to suspect the forgery before even thinking about comparing the signatures. Maxwell was dead; he'd died in Fort Sumner in July of '75. Obviously, Frank could not talk to him and ask if he'd sold Murdoch 57,000 acres of the land grant.

On top of this, Maxwell's recordkeeping was notoriously sloppy and careless. Murdoch heard that Lucien would keep gold nuggets and cash lying around openly and that he beat his Mexican workers. Maxwell was also a broker in human beings, and Frank was a staunch abolitionist. Even if Frank suspected Murdoch had obtained the land by fraud, how would he possibly prove it? All the paperwork had been filed with Dr. Spencer when he was still the surveyor general of New Mexico, and it was all perfect. Even if Frank wanted to examine the copy of the Maxwell sales contract, Fort Sumner was two hundred miles away, and it would be easy to claim that the copy was simply lost or stolen in Maxwell's move south.

Townsend's rules. Issue, rule, application, conclusion. He moved through them and became more confident that claiming the land and how he'd gone about it was unassailable. Frank, he surmised, would have too much work from the Lincoln County War and the ambient violence of other land deals to bother interrogating a colleague and a friend. While Murdoch did not feel smug at the end of his analysis, he did feel safe and very confident.

Raised voices from the other side of his office door pulled him away from his personal *voir dire*.

"I don't care if he said he didn't want to be disturbed, I don't have time to come back off the range during calving season!" Jim McDaniel shouted.

Murdoch walked quickly to his office door and opened it.

"That's all right, Paul. Jim, always good to see you. Come in."

McDaniel stared daggers at Paul and strode abruptly into McNeil's office.

"Have a seat. I can always make a little time for you," Murdoch said in a friendly tone. He could tell that McDaniel was upset about something, and he wouldn't need to pry. He waited for Jim to speak.

"Murdoch, I was out with my boys this morning branding..."

Murdoch sat back down as his desk, "Are my boys misbranding any of yours? I'll take care of that."

"No, that's not it. The other way around. You're going to think that we're misbranding your cattle because your survey markers are off. We were out on the western edge of my property; we hadn't been back there in a while. Not since you had your ranch surveyed and you filed your patent. And Murdoch..." Jim shifted with the weight of his accusation. "I saw your survey markers all over the place."

"How? I don't understand. Spencer approved both of our surveys."

"No, not quite. Benjamin Clark is the one who filed my land patent and approved the survey. That sonamabiche died two months into his job, and then Dr. Spencer took over and approved yours."

This was serious, more than Jim knew. "How much land are we talking about, Jim?"

McDaniel stood and paced, "At least a thousand acres, maybe more. You've got to request another survey since you were after me."

Murdoch had just put the issue of his land surveys out of his mind, and here it was again. He'd believed that Frank could not possibly impeach his land acquisition. Now this. He considered conceding the territory, but that would not avoid scrutiny. The last thing he needed was Henry Atkinson, the present surveyor general, to pull the original records and confirm the boundaries. He decided to try to rely on authority.

Murdoch remained calm and in control. "You know my legal background is in real estate. Once a patent is filed, it is irrefutable and permanent. You are welcome to hire an attorney in Santa Fe and fight it, but I believe it would be a waste of time and money."

McDaniel was animated, and pointed an accusing finger at Murdoch, "McNeil, you know damn well that your survey is wrong." Jim became more confident in his allegations.

"I'm not quibbling with you over one thousand or even five thousand acres if you run your cattle there. I'm not going to throw good money at a resurvey. Run your cattle there all you like with my blessing, and I'll just tell my boys you've got my permission." Murdoch tried to salvage the relationship. "We don't need to resort to a legal dispute here."

"Damnit, McNeil, something smells bad about this. I don't know if it was the Dutch Maxwell Land Grant Company, or if they led you into their corruption, or if it was Doc Spencer, or if you did something, but it's not right. I'm beginning to think that you sat in New York, big fancy lawyer, and thought you'd come down here talking a big game about how it's not right to push people off their land. You say you're not choosing sides. It looks like you are to me. Looks like you chose your own side."

Murdoch stood, walked from behind his desk, and faced McDaniel. "What's the difference in any of this, Jim? The grant is a mess. We have to work it out ourselves. Just run your cattle there."

"The difference is, it's my land, and it should say so on paper."

"I'm not cutting up my ranch on your say so. File a request with Atkinson then."

"It's not my responsibility. You came after me; it's your responsibility to make sure the survey is accurate. I know mine is."

Murdoch told him to get a court order, then stood by his door, signaling that the conversation was over. "If you want to force the issue I will take another survey, but only when I get the order."

Jim spat. "The goddamned courts. The courts are as crooked as you are. If you don't make this right yourself, then I will find a way to make it right myself." Jim turned and left Murdoch's office.

Paul Maestas, the foreman, poked his head into the office. "Mr. McNeil, not sure if you meant to leave your door open, but we all heard that he threatened you just now. Do you want me to fetch Sheriff Burleson? Maybe you should let him know before this goes any further."

"Glad you overheard. I knew he was mad about something when he came in and thought a witness might be helpful. I don't think I need to talk to the sheriff. I haven't known Jim for that long, and Anne knows Emma much better, but this doesn't seem like him. Maybe he'll cool off. Everyone gets a little hot now and again."

Paul rolled a cigarette. "Jim's got a reputation for holding a grudge. Mr. McNeil, would you like me and a couple of the teamsters to ride out with you to the ranch this evening? It's getting close to quitting time."

He shook his head, "No, Paul, I don't think that will be necessary. I would hate to take up your evening."

"The offer is open. And keep your eyes open, too. You're new out here, and I've seen men shot over less."

"As I say, Anne and Emma are quite close. We sit together at church, and we even eat together on occasion. I just can't believe he'd act against me."

"Your judgment is your own, but civility often stops when church service does. Please watch your back. I rather like working for you."

Paul's words made Murdoch feel uneasy. As his horse trotted south out of Cimarron, He peered nervously over his shoulders. About halfway toward home, he'd convinced himself that he was right, that Jim was just blowing off steam. When the two men met a year ago, Murdoch had found Jim difficult to get to know, but he thought nothing of it given the customs of the West. In light of the altercation at his office, however, he wondered if he had just made an enemy. He wondered how dangerous that enemy would be.

He resolved not to bring up Jim's anger and their quarrel to Anne. It would just upset her. He would deal with the matter as it came—no reason to give it a nudge. Murdoch arrived home, put up his horse, and went inside. Anne greeted him with a look of deep concern instead of her usual cheerful smile and pleasant hug. This was turning out to be a challenging day.

"Anne, what is the matter?"

"Oh, Dock, it's Emma." He felt ashamed at his relief. Anne continued. "She was supposed to come by this morning with Sarah and Alice. We were all going to work with Consuela in the garden, and we were going to have a nice visit. She didn't arrive, so I rode over there."

"And?"

"I didn't make it all the way there."

"Why? Is there something wrong with Skip?"

"No, thankfully. I ran into Dr. Gregg before I was halfway. He was just coming from McDaniel's." She paused. "Oh, Dock, Emma has tuberculosis! And she is so very sick!"

"Does Jim know?"

"I imagine he does by now. I saw him ride by earlier this afternoon. I waved and called out to him, and he looked in my direction, but he didn't even wave back. He just kept going. Maybe we should ride out and see if they need help."

Murdoch had no intention of seeing McDaniel after today's confrontation. Given McDaniel's volatility, it would not defuse the situation. He offered an excuse, "I wouldn't want to expose the boys to tuberculosis."

"You're probably right. I'll ride over there tomorrow anyway after Consuela gets here. She can watch the boys. I seem to be resistant to consumption. I didn't catch even a hint of it when I worked at Bellevue."

"I don't think you should expose yourself to that disease. It's just dangerous, and we've two boys that need you. I need you. I know you care about her, and I may not show it or say it as often as I should, but I do love you. I can't lose you over my stupidity or..."

Anne placed her hands on her hip, "Mine? Was that what you were going to say? I love you, too, but I can't change who I am. I cared for the wounded and the sick in the war. I just can't stop caring because we had to move out here."

Murdoch moved to her and held her tightly, which he thought he didn't do often enough, "I do have a good piece of news from today as well, I got a telegram from Frank Angel today! He's coming out to Cimarron on business. He gets here the twenty-second of this month."

She laughed, "Is he going into the freighting business or the cattle business, or is he selling cholla to naïve New Yorkers as back scratchers?"

"None of these! He finally got his government appointment, and as luck would have it, he'll be the investigator for that awful business in Lincoln County. He'll stay with us for a few days." Murdoch purposely did not mention that he was also assigned to investigate land fraud while here.

"You should ask him to bring some sweet vermouth. We have something very much like whiskey," she teased.

"Already done. But I suspect he will complain about my bartending skills regardless," he said.

***

The stage arrived in front of the St. James Hotel at 5:00 p.m. on April 22. Six jostled, dusty, cold, and sleep-deprived passengers exited the coach. It had taken six days of rail travel and two days of nonstop coach travel to make the 1800-mile journey, the last leg of it in a Thorough-Brace Concord Coach that was intended to get passengers to sway with the motion but instead just seemed to knock them together. Frank descended looking like he needed a good home-cooked meal and a good night's sleep.

"Frank! You've survived your first trip to the territories! Welcome!" Murdoch felt the isolation of New Mexico lessen at least a little bit with the arrival of his old friend.

"Murdoch! This coach trip over Raton Pass must be how President Hayes tests the endurance of his new investigators."

"They haul a nine-passenger coach up one side and manage to control it down the other side without a crash somehow. Are they still using a six-bronco team on the way up, mules on the way down?" Murdoch asked.

"Yes, and it's heart-pounding both ways."

"How's Henry? Is he doing well?"

"Yes, he seems fine. Tough man. You'd never know they were in that wreck."

"If not for you, we'd have had a worse time than we did. Anne and I were so happy to hear about your appointment. You were stuck in bankruptcy court, yes?"

"Not exciting, but it paid the bills. Now I'm here. If I can be of service on this assignment, I think I will be in line for an assistant district attorney position back East. At least that's my hope."

We're all paying our dues in New Mexico; only he's got an escape, Murdoch thought. "And how is Ada doing?"

"I've not seen her in some time, but Henry says she's doing well. Murdoch, I appreciate your invitation to stay at your place, but I must wonder about your cryptic message."

"It's not cryptic; it's Spanish. It means 'my house is your house.'" "Murdoch said as he helped Frank load his trunk into the carriage.-

They boarded and Murdoch let the reins fall lightly on his Morgan horses. It was a chilly evening, and the horses' breath burst from their noses in great clouds as they trotted back to the hacienda.

"Is Lambert's really that violent?" asked Frank.

"You've heard?"

"Well, what makes it to the New York papers is... concerning, I should say. It's got a reputation, and we get sensational stories in the *Times* or the *Sun* about someone getting shot over cards, or women, or just because they don't like someone's face."

Murdoch nodded. "Let's just say I'm glad you're staying with us. The rest of New Mexico could use some caution, too. Word will spread quickly that you're a government agent, and there are people on all sides of your investigation who will believe you've been sent out here to make trouble. I know you've been told of the violent situation out here, and I'll do anything I can to help. My first suggestion is to get an excellent meal followed by a good night's sleep, and we can talk further on the way back to town tomorrow morning. I've set up an office for you in the freight."

Frank was suitably impressed with the hacienda and the vast sweep of the McNeil Ranch. He did not ask any questions about the mechanics of the ranch's acquisition, nor did Frank offer any details of his assignment. Murdoch expected this, but he knew that the acquisition would eventually come up in conversation. He'd planned to give Frank just enough information to satisfy him but not enough to become suspicious. After all, Frank was already somewhat acquainted with the land deal since he was at the anniversary party when it was announced that the McNeils would be moving to New Mexico permanently.

The next morning Frank and Murdoch took the carriage into town.

"Murdoch," Frank started as the Morgan horses moved through the early spring air, "what can you tell me about the Colfax County War? And what have you heard about Reverend Tolby's murder beyond what's already been in the papers? Something I won't hear from Governor Axtell or the Sheriff here. I don't expect them to be honest if they might be implicated."

"There are two sides here, just like in court, and it's complex. We have the Maxwell Land Grant and Railway Company that bought Lucien Maxwell's 1.7 million acres, or so they say. Lucien Maxwell got the grant in turn from Mexico. On the other side are the people who settled this land to ranch, farm, or become prospectors. Some of them have lived here for generations, from long before the Mexican-American war. You've read the grant details and all the background research so you know that Article 10 of the Treaty of Guadalupe Hidalgo was not ratified. The article would have guaranteed Mexican property rights, so every Mexican here exists at the mercy of the U.S. Congress. There are still others: White settlers who followed Jacob Cox, the Secretary of the Interior, when he ruled that the Maxwell Land Grant was only 97,000 acres after all. Then Columbus Delano replaced Cox and opened up the land to homesteaders, who came here like they've done everywhere else in the West. Everyone claims the same land."

"And that breeds violence," Frank said.

"Yes, because the enforcers of the Maxwell Land Grant and Railway Company have started coming in and kicking people off land they believe is theirs. They won't go quietly either. Frank, this isn't new. The same thing happened to my family when I was a child. We called it the Highland Clearances, and it was ultimately at the hands of English land investors, too. We'd worked the land for generations and knew no other place. We were all rounded up by force and sent on ships with no provisions to Canada or Australia. We escaped to America, but I lost my entire family in the voyage. I hold that they were murdered."

"I remember the toast you made at your anniversary party. Your father taught you to do anything you can to acquire land, and anything you can to keep it. You have a better understanding of these people than I can get in official reports and legal filings."

"Do you remember what Anne said at the party? She said one of the reasons she wanted to move out here was to get away from the gangs, violence, and corruption in New York. We moved from New York right to a turf war in New Mexico. We just keep our heads down, happy that Townsend bought the ranch direct from Maxwell when he did, so we don't have to choose sides."

"What about the Ute and the Jicarilla Apache? Aren't there still confrontations?"

"No, the *Cimarron News and Press* routinely announces detachments of cavalry from Fort Union or from El Paso. They escort what remains of the Ute and Apache to their reservations. The wars and removals have almost completely eliminated their population and their culture. They were the last of the tribes to lose their homelands out of everyone out here."

"And Tolby?" Frank asked.

"You can get a complete accounting in the papers. Shot three times in the back, his horse and belongings weren't touched, so it wasn't a robbery. Nobody's ever been convicted of killing him. Tolby criticized the Maxwell Land Grant and Railway Company and encouraged the settlers to fight to stay. He also believed in using the Maxwell Land Grant to establish reservations for the Ute and Apache instead of sending them to the desert in Arizona."

"Did that get him killed?"

"Maybe, I don't know. The company people will deny it, and so will everyone allied with them. The settlers swear he was murdered by the company's enforcers."

"And your opinion?"

"I can argue it both ways and win the case. He might have been at the wrong place at the wrong time."

Frank said he'd thought the same. "At least I'd be the one with the happier client. Who else should I talk to?"

"Springer. He's the attorney for the land grant company and the real power in Cimarron. He'll come off talking like he's on the side of the ranchers and the settlers when he talks to them directly, but he works for the land grant company, sure as anything. Talk to Reverend McMannis, too. He's anti-land grant. If you want to know how people are claiming land rights in any case, the surveyor general in Santa Fe is where you start. He can give you the best answer, but it might not be the honest one."

"Henry bought the ranch in '68 if I recall right."

"'69," Murdoch corrected.

"Quite a coincidence that Dr. Spencer was the surveyor general, right?"

"No coincidence at all; that's how we got into it. Dr. Spencer took care of Henry after the wreck in Central Park if you remember. He mentioned that he was up for the appointment and that Lucien Maxwell was supposed to be selling off his property. That's what got Henry interested. Dr. Spencer said after the war, he rethought whether he wanted to be a physician, and he'd had enough of blood and pain. He sought a government post and went West. You did your research well."

Frank told Murdoch that his interview schedule demanded he be in New Mexico at least through August. Murdoch invited him for an extended visit once he was done with his investigation in Lincoln County. Frank would be busy, indeed.

Murdoch continued his summary. "There's a lot of fraud here, and I wouldn't know how you would stop it or even prove it. There's an umbilical cord running from here to New York, fueled by bankers, attorneys, and politicians. They, in turn, serve foreign investors from England and the rest of Europe, and those investors are claiming they own almost two million acres when the original Maxwell Land Grant was only 97,000. That doesn't sit well with most people out here. What's more, this type of fraud likely extends beyond the Maxwell and all over the southwest clear to California. And you know what, Frank?"

"Go on."

"No one is going to care as long as the cash register keeps ringing."

They pulled up to the warehouse. "This is the freight. I'll have a man saddle a horse for you. Please make yourself at home and consider my office your office."

Frank made his notes and tracked down the interviews he would need to conduct in Cimarron, then went on to Lambert's, where Murdoch and Anne held their anniversary party. Their cowhands and Diego and Consuela came, and unlike their Moving Day parties in New York, anyone who wandered into Lambert's came back out having had a good time regardless of their invite.

A few more bullet holes were introduced into Lambert's ceiling, another big difference from the Townsends' brownstone. Frank, nervous and jumpy by the impromptu gunfire, had to quell his spirit with a Manhattan, New Mexico style – and he lamented that he'd forgotten to bring the sweet vermouth after all.

Sometime later after he'd finished his interviews in Lincoln County, Frank returned to Cimarron to pay his farewell visit. It seemed everyone in Cimarron knew he'd been at least somewhat responsible for Governor Axtell's dismissal in favor of Governor Lew Wallace, but he could not quite determine if this was a good reputation or one that should have him watch his own back. Murdoch made sure Frank got to the stagecoach stop safely on August 16, then returned to his freight office. As soon as Murdoch departed, a man approached him.

"Are you Frank Angel? You've been looking into the land fraud?"

"Yes, what can I do for you?" He wished he carried a gun, just in case.

"I'm Jim McDaniel. I'm a neighbor of Murdoch McNeil. You ought to check into his land claim. Something about it is not right. His survey is way off at the very least, and I'll bet he doesn't even own that land."

"What makes you think that?"

"Just check it. You'll see," said Jim, walking off.

Just then the stagecoach pulled up. "Driver, do I have time to send a telegram?"

"Yes, but be quick about it."

Frank slipped inside the telegraph office and filled out a missive to Luz Maxwell, Lucien Maxwell's widow.

> PLEASE CONFIRM LAND SALE LUCIEN MAXWELL
> TO HENRY TOWNSEND JANUARY 1869 STOP REPLY
> TO FRANK ANGEL INVESTIGATOR DEPT OF JUSTICE
> WASHINGTON DC STOP

Probably nothing, he thought, but this was a strange territory, and Murdoch had lately been keeping peculiar company. It seemed that everyone in New Mexico held a grudge of some kind against everyone else, and this Jim McDaniel likely had another issue with Murdoch over cattle or just hurt feelings. Nobody can say I did not do my job, in any case, he thought.

That was where he let it lay as he arrived back in New York, and filed his report with President Hayes in September. Luz Maxwell never replied, and Frank let the issue slip entirely out of his thoughts. By October, he'd filed his reports on the violence in Lincoln and Colfax Counties as well as the claims of land fraud. As he finished his reports, he thought it miraculous that he had not been attacked or threatened. As a bonus, he had been able to spend time with his old friends.

Murdoch and Anne received a thank you letter from Frank in November with a newspaper clipping from the *New York Herald*:

> Mr. Frank Warner Angel, of No. 30 Fourth street, Williamsburg, has been appointed Assistant United States District Attorney under Mr. Tenny, in Brooklyn, in place of George W. Hoxie, the absconding defaulter. The new appointee has been practicing mostly in this city for the past ten years. He took the oath of office yesterday afternoon.

Murdoch pitied the criminals Frank would be bringing to justice. In court, he was like a puppy with a sock: Once he detected a wrong he felt he could right, Frank would not let it go. Anne remarked that she looked forward to a time when they could all sip their cocktails together again, and with those drinks made the right way. But Murdoch could only think of Frank as a puppy – and his own ranch as the sock.

Chapter XIII: Kewanee

May 15, 1879
Carlisle Indian Industrial School
Carlisle, Pennsylvania

"The man in charge of us pounced on the boy, caught him by the shirt, and threw him across the room. Later we found out that his collarbone was broken…"
Lone Wolf, Residential School, Fort Shaw, Montana, 1894

The silver brooches attached to my shawl clanged together as the matron at Carlisle Indian Industrial School ripped it from my shoulder. I caught it before it slipped away, pulled it free from her, and launched it back at her face like a bullwhip. She clutched reflexively at her cheek where one of the thick, heavy brooches struck her.

"She cut me! The little Indian bitch cut me!"

I spit in her face, shouted, and called her the dog she is, "Nemosh!"

Blood from the cut seeped out from under her hand that she pressed against her cheek. The kerosene lantern had little effect against the midnight gloom in the small room where the teachers and staff, all women, had taken us from the train we arrived on. Blood ran freely down her cheek and seemed to change from bright red to the dull, brackish color of polluted water in the flickering lantern light. They were all dressed in dark clothing, covering them to their necks. In the darkness, all we could see was their ghostly light-skinned faces moving about as if their heads were detached from their bodies.

The matron slapped my face. "You will speak only English at Carlisle! You ignorant animal!"

I reached out to grab her, and she struck me again. I did not wince. I am determined, even at twelve years old, not to show any emotion or fear to this so-called teacher.

"Get those filthy heathen clothes off of her and bring me scissors!

After you strip her, cuff her hands behind her back!"

Two women seized me, tearing at my buckskin dress with ruthless determination. The buckskin resisted, refusing to tear, but instead entrapped, pulled, and painfully twisted my arms as they pried the dress from my skin. The beads, which once proudly adorned my dress, burst off like buckshot, scattering across the floor. The younger children cried in terror, while the older ones stood paralyzed in shock, retreating into the dark corners of the room. But there would be no refuge from the nightmare for any of us. They snatched my shawl from my hands and flung it to the matron. With a cruel hand, she stripped the brooches off before hurling the shawl onto the growing pile of clothes they had taken from the others. They would later burn them.

She picked up a yellow card from the stack on the table and glanced at it. "Kewanee. Well, that's your old Indian name. You're Carrie-Mae now. Turn around and get on your knees."

I stood in silence and defiance.

She addressed the other matrons, "Sisters, take that broom and put it in front of her and make her kneel on the handle!"

They grabbed me roughly by my shoulders, spun me around, and kicked the back of my legs, making me fall onto the broom handle. I was too angry to acknowledge the pain. Instead, I screamed at them, "My name is Kewanee! You will never be able to change it!"

She gripped my long hair in her fist and pulled it straight up, bending my chin to my chest. "All of you, you heathens, pay attention to this! If you strike out at us, this is what will happen to you!"

She picked a willow switch off the table and began whipping it at my back. I flinched with each strike, but I refused to cry out. I have never felt such hatred. She finished. Her breathing turned fast and heavy, and I could smell her foul breath. Then, the grating sound of scissors cutting through my hair. The cut hair slid down my back, raw with welts and cuts from the whipping. The hair settled on my bare feet.

She threw the scissors onto the table. "We'll see what Captain Pratt has to say about this in the morning! Take her downstairs to the bathhouse. Bathe her and douse her head with kerosene. She's probably full of lice. Put her in the basement for the night, and handcuff her to

217

the radiator."

I spoke in fluent French, "And you call us savages?"

I pressed the back of my hand to the corner of my mouth, tasted blood, and started to speak again. She drove the broom handle into my stomach. Darkness came, but I could feel them pulling me down steps, yelling words at me that I only half-heard.

They were not finished with me. The cold bath should have been a relief to the crisscross cuts the willow switch made on my back, but purposely directed kerosene fell from my head into the wounds, my eyes, and my mouth. I coughed, and my eyes burned. I could see nothing. Scrubb bushes to my back made the pain unbearable. Periods of unconsciousness were the only moments of reprieve, and they did not come often. I vaguely remember a nightshirt being pulled over me after pulling me out of the wooden tub. I did not feel the handcuffs tighten around my wrist or hear them rattle and click as they closed around the radiator pipe.

"Kewanee." Who was calling me? I started, tried pulling away from the radiator only to feel the handcuff cutting into my wrist. Was I awake? Where was I? The oily taste of kerosene lingered, my eyes burned, and there were blisters on my arm where I had fallen against the radiator burning them. But now I remembered everything. The taste of the kerosene brought it back.

"Kewanee." That voice, a woman's. Older. Familiar. My eyes were blurry from the kerosene. A softened form, not quite whole, not quite transparent, floated in front of me. I thought of the visions that were told to us in our stories from our elders. Grandmother.

"Kewanee," she called again. Grandmother. It was Grandmother.

"Kewanee, remember who you are. Remember where you come from. Remember Archange, your great great grandmother, daughter of Chopa, and Naunongee, the great warrior and leader. Remember the silver brooches so many on our shawls that we grew strong wearing them. The land that is in our hearts by the Great Lakes is still ours. No one can hurt you. Be Strong. Survive."

218

Chapter XIV: Christmas Morning

Friday, December 24th, 1879
McNeil Ranch
New Mexico Territory

"The stockings were hung by the chimney with care..."
Clement Clarke Moore, A Visit from St. Nicholas, 1823

William McNeil was still awake. He had not fallen asleep, and it seemed like hours had passed since he was put to bed. His eyes were propped open by Christmas Eve adrenaline, his ears alert, and he searched for the slightest sound. A jingle. A scratching sound on the rooftop made by anxious reindeer. Then he heard a sound in the cold night – a muffled clatter - and crept noiselessly out of bed, just as his father's Native employees taught him to do when hunting for deer and elk meat. His twin brother, Wallace, stayed slumbering in bed next to him.

William crept down the hall, making as much noise as a fishing worm winding through wet grass. He peeked around the corner from the top of the landing to the parlor below to see his mother and father giggling, placing gifts under the tree wrapped in that brand new Christmas paper Mother ordered from a catalog last September. It was not Santa. He hurried back to bed.

Wallace stirred. He yawned, "Did Santa come?"

"No," William whispered. "It's Mom and Dad. Quiet, or they'll hear you."

Wallace turned to his side. Wallace woke at the sound of a feather landing on the floor but fell asleep again quickly. William awaited the click of his parent's bedroom door closing and latching from the floor below him, but nothing came. He figured Santa would show up later after his mother and father were asleep and stacked more presents underneath the tree for him to open. He could not wait to open them all – and indeed, he would not wait. William was not a patient boy. He drifted off to sleep, anxious and excited for Christmas morning.

***

He awoke, gripping his cover with both hands. It was still dark and cold. William cocked his head to the left and peered at Wallace. The heavy patchwork blanket that covered him moved slightly up and down with each quiet breath he took.

Should he wake him? The thought slipped through his mind, then turned aside. They would just argue over which present each of them would open. Wallace would end up crying, waking up Mother and Father. He had waited long enough, but he needed to make it out of the room and down the stairs without alerting his brother. The house itself was the obstacle, the noisemaker that could wake Wallace.

Father had built the large adobe home three years before, and the large round roof timbers were still settling. William had practiced creeping ever so lightly across the wide slats of alternating walnut and maple flooring that covered all the rooms of the house. The tongue and groove joints were set very tight, but the floor was still new and would complain with a creak or two. This particular challenge to his stealth he could not resist, and the reward for his success lay underneath the Christmas tree.

William turned over in bed onto his side so that he faced away from Wallace. He lay still to make sure his brother's breathing remained deep and steady. He grabbed the bedding and folded it over his hip, freeing himself. He swung his legs over the side of his bed, and he pushed himself up into a sitting position, feet dangling a few inches above the floor. His deerskin moccasins were near him, but he ignored them and slipped soundlessly out of bed.

William took his first step toe to heel the way he had been taught. He paused and listened. No sound. He took his second step and touched his toe to the floor. A slight creak caught his ear. He stopped, lifted his foot, and placed it onto another plank. No sound.

He picked his way down the hall and then the stairs, the soft woven

Diné rug muffling his steps and assisting his stealth. At last, he stood before the tree. His tree. His Christmas tree.

"Which one should I open first?" he whispered to himself. It doesn't matter, he thought. They all needed to be opened.

Christmas stockings. He was hungry. "Chocolate."

He looked at the four stockings lining the top of the ember-reddened kiva fireplace, pulled his off the hook, and emptied it onto the hearth. He ignored the walnuts, pecans, apple, and the sacred orange wrapped in tissue paper. He grabbed the chocolate in the brightly colored Christmas paper, tore the paper off, and then the Whitman's chocolate label – then took a huge bite out of the candy. He savored the taste and contemplated the orange that sat in the middle of the rest of the stocking's goodies.

"We'll get the orange speech again this year," William mused, then smirked.

Ignoring the name tags on the presents, he picked up one of the packages and gave it a quick shake. He wrapped his hand around the decorative bow, dug the finger of his other hand into the package, and pulled the wrapping apart. The present smelled sweet, not candy sweet, but sweet like Mother after her bath.

The front of the box pictured two ladies, one in her corset and the other helping her with her dress. He recognized the words bath and oil, which confused him even more than the picture. He could not read the words Rowland Macassar on the package, and to William, the big letters looked like the title of a book. Books, he thought, didn't smell like that.

William tossed the package aside, along with all thoughts of stealth and caution. The next closest package was an elongated slim box covered in bright paper, both ends sealed with tightly wrapped twine. He did not notice how loud the ripping and tearing paper sounded. He scratched and poked at the middle of the box and managed to start a small opening into which he thrust his forefinger. He began pulling at the opening. Finally, he was able to insert his small hand into the package and pull the item out of the box like gutting a freshly caught fish.

This was more promising. It was a toy with a blue wooden handle and a bright red rounded knob at the end. Attached to the other end were two painted red iron disks connected by a horizontal axle. William placed the wheels of the toy on the ground and began to push it forward and pull it back. The toy emitted a pleasant chiming melody. Without smiling, William let the handle fall to the floor.

The next box was a perfect square, tightly wrapped and about the size of a candy box, but much heavier. Probably something for mother, but he'd open it anyway. A glint of silver in the partially opened box caught his eye. The box was stubborn, so he set his teeth to work on the string, his sharp young teeth easily popping the string in half. He pulled the box open. Two belt buckles with large silver letters. A W and an M. He liked the look and feel of the silver buckles, and wanted them both though they looked the same. He instantly thought how he could hide one, and keep both.

Then, the thump of feet hit the floor above his head. Wallace was awake. As quickly as he could, William ripped open one package after another, neither caring for nor curious as to their contents. He was in a manic race to open everything before his brother set foot in the Great Room.

Christmas paper piled up around him up to his neck. He could just glimpse Wallace's bare feet at the top of the landing. Then the war whoop-broke loose.

"He opened them all! He opened them all!" Wallace screamed over and over again like the way Mr. Thomas yelled, "Fire, fire!" when the schoolhouse in Cimarron went up in flames. Wallace's heels thudded down the stairs, his twin still screaming his chant. Wallace missed the last stair and sprawled face down onto the wide-planked wooden floor. He coughed, choked, and let loose an unholy scream.

Murdoch McNeil's booming voice hollered down the hall along with his loud, thudding feet.

"Wallace! What the blessed saints are you screaming about? Who's opening all the presents?" he yelled.

Murdoch thundered into the Great Room. The commotion awakened Mrs. McNeil as well, and she came close behind. She was softly saying,

"Now Murdoch, now Murdoch," in almost perfect cadence with her stride. This changed to "Oh my, Oh my," as she came in sight of her twin boys in the parlor, one buried to his neck in Christmas paper, the other sprawled face down on the floor, yelling and crying uncontrollably.

Murdoch stepped across Wallace. Anne paused momentarily and asked if Wallace was all right. "He opened all of our presents!" he repeated. Anne was at her husband's side.

"Now Murdoch, he's only seven years old."

"Well, goddamn it, Anne, he's old enough to know better! William, damn you, you ruined Christmas!"

Murdoch stood over William, who sat motionless and without expression in the Christmas rubble, the war paint of chocolate smeared on his face. He looked up at his father and did not wince as Murdoch raised his hand above his head. His hand looked the size of a shovel to William. Better than the belt, he thought.

Anne grabbed Murdoch's wrist with both of her hands. The motion of Murdoch's hand pulled her off balance, but only briefly. She settled her five-foot-eight-inch frame powerfully onto the flooring as if she were bracing against the pull of a temperamental stallion. "Murdoch! Stop it! You will not strike our child!" She gave him *that* look. She could make a fifteen-hundred-pound horse do whatever she wanted with that look, and Murdoch knew it.

Murdoch looked at his wife, his face red with rage and covered in sweat, adrenaline still coursing through his body. Wallace had not moved from his prostrate position at the foot of the stairs. He looked like a frozen, weeping statue. Anne still held onto Murdoch's wrist but loosened her grip and began to gently rub his arm.

"Murdoch, he's only a child," she said softly.

"Well, he still should have known better. There's name tags." His voice trailed off. Trying to explain why he was so angry would be pointless.

"Wallace, go upstairs and get dressed. You and Father can get after the morning chores. William and I have some rewrapping to do. We'll have Christmas breakfast when you two get back."

Wallace headed upstairs, and Murdoch walked back down the hall.

It's true, William thought calmly; I knew that they all had name tags. I just wanted to open them. That's all. He wondered what all the fuss was about.

"Sometimes you just have to take what's yours," he whispered.

Chapter XV: Tuberculosis

Saturday, December 25, 1879
McNeil Ranch
New Mexico Territory

"Live life when you have it. Life is a gift - there is nothing small about it."
Florence Nightingale, 1854

Murdoch disappeared. Wallace popped up off the floor and ran upstairs, leaving the chaos for his mother to sort. By the time Murdoch and Wallace were dressed and headed out the front door, Anne had herded William to the kitchen table while carrying an armful of presents, plain brown wrapping paper, scissors, and twine.

Murdoch stood on the hacienda's wide front porch and looked out at the morning sky. Wisps of clouds teased out the shades of pink and turquoise that married the sunrise with the land. He rested his coffee on the porch's half-wall, a two-foot-thick berm of adobe designed to defend the house against the elements – and everything else. The thickness of the adobe walls kept in the heat during the cold New Mexico winters, and let the heat out during the New Mexico summers. Murdoch liked the hacienda – Anne loved it.

The McNeil Ranch was built along the Cimarroncito, a little stream that fed into the Cimarron River, appropriately named in Spanish for its "wild" nature. The Cimarroncito stayed steady, but the Cimarron flooded regularly. Murdoch had thought to locate his ranch closer to the rough town of Cimarron, where he'd built his freighting headquarters, but the town and the river were unpredictable. As hectic as this morning had been, it was nothing compared to the chaos of the little canyon, the big river, and the wild town in the middle of it all.

Murdoch sipped his coffee and Wallace had stepped onto the porch unnoticed.

"Should I start on the barn first?" he asked.

Wallace's voice startled him out of his trance. As the light grew, the mesas and buttes in the distance were losing their sharp-edged appearance. He wanted to tell Wallace that he shouldn't have lost his temper with his twin brother. He wanted to tell him that this might be the last Christmas when they'd get almost everything they had asked for, and a few things he wanted them to ask for as well. He wanted to tell him that his freighting company was going to hell in a handbasket because the damn railroad had made it to Santa Fe. Wallace was not old enough to understand. All he knew was Dad had lost his temper. Murdoch felt awful about it, but he couldn't say he was sorry.

The railroad meant progress, but it also meant they'd be undercutting freight costs. They'd either attract the teamsters away from the freight or put them out of work. And then, when freighting companies like his own went out of business, they'd hit everyone with whatever prices they wanted to set. But all of this was not for Wallace, who had already absorbed too much of what he heard.

"Go on and feed the barn stock. Check the water, break up the ice."

"Is Christmas really ruined?" asked Wallace.

Murdoch thought of Christmas on Barra and in New York City as a boy when he was alone and frightened. He'd vowed to himself that when he grew up and had children of his own, they would never endure a Christmas like the ones that still haunted him after all these years. He showered them with presents, and made sure that each Christmas, they'd received candy and an orange in their stocking. If a year had been lean at the McNeil home, Christmas never was.

Murdoch's voice softened with contrition. "No, Wallace, Christmas is not ruined."

"Yeah! It's Christmas!" Wallace squealed, trotting off to the barn, the morning's escapade already forgotten. Usually, Anne and one of the twins helped with the milking, but not this morning. Murdoch drew a breath of frigid air sharp in his lungs and headed to the barn to help Wallace.

He'd only taken a couple of steps when he saw a rider cresting the distant hill to the south at a gallop, heading for his ranch. Christmas morning, and barely sunup?

"Wallace! Get out here now!"

The barn door flew open. "Yeah, Papa?"

"Get up to the house. Tell your mother we've got a rider heading in fast. It looks like McDaniel; can't be sure in this light. Tell her to bring my rifle." Murdoch had his Colt pistol on his hip as he always did, but had given up carrying his Winchester rifle when he did chores closer to the house. It was clumsy and heavy, not like the Colt that felt a part of him. But a Winchester was, from far away, a better visual deterrent.

Anne came out with the rifle, and the twins followed. She glanced at the bunkhouse, wishing Murdoch hadn't let the ranch hands go before Christmas. They could have found plenty of work for them during the winter months, but he had been so worried about losing money on his freighting business that he tried to save by reducing the number of hands on the ranch. He had kept a couple of the men on part-time, but they were in Cimarron.

"You boys sit up on the porch bench and stay there unless I tell you to go inside," Murdoch said. The twins sat close together on the bench, their lower legs barely reaching the edge of the seat. Anne stepped off the porch and stood by Murdoch, carrying her own rifle.

"Wallace said you think it's McDaniel. That's his paint."

"No mistaking that horse."

The flashy paint horse came closer into focus, and the sunrise was almost completely over the hills. Her breath came out, steaming against the cold air, and puffs of snow exploded with each impact of her hooves. The rider slowed to a trot, and Murdoch and Anne could see that it was their neighbor. "What the hell does he want?" Murdoch said, half to himself and half to Anne.

"I don't know, but I see worry on his face even at this distance." Anne sharpened her voice. "It's Christmas, I'll thank you to be civil, Dock."

Murdoch did not shift his gaze. "I'll be civil, but he's got that notion about the land, not me. Let's just see what he wants."

McDaniel sat back in his saddle, and the paint horse stopped in front of Anne and Murdoch. But he was not still, his weight shifting nervously from his right stirrup to his left. McDaniel swung out of the saddle and tied the reins to the saddle horn.

"Murdoch, Anne. Sorry to trouble you, but I'm headed on in to Cimarron. Got to get the Doc to come out. It's Emma. Her breathing isn't right; she's burning up."

"William! Wallace! Come get Mr. McDaniel's horse watered!" Murdoch hollered. The twins hopped off the bench and grabbed a pail.

"Are the girls at home?" Anne asked.

"With Emma."

"Murdoch, I'm going in to change. Get Skip saddled." She turned to McDaniel. "Jim, I'll get over to your place quick as I can. I'll take care of the girls until you get back."

The paint horse refreshed, William and Wallace stepped back as McDaniel swung back onto the saddle and took off for Cimarron without another glance. "Thank you, Anne," he yelled as he left.

Murdoch enlisted the twins to go get Anne's roan quarter horse. "Be civil, Dock," he said to himself.

"What's wrong with Mrs. McDaniel, Papa?" William asked.

Murdoch answered sharply, "Consumption. Tuberculosis."

Murdoch pulled the barn door open. Half-empty now in the quiet season, but Skip was in his stall as always. He got Anne's saddle.

Murdoch pushed down his irritation at William. He was not so much angry at him, even with what happened this morning, but by his irritation at seeing McDaniel on Christmas of all days. He chastised himself for that feeling. Emma was a good woman. She and Anne had become close friends after Murdoch moved his bride to New Mexico Territory nearly three years before. And Murdoch and Jim had gotten along well, too, at first. Jim helped him understand some of the subtleties of the territory's different cultures, always pulling at each other: The Indigenous tribes, the Ute, the Tewa, the Apache, and then the Spanish, the Mexican culture, and finally Americans and Europeans, all in different states of clashing and cooperating. It reminded him of New York City and all the immigrants from so many parts of the world. But here was an underlying tension that needed little to reach a flash point. The catalysts always seemed to be land and water.

Murdoch led Skip out of the barn and gave the cinch one last pull.

"All set. I should be going with you..."

"Dock, you know you need to stay here with the boys."

"Tuberculosis is contagious, Anne; you know that."

"I've been visiting Emma for the last two years ever since she was diagnosed. I'll be fine. Her girls shouldn't be left alone any more than our boys should be."

"We can take the boys with us." Murdoch grasped at something to justify being with her. "You know that Apache Victorio killed all those settlers south of here."

"That was way far south, near Alma, and that was back in April, and you know Victorio was killed by the Mexicans a couple of months ago." She checked the cinch, pulled it again, and slid her rifle into the scabbard. "I'll be fine. And I can't gallop near as fast with a boy as my baggage."

"Make sure you've chambered a round." If anything happened to her...

She didn't need to check. "I have." Anne swung easily onto Skip's back. She wanted to tell Murdoch that this would be easier if they still had their crew on for the winter full-time, but he already knew. The Cimarron was dangerous in a way that New York was not. An unorganized danger. Wild.

Anne galloped off with a slight click of her heel, cuing the horse with slight shifts in her body weight. Murdoch watched her disappear over the hill. Murdoch thought she was right about keeping the hands and about it being better for the twins to stay with him at the house. And she was also right that there were scant chances of raids on the area ranches at this time of year. If he'd hoped to control Anne by pointing out his concerns, well, he should have known better. Anne took to ranch life better than he did. He missed the city. He missed Central Park in the snow, Bethesda Terrace, the fountain, the tree-lined walkways, the people in their formal dress that matched the elegant iron and stonework. He missed the brownstone he and Anne had lived in with her father and mother. He missed their bench.

Murdoch dumped the rest of his coffee grown cold.

"You did it to yourself, Dock," he mumbled to himself.

***

His little paint horse tired from the twelve-mile gallop, James McDaniel slowed her to a walk as he approached the town of Cimarron. He passed St. James Hotel and Lambert's bar. The smells of Lambert's Christmas morning breakfast filled the air. Jim set aside his hunger – no time to hitch his horse outside to enjoy the bacon and sausage. He continued on to Dr. Gregg's home practice on 8th Street and knocked on the door.

"Hold on, I'm coming!" Mrs. Gregg called. "Who got shot at Lambert's this time?" She opened the door.

"No one that I know of, Mrs. Gregg. Is the Doc in?"

"Not yet, he got called out after he finished up with last night's gunfight. Should be back sometime this morning. Is it Emma?"

"Yes – too weak to be brought here, and her breathing is worse than ever. Color's bad too. Her hands and feet are so cold. I need Doc to come out."

Mrs. Gregg poured him some coffee. "He won't be there any sooner with you waiting here, Jim. Best get back to Emma and your girls. I'll send him out as soon as he gets back."

"Where's he at? I'll ride over, and we can head back out together."

"He's out toward Raton. It won't be quicker to send you out to get him. Now finish your coffee and get going – you shouldn't be leaving Emma alone any longer than you have to."

Jim furrowed his brow. "Tell him to hurry. Please. And Anne McNeil's staying with them for now."

Mrs. Gregg watched him ride off, but she wished she could ask him a few questions. Anne had been caring for Emma ever since Doc had diagnosed Emma with tuberculosis two years ago, and Anne had some nursing in her background. At the time of Emma's diagnosis, the McNeils and McDaniels were close. They were often seen together for socials and town gatherings. Their children played together, and some said that you couldn't slip a piece of paper between the four kids because of how close they were.

230

About the time Emma's tuberculosis looked like it was here to stay awhile, something seemed to change between the two clans. They no longer rode into town together. Jim and Murdoch no longer spoke unless forced. Anne and Emma were still good friends, but for Jim to stop by Murdoch's ranch himself to call for Anne – and on Christmas – meant that Emma must have been bad off indeed. And then it was bad enough for him to continue on to Doc Gregg.

The rumor was that their falling out had to do with land and a surveying issue, but that was all Mrs. Gregg knew, in spite of the way rumors and gossip traveled around in such a small, interdependent community. Without much to go on, people hadn't chosen sides yet, but everyone hoped this malcontent would not play out too badly. McNeil and McDaniel said nothing and were decent enough not to take part in any hateful comments. They were like poker players, each one looking for a cheat or a tell, and they had found nothing. Mrs. Gregg feared what would happen if they did.

***

Despite the scarf covering her face, Anne felt the cold bite of the winter air as Skip moved swiftly through the snow-covered hills. They both knew the terrain to Emma's well enough, and even covered with snow, he could avoid the prairie dog holes. She breathed slowly and deeply in time with Skip's gait and his rocking motion, so easy even at this speed. Riding erased her mind of its thoughts and worries. She had an eight-mile run alone with Skip and the scenery, and she never got tired of the ride to the McDaniels. She pulled up to the hacienda on Rayado Creek and brought Skip to a sliding stop. She hopped off the saddle and threw the reins over the hitching rail. Skip knew to stay where he was put. Then she ran up to the door and knocked loudly.

"Emma! It's Anne!"

The little patter of small feet ran toward the door and threw open the latch. Sarah was eight, and Alice was six. McDaniels's door was heavy, and so Anne helped the girls push it open.

Alice was failing to hide her worry. "Mommy won't wake up!"

"Emma!" Anne lost no time racing to her sickroom.

Emma lay on her bed. Her bedclothes and blankets were soaked with sweat and stained with streaks of dried blood. A worn dime novel, Ellis's *The Apache Guide*, lay face-down and torn upon the bed. Her lips were cracked, dry, and set in a face masked with white-green mucus. This sickly pallor was exaggerated all the more by the dark, puffy circles around her eyes. Anne pulled her bandana over her nose to mask the smell of a long, severe sickness, one awful miasma with so many different parts.

Anne knew the smell all too well. In her teen years the Civil War came, and so before she considered courting, she took nursing training at Bellevue Hospital back in New York. Tuberculosis was everywhere, and she'd become adept at easing patients. Though it was expected for a woman of her class to marry, it was still a difficult decision to leave nursing. But then there was Murdoch, deeply in love, as she was with him. Murdoch did not object, in fact, if she would choose to carry on as a nurse – but her father was a prominent attorney in the city, and he would not hear of it. As a compromise, she'd bargained to volunteer on occasion to keep up with her skills.

She called on that experience now. Anne placed the back of her hand on Emma's cheek and found that her fever was quite high.

"Sarah, Alice, fetch me a basin of cold water and some towels," Anne said. The task would help calm the girls and keep them busy. Emma's fever had to be reduced fast, so Anne stripped away the bedding and her clothes—there was no time for modesty. When the girls returned, Anne helped Emma sit up and ran the cold, wet cloths over her forehead, neck, back, and chest, trying to draw the heat away. Up close, Emma looked worse—her nailbeds were pale, and the circulation was slow to return when Anne pinched them. Emma wasn't just struggling to breathe; her whole body was starved of oxygen.

"Alice, remember when we picked that mullein and bungleweed last summer? Do you still have any?"

"Yes, I'll show you where it is."

But Emma stirred and began coughing, white mucus and red blood spattering from her dehydrated mouth.

"Oh God! My chest hurts!" she shrieked.

"Emma. It's Anne, I'm right here with you." Anne didn't know if Emma could see, and even if she could, she may not have recognized anyone at all.

"I know it hurts to breathe. Try anyway. Try to take some deep breaths." Anne cleared the sputum. "I'll get some laudanum. Alice, stay with your mom. Keep cooling her down with the towels, just as you saw me doing. Sarah, show me where the medicine is."

She continued on to the kitchen, and Sarah pointed to the cabinet holding the herbs. Everything was there, the mullein, the bungleweed, the laudanum, and all the other things Emma had tried to ease her condition. Anne lit the stove and put the kettle on, tossing in the bungleweed.

Anne remembered Murdoch's worry over her catching tuberculosis, but she had been exposed to tuberculosis so many times over the years that she felt she was not likely to catch it, or if she did, she had likely fought it off. Jim and the girls were not sick. Some people just caught a bad case, and some did not. Saving Emma was her concern.

The bungleweed would restrict the bleeding in the lungs and slightly sedate Emma. "Sarah, when was the last time your mother had laudanum?"

"Daddy gave it to her just before he left this morning."

No wonder she was in such pain. She had seen tuberculosis patients who coughed so hard that they fractured their ribs, and Emma was likely to be suffering like this.

"Will Mommy be okay? Or will she die?" asked Sarah.

"I don't know. She's very sick. Only God knows what will happen, so we need to be strong and take care of her until the doctor gets here, okay?"

Emma screamed from the sickroom. "No! No! You stay away from my babies!"

Anne hurried to see Emma standing in front of the bed, holding Alice in a chokehold with her left arm, wielding a large hunting knife in her right hand. Emma's eyes were wide with fright, as were Alice's. Emma was pointing the knife and screaming at someone who was not there.

Alice screamed. "Mommy! You're scaring me!"

"You goddamned Apache devils! I'll never let you take my babies! I'll kill them myself before I'll let you take them!"

"Emma! It's Anne! For God's sake, put the knife down! There's no Apaches here; it's just us!"

Emma tightened her grip on Alice. Both girls started crying uncontrollably. Sweat poured off of Emma, suddenly racked with a coughing fit. She splattered Alice with blood-streaked mucus. Alice took the chance to run, but Emma didn't notice. She shook the hunting knife toward the invisible Apache's, eyes glazed over with fever.

"I'll kill them, I swear! I'll kill myself!"

"Emma. Look at me." Anne kept her voice calm. "Look at me. Do you hear me?"

Emma finally looked in her direction.

"That's it. Just look at me."

"No! You're one of them! You want to take my babies!"

"Emma. If I was an Apache, I'd be talking Apache, wouldn't I? Come on, put the knife down. The girls are fine, but you're scaring them."

Emma looked past Anne as if she could still see the Apache. She shook her head and sank to her knees as another coughing fit overtook her. The knife fell from her hand, and consciousness fell from her body.

"I need your help to get her back into bed. Get under her arms and lift." She kicked the knife away. Once returned to bed, Emma drifted in and out of reality. For the next two hours Anne administered laudanum and tea. Her breathing returned to normal, and she coughed less as Anne continued to wash her with cool, moist cloths.

Anne looked out the window of the sickroom through the gaps in the latilla slats. By the position of the sun, it was now around 3:00 pm. The girls had fallen into an uneasy sleep in the front room, their faces streaked with tears and fixed with worry. Finally, she heard the front door to the hacienda opening, and footsteps on the wooden floors. The girls woke.

"Emma! Anne!" Jim was back.

"Daddy!" the girls exclaimed. They rushed to their father and chattered furiously about the morning's dangers.

"Slow down! It will be all right if you talk one at a time," said Jim.

Anne came to greet him in the big room. "Jim. Emma's okay. We had a bit of a time, and the girls were scared, but she's resting now. Where's Dr. Gregg?"

"He was out on a call when I got there; he's out toward Raton, but he should be here soon."

Jim quietly opened the sickroom door and stepped in. He sat down on the bed next to his wife, finally in an untroubled sleep. He brushed a strand of hair from her face and kissed her forehead.

Anne allowed them their moment but soon turned to Jim. "She had laudanum and bungleweed about half an hour ago. Her color's better. But Jim, the disease makes her see things that aren't there. She thought Apaches were in the house trying to take Sarah and Alice. They were pretty shaken up," Anne explained.

"I always keep my hunting knife in the bedside table. I didn't remove it when she got sick... I had no idea. Anne, if you hadn't been here..."

"But I was. I put the knife in the kitchen cabinet."

From outside the hacienda, a horse whinnied. There was a knock at the door. Without waiting for an answer, Dr. Gregg poked his head inside. "Jim?"

"Back here, Doc!" Jim called.

Gregg made for the sickroom where Anne sat in a large padded oak chair next to the bed. Jim hovered on the edge of the bed next to Emma while Sarah and Alice had taken up a watch at the foot of the bed. Emma was covered with a light sheet and lay propped up by pillows.

"Emma, Emma. Wake up. It's Dr. Gregg. I need to listen to your lungs, okay?" He turned to Jim. "Would you take the girls and step out for a minute? I won't be long."

"Come, Sarah, Alice. Did you have any breakfast or lunch?"

"No, Daddy," said Sarah.

"Let's get you something to eat then."

Dr. Gregg enlisted Anne as his assistant. "Anne, help me sit her up so I can get my stethoscope there."

Anne and Dr. Gregg pulled Emma forward. Though they were as gentle as possible and careful not to place pressure on her ribs, Emma stirred, and her eyes opened.

"I'm thirsty," she said, half-aware.

"That's good. Emma, let me listen to your lungs."

"Here you are, Emma. This tea will help."

"Anne, would you step over here?" She and the doctor moved to the corner of the room just out of earshot. "Not in front of Emma or Jim just yet – would you tell me what happened?"

Anne recounted the events in clinical detail. She explained Emma's hallucinations and the impact it had on the girls.

"Apaches... what do you think triggers that fear? Was there any Apache attack on this ranch?"

"Not that I know of, but Emma's always reading the dime novels and the newspapers. Those papers print mostly panicked rumors like they're facts." Anne's father had instilled in her a love of reading but also a belief in the truth.

"And those dime novels. They're written by Easterners whose only knowledge of the West comes from other dime novels. No wonder she's scared half to death; they'll say anything to sell a few copies." Dr. Gregg wrote something in his notes.

"I can't say for sure. This damned disease. Sometimes the fever breaks, and they get better, and then they turn. I'm going to tell Jim that I'm staying the night. Can you get more of the mullein tea into her?" Anne nodded. "And Anne..."

"Yes, Dr. Gregg?"

"It doesn't matter out here if you finished nursing school or not. You're a damn fine nurse. We even had female doctors in the war, a few of them, and I'd say you could have gone to medical school if life had taken you in that direction. If I know my business as well as I think, you saved her life today."

She said her goodbyes to the McDaniel family and to Dr. Gregg and went outside to the corral to check on Skip. She used the shovel to break the ice in the water trough, one less thing for Jim to have to worry about until it froze over again. Then she swung up into the saddle and cantered off toward home, letting Skip slow his pace as he wished. It was 4:00 in the afternoon already, and Christmas dinner was going to be late. The jerky in her coat pocket had been a good idea, and just now, it tasted like the best roast beef.

Though the ride encompassed several miles, they seemed to melt away quickly. Anne would be home before sundown, but not by much. The breeze carried the smell of piñon wood from her cozy fireplace long before she saw the smoke curling from the chimney.

She stopped Skip at the hitching post before the porch and sat for a moment, appreciating the sight of home. How I love this place, she thought. The adobe walls were thick and made her feel safe. The giant log beams protruding from the flat roof, anchoring the expansive porch, seemed more permanent and sound than the brownstones of her childhood. One of the shutters opened, and William's round face peered out, reflected by lamplight. From inside, she heard a squeal:

"Mommy's home!"

Followed by the thumps of running feet. Though she was chilled by the cold December night, she knew that she would soon be warmed.

The twins burst through the heavy carved oak door as she dismounted Skip.

"Mommy! Where were you for so long? Wait 'til you see what we did!" they chattered seemingly in one voice.

The boys enveloped her with hugs, and their arms were just long enough now to completely encircle her frame. Murdoch now stepped through the door, pipe in hand, the smell of tobacco mingling with the piñon.

"Boys! Give your mother some air! Hi, sweetheart. Is everything okay?"

"Rode hard," she said.

"And put up wet," Murdoch replied. Their code phrase for "we can talk about it later."

"Dock, is that my apron you're wearing?" she asked in disbelief.

Wallace could not hold on to the surprise. "Dad's cooking Christmas dinner!"

"Wallace…" Murdoch sighed. "You boys take Skip to the barn and put him up."

Anne giggled. "But my apron, Dock? I wish we had one of those fancy cameras. I'd love a tintype of you wearing that! I'd show it down at Lambert's!"

"My Levi's are perfectly seasoned with just the right amount of horse and cow stains. I'm not going to ruin them just to cook you dinner! Of course, I had to borrow your apron!"

Anne pulled Murdoch close, and they kissed deeply, holding it as long as they reckoned the twins would be busy with Skip. "Life is fleeting, Dock. Now let's see what you've done to my kitchen."

Murdoch knew she was referring to Emma, but he didn't ask about her. Anne would tell him in her own time what had happened. Death was always close in this land, but it could be close anywhere and everywhere. He had learned that at an early age. Smallpox, diphtheria, the flu, and other diseases killed so many out here, but disease was not confined to the West either. Anne and Murdoch's experiences with disease caused them to hold each other even tighter in the knowledge that life was as precious as it was fleeting.

Inside, Anne beheld the Christmas tree. The torn Christmas paper was all gone. The presents had been rewrapped as neatly as possible for two young boys working under the direction of their father. She could not complain. The smell of roast turkey filled the room, and the dining table had been neatly set. They'd lit candles and placed them into the small alcoves built within the walls. Normally, these would have been filled with images of Catholic saints and the veladoras, the prayer candles that stayed lit for seven days. Murdoch was not a religious man, but the men who built the hacienda were, and they insisted on this touch. Murdoch respected their custom.

The twins rushed into the front room, just as excited as they'd been on Christmas Eve. Nothing dampened their Christmas spirit. Anne and Murdoch finished preparing Christmas dinner together, and the family sat down and ate. Afterwards, they all opened their presents. The twins squealed with delight with each toy.

Then darkness settled in, the doors were bolted, and Murdoch sat in his favorite chair with his family gathered around him. As he did every year, he read aloud from "A Visit from St. Nicholas." It was not the night before Christmas as in the poem, but they'd made the holiday last a little bit longer nonetheless.

After "Merry Christmas to all, and to all a good night!" the boys were ushered off to bed, each carrying as many of their new toys as their arms could hold. Murdoch and Anne took one last kiss under the mistletoe that Murdoch had found clinging to one of the ponderosa pines in the hills. They climbed into their heavy log-framed bed and wrapped each other in their arms. Anne turned to Murdoch.

"Did you like your presents?"

"Yes, I don't know how you kept them from me! I even tried to check the post office!"

"You're so nosy!"

"A gold watch, an Elgin at that! And a pair of engraved Colt .45s right from the factory!"

"I have one more present for you, Dock," Anne teased.

"Well, I don't know where you could have hidden it. Is it you? Do I get to unwrap you?" he asked.

"Of course, you get to unwrap me, but that's not what I'm talking about."

"What is it?"

"I'm pregnant, Dock." She smiled wide. "We get to have our child in our own home."

Chapter XVI: Word Play

Saturday Night, December 25, 1879
McNeil Ranch
New Mexico Territory

"Do you eat, sleep, do you breathe me anymore? Do you sleep, do you count sheep anymore? Do you sleep anymore?"
Lisa Loeb

I lay next to Anne in bed, in the dark, staring at the dying embers in the kiva fireplace in the corner of our bedroom. Anne had insisted on a fireplace in every room in the house. Silly at the time, I thought, but now I appreciated it.

Sleep eluded me this Christmas night. Anne never had problems sleeping after our lovemaking. I usually didn't either, but I was troubled without being able to pin it down. Maybe it was having to provide for another child. When Anne was pregnant for the first time with the twins, I was elated, and Henry and Ada shared our joy. But this time was different. Maybe because we were in New Mexico.

The twins had been born in New York in the brownstone that we shared with Anne's parents. Anne was pampered during her entire pregnancy, and Ada led a cadre of well-meaning women who surrounded her with daily advice on everything from diet to the latest birthing techniques. She had access to the best physicians and midwives the world could offer. She chose the pain-free method, and labor was perfect, which was the exact result Henry Townsend's money and influence could buy.

She would have none of that in New Mexico.

She might give birth in this bed. She might be alone. She might be hurt. I liked Dr. Gregg; he was a competent physician, but he was also the only physician. What if Anne needed more help when it was too late to send for it?

That was it. That was responsible for my sleeplessness. She would simply have to go back to New York, where she would be safe, and the baby would be safe. As if in agreement, the last ember in the fireplace popped and sizzled. I kissed Anne's cheek and fell to sleep.

I was only too happy to have an excuse to skip church the next morning. We spent the day nestled into the hacienda, my only chores being to break in my new briar pipe and check that my new pocket watch kept the time well. Anne already playfully accused me of spending more time admiring the engraved Colt .45 pistols than I did her. As she'd been the one to give them to me, I argued it was functionally the same thing.

I still smelled the oranges, and I missed Elizabeth.

I did not bring up my concerns to Anne, but my worry was deepening and beginning to spiral out of control. I thought of the argument we had before we moved to Cimarron. I felt that I almost lost her then, and now, nightmare scenarios began to flood my mind of the myriad things that could go wrong. It would be better to form a good argument. Maybe bring it up at breakfast.

"Anne, Christmas night before you went to sleep, you said you were glad to have our child in our own home. You did mean in New York?" I half-asked.

"No, Dock, I mean here in our home. Our hacienda."

"I think it's best that I go back to New York with you and the boys. I can talk to Diego, and he and Consuela can handle things here. Paul at the warehouse can serve as ranch foreman enough for the off-season. We can retain some hands to work the stock through winter, and they'll be here for spring and summer to boot. You're right that I shouldn't have cut them loose, but I'm sure they'll come back; work is short. I can get you to New York with the twins and make sure you're set up, then I can come back here should I need to take care of anything in person."

Anne was silent.

"I'll send a telegram to Henry today," I said as Consuela placed my plate in front of me. *Huevos rancheros*, my favorite. She gave Anne dried fruit, boiled eggs, pine nuts, and tea.

"Thank you, Consuela. Murdoch, I want to have our baby in our own home. Consuela has been caring for me well. She's a curandera,

242

you know – she is as good as a doctor, maybe better. She's a *partera,* which means midwife." Anne was better than I was at picking up the odd Spanish term. "Consuela's delivered dozens of children, and even Dr. Gregg sends some of his patients to her."

Consuela added, "The baby will be fine and healthy, Señor McNeil. We've already started with the diet. I make a special tea for her to ease delivery and help her build the baby."

"The painless delivery from the twins—don't you want that?" I asked, ignoring Consuela's justifications.

"*Perdón*, Señor McNeil, but the *curandera* have heard about this painless delivery. They use a chemical that isn't good for the baby and the mother. We use *la lavanda*, the lavender, to help the muscles and relax the mother and baby. Then we use inmortal, the little white flowers you see growing in the open plains here. This is much like your painless delivery, but it is much safer."

"Consuela," I addressed her, "I am happy that you want to help. New York has the finest doctors in the country. They're highly educated and practice using all the latest medical advances. Even the Queen of England bore her children with chloroform."

Anne was straight in her chair. "Murdoch, I want our child here, in New Mexico, in our hacienda, in our bed. I want Consuela and the other curanderas to help me. Dr. Gregg, too, if you want." Consuela punctuated the argument with crossed arms and a stern look on her face. I felt as if I were a misbehaving child.

I was furious at the concerted interference of the two of them to put Anne's health aside and risk her, the baby, or both. Earlier this morning, I managed to push aside the dreadful thoughts of what could occur, but the chaotic scenes of a pregnancy gone wrong overwhelmed me. I would lose her to this godforsaken land and its backward and superstitious ways. I loved Anne, and I refused to let that happen. All I could see was her slipping away—like Elizabeth and my parents on the *Sarah.*

"Consuela, that will be all," I said in my most commanding voice. After she left the room, I looked at Anne. "If you want to take Consuela's herbs in your tea, then fine. If you want to take her herbs with you on the way to New York, fine. But I am not taking a chance with our baby born without a real midwife and a real doctor present. Consuela is a great person, but I won't have a Mexican witch doctor in charge of this."

"Consuela is not a Mexican witch doctor, Murdoch McNeil. She is a curandera. She has decades of experience. Her mother and grandmother were curanderas. I trust her."

"Your parents are not going to stand for having their grandchild born here with a Mexican as a midwife. They'll think she's a witch doctor, too. In their eyes, you might as well get some Apache medicine man to deliver our baby."

I didn't know what was wrong with Anne. Maybe she was too isolated here and had become too close with Consuela. She acted like a pouting child, silent and insistent. I did not want to ask Henry and Ada to step in, but I knew that if I did, they would agree with me. I would have to set aside my pride to send that kind of telegram but to protect Anne and our baby, I would do it.

"Anne, I love you. Please think about the baby and your own health. What if there was a problem? There's no guarantee that Dr. Gregg would be able to come here and help. He might be hours away on another call. Maybe we can bring Consuela to New York with us if you must have her. There just aren't enough medical personnel here to make you safe." It was a last-ditch argument, but being forceful wouldn't get her to see reason.

"I can't and won't ask her to leave Diego and her garden for so many months, Murdoch."

I would have to let the matter sit. I kissed her forehead. "Please think about it. I have to go to the freighting office today." Three years ago, I couldn't get her to leave New York without tears, and now I can't get her to come back. This place kidnaps the souls of some people. Not me, but clearly, it had taken hold of Anne.

Diego was hitching the team as I went outside. "Mr. McNeil, may I have a word?"

"What is it, Diego?"

"Consuela asked that I talk to you about Señora Anne. She thinks you might hear her better if her words come from another man. It is very important, Señor McNeil."

"If this is about Anne going to New York…"

"Only part. Consuela says Anne *es un tuberuloso*. She has tuberculosis. That's why she needs to stay here so Consuela can treat her. She knows, she is una curandera. Please, Señor, it's very important."

"Diego, that's absurd. Anne doesn't have consumption; she's pregnant."

"Consuela says that her weakness, her losing weight, and her loss of appetite is not from the pregnancy. It's from the tuberculosis. She's seen this so many times before. Without the medicine, she'll begin to cough and have night sweats. Her breathing will suffer."

I could not believe this playing at medical diagnosis. "I don't believe that's true. Even if it was, that's all the more reason Anne should be seen by the best doctors in the world. And they're in New York."

I could not be angry with Diego and Consuela. They had their beliefs and their quaint customs. I understood how deep Diego's concern must be for him to approach me like this and argue in defiance of his Patrón. I owned the very land on which they'd lived for so long. At any time, I could legally demand that they leave if I felt they were too much trouble. Of course, I would never do such a thing, but in their position, they had no way of either knowing that or trusting it.

"Diego, tell Consuela that I appreciate her concern. I really do. The best thing you can do for us is to keep the ranch running smoothly while we are in New York. I can get Paul Maestas from the warehouse to serve as foreman. Lawrence is probably halfway up the Chisholm Trail this time of year. Paul can put on half a dozen men, and they've been wanting work lately."

Diego gave a slight, terse nod. He was unconvinced, but it didn't matter. I climbed into the carriage and headed into Cimarron with a new flock of worries in my mind. I would send Henry and Ada a telegram as soon as I could, and I could almost hear Henry's voice. When Anne became pregnant with William and Wallace, he'd told me that a father starts worrying about his children as soon as their mother is expecting, and he doesn't quit worrying about them until either he's dead or they are.

Monday in Cimarron is not usually lively, so I was relieved to see the telegraph operator at his station. I fretted over the wording of my message. I couldn't remember a time since I'd begun my study of law when words failed me, but here I was, staring at a blank piece of paper.

"Mr. McNeil, Mr. McNeil, there's a gentleman behind you. Do you have your message ready?" the telegraph operator asked.

"Hmm? Oh, no, sorry. I'll step aside."

What was I going to say to Henry and Ada? What would they respond to? When I'd served as Henry's clerk as a young lad, his advice on legal writing was to focus on the facts. Keep it simple and unemotional. So I began to write.

ANN PREGNANT STOP INSISTS ON HAVING BABY HERE
STOP WANTS MEXICAN HOUSEKEEPER FOR MIDWIFE
STOP ~~VERY CONCERNED STOP~~

I crossed out the last line. No emotion, I reminded myself. I took the message to the telegraph desk. "Send this immediately, please, and have the answer brought to my office."

I received a reply within the hour. The envelope was addressed only to Anne. I took out my penknife, opened it, and placed the point upon the envelope seal. I started to slice through it and thought, this isn't right, and placed my knife back in my pocket. Whatever the message was from Henry and Ada I would know soon enough, and if I opened a private message meant for my wife's eyes only, she would become more insistent on her ways. I set the envelope aside and tended to business, though it did not leave my mind.

The freighting contracts had been tapering off since winter set in, and they would not be picking up this spring as they usually did. The railroad was slated to arrive in Santa Fe as soon as February. All of the other freighting companies scrambled to find other sources of revenue. I called Paul into my office.

"Paul, I hope you had a Merry Christmas."

"I did, and you as well, Mr. McNeil?" he replied with a hint of worry.

"I certainly did. I want to assure you and the other men in the freight that I have no intention of letting anyone go. I know we're all worried about what will happen when the rail reaches Santa Fe, and we'll certainly be losing business."

"We're all worried; thank you, Mr. McNeil. Some of the other companies let their workers go right before Christmas. It's been so hard on them and their families."

"I'm going back to New York this spring with Anne and the boys. I'd like you to serve as my ranch foreman and bring half a dozen or so of the men with you. We can offset our freighting revenue with increased cattle production, or at least Mr. Townsend seems to think so. Beef production is a growing business. The government is building more and more of those Indian schools, and we have a number of contracts with the Bureau of Indian Affairs already. As they finish those schools and fill them with children from the reservations, they will need a lot of cattle. We aim to provide it."

"Will we still run our line from Raton to Cimarron?"

"Yes, we'll continue to supply to Taos as well. Any men released from Townsend Freighting will be offered cowboy work on the McNeil Ranch. Would you let the men know?" Paul said that he would. He walked out of my office considerably more relaxed than when he'd entered.

Traveling back late in the chilly afternoon, I set the Morgan horse team at a walk. The team could sense my mood. I held the reins too tightly, and they responded by being difficult to control, shaking their strong heads and releasing clouds of breath into the cold air to punctuate their displeasure. I thought of Henry's accident in Central Park.

Usually, I'd want to enjoy the scenery, but just now, I wanted to avoid a confrontation with Anne for as long as possible. She would probably insist on having the baby at the hacienda, and I had resigned myself to the argument. I was wavering between worry and outright dread. She would not back down when she wanted something. I supposed that's how we came together in the first place, so I could not fault her for it.

Henry was aware of her stubbornness and was likely more than partially responsible for it. It seemed since we moved to New Mexico that she had become even more independent and strong-willed. I would have to make her understand that my desire to have the baby in New York came from my own anxieties. I wanted to have a clear conscience if anything happened to her or the baby. I wanted to be able to tell myself, as well as Henry and Ada, that I did everything possible to keep her safe, to bring her to New York.

Diego waited by the barn as I arrived. I nodded to him, and he to me, but we did not speak. He took the Morgans into the barn, and I went into the hacienda. Anne was sitting by the fireplace, and I went to the dining room buffet to pour myself an unusually large bourbon.

"Anne, I have said what I needed to say on the matter. I love you," and I kissed her on the cheek. "I sent word to your parents about the baby. They sent you a reply, and I almost opened it before I realized it was addressed only to you." I handed her the envelope.

She smiled and kissed me, took the envelope, and read the telegram. It seemed ages for her to absorb its message, whatever that may have been. She sighed and let her shoulders drop. She crumpled the message up tightly in her fist, then tossed the message and the envelope into the fireplace. She watched the paper flash into a burning yellow brightness.

"Murdoch. Buy tickets to the stage in Raton. Get some rail passes to New York. I'll have the baby there."

Chapter XVII: Frank

Tuesday, May 17, 1880
Grand Central Depot
New York City

"Ever-returning spring, trinity sure to me you bring,
Lilac blooming perennial and drooping star in the west,
And thought of him I love."
Walt Whitman, When Lilacs Last in the Dooryard Bloom'd, 1864

It was best to avoid traveling during northern New Mexico's notoriously unpredictable early spring, so we left for New York on Monday, May 9, and arrived at Grand Central Depot on Tuesday, May 17. I'd suggested traveling to arrive a few days ahead of our anniversary but Anne found her pregnancy exhausting and made it clear that she was not able to have a large anniversary celebration.

She never told me what Henry's telegram had said. Whatever message persuaded or ordered her to travel back remained between them, no matter how much it burned into my mind. I felt like a schoolboy seeing two classmates pass a note between them, knowing I would never be privy to its contents. I felt hurt, excluded, and jealous, though I knew this was immature and unjustified, and there were far more important things on my mind.

The freighting business had lost 80% of its revenue, much more than I expected. I would have to explain the loss to Henry. We'd survived the railroad's arrival in Santa Fe in February, but we had to fight for all the remaining crumbs with the other scavengers. I tried deeply discounting freight charges below our breakeven point, but the railroad matched and exceeded it to prove their point: we are bigger. The freighters only had our limited local capital. The railroad had foreign backers who had made the industry painfully successful.

Throughout the winter and the beginning of spring, Consuela cared for Anne. She gave her *burro* for the tuberculosis they both swore Anne had. She prepared *guayaca'n* and *huizache.* I didn't know their purpose and could barely pronounce them, but as useless as I thought these medicines were, surely they did no harm and were not worth fighting. Anne brought the herbs with her to New York.

Henry and Ada met us at the train station. "Darling! You look so thin!" Ada exclaimed. "You should be gaining weight, not losing it! Murdoch, Henry, see that the porter has all the luggage. You know how they can be."

"Yes, I'll see to it, dear," Henry replied.

"It's good to see you, Sir. I'm glad you were able to talk some sense into Anne." There would be no prying the telegram out of Henry either, and I wasn't going to ask.

"Yes, well, I'm glad she's finally here. I must agree with Ada; she doesn't appear at all well. Has she been seeing a doctor in Cimarron?"

"I can't get her to see our Doctor Gregg. She's been taking some potion from Consuela. Consuela has it in her head that Anne has consumption."

Henry looked concerned. "Has she been coughing up blood?"

"Not that I've seen."

"That witch doctor medicine is the first thing to go then. I'll have Johanna throw it out, and I'll send for Dr. Thomas first thing when we get to the brownstone."

When we arrived, Ada insisted that Anne go straight to bedrest, and Henry sent word for the doctor.

"Mother, I need my tea. It's in my bag. Can you please have Johanna make a cup for me?" Anne asked as she slipped into bed.

"We should let Dr. Thomas decide what is best for you, my dear. I hear you have the consumption?" she said with concern.

"Yes, I have a good friend, Consuela, in New Mexico. She is a curandera, which is like a doctor. She says I caught tuberculosis from one of our neighbors while I was caring for her. The tea is for my breathing."

"Murdoch says she's the housekeeper. The housekeeper was treating you?"

Anne flushed bright red at her mother's assumption and looked at me standing in the bedroom doorway. "Mother, I don't know what Dock told you about Consuela, but she's not really a housekeeper. She comes from a long line of curanderas…" She began to cough uncontrollably, snatching her handkerchief over her mouth. Ada poured a glass of water and waited for the coughing fit to subside. Anne pulled away the handkerchief, which was flecked bright red with blood. Her breathing became labored.

"Anne? How long has this been happening? The blood?" asked Murdoch.

"I didn't want to worry you, Dock, but I've been coughing a bit of blood since March. Emma was so much worse than this, and it just had to run its course. That's why I didn't see Dr. Gregg about it. Consuela's medicine seems to ease the coughing just as it did for Emma."

"Wouldn't Dr. Gregg have given you laudanum?"

"Laudanum is opium. Emma wasn't pregnant, but for me, it could harm the baby. Consuela tried to tell you." Her eyelids seemed heavy. "I'm so tired. Mother, can you please bring me the herbs from my luggage? I really need that tea."

Henry entered the bedroom with Dr. Thomas. "Anne, I've already instructed Johanna to get rid of that witch doctor's medicine. Doctor, don't you agree that she needs to take the medications you deem necessary?"

"Yes, generally. Anne, we don't know what those herbal medicines are. They might be fine, but we can't take the chance that they could harm the baby. Now, what's this I hear about you coughing blood?"

"I'm too tired to keep fighting with all of you," Anne said in an exhausted voice. She turned her head away from us.

"Anne, I prescribe rest and lots of it. I can give you some lavender tea just like you're used to from home and then laudanum for the cough."

Anne protested. "I won't take laudanum."

Dr. Thomas took the men aside. "Henry, Murdoch, I need to talk with you in the hall. Let's let Anne rest now."

Henry and I followed him out. He shut the bedroom door. "I have some concerns here. After listening to her lungs, I believe that she does have tuberculosis. I know she's had a lot of exposure from when she nursed at Bellevue and then when caring for her neighbor, and there's no way to know for sure when she contracted it. We know it's contagious, but it stays dormant so very long sometimes. Make sure you keep the bedroom window open so she gets fresh air." He went on to explain that tuberculosis can complicate childbirth and that the babies of infected mothers are often premature and underweight.

Henry started to say something, hesitated, and returned to Anne's room. Dr. Thomas reached into his medical bag for a bottle of laudanum and gave it to me. "The directions are on the bottle. See if you can get her to take it. Uncontrolled coughing fits aren't good for the baby either. Tell her that if she argues."

"What else, Dr. Thomas? I'm an attorney, as you know, and I suspect there is something you aren't saying."

He scratched the back of his neck and sighed. "She's going to get worse, and I can do nothing to stop it. When did she tell you she was pregnant?"

"Christmas night."

He made some notes. "I will check with Anne, but from what you say, she's probably due around late July."

"She said that's what Consuela told her, too," I agreed.

"Ah, yes, the Mexican witch doctor. Well, she was right about this, at least. She seems about seven months along now despite the weight loss. Fortunately, you traveled all the way back here to New York."

"Dr. Thomas, this is troubling me, and I have to know. Would she have been better off if she'd stayed in New Mexico? She wanted to stay."

"If I'd known she had tuberculosis? I would have advised her to stay. The climate in New Mexico is much better for consumption than the air we have here in New York. The patients always do better in dry air and where they can get distance from other people. I could have coordinated her care by telegram with the local doctor. We do that all the time now with the telegraph wires. Didn't she see her local doctor?"

"No, she refused to."

"Then nobody knew she had tuberculosis," Dr. Thomas sighed. But I remembered what Diego said. What Consuela said.

"Doctor, please don't tell Henry about this... I'm afraid he and I both insisted she come to New York for the baby's safety. At the time..."

He placed his hand on my shoulder. "I know, at the time, it seemed like the right thing to do. You didn't know what you know now. You can't blame yourself; you'll go mad."

Henry emerged from Anne's room. "She's sleeping. Ada's going to stay with her."

"Just the same, I'd feel better if she had a nurse," Dr. Thomas said. "I'll send a hospital midwife to stay with her."

The remainder of May and most of June saw Anne's condition deteriorate slowly at first, and then she seemed to worsen quickly. The clock in her body decided when the baby would be born, and unfortunately, it did not agree with the calendar. The baby was going to be early. Henry and Ada were frightened, and I tried to avoid thinking of the unthinkable. William and Wallace were only eight, and both were aware of how sick their mother had become. Wallace was mostly silent, and William seemed to delight in teasing him about his concern for his mother. I scolded William, who did not seem to truly grasp what was happening. Perhaps ignoring it was his way of dealing with the seriousness of the situation. Anne grew weaker, and I spent more of my time just sitting with her.

"Dock, we need to talk." Anne turned to the midwife. "Rachel, will you please give us some time?"

She left the room. In my heart, I knew the dreaded place where this conversation was going.

She patted the bed close to her and attempted a reassuring smile. "Sit next to me, Dock," she said, her eyes full of concern. "I was thinking about our last anniversary party here, in this house, and what we fought over. It seems so petty now. I want you to know how proud I am of you for risking everything to get our ranch. Whether Dad admits it or not, we would not have had the ranch or the freighting company without you. You gave me a life in the most beautiful, amazing place, New Mexico. I was free there. No one can take that from me."

Her words hung in the air, swirling in my head, and I was filled with an inconsolable sorrow that had nowhere to go. I could not speak.

"I know what's happening to me, Dock. I've seen tuberculosis too often to let it fool me. I'm not worried about me, and the baby will be fine, but he will come early. I'm really worried about you. I'm worried about the boys. I need to tell you some things while I still can, and please don't tell me that I will be alright. I won't be. Don't try to bullshit me, Dock."

"I don't know if I can do this, Ann." I knew I couldn't, but it didn't matter.

"I know it's hard, Dock. You've been through so much. Your parents, your sister. Having to fight and scrape so young, fighting and scraping instead of growing up the way everyone should. Now this, and you must bear this too. Dock, don't let Father talk you into leaving the boys here in New York to be raised by him and Mother. They're yours. Ours. I want them to grow up in New Mexico with their father on our land. I'm telling Daddy the same thing I'm telling you, so there's no mistaking what I want. I want our children to smell the lilac Consuela and I planted near the front door of our hacienda. Let the smell remind you all of me and, how much I love all of you, and how much I love that baby to come. A boy. I know it will be a boy. Don't let them forget about me, Dock."

"What is his name?"

She had already decided, "Frank. He was such a help to us when Daddy and Mother were in the wreck. It's a simple, honest name. We should name him after Frank." She added with conviction, "And Murdoch, do everything you must do to keep the ranch. Your father was right."

I fought to hide the anguish; I didn't want to show my weakness to her. She didn't need to concern herself with tears from me when she already had so much weight on her. I felt like I was being thrown overboard to join my parents and my sister. I could not stop this.

"Dock, do you remember the day of the accident? I know you do. But do you remember what you were whispering in my ear?"

"Of course, my dear."

"Whisper it to me again."

"'Ever-returning spring, trinity sure to me you bring, Lilac blooming perennial and drooping star in the west, and thought of you that I love.'"

I rested my head against her and thought about what was to come. I resolved to fulfill her wishes if the worst happened. She said the baby was to be a boy, and I knew she was right, though I did not know how. She fell asleep, and I left her there, my eyes now watery and red.

***

It was early in the morning of the first week of July when Rachel banged on the door to my room. "Mr. McNeil! Mr. McNeil!" she shouted.

I bolted from my bed and opened the door. "What is it? What's wrong?"

"Have someone go to Dr. Thomas's house and tell him the baby's coming."

The entire house was up in a panic. Henry threw a coat over his night clothes and hurried out the door. It was 2:00 a.m. By the time Dr. Thomas arrived, Anne was well into labor. She had trouble breathing, and she groaned with a deep, exhausted pain.

"Anne, I'm going to give you chloroform to help with the pain," Dr. Thomas said flatly.

"No! I don't want that!"

"Anne, it's the only way we can save the baby. Rachel, hold her still!" Dr. Thomas commanded.

I suspected Anne knew to fear the chloroform, but I didn't know why. "Dr. Thomas, what will the chloroform do to Anne? She's already having a hard time breathing."

"I'm here to make sure the baby is born alive. Murdoch! Leave the room! That's the best thing you can do for her."

Henry pulled my arm. "Murdoch, let's wait outside with Mrs. Townsend. Let the doctor do his job."

Anne cried out. "Dock! Don't leave me! Don't let them give me the chloroform! Please!"

Henry forcefully pulled me away as Rachel fought with Anne to cover her face with the mask. Dr. Thomas began dripping the chloroform. We waited outside, and from the other side of the door, I could hear Anne's weak, muffled pleas. Then I heard no more. Soft murmurs from Rachel and Dr. Thomas were the only sounds for two hours, and then there was a burst of crying from a baby. At that, I couldn't wait any longer, and I burst into the bedroom. The doctor was cutting the umbilical cord, and Rachel was wiping blood and fluid from the baby. I just stood in shock. Henry and Ada ran to Anne's bedside.

"You can't see her like this! For God's sake, step outside!" Dr. Thomas ordered.

Anne's face was blue. Her beautiful blue eyes were now fixed upon some middle distance, pupils wide.

"Rachel, cover Anne. Please, Henry, all of you must wait outside."

Henry guided away Ada, who now sobbed uncontrollably. I followed.

"What has happened? How can she be gone? I don't understand. They let her die. This isn't happening," Henry shakily stammered.

"She's gone," I said.

Henry wrapped Ada in his arms as she wept.

"I thought she was talking nonsense when she said she wanted the boys raised in New Mexico if she didn't live. I thought it couldn't happen. Oh, Ada, our baby is gone!"

Ada stopped crying. "She's on the other side now. God's will. I must tell the staff to prepare the house," she said in a voice with no bottom. She left the room, and she turned all of the family's photographs face-down on her way through the house.

The brownstone, once filled with anniversary revelers, now sunk into mourning. The mirrors were veiled. Black crepe and ribbons adorned every door handle. A laurel and boxwood wreath hung on the front entrance. Frank and Sarah Angel helped to arrange the funeral in Anne's beloved parlor, and Ada's closest friends helped to prepare Anne's body. I told Frank that Anne wanted our baby to be named after him, and he was as pleased as he could have been in the moment.

Frank choked back a tear, recalling his failed attempt to court Anne. "I loved her too," he admitted.

"I know. I believe she loved you too, Frank." She had so much love for so many people.

"Do you happen to have some good whiskey and some sweet

vermouth, Murdoch?"

"I believe so."

"You are a poor bartender, but you can redeem yourself. Manhattan?"

"Yes, several," I replied.

"And one for Anne."

"She'd like that."

The following days were tense at the Townsend brownstone. We were filled with blame, anger, and denial. Dr. Thomas said that Anne's lungs had been weakened by her tuberculosis. She couldn't breathe, and the stress of the birth killed her. I knew it to be the chloroform and whoever put her in the way of Dr. Thomas and his mask. I thought about Consuela's anger at me taking Anne away to New York. She would know exactly who was responsible for this, but it would be me living with the guilt.

Anne was right about her father. Henry blamed me, though not as much as I secretly blamed myself. He tried to persuade me to leave the children in New York, insisting I couldn't raise them in New Mexico on my own. Perhaps he was right. I made two promises to Anne. I knew I could keep my promise of raising our sons in New Mexico. Anne had transformed from being furious with me about how I acquired the ranch to loving the land, the hacienda, and New Mexico itself. She even said my father was right. But keeping the ranch amid all of the turmoil that was continuing with the Maxwell Land Grant, well, that was another matter entirely.

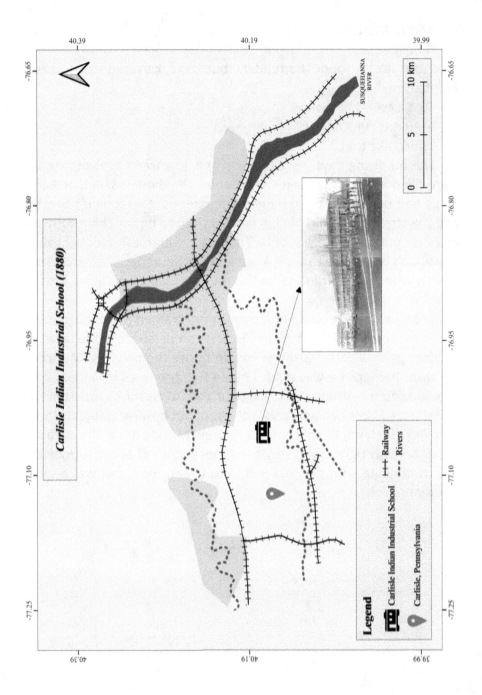

Carlisle Indian Industrial School (1880)

SUSQUEHANNA
RIVER

10 km

5

0

Legend

Carlisle Indian Industrial School

Carlisle, Pennsylvania

Railway

Rivers

258

Chapter XVIII: Captain Pratt

May 15, 1882
Carlisle Indian Industrial School
Carlisle, Pennsylvania

"Kill the savage and save the man."
Captain Richard H. Pratt 1879

"Good morning, Captain. Murdoch McNeil. Thank you for seeing me," he said extending his hand.

"Good to meet you, Mr. McNeil, please sit down," Captain Pratt replied.

Murdoch took a seat in front of Pratt's desk. Pratt was the superintendent of the Carlisle Indian School, which he'd founded in 1879 to assimilate Native children into the white culture. Each child was separated from their parents, by force if necessary; then they had their hair cut for the first time since this was not the Native way. They were issued white man's clothing and were severely punished for speaking their tribal languages. All this was necessary to save the children from the horrors and indignities of the savage existence, at least according to the Department of the Interior.

All those children must naturally be fed.

Henry Townsend, Murdoch's father-in-law, mentor, and law partner had applied his success in obtaining lucrative government freighting contracts into supplying beef for the U.S. Army and the Indian reservations. Townsend dispatched Murdoch to meet with Pratt. Pratt's school, Townsend had reasoned, was much like a reservation, only just for Native children. Native children who would have their Indianness stripped away by force through education. The Carlisle Indian Industrial School would be the model for scores of other such schools to follow – and they would all need to buy beef to feed thousands of students and staff.

"I've spoken with Hiram Price, of course, the Bureau of Indian Affairs Commissioner, and he speaks highly of Mr. Townsend and your ability to supply your beef contracts for the Army."

"Thank you. Mr. Townsend and Mr. Price have known each other since Mr. Price's days in Congress. I believe they met through Edwin Morgan when he and Price served on the Senate Committee on the Pacific Railroad. Our firm assisted with the land grant issues related to the Transcontinental Railroad."

"Yes, Price is a good man. He has a soft spot for children and has accomplished fine things for the Iowa Soldier's Orphan Home. He has some Pennsylvania connections as well."

"Your school, I understand, is a model for a number of Indian schools currently in the planning stages. I want to make sure that we supply the quantity of beef that you need, and then expand to supply the other schools as they come."

"I see. So if you do well here, you'll want to count on my support as you supply the other boarding schools, yes?"

"I appreciate your candor. Yes, that's why I asked to meet you directly."

"I'm sure since you have the support of Mr. Price that the McNeil Ranch will be able to handle our needs. I'm quite proud of our school. Would you like a tour?"

"Before that, there is one other thing I wanted to ask you about."

"Yes?"

"Mr. Townsend mentioned your outing program, and I wonder if I might volunteer my ranch for a placement."

"Very kind of you. New Mexico Territory?"

"Yes, that's right."

"We prefer to place our students a little closer to the school, but we have students from the West. Perhaps we can place a young man with you to learn ranching."

"I was hoping for a young lady, perhaps fourteen to sixteen years old. You see, I have two twin boys who are nine, and a little boy who will be two in July. They could benefit greatly from a surrogate older sister."

"We generally do our placements at the beginning of the summer, but we'll see. Let's talk as we tour. This way," Pratt said as he rose from his chair.

The two men talked as they walked the extensive school grounds. The superintendent's office was in the administrative building, a large two-story structure painted a dull red color with a steep, pitched roof. On either side of this building were attached wings twice the length of the center with almost flat roofs. These wings held additional offices and classrooms. The male students walked the grounds wearing military-style uniforms, and the female students wore modest, full, ankle-length dresses.

Murdoch and Pratt visited a few classrooms, and he could tell by the students' demeanor that discipline was strict. He was not accustomed to seeing Natives with their hair cut short, and he asked Pratt why this was. "Even the girls all have short hair. Is that not a sacrilege to them? They usually only cut their hair in mourning."

"Ah, our rules may seem strange to you at Carlisle. We have strict military discipline. We cut their hair as soon as they arrive, and we burn it, we burn their clothes, we take away any Indian adornments they wear, and they are forbidden to speak their Native language or perform any of their heathen dances."

"I find that..." Murdoch started, and then he suddenly felt sick to his stomach. "Interesting," he finished. He found the policies too familiar to his own displacement as a Highlander.

Pratt continued: "You see, you have to kill the Indian to save the man. That's what these schools are designed to do. You're an educated man, an attorney, I believe. Surely you can see that they all must assimilate into the white culture. On the subject of civilizing the Indian, I am a Baptist, because I believe in total immersion of these Indians into our American way of life. When we get them under, we hold them here until they are well and thoroughly soaked."

"Until nothing of the Indian is left."

"That's right."

"Well, I'm not here to debate the finer points of your educational theory."

"Indeed you are not. In the next classroom we train the young ladies to be seamstresses," Pratt said as he opened the door.

"How clumsy of you!" shouted the teacher, not seeing that she had visitors and they'd entered the room. "You knocked off those spools of thread! You pick them up right now!" She grabbed a little girl about seven years old and flung her to the ground next to the tray of spools she'd dropped. The girl, terrified, started to cry. Some of her young classmates also started to wail.

An older girl, about fourteen or fifteen, stood up and began to dance around the spools of thread on the floor. She lifted her left foot slightly off the ground, set it down gently, then lifted her right foot and moved in a clockwise fashion with her hands on her hips. With each step she sang undistinguished syllables. The children grew quiet and comforted, and they watched.

"Carrie-Mae! You stop that heathen dancing immediately!" the teacher cried.

"My name is Kewanee!" the girl said.

The teacher grabbed her arm. "You will do as I say, Carrie-Mae!"

"I'm too big to throw on the ground like you do with the little ones, Miss Wells," she said.

The children were calmed by the older girl, and they began picking up the spools of thread and placing them back onto the tray. The teacher, embarrassed, finally noticed Mr. Pratt and Murdoch.

"Miss Wells, if you will escort Carrie-Mae to detention, I will look after your class."

The teacher looked at Carrie-Mae. Mr. Pratt opened the classroom door, and they both walked out. "You see what I mean? You must hold them under. That's why I prefer that when we place them in the outing system, they go with Quaker families. They do not hold with the sins of dancing."

"I had a Reverend back in Scotland as a boy. Reverend Beatson. I dare say he would agree with you. You remind me of him."

Pratt had no way but to take it as a compliment. "He sounds like a wise man."

"*Heh, ceilidh,*" Murdoch mumbled.

"What was that?"

"Ceilidh. It's a Gaelic word. I'm a Highlander, Gaelic, from the Isle of Barra. I was born there, and that's where I lived before I came to the States. A ceilidh is a social gathering where we dance, sing, tell stories. Her dancing just now reminded me of a Highland dance. Seems she's good with young children."

"She's not a good candidate for the outing system, if that's what you're getting at," Pratt said. "She's been here since she was twelve, and I can't tell you how many times she's run away. We have to force her back here all the time. She goes to detention at least once a week, sometimes two or three. One of our hard cases. She's stubborn, unruly, and doesn't respond to punishment."

"Is she good at reading, writing, math, the basics?" Murdoch asked, ignoring Pratt's criticisms.

"Her teachers say she is, but her behavior destroys whatever potential she might have."

"Then place her with me. I can take her to tutor my children as a favor to you, and then she won't be your problem any longer. I'm sure Mr. Price would be informed of how helpful you've been to Mr. Townsend's law firm. Where is she from? Does she have any family?"

"When they come here, it's to be away from the family. Savages cannot raise up children. Carrie-Mae doesn't have parents in any case; they died of tuberculosis. We rescued her from the Potawatomi reservation in Oklahoma. We had such hopes for her since she's not full blood, her grandfather was a Frenchman. Some fur trapper from the Great Lakes. Perhaps with enough of her French blood, she can do you some good. I will need to consult with Mr. Price."

Murdoch understood the authority it would take to win over a man like Pratt. "I understand. I'll notify Mr. Townsend that he may expect your telegram today. My children are Mr. Townsend's grandchildren, and I am sure that when I explain what a wonderful help she will be to them, he will make sure Mr. Price is as helpful as possible. You understand, Captain?"

"Yes, I understand the politics, Mr. McNeil."

"I know you understand the politics from your end of things,

Captain, but I daresay we all have more to learn in this country about the other fellow's view. I can find my way out. I'll be back at noon tomorrow to collect Carrie-Mae. We'll need to be on the train by 1:00 o'clock. Thank you for your help." He made his way and then turned his head to address Pratt again. "I'm sure you have a wonderful school here, and you know your educational business. We've agreed on that. I can't help but think that while your heart may be in the right place, your methods may do more harm to the Indian than even killing them on the battlefield. Good day."

Murdoch arrived at the telegraph office in the Carlisle railway station and sent a message to his father-in-law.

> BEEF DELIVERY AT INDIAN SCHOOL SET STOP SEND
> PRATT CONFIRMATION FROM PRICE STOP CONFIRM
> ALSO ADOPTION OF STUDENT CARRIE-MAE DARLING
> STOP PRATT REQUIRES DIRECTION FROM PRICE STOP

Murdoch left directions that the reply was to be immediately relayed to his room at the Mansion House Hotel, and he expected a response within two hours. Then he booked two tickets and space in a sleeping car for the train to Raton, New Mexico.

"Luggage?" asked the clerk.

"Yes, but I'm not certain yet how many bags."

Once he got to his hotel, his reply awaited him. It came from Hiram Price himself.

> PRATT INSTRUCTED TO ASSIST DARLING PLACEMENT AT
> YOUR RANCH STOP CHARMING EXPERIMENT STOP

Murdoch chuckled as he read the message, and he wondered if maybe he'd burned a bridge during his visit. If so, it was worth it. His argument with Pratt today made him miss the courtroom with its heated exchanges and verbal jousting. He missed winning. Perhaps that was why he acted as he did in the moment: His anger up by seeing the child thrown to the ground, his blood pumping in his veins heated by Pratt's lack of compassion. Pratt had been a captain in the U.S. Army, but these were not soldiers he oversaw. Now he had one less troop on his hands, and Murdoch was glad of it.

He folded the telegram and placed it in his pocket. He'd hoped that taking care of some business would occupy his mind, but he could not help but think of the young Potawatomi girl whose spirit prompted her to stand up to her teacher and comfort a small child. She reminded him of Elizabeth and how one of her last happy moments was dancing aboard the *Sarah*.

"Maybe that's just what my boys need," he said to himself.

Chapter XIX: Carrie-Mae

May 16, 1882
Carlisle Indian Industrial School
Carlisle, Pennsylvania

Once I spoke the language of the people, now I speak the language of
the conquerors. I have two hearts and both are broken.
Linda Hogan, "The Two Lives," 1993.

    I settled into my seat on the train across from Mr. McNeil and
averted my eyes from his. At the white man's school, we were scolded
for looking away from our teachers' eyes. "Pay attention! Look at me!"
they would shout. But to the Potawatomi, looking into another's eyes is
a sign of disrespect. So which is it? How do I unmake myself from what
is natural? It was easy not to smile anymore, and my eyes are where
my soul lives, and they could steal that like they stole everything else.

    I wrap my arms around my shoulders, where I used to wear my
shawl with its silver brooches. It was my great-grandmother's shawl,
which she created for me even before I existed. They took the shawl
away from me at the school, too. My arms still feel its absence.

    My long dress covers my arms down to my hands. I sometimes pull
up my left sleeve and rub the scar on my wrist from where the handcuff
dug into my skin. The other end of the handcuff was on the radiator in
the school basement. The hot radiator that left burn scars when I would
fall asleep and be woken by its scalding touch. The matron chained
me there often and said proudly that the school had special handcuffs
made for our small children's wrists. But I didn't find them special. The
scar reminds me to hold onto my hate. And this white man, Mr. McNeil
– what does he want of me?

    Before we left Carlisle, Mr. McNeil and I had a long talk. He asked
Mr. Pratt to step out, but I knew he had his ear pressed to the door. Mr.
Pratt didn't like Mr. McNeil, so I want to like him. I say that Mr. McNeil

and I had a long talk, but he had a long talk, and I had a long listen. He hadn't had anyone to listen to him in a long time. Mr. McNeil chose me to come to his ranch in New Mexico, not to learn ranching as some of the boys at Carlisle had been made to do, but for me to help with his family. Mr. McNeil had three boys and no longer had a wife. He asked if I had heard of tuberculosis. Children here died of it, but my parents died of it before I was made to come here.

There are many ways for boys to be placed in an outing away from Carlisle and for girls to be placed in an outing. I'm fifteen years old. The age when Indian women disappear to be wives and house servants or to have the white men at the school try to treat us as their wives in the night, not only at fifteen. Others, younger than me, whisper their nightmares to each other. I asked Mr. McNeil if that was what he wanted from me. He looked like he'd eaten bad beef and said, "I am not Lucien Maxwell." I don't know who Maxwell is, but Mr. McNeil said he had taken a wife who was barely thirteen.

Mr. McNeil said that he'd always wanted a daughter and that his boys needed a big sister. I would be adopted by him and carry his name. This was familiar to me as the Potawatomi adopted many people from other nations: My grandfather was French, and he married my grandmother and came into our people when they were on the lands to the north, near the Great Lakes. Grandmother learned French and taught me to speak it, too. Now, the country of the white men tells us to stop adopting others, but I can be myself adopted.

Mr. McNeil said that my life would be easier if I carried his last name as his daughter. He would tell the people around him that I lost my parents in an Indian raid while on a wagon train bound for California. I have fair skin and look more like my grandfather, so nobody would know that I was native unless I chose to reveal this. This, too, felt natural, as my Potawatomi elders were in the habit of using our light skin to slip between the different races. Sometimes, this was an acknowledgment of our European kin, and sometimes, this was simply a good business decision. The elders said we'd always done this, but I didn't want to pretend when the Carlisle School came for me. I rubbed the scar on my wrist just then, and Mr. McNeil noticed.

"How did you get that scar?" he asked.

I did not answer.

"It's fine if you wouldn't like to say. Most of my scars aren't on my skin. I was taken from my home, too. I was nine, and they burned it to the ground. We left on a boat. From Barra. That's an island in Scotland."

His voice was unsure, like he hadn't been practiced in talking about it. I pulled my sleeve back over my wrist. Mr. McNeil was looking out the window. This rich white man: how could he have lost his home too? How could he have gone through this as a child? I puzzled over this man who had long ago been treated similarly to my elders.

"Why did they burn your home?"

"Because I am Gaelic. Gaels are a group of people who were not well-liked in Scotland because we lived simply, among ourselves. They removed us from the Hebrides – those are islands – where we'd lived for many generations. They did this so the landowners could raise sheep where we'd once had our farms. They forced us onto ships and sent us to who knows where – Canada, the United States, Australia, sometimes just to die. My parents and my sister died of a disease called typhus on our way to America."

"So your people were removed from your home, too."

"You could call it that."

We talked very little after that, as we were beginning to understand each other. On the train, I spent my time reading books that Mr. McNeil had brought with him for his own reading. My grandmother used to give me books in English and French, too and taught me how to read. After my parents died on the reservation in Oklahoma, I went to many different families and then finally was made to go to the new school in Carlisle to be "civilized." At Carlisle, they did have some books, and I'd already read *Jane Eyre*, which I liked because it was about an orphan and *Robinson Crusoe*, who was stranded in a strange land. Then, they had *Godey's Lady's Book* to teach us how to act in a civilized home and the Bible to save us from the happiness of our tribes. Mr. McNeil's favorite book was good; it was about Marco Paul, who wanted to know everything.

"I've had that book for a long time," he said. "I used to live on a place for orphans called Randall's Island, and someone gave me that book there."

"What was it like at your orphanage? Most of my friends at school had parents, but they were taken from their families and sent to the school to 'kill the Indian in us.' That's what they told us." He ignored my question. "Can you read a page from Marco Paul?"

"I was just on page six. 'There were two modes of acquiring knowledge, said Forrester; the study of books and the study of things.'" I read two paragraphs and paused, finishing with, 'Instead of taking the statements or explanations of others.'"

Mr. McNeil recited next, "' Which is best?' asked Marco." He smiled. "That's the next line, am I right?"

"How did you know?"

"I remember what I read, and that book was my favorite when I was about your age. Miss Walker was my teacher at Randall's Island, and she gave me the book."

I did love to read. "Do you have many books at your ranch?"

Mr. McNeil smiled. "Yes, I have a whole room. Our own library. Books from floor to ceiling!" He made a grand sweeping gesture. "You may read them all if you'd like."

At the end of the second day's journey, we arrived at a large city that Mr. McNeil said was Chicago. We wouldn't change trains until we reached a place called Cheyenne, Wyoming, but we could get off the train and walk to loosen our legs.

"I know a little about this place called Chicago. This is where my people were from before we were sent away on our trail of tears."

"From here? From Chicago?"

"Chicago, Wisconsin, and Indiana. Before that, Canada. They kept moving us around. At one time, we were three nations in one: Ottawa, Chippewa, and Potawatomi. Then we were scattered."

As we headed back to board our train, I began to think that this person at least could have some understanding of me. I didn't want to trust him, and I hadn't decided whether to stay or leave. He said that I was free to return to Oklahoma or wherever I would like at any time. I believed he'd probably put me on the other train to the reservation in

Oklahoma and Indian Territory at any time if I were only to ask.

But going back didn't feel like a good option for me. What awaited me there? The Indian Agent told my parents to sign the paper accepting U.S. citizenship in exchange for a bit of land the U.S. would choose for us. Many people signed the papers. Then they taxed the land, and when we couldn't pay the taxes because everything had been taken from us and the land couldn't be farmed, we were made to sell to the whites. They set foot on their land, and just as soon, they lost it, and then they died.

Something pulled at me to stay with Mr. McNeil. I always was afraid, but I wasn't at Carlisle anymore. Maybe the fear didn't come entirely from Carlisle. I was more afraid of going back home to nothing and nobody than continuing on this path. I didn't like it, but fear came from somewhere that scowled and barked at me like a hungry coyote. I didn't want to go home, wherever home was, but how could I be more afraid of being back with my own people than being with this stranger?

It seemed he wanted to wring the Indian out of me, too. "You could pass for white," he said, and my life would be much easier. It was a different kind of lying. I knew what Carlisle was like. I knew a little bit about what the reservation was like. I didn't know what this new life was like.

The train picked up more passengers in Chicago. We returned to our seats, and three nicely dressed women sat in the row behind us. Their conversation reached my ears; it was French—not the Acadian French my grandmother spoke, but I could understand.

"*Un bel homme est assis devant nous!*" One of them said.

"*Oui, et la jeune femme doit être sa fille. Pas de mère.*" They giggled.

"*Il a de l'argent. Nous pouvons prendre la fille aussi, et pouvons gagner de l'argent sur le chemin des camps d'or.*"

What they suggested was offensive. The women said they saw a handsome man of means, assumed I was his daughter, and schemed to rob him and take me to make money for themselves as they went to the gold camps. Whether by persuasion or force, I had heard of girls my age caught up in such schemes.

I turned bright red with rage, rubbed my wrist scar, stood up, and turned to face them.

I spoke in perfect French, *"Mademoiselles, mon père n'est pas ce que vous pensez. Garder votre conversation civile! Ce n'est pas un bordelo!"* That last word I learned from overhearing my grandfather. I'd hoped that my French was refined enough to give me some authority. I told them that Mr. McNeil was not what they thought, and this was not a brothel where such conversations were welcome.

Mr. McNeil had observed our argument and evaluated it without interfering. "You speak French. Well, I am shocked but not surprised. What did you say to them?"

Before I could decide how to answer, the women rose to exit the train car. One of them stood near Mr. McNeil and said, in practiced English, "Monsieur? You have a very lovely daughter who is very protective of you. You are lucky."

"Just talking between women, Father," I said loud enough for them to hear. The women left.

Mr. McNeil nodded, folded his coat, slipped it under his head, and closed his eyes. I had not actually intended to call him Father, even for effect. He wasn't my father. The word slipped out as if I was pleading to find my real father's spirit. My father taught me to separate a person's speech from their actions.

"Trust in what a person does, not what they say. Words float through the air like feathers. They carry little weight, and they have none of the gravity of truth," he would say.

On the evening of May 22, we finally arrived at the McNeil Ranch, where we had taken a stagecoach for the last part of the trip from Raton to Cimarron. A man named Diego picked us up in Cimarron in a fine carriage. The country was beautiful in its own way, and I felt a part of it immediately. We arrived at the house – a hacienda, he called it – and I paused at the entrance, the smell of the lilacs planted there just teasing out the new air of spring. Everyone was gathered at the front room, and even though it was late May, the fireplace was lit against the spring's evening chill.

"Carrie-Mae, this is Consuela. She's been working very hard caring for the boys and the house. Consuela, I hope you find that Carrie-Mae is a great help to you."

I remained unsure about this with my whole heart, though Mr. McNeil had shown nothing but kindness to me. I settled that I would join this family as I had no other.

"Boys, say hello to Carrie-Mae." Mr. McNeil turned toward two boys who were identical in their appearance, but seemed different nonetheless. There was also a much smaller, younger boy who inhabited corners and shadows.

"She's part of your family now. She's your big sister, and she'll be tutoring you in math, reading, and writing. She'll help with Frank, too."

Mr. McNeil said I would know William by how he spoke first, and he did. "What do we need a big sister for?" he said.

The other one who looked like him spoke now. This was Wallace. "Yeah, we have Consuela, and we're ten years old now; we already help with Frank."

"She needs a family, and Consuela needs help around the house. Your education is important. There is no suitable English-language school in Cimarron for you. Just the parish school, which teaches everything in Spanish."

Consuela, defending her culture exclaimed, in Spanish, *"No hay nada malo en la escuela católica y ambos hablan español bastante bien!"* There is nothing wrong with Catholic school, and they both speak Spanish pretty well!"

"I know you're upset about it, Consuela, but they'll be working in the business world speaking English, and they need to be taught in English. It's nothing to do with how good or bad the parish school is." Better than some schools, anyway, I thought.

"Consuela can teach us in Spanish anyhow," William said. "That's what Mom wanted."

"Carrie-Mae will take up your education where your mother left off, and that's the way it will be. You're not Catholic, and I cannot have you educated in a Catholic school in a language you won't be doing business in. Until the damn territorial legislature quits whipping up the Catholics and the Protestants against each other and using their education as the pawns in their juvenile disagreements, you'll have to be taught here at home. I expect you to all go off to college when it's time."

Consuela dropped the dispute, but my instincts told me that when it came to arguments, she had other ways of winning than arguing. "Diego, would you bring Señor McNeil's bags to his room? Carrie-Mae, did you leave your luggage on the carriage?"

"No, ma'am, I have only this little bag. I lost everything else in the Indian raid," I said, remembering the story Mr. McNeil had drawn up for me.

Now William was interested in me. "Indian raid!" he exclaimed. "Did you see anyone scalped?" And he pranced around, chopping his hand. I ignored his comment.

"William, that's not proper," Mr. McNeil said.

"In town, they all talk about how bloodthirsty they are!" Wallace said.

"Who is this 'they'?" Consuela asked.

"You know, the savages!" William replied.

I was used to comments like this but found them no less disgusting. We are called savages to make us feel ashamed of who we are. I could tell that Consuela was disgusted too. There was nothing savage about my look and attitude. In fact, here I am passing for white. Had I not been born on the reservation, I could have slipped into white society with no notice or suspicion. But in Oklahoma, they came for us. Are "they" more savage than they said we are? They put us on a list, the tribal rolls, tracking every man, woman, and child. They listed all of our possessions.

Then, in 1879, they came back to loot our tribe, our cherished objects, and even our children. As to the children, they took us to Carlisle. I was twelve then. I had never heard the terms half-breed or savage until Carlisle. Now I stood in this white man's living room pretending to be white, in danger of losing what little of myself I'd held onto despite Carlisle. Life was better here; it sure couldn't be worse, but I'd have to make a special effort to hold on to my ways in private.

Mr. McNeil's voice distracted me from my troubles. "Boys, take your sister upstairs and show her to her room."

Wallace motioned that I should follow him up the stairs to a

273

bedroom at the end of the hall. William picked up Frank and followed us. I had never had my own room, but here, I would.

"Our room is right across the hall from yours. Frank sleeps in Dad's room," Wallace said.

I placed my bag on my bed and crossed the hall into the boys' room. Two beds were lined up on one wall, toys strewn about the floor, the top of the chest yawning open as if asking them to pick up and put them away. William sat Frank down in the middle of the floor, and he began to play with wooden letter blocks. I sat on the floor with him.

"How old is Frank?" I asked.

"He's almost two," Wallace said.

William sneered. "He's why we don't have a mother. Runt killed her when he was born."

"Runt's what we call him when Dad's not around. He was born early, and he was really tiny when he came out," Wallace stated matter-of-factly. "If you're going to be his sister, you call him Runt too."

I'd heard plenty of disrespectful speech aimed at children at Carlisle but very little among children themselves. On the reservation, this would have been unthinkable. We'd been at the receiving end of so much abuse, from the Indian agents to the matrons, to the male staff, and sometimes even from our peers when they were forced to be part of disciplinary tribunals. We were made to be cruel to each other, so the staff bore no responsibility for sending us to the school's jail. But outside when we were forced, I was shocked to see children this young be so inventive with their cruelty toward one so tiny and blameless.

"Do you understand how hurtful these words are, William and Wallace? You're certainly old enough to know, aren't you?"

William scowled.

"Dad doesn't like us saying that," Wallace said.

"I don't care. It's true, and I'll say what I want," William said.

"What's true?" Murdoch said as he entered the room.

I just smiled. "The boys were telling me that Frank was born very small."

"Yes, that's right. He was born very early because my wife had tuberculosis," he said sadly. I tell the boys that he's likely to catch up

274

to them, maybe even grow bigger. Boys, Carrie-Mae will start with your lessons tomorrow, right after your chores. You have a busy day, so better be off to bed." Murdoch picked up Frank. I followed him back down the stairs, where Consuela waited.

"Carrie-Mae, you are always most welcome here. The boys will have a good tutor. Señor McNeil, may I show Carrie-Mae where to put Frank to bed?"

"That will be fine, Consuela. Carrie-Mae, my room is off the large hall."

"Frank is never a problem," Consuela told me as I carried Frank to Murdoch's large bedroom. "He's the sweetest boy. William, well, you must be careful around him. His temper. I've never seen a boy so angry, and not just because his mother died. He has always been like that. He throws things, and he threatened me once with a kitchen knife. Diego was there and took it from him. I don't know..." She shook her head. "I was sure he wanted to kill me. He was only nine years old then." She shivered as if a cold wind came through her soul.

"Señor McNeil didn't believe me about William. Earlier, he didn't believe me that his wife had tuberculosis."

"What about Wallace?" I asked.

"He's afraid of William and will do whatever his twin tells him. Your room has a solid door and a good lock. Make sure you use the lock at night."

After we put Frank to bed, Consuela left, saying she would be back in the morning to help with breakfast and show me where the children were with their lessons. Murdoch sat in a prominent chair, ornately carved blond oakwood with a deep crimson cushion. It seemed out of place among the plain adobe walls.

He had quite a large glass of whiskey in his hand, and it was almost empty. He got up and poured himself a second. I don't care for the smell of whiskey.

"Food is in the kitchen if you're hungry, Kewanee."

"I'm not hungry, thank you. I don't know what to call you. I know you said I have your last name, but I'm not ready to call you Father."

"Call me Dock," he said, gulping from his glass.

"Dock?"

"Yes, Anne calls me Dock. Called. I miss hearing it. Someday, I'll tell you how I got the nickname, but for now, you should get some sleep," he slurred.

I have never felt such sadness tumbling out of a person. I walked up the stairs, and halfway, I looked down at him. He sat in his too-large, too-ornate chair, rolling his glass between the palms of his hands, his gaze far away as if the home had no walls.

"Goodnight, Mr. Dock," I said.

Chapter XX: Consuela and Kewanee

May 23, 1882
McNeil Ranch
New Mexico Territory

"I'm nobody, who are you? Are you nobody too?
Then there's the pair of us-don't tell!
They'd banish us, you know."
Emily Dickinson, 1891

I awoke to a familiar smell. At the Indian School, it was a forbidden smell. My parents used sage smoke—we called it smudging—to remove bad feelings and cleanse away negative things. It would take too many sage bundles to clean Carlisle Indian School. My senses looked for the other medicines of our prayer fire: sweetgrass, tobacco, and cedar, but they weren't in the air. There were clothes laid out for me. I put them on and went downstairs.

The smudge stick lay in a beautiful jet-black clay bowl, its sage smoke gently drifting upward. By instinct, I placed my palms into the rising smoke and pulled it over the top of my head. I turned my palms downward as if scooping water from a waterfall and pouring it over myself. I took my left hand, pulled the smoke again, and washed down my right arm in a motion. I did the same with my right hand. I felt clean. I breathed in the sweet scent and closed my eyes. I was free of the filth of the Indian School. All I had left were the ghosts.

"Who are your people?" Consuela asked.

I slowly turned to face her. She stood in the entryway to the great room. I couldn't tell if she was frowning or smiling. The sage brought good memories, a tidal wave of cleansing memories, and now I could free those memories to live in my new place. The dark memories—my too-tight dress, my too-tight handcuffs, Pratt's too-tight voice—were washed out into the void where they belonged. The sage healed. I risked honesty.

"Neshnabek," I said. "People who don't know us call us Potawatomi. It means People of the Place of the Fire."

"And Neshnabek?"

"The True People," I answered. "How did you know?"

"Many people practice cleansing. You moved your hands through the smoke as if it were water. Yesterday, you looked sad and angry when William said what he did about us Natives, and that was not an expression I see on those with light skin."

"It's difficult to hide my emotions when I'm treated poorly. But you said 'us Natives'?"

"I am Spanish, true—my mother was Castilian from Mexico City. My father was Tewa, and others call his people the Puebloans. In the Tewa tradition, the man is chosen by the woman and goes to live with her and her family and is required to marry within one's own tribe. My father loved my mother so much that he traded his existence as Tewa for their love, but he passed the traditions and customs on to his children."

"That must have been difficult for him."

"Yes, the Tewa and the Spanish have a history of war and hate. The Puebloan revolt against the Spanish happened two centuries ago, but between the groups, it was also yesterday, today, and tomorrow. The Spanish don't care much for the Tewa, and the Tewa don't care much for the Spanish."

"I was raised similarly—we were all displaced today, yesterday, tomorrow. There is no beginning or end to time; it's all to be lived with. That's why our tears happened today, yesterday, tomorrow for us, too. The Anglos don't understand this."

"There are underlying cracks in the pottery of the different cultures here," Consuela continued. "The glaze covers them, and they can't be seen. The cracks remain, and sometimes the pottery breaks, even though it's handled carefully. Why pretend to be white? You're like the pottery."

"I think that Mr. Dock wants to protect me from those who hate us, steal our lands, and want to destroy who we are. He's afraid for me, so he has adopted me and has given me his name, using a story about an Indian attack so that people will accept me as white. When Dock was a boy, he was forced from his home too, and like me, his parents died. He was alone, like me. Now his wife is gone too," I said.

"Anne was his great love, like my father's for my mother. I miss Anne too. She was a dear friend and cared about everyone, no matter their clay. She loved the smell of sage, so I light the bundle each morning, and it will find its way to wherever she is." Consuela looked as though she carried a weight just then. "There's not much laughter in this house since she walked on. Mr. McNeil blames himself for her death, and he thinks I blame him too. You and I will have to keep the pottery in this home from breaking."

"Is he the reason that Anne died? Do you blame him, too?"

"I'm a curandera, a healer, yet he wouldn't listen to me. Anglos often don't, even when they try to respect our ways. Anne and I looked forward to the day I'd help with her baby as I was trained. She had tuberculosis, and I thought she needed to stay here, close to the garden, with my medicines."

Consuela hesitated, wondering if she'd said too much, but now wasn't the time to hold back the truth from someone who'd already been deceived too much.

"Anne and Mr. McNeil fought, Mr. McNeil and Diego fought, and I tried not to fight with anyone. Then Anne got a telegram from her father in New York City, and that was that. She became very sick after she went to New York, and she couldn't withstand the childbirth." She paused. "But I don't blame him for her death. The Creator makes that decision."

I need more than just sage; I need our medicines from each of the four directions. I believe Consuela will help, even though we've only just met. There's a kinship between us—I can sense it.

"I need to gather our four medicines for the prayer fire. Our sweetgrass is the gift from the north. It's the wishkpemishkos; it keeps evil at bay. Our cedar, kishki, is of the south and protects the body from disease. Sema is the tobacco from the east, and the creator sees its powerful smoke, while the sage, wabshkebyek, is of the west to purify

279

the home."

She grabbed two baskets. "They took my eagle feather from me at the school... I need to move the smoke skyward on an eagle feather if the creator is to receive our prayer." They had cut my eagle feather to shreds at Carlisle, so the creator wouldn't be able to hear us.

"We have all of these things; the four medicines are abundant here. We can gather them before the boys come in from their chores. My father left his eagle feathers to me. Let's do this quickly. William sees everything he can, and if you don't want the whole territory to know you are Neshnabek, don't leave any clues. Once he latches on to an idea, he doesn't quit until he finds someone out."

I knew William for less than a day, but I knew this without Consuela telling me. She reassures me. "He won't find out from me. And Mr. McNeil was right; you will have an easier time passing as Anglo. It's hard enough being Castilian and Tewa, and I don't think it would be easier for you to be treated like a squaw. Harder, probably, if William finds out."

We took Frank with us, our silent witness. We walked a short distance to her healing garden and gathered what we needed, nothing more. As we gathered, we talked of what we would teach the boys and how we might handle them. Consuela put our kit in a cedar box just before William and Wallace came back into the house.

I was relieved at Consuela's knowledge of the boys. William did not like me, and he made it clear I would neither be his mother, nor his sister, nor his teacher. He was intelligent but argumentative, with a temper as quick and explosive as a snakebite. Consuela warned that he would test me on the first day and was nice enough not to say "and every day after this."

"I don't want to do math! You can't make me! I already told you, you're not my teacher!" he screamed.

"William, you have a lot to say today!" Consuela handed him a pine staff. It was beautifully carved, about five feet long. I recognized it but did not let it show on my face. "Would you like to tell your sister what this is, and who made it?"

"No."

"These are the rules: If you have the staff, you must speak or pass it on. Do you want to pass the staff to your brother? He could tell your sister what it's used for. Or maybe Carrie-Mae should have it. Or maybe Frank can say…"

William could not stand the insult that a toddler would be better to hold the stick than he would. "It's a talking stick! You and Mom made it! And I hate you!"

He threw the stick at me. I stepped out of the way, and it clattered on the floor, landing against the wall with a crack. I almost said something, but Consuela shot me a look to tell me it wasn't necessary. She walked over to the talking stick and held it out again to William.

"If you want your sister to have the talking stick, you have to hand it to her."

He took the stick, drew back as if he were going to throw it again, and then handed it to Wallace.

"Dad said you speak French. Can you talk some French?" Wallace said. He handed the stick to me. William turned bright red, and his breath turned shallow and fast. His jaws clenched, and through his teeth he made a whistling, wheezing sound. He started throwing things around the room. What kind of family have I come to? Consuela stood calm and waited for William to finish.

When he tired of his game, Consuela spoke. "William, I'm sad that you can't have lunch with us, but I'll make food for you once you straighten up the room and put everything back in its place. Now, before the math lesson begins, we'll all tell you something we like about you. I admire how much you like to write your lessons. Wallace?"

"William, I like how strong you are!"

"Carrie-Mae?" she said, using my new family name.

I was at a loss for words. I was familiar with this custom but didn't know which other tribes used it. Was this also a Tewa custom? This operated on reasoning that was familiar to me. When someone acted against the tribe's rules, the member was punished, but after punishment, each person would tell the transgressor something positive about themselves. The transgressor then knew that, despite their punishment and what they had done to earn it, they were still valued and that our love for them would be strengthened by our forgiveness.

"William, I admire how much you love your mother," I said. Even though I had known William for such a short time, I knew this.

He just scowled.

Mr. Dock arrived home from work at the Cimarron freight office. Consuela and I made dinner, but our little makeshift schoolroom was still a wreck. William was brilliant, but he was stubborn. Consuela expected this, and I think she was even used to it.

"I see you were teaching math today," he said, trying to make light.

Consuela asked to see him in his study. The twins were occupied with playing in their room, and Frank sat with me on the floor while I read to him about Marco Paul from Mr. Dock's favorite book. Consuela and Mr. Dock emerged from his study, and Consuela looked like she had gotten hold of some bad medicine for a good purpose.

"William! Wallace! Come down here!" he commanded. And they clattered downstairs. "I understand, William, that you misbehaved rather than do your math. You threw a lot of things. Before supper, we will get this room straightened up together. If we all pitch in, we can have supper soon." His voice moved from a command to a request to a plea. "Carrie-Mae, you can help us too."

William's smug expression surfaced immediately. "William is the cause of this. He should be the one to straighten up the classroom. I need to help Consuela with dinner."

To show I meant it, I marched into the kitchen.

"Consuela, he's making Wallace help in there, and I'm furious! He wanted me to clean up the room! Well, I won't do it—I just won't! I'll go back to my people in Oklahoma. I'm too old for the school to catch me again!"

Consuela asked, "What is your true name?"

I glanced toward the kitchen door to make sure no small feet were casting a shadow at the bottom. "Kewanee."

"Kewanee. If you leave here, that is exactly what William would want. I cannot make you. You're free. But they need you, and I need you. And now you understand why I cleanse this place every morning."

"How can I break bread with them now? I can't sit at the table with them this evening."

"I'll fix a plate for you at the table, and you can take it upstairs if you wish." And so she did. She didn't speak a word to the boys or to Dock, and I was silent also. However, I didn't go upstairs. Eventually, Diego came in to get his plate, and then Consuela went back with him. I finished my meal and, still without speaking, went upstairs to await the next day and decide what I should do.

The following day, I woke up early to greet Consuela and not have to face Dock or the boys and their questions alone. They hadn't woken up yet, being accustomed to the smells of breakfast as their cue. In the kitchen, Consuela showed me her father's eagle feather. I had my own eagle feather before the school came for me, but this one was far prettier. It was a foot and a half long, a dark brown color that lightened to the color of chocolate toward the tip. With such a feather, the creator was sure to hear our prayers. Consuela put it in her cedar box to protect it.

I wasn't ready to eat with Dock, and the twins at the breakfast table, and nobody asked me to. Then instead of asking if the boys wanted their lessons, he announced that William and Wallace would be going with Diego today to help brand the new calves.

"If you expect to inherit this ranch someday, you must start acting like cowboys. You will resume your lessons in the fall, but you are to work the range through the summer."

After they all left to go to either their branding or their freighting, Consuela and I ate our own breakfast together, which put me in a sound mind to smudge the hacienda. I prayed outside first to the four directions. For three years, I could not pray in my own way. I prayed for peace in this family. I prayed that the creator gives people a way to walk a good path even if they don't know how. Each of the four directions must come together to show us this way, and they'll do so in their own time.

Afterward, I used the eagle feather to help smudge each room, moving the smoke with the four medicines over Consuela, and she did the same for me. We have the four directions over us. We cannot be broken.

After smudging, we had only Frank to watch over, and I liked him the moment I stepped into the hacienda. He was never a bother and stayed like a shadow, trying to escape notice while still being around us. I was still tense around William, who did his best to show me that he was glowering at me, and I did my best to ignore him. But I started eating at the dinner table with Dock and the boys. On Saturday morning, seeing that I was including myself, he said he would show me the wide sweep of the ranch and that Consuela could take care of Frank. Dock asked William to saddle a horse, Skip, for our ride.

To my surprise, William did not complain or whine, even though Skip was his mother's horse. When he handed me the reins, I took them and checked the cinch, which was loose and would have slipped the saddle upside-down had I tried to get on. I tightened it and glanced with my side eyes at William, who wore a smirk. Having avoided disaster, I placed my left foot in the stirrup and swung onto Skip with my right leg.

And Skip leaped into the air. Not out of spite like a mean horse, or because he was soured from not being ridden, or even because he didn't like anyone but his departed owner. But because he needed to buck. He shrieked in pain.

I swung my legs back to avoid getting hung up in the stirrups and jumped off to the side, landing on my feet. William was laughing but stopped when I didn't fall or get trampled.

Murdoch reacted in shock, "Carrie-Mae! Are you alright? William! What did you do to Skip?"

I didn't even have to brush off my leather dress. I was fine. Growing up with horses and being bucked off was nothing new. I'd practiced this move on the reservation with the horses there. I just didn't expect it here.

Everyone talked about their horses like people, and when anyone spoke of Skip, they bragged that he was the best-trained horse on the range. He was spunky but not dangerous. I suspected something. "I'll go put up Skip and get another horse," William exclaimed.

"No, you won't," I asserted. "I will check Skip and put him up. I'm checking this saddle blanket first."

Dock stood silent. William moved toward Skip and tried to grab the reins, but I pulled them away.

"Back off!" I yelled. "He is upset enough!"

"William, let them be. Get over here," Dock said.

I carefully pulled off the saddle, taking care not to drag it across his back, and lifted off the saddle blanket. A foot-long piece of barbed wire was snagged on the underside of the blanket. It was positioned so that the wire lay directly on Skip's spine. The barbs had rubbed away his coat, and his back was bleeding. I was sick at the thought of someone doing this to a horse.

"Dock, you need to see this," I said.

He looked at the ground and shook his head. "Come with me, William." He checked the wound and stared at his son. "Why?" was all he could say.

Never one to stand by in shock, I went into action. "Where's the salve? Tack room?" I called for the other twin. "Wallace!" And when he came running out, "Show me where the salve is! I need to put up Skip and take care of him." Wallace nodded and led me into the barn. I said, "Dock, I might be a girl in your world, but I'm nearly full-grown. Deal with this or I will. That little shit has to sleep sometime."

Dock said nothing, but I saw a glint of fear in William's eyes for the first time—then something like surprise at the emotion. Wallace helped me put the salve on Skip's back, and like it usually is with horses, all was forgotten with a bit of hay and a little grain. I sat in Skip's stall and closed my eyes. Skip was getting used to my smell without feeling pain this time, and I was enjoying the earthly, connected scent of horseflesh.

Dock came in shortly. "I'd still like to go for that ride. We have other horses. Wallace says he wants to stay here, and I have William stacking wood, enough to heat the whole range for the winter. That should keep him out of trouble until we get back."

"Why is he like that? Is he hurting from his mother's death?"

"I don't know. William always had a streak about him even before Anne died. Then he got worse. Anne had a way with him. Sometimes, I think I should send him back to New York to live with his grandparents, but I promised Anne I'd raise the children here in New Mexico. Anyway,

I couldn't just send William; Mr. Townsend would want Wallace and Frank too." He struggled to retain a tear. "Anne loved that horse. He knows that."

He opened a stall with a grey roan horse. "I'll saddle her up."

"I'll do it," Carrie-Mae insisted. "She can get to know me a bit as I tack up."

"The way you sat, Skip, I should have you breaking the colts with the rest of the hands."

"I've done it before."

"Well, you can break William then. Let me know when he misbehaves, and I'll back whatever punishment you and Consuela decide is best. I'll let him know that, too. He'll be so tired from stacking all that firewood, his butt won't see a saddle any time soon."

Delayed by these antics, we rode well into late afternoon, ignoring any need for lunch. We'd filled our canteens as we left and refilled them at the spring that fed the Cimarroncito on the way back. The ranch was spectacular, and I loved the clean, light, cool air. We reached Diego and Consuela's home, and Murdoch asked that I stay with the horses so he could talk privately with them. He came out afterward with Frank in his arms and lifted him up to me. I gladly took the little one, and he giggled as I nuzzled the ticklish spot on his arm.

"I talked with Diego and Consuela about William. I let them know that I cannot tolerate his behavior and that he must work quite hard if he misbehaves. I hope that's the end of it," Murdoch said.

I'd hoped so, too, but it was not the end. That night I awoke with a nightmare from the Carlisle Indian School. I was so ashamed of what had happened, but I resolved to bring Consuela into my confidence. She would be the first and likely the only person I would ever tell. I sat on the side of my bed, shaking and covered in sweat.

Something in the air changed.

I felt the floor through the soles of my feet. A slight vibration. The floor popped, and the doorknob turned, then wriggled loudly.

I knew who it was, and I was not afraid. There were worse monsters in the night to come after girls. I opened the door prepared to confront the prowler, but I wasn't surprised to see nobody there. My senses told me another Native must be about from the movement. How could it have been William? But it must be him. At supper the following evening, I had my answer.

"I know we usually hunt in the fall, boys, but our Ute friends asked if we can use some elk meat, and I'd never turn that down. Did you want to go with them again?" Murdoch offered.

"Yeah, last time they taught us how to move through pine needles without making any noise!" Wallace said. "William was really good at it, weren't you, William?"

"Yes, I am," William said with no humility.

That night after the boys went to bed, I crept into their room and stood next to William as he lay sleeping. They couldn't hear me. I was too quiet.

I sat down on William's bed as gently as a golden aspen leaf falling on the forest floor. He didn't awaken. I moved my face close enough to his that he could feel my breath on his cheek. He woke up, startled. Wallace sat upright; he was awake too.

"My door is always locked," I said, never wavering my eyes from William's. "Even if you could open it, I would be awake before you ever reached me. I can take care of myself. I am not afraid of you, little boy."

I walked out of their room and shut the door.

Chapter XXI: William

June 13th, 1885
McNeil Ranch
New Mexico Territory

"Said Aristotle unto Plato, 'Have another sweet potato?'
Said Plato unto Aristotle, 'Thank you, I prefer the bottle.'"
Owen Wister

"Goddamn it!" Murdoch took a large pull from his whiskey bottle. "Now Commissioner Sparks is trying to have all but 99,000 acres of the Maxwell set aside! Damn Washington bureaucrats!" He'd just emptied the whiskey glass and, having no use for it with the bottle here, had set it on the low table next to his leather chair. "He says the Colorado and New Mexico suits should be 'vigorously prosecuted!'" He launched his glass into the fireplace.

The boys jumped at the glass breaking. Murdoch had come home after stopping at Lambert's. He was drunk when he arrived, and he continued drinking when he got to the ranch. The twins had worked the spring cattle all day, and Frank, only seven, stared wide-eyed at his father's temper, at something he could not understand.

"How does this affect us?" Consuela asked.

He picked up the telegram he'd received from Townsend and read it out loud, though his words slurred.

"Article in *Times*, June 12. Sparks recommends reduction of Maxwell to 99,000 acres. Will lose ranch if suit successful."

"Henry sent that, and I don't think he'd mind at all if I had to give it up and move back to New York City. He has never gotten over wanting the boys back there. He has never stopped blaming me for Anne. He'd sure as hell not hire me back."

"But you bought the land from Mr. Maxwell," Consuela stated.

"I don't think it was Mr. Maxwell's to sell. Colorado and even New

288

Mexico are now bringing lawsuits against the Maxwell Land Grant Company. If they are successful, then the land enters the public domain. We could lose it all."

"Carrie-Mae, help me bring in the dinner. Boys, wash up and set the places. Frank, you come in the kitchen with us," Consuela asked. She did not think the boys should worry about losing their ranch.

She was also worried about the change she saw in Murdoch. He'd been drinking more and more since Anne died. Soon after, he lost the contract to supply the Indian schools with beef. It happened on January 21, his birthday, as though someone cursed him.

That year, Hiram Price, the Commissioner of Indian Affairs, resigned. Price was a strong supporter of Mr. Townsend and had extended the contract to McNeil Ranch as a favor.

Captain Pratt, in charge of the Carlisle School, claimed that Murdoch's beef was substandard and that many of the cattle had arrived infected with disease. Checking with the lots in Pennsylvania proved this untrue, but Pratt intensely disliked Murdoch and made sure the claim filtered up to Indian Affairs. The rumors that the cattle were bad spread through the rest of the federal government, and now there was a rift between the McNeil Ranch and all the federal contracts, and between Henry Townsend and Murdoch.

Another telegram from New York. Long holding the blame for Anne's death against Murdoch, Mr. Townsend became convinced that he'd also been mismanaging the business.

TOWNSEND MCNEIL DISSOLVED STOP
PARTNER DISSOLUTION PAPERS COMING STOP

The last tie to New York had been severed. Thirty-one years was the longest relationship he'd ever had—longer than Anne, longer even than his parents.

Henry Townsend would now only be the grandfather to the McNeil children. He would be nothing to Murdoch. A surrogate father, a mentor—had it ever been genuine if it could be ended so abruptly? And by telegram. He felt numb, emotionless, and detached. He had no capacity for empathy, and those around him suffered for it.

William was incredibly hostile, and Murdoch was indifferent to it. He couldn't see the anger in him through the veil of alcohol, nor could he see the worry in the faces of those around him who cared about him. His overwhelming grief drove all emotion from him.

Had he cared, he would have seen Wallace spend more and more time on the range and avoid home as much as he could. It didn't matter. None of it mattered anymore. Murdoch drained the bottle.

The next day, he cast about trying to make work for himself in the wake of the dissolution. Afterward, he sloshed home in the saddle and thought that the twins had been more argumentative, not less so after he adopted Carrie-Mae. Whatever had happened between them, he knew William and Carrie-Mae were at the center of it.

Carrie-Mae had not forgiven William after he injured Skip, and Murdoch, if he allowed one of those increasingly rare moments of honesty with himself, admitted that he hadn't forgiven William either.

Carrie-Mae reminded him so much of Anne, or rather the daughter Anne might have had if Murdoch had listened to anyone but himself when it had counted. Carrie-Mae was smart like Anne. She was headstrong like Anne when she had the courage of her convictions. She had strength and poise and was not intimidated. She was eighteen now, ready to be sent off to school.

Murdoch would soon counsel her to court a young man who would listen to her and allow her the respect of knowing her own mind. Until she went to school, Murdoch insisted that she become the primary tutor to the twins and Frank. He suspected that Consuela continued her education in Spanish and the healing arts once he went into the office, and he did not so much as approve as to allow it to happen passively.

This tutoring had to fit around ranch work now, not vice versa. The twins were thirteen, and the cows were just now throwing their calves. Murdoch's business had lost so much freighting revenue to the railroads. The beef contracts dwindled, and so did the number of hands kept on the ranch. The boys could no longer enjoy the comforts they once had, and now they had to work full-time, just like regular hired hands, taking orders from Diego.

"Dad, we have to talk to you," William said as the children sat at the dinner table.

"Boys, maybe not the best time. He has a lot on his mind," Carrie-Mae cautioned.

William pressed. "It's important."

Wallace picked up the thought. "We're working just as hard as the other cowboys. We should get paid the same as them."

Murdoch set his fork down mid-bite. "Is that right? Shall I also take your found out of your pay? You know what that is, yes?"

Wallace snorted. "Room and board. And you don't do that with the other hands."

William crossed his arms. "Yeah, we asked them."

"You're both thirteen. Too young to come on at other ranches and earn your way. Give it five years. Then, you can pull a man's load and not have to be taught everything by a foreman. It takes Diego longer to teach you both how to cowboy than it would be to have one of the hands do the work. Christ, if I paid you what you were worth, you'd wind up paying me. I had to serve an apprenticeship, too. Now eat your dinner."

"You always talk about working for Grandad when you were twelve. He paid you too; that's what you said." Wallace displayed an unusual defiance, and it galled Murdoch that he had a point this time.

Murdoch pushed himself back sharply from the table. His heavy wooden chair screeched against the floor. He filled his glass and poured it down without pausing. He felt like exploding with rage, but instead, he laughed. He laughed so hard that he sat back down with tears streaking his face. He wiped them with his napkin.

"William, sometimes I just want to wring your neck, then you argue. You come up with some point so convincing, some fact, that I just can't argue with. I have a mind to send you to law school early. You're right."

William beamed.

"Your Granddad took me on at twelve, about your age, and made me into an apprentice law clerk." And now we're nothing, he thought. But Murdoch pushed that aside. "It is up for debate as to whether clerking

291

is as hard a job as cowboying, but that is an argument for another time. I will pay you both $20 a month and found. The last day of the month, you'll stand in line like everyone else and get your pay. If you don't like the offer, just like I tell the rest of the hands, you can negotiate a better rate somewhere else." He took the whiskey bottle up to his bedroom and let the proposal lie.

"That's half what the other men get paid!" William said.

"Yeah, but twenty bucks!" argued Wallace, who smiled at the thought.

"You boys are... Well, you should just look around you. Don't you know how lucky you are?" Carrie-Mae had enough.

"I don't..."

"Not another word, William. Not another word," she cautioned.

The following day, Murdoch struggled into the freighting office. He could not remember the last time he'd felt well. He arrived later each day and left Lambert's bar later each night. Both Consuela and Carrie-Mae tried to exert some influence as gently as they dared. Consuela told him she was worried, and he would just say, "I know, I know."

Carrie-Mae told him he was needed by the ranch's boys, her, and everyone. She tried to build him up, but he was drowning in grief and the bottle.

After Paul let Murdoch have his morning "adjustment," the foreman gingerly opened the office door.

"Boss, you've got a foreign guy out here askin' to see you."

"Just a moment. I'll come out there," Murdoch said.

"I'm Marinus Pels from the Maxwell Company," the man said, extending his hand.

"Murdoch McNeil. What can I do for you?"

"I manage the Maxwell Land Grant property for a group of Dutch investors. I understand you're both an attorney here and a ranch owner who purchased the property from Lucien Maxwell some time ago."

"True, and it is common knowledge. What is it you want?"

"Americans are so direct. I like that. As you know, there are many squatters on our property here. Five hundred fifty-two to be exact."

"I don't have anything to do with the land grant. Not the settlers, not the legal wrangling, and certainly not the politics. I pay attention to my cattle and my business. So I will tell you the same thing I told a certain preacher when I moved out here: I have no interest in being the least bit involved with the Maxwell. I do not wish to work for or with your company. Frank Springer is the attorney you want, but I suspect you know that. And if you want to know about my land, the patent is on public file with a full description of the property."

Pels continued as if he'd not heard the speech. "I wondered about your neighbor, Mr. McDaniels. He's on my list of settlers who haven't paid their rent. He's hard to contact."

"He has clear title too; he owns his land."

Pels riffled through some papers. "No, unlike your land, which, of course, I checked – your land patent, bill of sale, legal description, it all looked perfect. Unlike McDaniel's..."

"You're Dutch? European?"

"Yes."

"Then you've heard of Patrick Sellars, Gordon of Cluny, the Highland Clearances?"

"Necessary for their needs at the time." Pels had not detected any accent in Murdoch and answered honestly.

Now Murdoch could not help but revert to a more Gaelic tone and attitude. "I'm from the Isle of Barra. A Highlander. Not American, though I am now. My family was forced from my home in 1851. 'Needs at the time,' but it affects real people. In your case, you're clearing out 552 of them the same way. People with families. People who were already here. I could not care less, Mr. Pels, about your damn clearances."

Pels grew red. "Anglos, Mexicans, Aboriginals, they all need to pay rent, buy the property they're on, or leave. We don't round them up and ship them off. We even pay them for their livestock and improvements. The offer is very generous."

"With the challenge in the courts? You Dutch are gambling an awful lot on our legal system."

"You said that you were not interested in the Maxwell Grant?"

"I'm always interested in legal opinion and argument. I'd never have become an attorney if I wasn't. My interest is purely academic." But I am still a Highlander, after all, he thought.

"Then what is your academic opinion? Do you think this will go to the Supreme Court?"

"I do."

"Hazard a guess as to their decision?"

"I could argue it either way and win, as I told the attorney general in New York. He's a good friend of mine as it happens. My own academic opinion," he said with sarcasm, "is that I can't imagine our own United States government meant to give away almost two million acres of good homestead land. I can't see the Supreme Court nullifying Homestead Act claims given legally and honestly when this land was legally and honestly open for settlement. I do not believe that this country will rule in favor of a foreign government in order to have a few individuals become rich."

"Mr. McNeil, look at Lincoln County, an Irish concern battling for control against the English, Catholics and Protestants at each other's throats, but it's all about selling New Mexico to foreign concerns. If the Supreme Court rules that all but 99,000 acres must go back into the public domain, then all the European shareholders in the Maxwell Land Grant Company will see their money disappear."

"Investors always take risks. How is this any different?" Murdoch's eyes gleamed at the argumentation.

"They invest in not just the land, but in the confidence of the American economy and the policy officials that make it succeed. People like this Chaffee fellow, Chilcott, Holly, and all the others in the legislatures. If the Maxwell Grant is annulled, foreign investment loses confidence and leaves – not just in the Maxwell Grant, but also the railroads, banks, buildings, coal, silver, gold, and all mining. It will leave along with any sense of trust."

Pels shrugged his shoulders. "Maybe it's better for the squatters—" Pels then corrected himself—"pardon me, homesteaders and Mexicans. Maybe nullification is even better for the Ute and Apache that your government has decided must be expelled from their own lands. You know where the decision comes from. Back in New York, the money and the laws flow in tandem. Maybe the Court will dress it up in legal

294

rhetoric. But, Mr. McNeil," Pels argued, "if the Court rules against the Maxwell Land Grant Company, wouldn't your ranch be nullified as well, being part of Lucien Maxwell's boundaries?" Murdoch felt chilled by the argument. Pels was right. He told him so but qualified it.

"My opinion isn't just about what's best for me. I want the strongest legal arguments. Yes, as you posit, money influences policy and law, but it doesn't necessarily do so here in New Mexico. The Territory easily defies both policy and common sense. I'm not naïve. Perhaps you are right, not in the matter of justice, but in a matter of the way the Court operates. Soon enough, we will hear from the Supreme Court, and we will either reargue the case, or we will react some other way."

Just then, Diego interrupted with William and Wallace in tow.

"My apologies, Mr. Pels. Diego, what can I do for you?"

"Lo siento, Señor, but we need to pick up corral fencing. I've set the boys to work on it and thought I'd bring them into town to help load the wagon."

"Mr. Pels, may we resume this another time? As I said, I'm not sure how you find Mr. McDaniel." He wouldn't be one to help harass an honest man if he could help it.

"Dad, I just saw him head into Lambert's," Wallace said.

"That's good," Mr. Pels said. "I'll head right over there. Thank you, young man." He left after his quarry.

Diego pulled the wagon around to load the timber. William hung back in the warehouse and watched Pels cross the street to Lambert's.

"Hadn't you better catch up with Diego and Wallace?" asked Murdoch.

"Dad, half-pay isn't right."

"You're still on that? I have other business just now. You're paid what you're paid, and you're not in a position to argue the point. Now get back to work; they have enough to do without having to do your share as well." And he closed his office door behind him.

William stood a moment, slapping the palm of his hand with his leather gloves. "Damn old drunk," he whispered. "I'll get what's due me, one way or the other."

Unaware of William's resentment, Murdoch sat at his desk, tired and shaky. He pulled the whiskey and glass from his bottom desk drawer, telling himself he poured just enough to keep off the shakes. Half-heartedly, he turned to his messages, fishing for freighting jobs and trying to save as many Army beef contracts as possible via telegram.

He thought about McDaniel having to deal with Pels. McDaniel had gotten his land via the Homestead. He'd said he had some more Homestead Act claims too. Who knows how many of them Pels planned to seize, or if that would even stop at the ever-shifting boundaries of the Maxwell.

By late afternoon Murdoch finished the freighting work and decided to have a quiet supper at Lambert's. He hoped he wouldn't have to talk with anyone and didn't want to go home only to sit at the dinner table and argue with William. He was so tired of hearing about the damn Maxwell Land Grant and the court challenges and the legal turmoil. The land was unstable, not physically but legally, and the controversy bubbled up like a spring poisoned with alkali water.

In his corner of the world, Murdoch's day had been somewhat successful. He disputed Pratt's slanderous and libelous claims with the forts and the other Indian schools and even prepared a potential suit against Pratt since he had demonstrable damages. He contemplated whether to officially file the suit while he tucked into his steak. His peace was interrupted by McDaniel coming through the door, drunk.

"There he sits!" Jim roared. "Mr. McNeil of the great McNeil Ranch! You should all know that Marinus Pels of the Maxwell Land Grant Company was in his office today taking a meeting! Sure, McNeil says he's not on their side, but hell, he's here workin' for 'em!"

"Jim, please," Murdoch begged.

"McNeil even told that son of a bitch, Pels, that I was over here so he could come demanding rent money for property that isn't even his! How many of you have had that little Dutch snake getting in your face about the rent? And if you haven't yet, you will! How much they pay you, McNeil? Desperate for money since you wasn't Townsend Freighting Company anymore? Your own father-in-law giving you the heave!"

"That's enough, Jim!" cried a voice from behind the bar. Bobby had seen worse violence in Lambert's with less at stake. "You can't come in here anymore. Now get out yourself, or I'll toss you out!"

McDaniel looked at the crowd for support, but they were all murmuring and shaking their heads. Someone yelled, "Go on then, or we'll get the sheriff!" McDaniel walked past Murdoch and refused to look at him.

"I'm sorry, Mr. McNeil," Bobby said. "I should have banned him from here a long time ago. We all know what you've been through, and we know you aren't tied up in this Maxwell business. You've got as much to lose as anyone."

Murdoch remembered the most important lessons Henry had taught him, and he was ashamed that he'd been forgetting those lessons in the wake of their partnership dissolving. "You are always on stage," Townsend would say. "Emotions are a tool. Use them to provoke the right emotions in others. Your own emotion should never be unplanned." At least he wouldn't drink any more tonight, not until he got home. He finished his meal and rode home, sneaking looks over his shoulder.

The family was just finishing dinner when Murdoch finally arrived at the hacienda. He paused to breathe in the lilacs at the entrance, though he had lately been in the habit of walking past them, closing his nose to the memory. Anne had wanted the lilacs to be a special and pleasant reminder of her love for him, but now they just reminded him of how lost he felt without her. This night, however, the lilacs seemed to erase his self-blame and help him heal. He made a mental note to ask Consuela to cut some blooms and bring them inside.

Consuela had already left with Diego for the evening, and Carrie-Mae was cleaning the table with the boys. William was unusually talkative and cheerful, but Wallace started in with his chatter first.

"Dad? Les wants to work with me on my shooting. Is that okay?" Wallace asked.

"Who's Les?"

"One of the new ranch hands. Diego says he's real good."

"Target practice then? You shoot well enough, but I'll practice with you when I get home tomorrow night. We can take the Winchesters out and kill a few bottles."

"No, I mean really shoot."

"Really shoot?"

"Yeah, Diego just hired Les, and he showed us how fast he draws. He's so fast!"

"A six-gun?"

"Yes, most of the boys our age are already shooting Colts. Some of them go .45, and some of them go .38."

"You want to learn how to fast draw? It's not a game, son. The quick draw is meant for killing. It's not a sport." Murdoch paused. "I'll talk to Diego about it. I don't know Les, but Diego does. How's the corral coming?"

"Fine, Dad," said Wallace, trying not to be impatient.

"I know how an apprenticeship works, Dad," William scoffed. "It's when someone makes you work and doesn't pay you enough."

Murdoch patiently ignored William's comment. "An apprenticeship is about training. Apprentices make much less than journeymen. Before I worked for your grandfather, I was a printer's devil, working in a print shop. Since you're apprentices and still learning, you make half wages, and that's fair."

"Sure, Dad, that makes perfect sense," William agreed quickly. "Right, Wallace?"

"I think it's great! I'll be able to get a Colt .45 and holster in no time!"

Murdoch eyed William suspiciously. He couldn't tell if his son was being sarcastic or serious. "Maybe save for college," Murdoch suggested.

Carrie-Mae interjected. "Murdoch, may I borrow the Marco Paul book? I never finished reading it when I first came out." Murdoch reminded her that she had full access to his library. "I know, but that book is special to you. I like to ask permission."

He went to the library to retrieve the book, but it was not on its shelf. I know I put it right here, he thought, and now there was an empty space instead. He asked the twins if they'd borrowed it, though since they usually had to be prodded to read, this was unlikely. They said they didn't.

"I don't have it either, Daddy!" said Frank, who could barely read letters.

"It's not there, Carrie-Mae. Ask Consuela tomorrow, or I can. Maybe she borrowed it and forgot to tell me. She probably has it."

"Then can I start with your law books? I know most of them are in your business office, but the ones you have here would be a fine start. Which one should I begin with?"

"Why on earth would anyone want to read legal procedure?" Murdoch asked.

"You said to start thinking about college..." She pulled out a letter from the Union College of Law in Chicago. "I wrote to them."

"Can you be admitted to the bar, being a...?" Murdoch looked at his sons and didn't finish the sentence.

"A woman?" Carrie-Mae covered. "There's already been women graduating law school."

"Boys, look after Frank. Carrie-Mae and I need to tend to Skip. Diego says he's got a cough. He's getting old, you know." They walked out together, and Murdoch paused at the entrance.

"Anne planted these lilacs. I know, I say that often. They seem to have a deeper meaning for me lately. It's a little less painful walking by these, smelling them, and remembering her. She'd admire you for going to law school, and she'd insist that you go. She wanted to be a nurse, you know. Dr. Gregg said she could have even gone to medical school."

They walked to the barn well out of the range of their voices.

"Carrie-Mae. Kewanee." He so rarely said her true name. "If the school finds out somehow that you're Potawatomi, they'll dismiss you. Even if they never find out you're Indian, finding a judge to admit you to the bar will not be easy. Maybe impossible."

"There's women that have done it."

"I know, and most of them have husbands who are solicitors. They have a reputation of merely being female law clerks. They don't argue cases."

"I could clerk for you."

"I'm not practicing anymore; you know that."

"You said this would be a better life here in New Mexico. More opportunities. If I'm to have a better life, I must be able to have a say in its direction and meaning. I can't live a better life if I'm to marry a rancher, have children, and try to scrape something out of the dirt only to see some foreign land company come along and take it all. I've seen what goes on here. Folks are being shoved off their land after they work it and improve it for years."

Her tone grew more resolute as she continued. "I've already been through this, as has my family and my nation. Our tribes are learning quickly that if we are to keep this from happening, we must learn legal language. White legal language. We must learn the rules of the fight if we are to win it. I can't forget who I am or where I come from, and I am an Indian from ancestors who have been fighting and losing for a century. I know where the battleground is. It's not here. It's in the court."

Another thing I've done to myself, thought Murdoch: I've created children who win arguments with their parents, adopted or not if she can argue that well, then she must become an attorney.

"Let me see that letter. You'll need letters of recommendation from solicitors. A judge would help. Grandfather Townsend can write one. For now, look through case law and read the rulings, but don't forget context. If you still feel this way by August, I will help you apply."

***

The lilac bush decorating the hacienda entrance with its plumes and perfumes began to die. Slowly at first, like they were gasping for air, then quickly. By mid-June, the leaves looked as though they had just had a choking ice storm. The purply blooms withered and fell, leaving the branches brown and bare. Here and there, a few splotches of green and purple clung to life, which only made the bush look ghastlier.

Consuela thought if a plant could scream, this is what that scream looks like. She tried everything she could do to save it, perhaps because it was Anne's and probably because she couldn't save Anne when she had the chance. Consuela watered the bush, and maybe she babied it too much, but this did not seem to be a case of drowning.

She worked aged cow manure into the soil, caring for the lilac bush like she would have cared for her friend. Nothing worked, and the lilacs continued to struggle, wither, and die.

"Diego, have someone dig that lilac out. It won't make it. I can't stand to look at it every day, like it's choking. Like it's Anne. Please tell Consuela it's not her fault, and I value her efforts a great deal. What the hell could have happened to that bush?" Murdoch wanted answers, but sometimes, New Mexico took beautiful things and destroyed them.

Diego decided to dig it out himself. Even the grass around the bush was dead, changing from lush green to yellowish brown the closer it got. He pulled out the roots and smelled them with his trained farmer's nose. Salty. The soil reeked of salt. He grabbed a handful of dirt and rubbed his hands together until the excess fell off, and then he smelled his hands. Salt. Someone had been putting salt water in these roots.

He'd seen William watering the lilacs from a bucket early one morning before his chores. He'd smiled then to see William caring for another living thing, caretaking his mother's legacy. Now Diego found the bucket in the barn. It was dry. There were salt crystals in the bottom.

"I don't know what to do about this, Consuela. I don't want any more of their family problems. The boy is a monster," Diego said. "Should I tell Mr. McNeil?"

"He might not believe you, but then he might. If he does believe you, I don't know what he'll do to William, and I don't know what William will try to do to us. I wish Anne were still here. She had a way of keeping him under control. He pulled that knife when he was nine. You stopped him then, but now he is much bigger. More dangerous. Should we leave this place?"

"We need the income, and our home is on his land. We must tell him. But how do you tell your Patrón a thing like this? How do you tell him his son has been so cruel to him?"

**

301

"George, I'll have a box of those cigars and have your man put a case of whiskey in the back of my carriage."

"Sure, Mr. McNeil. How have you been getting along?"

"Well, thank you. Say, how's that for a coincidence?" Murdoch said as he looked through a few used books on the store's corner shelf. Most of the books were dime novels left here by disillusioned thrill-seekers, but not all were. "I have this book about Marco Paul! It was one of my favorites as a boy," he said, opening the front cover.

Then he saw it.

"How did you get this book? It's mine. You see? It went missing recently, and here's where I wrote my name on the front cover," he said, holding the book out.

"Barbara said one of your boys came by selling a few books. Barbara?" George called out.

She came from the back. "Oh, hello, Mr. McNeil. Good to see you."

"How did you come by this book again?" asked George.

"Your son, Mr. McNeil. Not sure which one; they look alike to me. He said you knew, and that you were paring down your library. Brought in some law books too. I didn't think much of it since you say you don't practice anymore. Was that not right?"

"I am embarrassed to say so, but no. He was not to sell these. Whatever he sold you, I would be happy to buy them back, whatever your asking price."

"I'm sorry to say that we've already sold the law books. All we have left is the Marco Paul. Please take it, no charge, and my apologies. I should have known to ask you first."

Murdoch left the store with Marco Paul once again tucked in his arm. He'd made a decision. He thought of William, recalling the time long ago when he had opened all the family's Christmas presents. He and Anne had eventually laughed about it, but now he wondered if that seemingly small incident was something he should have taken more seriously.

His own Christmases as a boy had been sparse yet full of family, caring, love, and wonder before they were forced out of Bara and sent to America. In this new country, he experienced a Christmas chained to an orphanage wall. The knife incident had terrified Consuela, making her afraid of him, but Murdoch refused to believe it had happened. It did happen. Murdoch knew it but was too stubborn to admit it to himself. What kind of man would William become? Who was he?

Murdoch tried to give William and Wallace everything they wanted to make up for what he lacked as a child. Perhaps it was too much. "I tried to be a good father," he thought, "but I wasn't." The realization shook him to his core, and he questioned himself: If he could not be a father to his children, what was he?

He sent a few telegrams, replied quickly, and bought tickets to the Raton stage the next morning. They would take the railroad to San Francisco. He wondered what Anne would think of his decision. He hoped she would understand. He wished she were here. Maybe if she had been, he wouldn't have needed the tickets. He missed Anne's counsel when it came to the children.

He left the freight office and headed home with the carriage at a comfortable walk. He was in no hurry, and he felt strangely assured. As he crossed his property line, Diego approached him at a gallop.

"Señor, I must talk with you; it won't wait. I found what was killing the lilac bush. I don't know how to tell you."

"William." The air left him heavily.

"He poured salt water on the lilacs. I thought he was watering it because of his mother. When I pulled the bush out, I smelled the roots and the dirt. I found the bucket he used and there were salt crystals on the bottom. It took him so long to kill the lilacs like that."

Murdoch grimaced. "At least the last ten days, I could see him from my window. Don't mention anything about this to the rest of the family or the hands. Even Wallace. I'll take care of it."

"Consuela is afraid of him, Señor McNeil."

"You both should stay away from the hacienda tonight. William and I are going to California tomorrow morning, to the Belmont School for Boys. It's a military school. I will be back alone in about ten days. Check the telegram office in case I need anything from you."

Diego tipped his hat and rode to the warmth and safety of his own adobe home, and to his wife, relieved.

304

Chapter XXII: Fire and Snakes

May 1, 1888
McNeil Freighting Company
Cimarron, New Mexico Territory

"Revenge only engenders violence, not clarity and true peace. I think liberation must come from within."
Sandra Cisneros

The oily smell of the kerosene burned his throat, but he paid little attention as he flung the five-gallon can in all directions. He focused on coating McNeil's office, soaking the desk, his damned law books, and his filing cabinets. It was 2:00 in the morning and still dark. He tripped over a box, and the can fell from his hands, the kerosene splashing onto the floor and his clothes. He thought I'd have to be careful when I light the match.

The freight office contained more than paper. The company held explosives for shipment to the railroad. He judged that with any luck between the kerosene and the stores of dynamite, they'd see this explosion all the way to Springer. He moved quickly to the barn, where he didn't need to waste any kerosene. The hay would catch quickly enough. The draft horses shifted sleepily in their stalls. He opened the gate and let them out to go stray.

He'd start the fire outside in the freight wagons and place a rag in the kerosene jug's spout. From there, the fire would spread quickly to the inside of the building, the barn, and the corral. There would be nothing left. He took out his tobacco pouch, rolled a cigarette, and pulled the matchbox from his pocket. He took a long puff, then slid the cigarette inside the matchbox. This he placed next to the jug. The improvised fuse would leave him a short time to get away, mount his horse, and ride up the hill to watch the place burn – and explode.

He'd ridden his horse away behind Lambert's and then moved

south out of town to the high ground. He'd barely gotten up the hill before he saw out of the corner of his eye the bright flash of the freight yard as it started to go up. Then, a great concussion that rattled his teeth spooked his horse and threatened to unseat him. He might have heard windows breaking in town if he'd been closer. He enjoyed the sight thoroughly and smirked.

He saw people pouring out of the St. James Hotel now. Others came running from the mill, the livery, and all directions toward the blaze. The fire was too intense to put out with their buckets. They were powerless. He heard a rider approach from town and ducked his horse behind a boulder. The rider galloped past, not noticing him.

***

The rider jumped off his horse outside the McNeil hacienda and pounded on the front door. Murdoch groggily opened up. The cowboys in the bunkhouse awoke and ran onto the porch to see what the commotion was.

"The freight's on fire!" the rider yelled.

The men quickly saddled their horses. Murdoch, still half-drunk, changed out of his nightclothes. The men had saddled a horse for him, and Wallace raced out to see his father half-fall out of the stirrup.

"Dad! You're in no condition!" Wallace called out. "We'll ride out; you stay here!"

"Let me alone. I'm going," he said and managed to climb up.

The cowboys rode out fast, Murdoch following, and Wallace trailing behind his father with growing worry. They saw the ominous orange glow on the horizon. As they got closer, the vision became apocalyptic. The entire building was engulfed in roaring flames, sending thick, black smoke spiraling into the night sky. Even at a distance, the acrid smell of burning wood and ash filled their nostrils, stinging their eyes and throats. The town had given up on saving the freight building and was wetting down the St. James Hotel.

As Murdoch crested the hill south of Cimarron, his horse stumbled on a loose rock. The horse recovered, but Murdoch, in his inebriated state, could not hold on. Wallace watched as his father was thrown headfirst from the saddle, his body pitched through the air before smashing into a large boulder. He did not move.

Wallace reached his father, jumped down and ran to his side. Blood pooled around his father's head and soaked into the dirt, the metallic smell of blood mixed with the smoke in the air. Wallace cradled Murdoch's head in his lap and he rocked back and forth, crying. The blood was warm and sticky against his skin and quickly soaked through his blue jeans.

"Father." Wallace's voice was a hoarse whisper, his throat choked with smoke and terror. In the darkness, he was not able see his father's open lifeless eyes that stared up at the sky. He couldn't feel his Father's chest rise and fall. He knew he was gone. He wanted to scream, to do something, anything, but he was frozen, his body numb with shock. The reality of his father's death crashed over him, and his tears mixed with the blood on his hands.

William, where are you? Wallace's mind turned to his brother, and he pictured William at the military boarding school in California, safe, far away from this nightmare. A sob caught in his throat. If William were here, would he even care?

"Someone, please! Get Doc Gregg!" Wallace's voice broke as he called out, desperation lacing every word. He looked around wildly, hoping someone had heard him, that someone could make this nightmare go away. The flames roared behind him, an unstoppable force, as the darkness closed in around him.

From the other side of the boulder, the arsonist saw the man fall. He saw the boy jump off and run to him. He heard the boy cry out for the doctor. He watched as Doc Gregg galloped up. The doctor kneeled beside the boy and his father, and someone brought a wagon. Even though the fire still raged, the night was quiet, except for the sound of Wallace sobbing. The arsonist slipped away unnoticed. *God knows I didn't want that to happen,* he thought. *I didn't mean it. God forgive me.*

He rode up to his house. He slipped inside quietly, but Emma was still awake.

"You smell like kerosene," she said. McDaniels said nothing. "My God, what did you do, James? What did you do?"

He sobbed against her shoulder.

***

Carrie-Mae had spent the last three years at Union College of Law in Chicago. She was in the previous two weeks of class preparing for her final exams. She excelled at the law, though she didn't have quite the recall of Murdoch, who she now called Father without hesitation. When she was home for Christmas during her first year, she'd called him "Father" for the first time since confronting the French ladies on the train. Something about being away from the family had made her feel closer to them.

Now, there was a telegram.

She showed her professor the telegram and asked one question.

"What do I do?"

She took her exams early, passed them easily, and headed home. Union College promised to send her diploma after her.

William was seventeen now. He'd promised to come home from military school for the holidays each year, and then every year, he'd not show, simply to hurt his father. The last Murdoch had heard of William directly was him vowing to escape from what he called his prison. His behavior angered and alienated Carrie-Mae and Wallace, but their feelings did not affect William. When he received the telegram, he informed the superintendent of the military academy that he'd be returning home for his father's funeral and would not be returning.

Diego met Carrie-Mae and then William at the stage in Cimarron. They passed the burnt and blackened shell of the McNeil Freighting Company. The town of Cimarron still smelled like charred wood. Carrie-Mae thought it smelled like a morgue, a perverse memorial of twisted metal, charred timbers, and broken dreams. Twenty-five jobs went up in flames with it.

Carrie-Mae cried when she saw it. William smirked, though she saw that he might be smirking at her sorrow just as well as the injury done

308

to his father's work. If he'd known that half the town suspected him of having snuck back to set the fire, he might have been even more satisfied.

The funeral was at the ranch and was attended by almost everyone in town. Telegrams of sympathy poured in, mainly from New York. Despite his troubles, Murdoch McNeil was admired and well-thought-of by more people than he could have imagined.

Townspeople had suspicions, and there was talk about who set the fire and why. Most believed it couldn't have been an accident, but nobody had seen anything that would necessarily point to an arsonist. Rumors flew hot, and all of Cimarron was wrapped up in the why and how.

Murdoch McNeil was buried next to Anne McNeil on their ranch, in a part of the world he wanted nothing to do with but that Anne had loved and called home.

The year before, the Supreme Court decided that the Maxwell Land Grant and Railroad Company had the exclusive title to 1.7 million acres of land. Their agents filed legal action against all who lived on their land without paying rent. Some residents had lived on the land for generations, and the Maxwell Land Grant and Railroad Company forced them off just the same. It was no wonder that many people in Cimarron thought it was their agents setting the fire.

Maxwell's agents spread gossip that one of the squatters did it. As to Murdoch's death, everyone knew he was drunk, and Wallace witnessed it. The horse may have stumbled, but the horse was blameless. The attorney, in the eyes of the town of Cimarron, had been killed by his struggles with the drink.

Murdoch had amended his will just before Carrie-Mae turned twenty-one. After Anne died, he didn't have the heart to look at it. His health was failing more than anyone knew, but Murdoch got around to it for Carrie-Mae. He wanted assurance that his children would be cared for, and he did not want them to have to return to New York to be cared for by their grandfather.

Thomas Hernandez, who practiced law in Las Vegas, New Mexico, was chosen as executor. While he had the technical skill and experience to write his own will, Murdoch had also been taught that a man who serves as his own attorney has a fool for a client. The week after the funeral, Thomas Hernandez made the trip to Cimarron by coach and requested a meeting with the McNeil children, Diego and Consuela.

"Before his death, your father and I talked at length. He decided that, given her legal education and her age, Carrie-Mae would become the guardian of William, Wallace, and Frank McNeil until they reached the age of majority."

William fumed and interrupted. "How is this legal? She's a woman; they can't do that!"

"Your father knew the law, William, and I imagine that Carrie-Mae – congratulations on the bar, by the way – knows the law almost as well. This is New Mexico Territory. It's legal for single, married, or widowed women to own, inherit, and buy property. They may serve as legal guardians as well. Carrie-Mae, you'll find that some men will present themselves to you with the idea of marrying into money. At least once word of the will gets out. We will talk about that later." He sipped some water. "In any case, his wish is that Carrie-Mae take full legal responsibility for you boys and the ranch."

He turned to Diego and Consuela. "It was his wish also that you two stay on and help Carrie-Mae. He has also deeded a portion of the ranch, where your home and gardens are, to you." He handed Diego the deed.

William blurted out, "So the damn drunk didn't leave us anything?"

"If you will be patient, young man, and let me continue."

Hernandez was irritated, but he'd been warned beforehand about William's attitude.

"In the last few years, his business was not as fruitful as he'd have liked. Nevertheless, he put away a small fortune, which he invested well. McNeil Freighting has no debts to settle, nor does the McNeil family. Since you are focused on the next part, William, I will read it to you.

"'Sound mind et cetera. Once the minor child reaches the age of majority, he is given one-fourth of the total liquid assets, stocks, and bonds held in trust by the executor. If the minor child graduates from college before the age of twenty-one, at that time he will be entitled to one-fourth of the total liquid assets, stocks, and bonds.'"

William was by now enraged. "That's still not fair! Carrie-Mae isn't even a part of this family! I don't give a damn if Dad adopted you or not; you're not blood kin!"

Wallace shook his head, his voice low and tinged with bitterness. "You think blood makes a family? Where were you when I was holding Dad in my arms, watching him bleed out? He was dying, William. You weren't there then, and you're not here now."

William stormed out of the room, looking back to see if Wallace would follow him. His twin stayed rooted to his chair, eyes fixed on the floor.

Hernandez sighed in exasperation. "Death is always hard on a family, I know. I hope he will calm down. If you like, I can read the entire will to you. There's a list of his belongings, things that were special to him, and he's designated these things to each of you."

"No, it doesn't seem necessary at the moment. We can read through Dad's will when we're ready. You have a copy in your own files, correct?" Carrie-Mae asked.

"Of course," Hernandez gathered his satchel. I must be going. I stopped at the bank and signed the papers so you can access your father's accounts. I'll be transferring the legal holdings into your name, Carrie-Mae. It will take some time. I can get you an approximate total of his liquid estate, not including... oh, I'm getting into the details again. You've just finished law school, and here I am talking to you like a layman."

Frank sat with Consuela in the front room. Wallace looked down at his hands. Diego didn't know quite what to do with himself. Carrie-Mae walked Hernandez to the door. After she saw him out, she turned.

"Well, it looks like we have a ranch to run!" she cleared her throat. "Diego, Consuela, I hope you..."

"We'll stay on, of course," said Consuela. "Where would we go, after all this time? This is our home, too."

"Diego? You handled the budgeting for the ranch, so will you put together some figures for me? Most of the freighters are out of a job

311

thanks to the fire. I want to see if we can afford to add any of them to the work here. I don't even know who the manager was over there! Can you find him and have him come by?"

She turned to Wallace. She remembered what it was like to see her own biological father die, though not as violently. "Wallace, stick close to Diego. He'll teach you as much as he can, as fast as he can. You'll be all right. We will make sure of it." Wallace nodded.

"Do you want me to try to talk to William?" asked Diego.

Wallace spoke up. "No, leave him be."

"Miss McNeil, I must tell you that the fire was not an accident. And that is all I have to say about it," Diego said. He was not one to fall into rumors.

"I know, Diego," she responded. "I suspect we'll never know who held such hate for Dad. Who would even be capable of such a thing?"

***

It was a full month before William had the chance to go through his father's desk. Carrie-Mae met with a judge about her law license in Santa Fe. Frank was with Consuela, who he looked at as a real mother. Wallace was out on the range with the rest of the hands. William shook his head in disgust. Imagine Wallace as a cowboy, he thought.

He didn't trust Carrie-Mae. He wanted to know just how much money he was entitled to. He'd read the will, but all it said was he'd get one-quarter of the assets when he turned twenty-one. Christ, four years away, and he thought this was utter bullshit. There had to be another way to get what was rightfully his.

It infuriated him that Carrie-Mae, an adopted sister, would get a full share. She wasn't even blood, he kept repeating to himself, his anger boiling over. She had no right to the McNeil fortune. Maybe he'd hire his own lawyer to outsmart her. She wasn't family, and she sure as hell didn't deserve a dime of their money.

And then he saw a yellowed card in the back of Murdoch McNeil's desk.

The card said, "Carlisle Indian Industrial School" and then

underneath, in smaller letters, "Descriptive and Historical Record of Student." The following line read, "Carrie-Mae Darling. Agency: Oklahoma. Nation: Pottawatomie." William's eyes widened, and he fell back into the chair.

"What is this?" he said out loud.

On the next line was the date she arrived: May 3, 1879. She was discharged on May 16, 1882. Reason: Outing. Adoption to Murdoch McNeil. Beneath that were remarks. William read them. She was always in trouble. His father had adopted a damn Indian. A squaw, he thought. He couldn't believe it.

I can destroy her, he told himself.

Law school? No way they would have admitted her if they had known she was an Indian. He was sure they would revoke her degree. His three years of military school had taught him to think strategically and with precision. What else could he do?

Option one: Do nothing. Wait four years. Take the money and leave this shithole. Option two: Tell Carrie-Mae nothing and send the record to the Union College of Law with a letter telling them exactly who she's been. Option three: Show her what he'd found and force her to give him her share of the inheritance in exchange for his promise not to tell the law school. Option four: Show her the record and let her wonder what his next steps would be.

William liked the last option the best. It would be four years of seeing her wonder and worry.

Worth waiting for.

The following evening, after supper, William asked to speak with Carrie-Mae in their father's study. There, he grinned and pulled out the card.

"I found this in Dad's desk," he said triumphantly. "You're just a god-damned Indian squaw! I knew there was something about you that you didn't belong in our family."

She reached out to take it, but he pulled it back. "Oh, no, you don't. I'm sending this to your precious law school. You spent three years there getting your law degree, and I'm going to watch them take it all away from you. No way they'd have let you in as a squaw. Isn't that fraud?"

"Why do this, brother? Why? Skip your own mother's horse. The lilacs. Stealing from your own father. How you treat your own brother! Now this! I might have been able to understand some of it – being angry, selling the books – but the lilacs?"

"Mom's dead. The lilacs should be too."

"But why? Do you need your share of the money now; is that it? I couldn't even give it to you if I wanted to. Mr. Hernandez is the executor, not me."

"Oh, I can wait for the money. You know what I really want, Sister?" He spat the word at her. "I want you to leave and never come back! If you leave, I won't send them the card. Unless you come back."

"You think I care a toss about a piece of paper? Let me tell you something about our father you must not know. You think he cared about this ranch, the land, the money he made. Well, he didn't. He told us how he lost his home as a boy, but in the end, he'd made peace with it. Dad said he wished he had never gotten our land the way he got it. I don't know what that means, but he did."

William opened his mouth as if to silence her, but she was not having it.

"No, you're going to listen for once. He cared about education. He gave us all an education. That's the one thing people can't take from you, ever, because it's in your head. Why do you think he sent you to military school? He cared about you, you fool! He cared about all of us. He could have forced you to go to college, even, but he thought you would do better where he sent you."

She paused and controlled her breathing. "They can take back their diploma, but they can't take back what I know. And I am not afraid of you!"

"You should be. If you think the only thing I can do to you is send this card to your law school, you're wrong. You could just disappear. Indian women disappear all the time, and no one gives a shit. No one will look for you! Hell, even if the sheriff comes looking for you, all I have to do is tell him that some squaw came in here and weaseled their way into our family. You'll be long dead and nothing but dry bones before anyone finds you! Dad's real children will split all the money three ways, not four. So, you can either go away on your own, or I will make you go away, and you'll never be able to come back. Not ever."

He turned and left.

Consuela had been sitting on the front porch near the open window to the study. She brought sage bundles, sweetgrass braids, cedar, and tobacco. Carrie-Mae had been gone from home for so long, and Consuela was ready to help her smudge. Now that William was home, this was a requirement, all four directions.

She didn't tell Carrie-Mae that she had heard everything from the open window, and she didn't tell her what she was planning. She knew William was planning to kill her, and Consuela would not let that happen. Carrie-Mae didn't need to trouble herself with that. Consuela gave the four medicines, made some small talk with her, and said she would return in the morning to help with cleansing. Afterward, she would send Carrie-Mae into town and make William and Diego breakfast.

The following morning, they smudged. William slept late, and by the time he had awakened, Carrie-Mae was already in Cimarron with a list of baking supplies and a few pie tins. Consuela went to the boys' room and asked William if he wanted some bacon and eggs. "I'm making breakfast for Diego, too," she said.

William came down to sit at the table. They all had breakfast. William was quiet. Consuela was not.

"Diego, I heard again about that miner that was supposed to have hoarded a bunch of gold from the Aztec Mine."

"Just stories, mi amor. It's gone on for ten years. It's all gossip, why listen?"

"I thought the same too, but Miguel has a map, and Maria told me about it. He won it in a poker game at Lambert's. Tells you right exactly where he left the satchel!"

"Who cares? It's not our map." Diego was no treasure hunter.

"Don't be mad at me, please."

"What did you do?"

Consuela fixed her face like she was apologetic. "The money."

"What money?"

"The money that Maria and Miguel owe us. The Sanchezes owed us that $250. I traded it for the map."

William listened intently to this conversation but acted like he was still half-asleep and tired from his long journey home. He yawned a couple of times for effect. He'd heard the stories, too. A miner worked the Ajax up on Mt. Baldy, squirreled away gold nuggets, and smuggled them out without anyone knowing. Then, the prospector got drunk at Lambert's and bragged about his fortune. The next day, he was killed in a mining accident. Ever since then, people had been looking for the hoard.

"Oh, no, mi amor!" Diego was upset. "Tell me you are just kidding with me!"

"This is the real map, Diego!" She pulled out a hand-drawn map. It was yellowed and had been folded and refolded so many times that the corners were ragged. "You see? Here's the Palisades Sill, which looks like cathedral steps on the south wall. It's easy to find, but only if you know where it is. See?" The map covered half the table when unfolded, and she bent it a little to hide it from William's view.

A shot rang out from outside. One of the cowboys knocked on the door and came in. "Boss, we've got a mountain lion out here, I think." Diego jumped from the table and ran out the door, with Consuela close behind.

In her haste, she had forgotten the map sitting open on the table. William grabbed it. "That's the one thing you gave me, you old drunk. Just like you, I remember everything I see. This is better than any diploma from any fancy school."

He grabbed a paper from Murdoch's study and jotted down the details. Then he replaced the map on the table, turning it just so as though he had never touched it. Consuela would never know that it had been moved. Then William went outside and left his plate on the table. The help should clean it up, not me, he thought.

Consuela watched as he rode off. She smirked, but William did not catch it. It was three miles to Cimarron and another seven up the Canyon to the Palisades Sill. William planned on cashing in the fortune and living anywhere he wanted to for at least the next four years. The treasure was sure to be there. Consuela was level-headed and had often dismissed the rumors of the gold. For her to spend $250 on this map meant she was absolutely certain that the gold was there.

Well, he thought, it won't be there by the time she gets around to it. She'll just think that it was another tall tale. Diego will be furious at her for wasting their money.

William reached the Palisades Sill along the Cimarron River. He checked his copy of the map. The canyon air was heating up, and the steep walls of igneous rock reflected this warmth coming from all directions. There was a secondary ridge of bare cliff that ran at a steep angle up to the face of Palisades Sill. Enough space between these ridges allowed for a climb up to the top, though it would be difficult. He secured his horse, crossed the river, and climbed the Sill.

The rocks were sharp and loose. They gave away easily, and William slipped down the Sill. He turned sideways and stepped gingerly up the loose rock, placing a hand, then another, then a foot, then another. He searched for handholds. His leather gloves began to shred. No matter a few cuts and scrapes, he thought. I'll be rich. I can buy a thousand bandages.

Three-quarters of the way up the face of the Sill, William reached a landing just where the map said it would be. The landing was about three yards square, not so big that anyone would see it from down below. He pulled himself up and took a breath. There was an opening in the rock. It wasn't really a cave, but it was big enough to hide a satchel. This must be it, he thought. The satchel has to be in there. He approached the opening and took out a box of matches. He lit one and peered inside.

The timber rattler struck William below his left eye. It was all muscle, and it was like getting hit with a club across the face. It knocked him back, but not off the landing. William was stunned for a moment, and then the pain hit him. The rattlesnakes in their den, awakened from hibernation by the rude intrusion of his match, came out of the cave. They struck him again, and again, and again.

***

Diego and Consuela came back from their mountain lion hunt empty. The beast proved elusive. Consuela smiled at the cowboy, who alerted them to a nonexistent quarry. He'd played his part and wouldn't be asking any questions. Diego was prattling on about her paying $250 for a fool's errand. Later, Miguel paid Diego the $250 the Sanchezes still owed, and he acted like Diego must have been crazy to think they had a map to the Aztec Treasure. Diego searched for the map to show him but could not find it.

"Up on Palisades Sill, you say? Ridiculous! It's full of rattlesnakes!" A miner would never put a cached fortune up there. Not even the vaqueros liked to go there, though the younger ones would challenge each other to climb the Sill and catch the snakes for a nice, tasty rattler dinner.

When William did not come home by evening, Carrie-Mae worried. When he had still not arrived home the following morning, she had the ranch hands form a search party. She even contacted his school in San Francisco, thinking maybe he went back. Perhaps the talk of getting an education came through. But he was not there. They searched Cimarron Canyon. Not even his horse returned. Consuela was not surprised; a fully tacked horse left unattended would not be unattended for long in the Canyon.

Wallace was not surprised at his brother's behavior or disappearance. He surmised that he'd show up when he could cash in and not before. Wallace, finally seeing his brother for who and what he was had outgrown him. He no longer needed or wanted his approval for anything.

The days stretched into weeks, and then months.

318

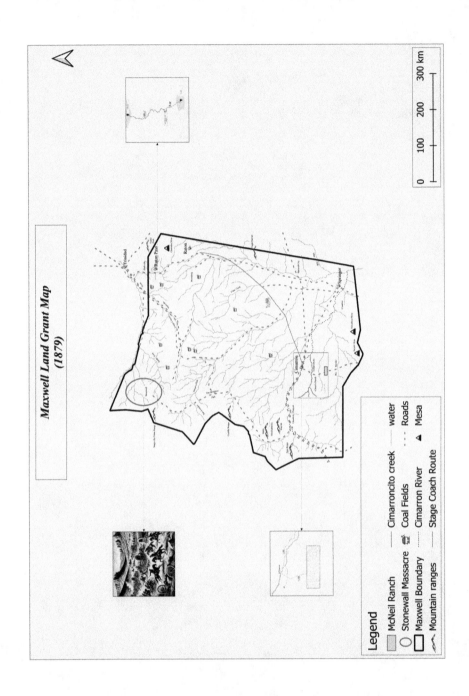

Maxwell Land Grant Map
(1879)

Legend

- McNeil Ranch
- Stonewall Massacre
- Maxwell Boundary
- Mountain ranges
- Cimarroncito creek
- Coal Fields
- Cimarron River
- Stage Coach Route
- water
- Roads
- Mesa

| 0 | 100 | 200 | 300 km |

Chapter XXIII: Wallace

August 23rd 1888
McNeil Ranch
New Mexico Territory

"Without the powerful aid of the Federal Government, the battle between the settlers and the company might have been a fairer one. Government collusion, corrupt, or legal was the deciding factor....."
Maria E. Montoya, Translating Property, 2002.

Wallace stood on the front porch of the hacienda and sipped his coffee, the bitterness accentuated by it having gone cold. The morning sun blazed at an angle that obscured the features of man and horse that approached from the east.

He finished his coffee not minding its temperature or taste and set the metal cup on the adobe half wall as he stepped off the porch. He slipped the leather catch from the pistol's hammer and rested his hand on the Colt .45 buckled around his hip.

"You've a lot of nerve, Pels. What the hell do you want?"

Pels glanced unconcerned at the pistol. "Young Mr. McNeil. The last time I saw you was in your father's freight office. I believe you helped me locate Mr. McDaniel. From lad to young man now. I am sorry to hear about your father."

Wallace had grown tall and lean and had inherited his mother's cat eyes that changed from an angry grey to blue. Wallace spat, "Yeah, some say it was your men that torched the freight."

The heavy oak door opened sharply, and Carrie-Mae stepped confidently onto the porch. "Mr. Pels, this is not the time..."

"Miss McNeil, I apologize, but I do have important business, and I don't think there is a good time."

Carrie-Mae tossed her long hair back, turned, and strode back through the door. The footfalls from her boots echoed with authority.

She did not close the door. Pels followed her and whispered to Wallace as he passed.

"It was not me nor any of my men that destroyed your father's freighting building, but I know who did. We'll talk."

Wallace, with no emotion on his face from Pels's statement, headed toward the open door but paused. If Carrie-Mae needed him there, she would have told him, and he trusted her. Besides, Consuela was inside, too. He shook his head slightly and thought that he would not want to be the one who tangled with either of them, much less both of them.

He unconsciously pulled the revolver from the holster just to feel it in his hand. Five years before, he asked his father if he could take shooting lessons from Les, and under his guidance, he'd developed the speed and coolness of an expert gun handler with the calmness of an undertaker. He holstered the weapon, satisfied, having heard the sound of steel sliding against leather. He would wait for Pels to have his say.

The shock of his father's death had passed, and now Wallace hunted for a place to stable his anger. Blame was restless, bouncing from the guns hired by the Maxwell people to the hotheaded settlers. He did not know who to blame. He felt cheated and very alone. Even William had run out on him and had not been heard from since his disappearance in late spring. And now here's Pels, he thought, saying he knew who set the fire that resulted in his Dad's death. Anger simmered in him, and he searched for the catalyst that would bring him to the boiling point, and he may have found it. He raged inside, and only he knew it.

Pels followed Carrie-Mae into the living area and sat in the ornate crimson chair without asking or being asked. He opened his worn, dusty satchel, removed some papers, and tapped them into place between his hands. "Now, then, I understand you inherited control of the McNeil Ranch after your father passed; my condolences, by the way."

There was no emotion in his voice. "When I last met with your father, that was some time ago; yes, in the summer of 1885, we discussed my audit of the squatters. I was actually looking for Mr. McDaniel, and the subject of the purchase from Lucien Maxwell and the survey of your ranch came up. I mentioned that I, of course, checked the deed, bill of sale survey, and the like."

Carrie-Mae, still standing, placed her hands on her hips, "I don't need a law review, Mr. Pels. I'm an attorney. Save us both time and get to the point."

He ignored her sharp tone. "I talked with McDaniels a few times trying to convince him to leave his ranch quietly; he didn't have ownership, you see. Then the Supreme Court decision finally convinced him he had no claim, and he left, but before he did, he kept insisting that your father had no claim on his ranch either and that his survey was off. I checked his paperwork again, including the bill of sale from Lucien Maxwell. I checked the signatures carefully this time."

He handed Carrie-Mae the bill of sale, the survey, the deed, and a letter signed by Luce Maxwell, Lucius Maxwell's wife. Pels's eyes narrowed as if he were a cougar that had just trapped a fawn. "You're an attorney. Look at the signatures."

She rifled through the papers, halting at the letter from Mrs. Maxwell and then at the bill of sale. Her jaw muscles tensed, and she crumpled the documents slightly, "You're saying that Murdoch forged the signatures on the bill of sale? How do I know that these documents are real?"

"Come now, you know, all I had to do was to have our attorney Frank Springer subpoena the documents from the land office. In any case, Mr. Springer deposed Luce Maxwell at Ft. Sumner regarding this. She never heard of any sale to Henry Townsend in New York and testified that the signature on the bill of sale is not Lucien Maxwells."

"You're asking us to leave the ranch."

"The land belongs to the Maxwell Land Grant and Railroad Company. I came here as a courtesy to show you those documents and to give you a fair offer for the improvements made on the land, although it's the company's contention that you knew full well that the land was acquired by fraud. We don't legally have to compensate you for anything if the land was not acquired in good faith."

Pels stood, took a kerchief from his breast pocket, wiped his brow, and held out his hand, "If you've finished examining the documents?"

Carrie-Mae handed them back, "Our family attorney is Thomas Her-"

"Hernandez in Las Vegas. Yes, I know." He put the documents back into his satchel and removed an envelope. "I'm meeting with him as well to show him these. You'll do well to follow his advice, which will be to take the offer. Relocate. Start a new life."

Carrie-Mae could no longer control her rage, "You say that as if starting a new life is nothing! This is what you do? Go from country to country, ranch to ranch, kicking people off their land! Ruining peoples' lives! To you and people like you, we are no more than shadows! Land shadows! Get out!"

Wallace heard footsteps approach the door; their voices became distinct as they approached. Carrie-Mae had a seriousness in her face that Wallace had never seen before.

Pels extended the envelope to Carrie-Mae. "I understand you're upset, but I'm just doing my job. If it were not me, it would be someone else. In this envelope is an offer, a generous offer, I believe, for the improvements on the property. Have Mr. Hernandez look it over if you'd like. Tell him we will assert that you knew of the fraud that Mr. McNeil perpetrated to acquire this property, and if the offer is refused, we will not make another. We will ask the court to order you off the property. I'll be at Lambert's for a week. Contact me there."

He nodded at Wallace as he stepped past, mounted his horse, and trotted away.

Wallace stood, "Well, that's it then, isn't it? The ranch is gone."

Carrie-Mae sighed and wiped away a tear, "Wallace, it never was ours. Maybe the Utes, the Apache, and the Tewa have the right idea about it. I don't think you can ever really own land. It seems to just tangle everything, then shreds into pieces."

Wallace ambled toward the barn to retrieve his horse, "I'm headed out. Back by supper."

Wallace knew that Pels couldn't be far ahead of him on the road to Cimarron, so he set his horse at a trot and scanned the road ahead. It was not long before he spied Pels sitting at a standstill on his horse at the top of a hill that looked down over Cimarron. That hill, where he first saw the freight buildings on fire that night, and where he also watched his father die in his lap on that night and every night since in his nightmares.

Wallace slowed his mount from a trot to a walk, halting a few feet from Pels.

"Who started the fire, Pels? Who's responsible for killing my Father?"

Pels met Wallace's cold stare. "The same man that I was looking for when I last saw you, Wallace, McDaniel. It shouldn't be a surprise."

The saddle leather creaked as Wallace shifted, "I hear he pulled out and that you got his land. That true? And how do you know he set the freight on fire that night?"

"When I confronted him, telling him that he had no deed to the property, he went into a rage. You know how he could be. So did your father. He admitted he burned your Dad's business to the ground because his survey was off, and he was afraid I'd find out that he, too, was on his land without title, so when your Dad wouldn't resurvey and make his title appear legitimate, McDaniels took it out on your Dad. I don't think he meant for your father to die."

Pels paused to let his explanation sink in. "Look, I take no pleasure in this, in any of it. The McDaniels family is gone. I tried talking with Sheriff Burleson, and he told me he investigated the fire, and there was no evidence that McDaniel had anything to do with it."

Wallace's voice softened and sounded hollow, "Now, after all of his hard work, we're left with nothing."

Pels nudged his horse closer, "Not if, as your father would say, you play your cards right. I'm betting you're a lot like your father. He was very direct, and I appreciated that. I'm going to be direct with you. No bullshit. What do you want most, Wallace? Since I'm being direct, I'll tell you what you want. The same thing your father wanted. You want land, and you can have it. Maybe not the same piece or the same amount, but with your share of what I'm paying you for improvements on the ranch and what I'm going to pay you to come to work for me, you'll have your own place."

Wallace shook his head and let sarcasm form his words. "Why would I ever want to work for you, and what do you think I can do for you that you'd pay a stack big enough to buy a ranch? Besides, all the land is tied up in that God Damn Maxwell Land grant. You of all people...."

Pels stood up in his stirrups and hissed, "Do you know who I am, Wallace? Say it! God Damn it!"

"Manager of the Maxwell Land Grant and Railway Company. I don't know who the hell you think you're fooling with, but I'm no kid, and this .45 on my hip can have a quick way of addressing stupidity, Pels."

"There, you realize it. You know it! It's all around that you're as fast and accurate as anyone, and whether or not you realize it, Les turned you into a shootist because he's a shootist himself. The only difference between you and that cowboy down south is that he's killed men, and you haven't yet."

Wallace reddened. "I'm not killing anybody, Pels!"

Pels's horse, sensitive to his increasing temper, shook his head and pawed at the ground, "You will, Wallace. It's up to you whether you want to be on the right side of the law with that pistol or the wrong side. That kid down south was on the wrong side, and see where that got him."

Wallace calmed, "There's still the issue of the land; it's all tied up, and you're kickin' people off, not sellin' to anyone, far as I know."

"Wallace, as manager of the Maxwell, I can sell to whom I choose, no questions asked. For Christ's sake, I sold 5000 acres in Stonewall Valley to the Governor of Colorado and his investors, so I can sure as hell sell to you! You have my word."

Pels let his words sink in. "Listen, the Sheriff down in Trinidad is hiring extra men to go over to Stonewall and kick a bunch of settlers off the land there. The settlers set the Maxwell cattle foreman's house on fire and ran E. J. Randolph and his wife off their property. They threatened to hang him and his wife! Do you know them? Threatened to hang E.J.'s wife, for God's sake! They're going to kill someone down there before it's all done, and the county sheriff won't let that happen. Neither will I."

Pels stated convincingly, "You'll be doing the right thing, Wallace. You and your fast gun can help stop the killing and put this Maxwell Land Grant issue off the table at last. You'll be following what the Supreme Court says is the law. Hell, even your own president sent an open letter to the settlers telling them to back off and follow the law."

Wallace sounded incredulous, "Dad knew the Randolphs. They burnt their house down and ran them off? Same as what McDaniel did to us?"

Pels did not rope calves, but he thought this is what tightening that rope around that calf's neck and slamming it to the ground feels like. Now all he had to do was tie those hooves up.

"That's right, and just like what happened to you and your Dad, they don't know who set the fire, but they're sure it's one of the settlers. Sheriff Burns has twenty-five deputies, including Pinkertons. I'll be bringing ten men, including you. With those Pinkerton fellows there, you won't have to draw your weapon; just help serve those ejection notices. Part of the sign of force we need to keep the peace and get those squatters off the Governor's property. You'll need to ride up to Trinidad on the 24th. We'll leave the next day and meet the rest of the posse at the Pooler Hotel in Stonewall. Half pay when you get to Trinidad, the other half when we're done. More after that if you work out."

Pels reined his horse in the direction of Cimarron and trotted off, not waiting for Wallace to react to his offer. He knew he'd be there. Calves always follow their mama.

***

August 25, 1888
Stonewall, Colorado

Wallace spoke briefly with Carrie-Mae, saying he'd be on the range with Diego and the other hands working cattle for the next few days. He had been solitary and distant since Murdoch's death, keeping to himself, so she was pleased that he wanted to be back on the range again. Being with Diego and Les who he idolized, would be good for him, she reasoned.

Carrie-Mae was to meet with Hernandes about Pels's visit. Wallace wouldn't tell her that he decided to take Pels up on his offer to work for the grant company until he returned from Stonewall. Wallace looked forward to being deputized and was pleased but not surprised that word of his skills with a six-gun had spread. He thought of Murdoch and wished his Dad had taken the time to see how fast he could throw that Colt. Always had been too busy, and, he thought, I won't be aiming at his empty whiskey bottles now.

He traveled to Trinidad, collected half his pay, and joined the posse of twenty-five men. Sporting his badge newly pinned to his vest, which he carefully polished, he rode with the rest of the deputized men, company agents, and Pinkerton detectives out of Trinidad and toward Stonewall to eject the squatters illegally occupying company land. As much as his father refused to become part of Maxwell's madness, Wallace embraced it, feeling the power of the law riding with him. After all, he thought, as he plodded along with the company, the United States Supreme Court said they're squatters. The agents and deputies joined the other company men at the Pooler Hotel in Stonewall. They were to serve the ejection lawsuits the next day.

The morning broke clear, and the sun streamed through openings in the dike formation that gave Stonewall its name. Sheriff Burns stood with some of the Pinkerton men and his deputies in front of the Pooler Hotel and swallowed hard: "Pels! Get out here and bring all the men, now!"

The settlers had begun to arrive that morning. The Reverend O.P. McMannis, the pastor who was so vocal against the Maxwell Land and Railway Company, had come up from Cimarron and brought at least a hundred settlers with him. McMannis and one of the ranchers, Richard Russell, who had established his homestead in the valley seventeen years before, approached the hotel as Pels emerged.

"Yeah, I see 'em. There must be one hundred fifty settlers there! Don't falter!"

McMannis was beyond angry. He was consumed by years of edgy entanglements and simmering rage caused by the Maxwell Land Grant injustices, which included the brutal murder of his good friend and fellow preacher, Frank Tolby. The final blow was the decision by the highest court in the land, which gave the Maxwell Land Grant and Railway Company unprecedented power to remove all settlers irrespective of ethnicity or original homestead claim status. There was no room for negotiation.

Pels had put aside the need to gently persuade squatters and aboriginals by using tactics that attempted to build a sense of trust and fairness. Instead, he wielded the Supreme Court decision like a blackjack. The puppet strings of Supreme Court Justice had reached from Washington D.C. to Stonewall, Colorado. They reminded McMannis and those who followed him of the unequal balance of power in a world where justice often bowed to the interests of the rich and powerful.

Wallace stood on the porch, thinking that the situation was unfolding in a way unlike what Pels had described to him. He would not be just handing out ejection notices, and he didn't see where the Pinkerton detectives were a deterrent. Unlike the new deputies, who showed a range of emotion on their faces, the Pinkertons whispered to each other in poker-faced monotones and then retreated unnoticed into the hotel. The mob was angry, focused, and resolute. He could feel the atmosphere, heavy and thick with hostility.

McMannis leaned into his speech, pointed a stiff finger at the posse assembled in front of the Pooler hotel, and spoke in a menacing tone. "You all need to pack up and leave. There's nothing for you here, and we don't recognize any authority you think you have!"

Sheriff Burns urged calmly, "Now, boys, give us a chance to talk this through. We'll go back into the hotel and let this thing simmer down. There's no cause to let this turn violent here."

"Alright, talk it through, but our patience is done here."

The last of the posse was back inside the hotel. Sheriff Burns said, "Carlos, Jimmy, head out the back way and make your way back to Trinidad. Cable the Governor! Tell him that we have the makings for a war down here. Tell him we need the militia! Now go! The rest of you men, grab the mattresses from the beds and plug those windows with them."

Five minutes after the men had left out the back way to sound the alarm, a volley of gunfire let loose from the second story of the hotel. The Pinkertons had opened fire on the settlers out front, and the fight was on. Wallace drew his Colt and looked through the window. He could see two men down, the sand beneath them turning crimson. He was nauseated and sweating with fear.

"Open fire, men!" Pels shouted, "Kill them before they kill us!"

Wallace's eyes widened as he saw the settler that had been standing next to McMannis before the fight running hard toward the hotel, his pistol drawn. He aimed at the man's shoulder and fired. The man went down. Not aiming to hit anyone else, he emptied the gun's cylinder and reloaded.

"Russell's shot! He's down!" Pels yelled.

Sheriff Burns holstered his pistol, picked up a rifle, and chambered a round. "That's nothing to be proud of, Pels; Russell has four boys and two daughters! That's the worst thing that could happen to get those squatters fired up! This has turned into a God Damn disaster! Who the hell opened fire? It wasn't on my say-so! God Damn it! Pinkertons! Anyone in here hit?"

"Don't think so, Sheriff, but there are two more settlers down; one's dead for sure. Looks like Russell is still alive. He's moving in the middle of the street, but it doesn't look like he can get to his feet."

Gunfire from the settlers and the posse continued through the afternoon. Splinters of wood from the facade of the building flew as the bullets tore through the walls and ricocheted, but no one inside the hotel had been hit. Russell continued to bleed out.

Wallace realized that no one knew he had been the one who shot Russell. Two of the other deputies claimed with pride that they had hit him. Wallace was sick to his stomach at having shot the man. He went to the back of the hotel, pushed a mattress off the window, retched, and vomited until there was nothing left in his stomach.

Pels saw him and laughed. "What did you think would happen, McNeil? Get back at that window and fire that weapon! They're trying to kill us, you fool!"

"Pels! I killed the wrong man! You're the man I should've killed!

Wallace drew his Colt, and Pels turned white. "You'll hang, Wallace!

You'll hang!" And stomped off.

Twilight came early in Stonewall Valley, the sun swallowed up by the steep mountains that encircled the area. It became difficult to see. The gunfire quieted and finally stopped, allowing Russell's boys to go to their father and carry him off the street. Wallace witnessed the scene, which pulled him back to watching his father die in his lap, and he struggled to hold his emotions in.

Word came through angry shouts, random gunfire, and the agonizing sounds of grief that Russell was dead. Russell was non-violent, well-liked, and had argued for peace between the grant men and the settlers. He had reluctantly accepted an offer from Pels for his ranch, but when Pels couldn't come up with the money, the deal fell through.

The irony was not lost on Pels, though he felt no more responsible for his death than he did for aboriginals on Indonesia's Java, where he first made a name for himself working for the Dutch, clearing the citizenry there. To him, they were all the same. No more than weeds to be plucked out of the ground and discarded.

Sheriff Burns would not wait to see how the ranchmen would react to his death. He knew if he didn't come up with a plan soon, they would all die at the hands of the mob.

Sheriff Burns gathered his posse. "Here's the deal. There are a lot of them, and not many of us. Opening fire on them and killing some of them, especially Russell, well, that's as good as getting us all sentenced to be shot." He threw a side glance at the Pinkertons. "There's no way they are going to let us out of here. They may say they'll give us a cease-fire and passage out of here, but as soon as we step out that door, we're dead."

The Sheriff took a deep breath. "Two of you will need to sneak out the back and over to the barn. Take a kerosene lamp, dump it, and start a fire. They'll have to get the livestock out, and while they're busy with that, we vamoose out of here through the back and hide in the hills until sunup, then find a wagon and make it back to Trinidad. Jacob, when the boys head out to burn the barn you slip out easy like, and station yourself out back. If you see anyone watch in the back, take your hunting knife and…. well, you know what to do. Savvy?" They nodded in agreement.

The two men started the fire outside the barn, and it spread quickly. The silhouettes and shouts of the settlers fighting the blaze and trying to save the livestock in the barn signaled that it was time for the posse to slip away. They were not seen. Once a safe distance away, they settled in for the rest of the night. The next morning, the settlers attacked the hotel and found it empty. Three settlers died at the Stonewall fight, but the number of people that their deaths affected was far greater. The Maxwell Land Grant added the Stonewall dead to its body count that summer weekend, a blood sacrifice to having a resort built for the Governor of Colorado and his investors.

Wallace slipped away from the posse in the middle of the night and stood at the bank of the Purgatory River, the moon reflecting off the surface. The soothing sound of a meandering river was one of Wallace's favorite sounds, but the gurgling of the Purgatory River was not calming to him. He'd shot and killed a man for just defending his ranch. Same as his father would do. The badge he wore gave him the authority to pull the trigger. He ripped the badge from his vest and threw it hard into the Purgatory. He walked toward Trinidad in the moonlit night and murmured, "This is no dime novel."

When Wallace returned, he no longer wore his side-arm, and he no longer practiced shooting. She did not ask where he had been or what had happened to the firearm. She had, of course, heard about Stonewall, and Les had told her that he'd not been on the range when she asked him. That incident was in practically every paper in the nation, and she suspected that he was somehow involved and that Pels was the catalyst for Wallace's involvement.

Chapter XXIV: The Value of Land

October 1st, 1888
New Mexico Territorial Supreme Court
Raton, New Mexico Territory

"The earth does not belong to man, man belongs to the earth. All things are connected like the blood that unites us all. Man did not weave the web of life, he is merely a strand in it. Whatever he does to the web, he does to himself."
Si'ahl, Chief of the Duwamish

Carrie-Mae was steadfast in her refusal to accept Pels's offer, and claimed that the offer was far below what the improvements and livestock were worth. The Maxwell Land Grant and Railway company, through Pels, made the mistake of thinking they could bully Carrie-Mae into giving up their ranch without a fight. Hernandez agreed with Carrie-Mae and counseled her to reject the offer. Since there was a question of fraud, the case was not heard at the court of land claims, and instead, the case landed at the New Mexico Territorial Supreme Court.

"All rise. The New Mexico Territorial Supreme Court is now in session. Chief Justice James O'Brien presiding."

"Be seated," said Chief Justice O'Brien. "The case before this court Maxwell Land Grant and Railroad Company, represented by Frank Springer, plaintiff. Defendants are the estate of Murdoch McNeil, deceased; heirs are Carrie-Mae McNeil, Wallace McNeil, and the minor child Frank McNeil. The court understands that another heir, William McNeil, has been missing for some time, but the outcome of this proceeding will apply to him as well. Thomas Hernandez, esquire, the executor of the estate, represents the estate. Mr. Springer, you may begin your argument."

Springer issued an opening statement that discussed the importance of trust in land adjudications and the letter of the law. He kept it short, knowing that, while his words were pretty, the facts of law had always borne little relevance in New Mexico's Territorial Supreme Court. He called his first witness.

"Mr. Pels, will you kindly take the stand? State your full name for the record and your occupation, please."

"My name is Marinus Petrus Pels. I am the general manager of the Maxwell Land Grant and Railroad Company."

"Please tell the court your understanding of the ownership of the McNeil Ranch."

"The McNeil Ranch is some 57,000 acres located in northern New Mexico in the area of Cimarron. It was initially filed in 1869 by the law firm of Henry Townsend, who resides and practices in New York City, New York. The filing stated a purchase record from Lucien Maxwell, then the owner of Maxwell Land Grant. Mr. Townsend gifted the property to his agent in the deal, Murdoch McNeil, in 1877. I conducted a property audit last year in which I determined that the 1869 bill of sale was falsified by Murdoch McNeil, and Maxwell's signature was forged."

Attorney Springer moved the fraudulent bill of sale and the filing into evidence, along with a sworn affidavit by Luz Maxwell attesting that her late husband had never sold the property and that the signature did not belong to him. Then, Springer presented verified archival signatures of McNeil and Lucien Maxwell.

"Mr. Pels, you collected these signatures as part of your audit, correct?"

"Yes."

"What is your opinion as to the validity of these signatures?"

"The bill of sale and Lucien Maxwell's signature are obvious forgeries. Lucien Maxwell's signature resembles the style of Murdoch McNeil's signature. He was so sure of his ruse that he did not even attempt to cover it up."

"Objection," said Mr. Hernandez.

"Proceed," O'Brien said.

"Calls for speculation."

"Sustained."

Neither of the attorneys had any more questions for Mr. Pels, and Justice O'Brien asked Mr. Hernandez to proceed with his case.

"I have been instructed by the estate's heirs to plead no contest to the charge that the bill of sale was fraudulent. The statute of limitations has expired, so no criminal charges can be brought against Mr. Townsend or his law firm. I contend that Mr. Townsend was unaware his agent falsified the sale. At the time, Mr. Townsend was recovering from a serious head injury in a New York hospital, leaving Mr. McNeil to manage the firm until Mr. Townsend's release in the summer. The plaintiff's claim that Miss McNeil knew about the fraudulent purchase is also unfounded. She was not part of the household and had not yet been adopted into the McNeil family. We ask the court to order the Maxwell Land Grant and Railway Company to compensate the McNeils for improvements made on the property, as they have done in similar cases."

Chief Justice O'Brien questioned him further. "The court understands that you will represent the estate in talks to transfer and vacate the property; is this correct?"

"Yes, sir, that is correct," Hernandez answered.

"It is the order of the New Mexico Territorial Supreme Court that the property known as the McNeil Ranch, comprised of 57,000 acres near the Cimarroncito, and all real estate holdings contained therein, shall be returned to the ownership of the Maxwell Land Grant and Railroad Company. All Land and residences shall be vacated within ninety days of the court's order. The court further orders the Maxwell Land Grant and Railway company to negotiate with Mr. Hernandez in good faith and come to reasonable terms to compensate the McNeil's for improvements and livestock based on this court's ruling that Carrie-Mae McNeil is innocent of any fraud in this matter. She was, in fact, not even born yet when this fraud was committed.

Justice O'Brien stated forcefully, "Mr. Springer, how you could make this interpretation is beyond any reason except to say it is evident that you attempted to badger Miss McNeil into accepting any offer. The court intends to look closely at your clients' new offer and warns that if the offer is not reasonable, in the court's opinion, the court will decide what will be paid. Is this clear, Mr. Springer?"

"Yes, your honor."

"This court is adjourned."

Mr. Hernandez and Mr. Springer negotiated a fair compensation with the land grant company for the livestock, and they offered the same terms they'd provided many of those who'd settled on their land: fair compensation for the hacienda and other buildings on the property.

Mr. Pels saw an opportunity on the ranch, and he persuaded the rest of the Dutch company that the McNeil Ranch should be retained as a profitable venture and that Diego and Consuela should oversee operations since they knew it best.

For Diego and Consuela, their patron had merely changed once more, just as their ancestors had always known.

Carrie-Mae supervised as freighters crated up the furniture. Consuela hugged her tightly. "Mija, Kewanee, I will miss you."

"I will miss you, too."

"Where do you plan to go?"

"I think Dock would want me to take my parents' land back and to have Wallace and Frank with me. We're going to travel back to Oklahoma, to the Potawatomi reservation, buy land there, and chase anyone off who tries to get in our way."

Frank, then an energetic eight-year-old with sandy hair, was fiercely independent and roamed the ranch freely. Like his father, he loved to read and would pore through Murdoch's law books, constantly peppering Carrie-Mae with questions about them. Carrie-Mae knew she would find him in Murdoch's old study, wrapped up in law books even as the movers crated them up. All those books, including Marco Paul, went with them to the Potawatomi Nation. Carrie-Mae could see him as her future law clerk.

Carrie-Mae, Wallace, and Frank arrived in Oklahoma one dusty summer day. She was surprised that she still remembered the landmarks that first led her away from her parent's farmstead: The bluffs where, her father said, the Kiowa had run the bison off the cliff and harvested the meat below. The field with rings burned into the ground where the Pawnee would set their tipis. The lake where she still held a fuzzy memory of catching a gar and where she'd been terrified even to take it off the hook.

Carrie-Mae's allotment was 320 acres. All of it taken for taxes that should have never been assessed. The tax law was used as a ruse to take land from the Potawatomi, and they were just awarded for agreeing to become United States citizens. The sharecroppers who'd bought it from the government had gone bust and abandoned it. She repurchased the acres for the taxes they still owed, and then she and her brother built an exact replica of the hacienda right down to the massive porch. Let them take it now, she thought.

This place is like a fort. Life was comfortably still and calm. Wallace, though not free of nightmares surrounding the Stonewall War, as it came to be called by the eastern newspapers, was working through his part of what he considered a manufactured tragedy. Pels led him down the path, and Wallace, who needed to feel accepted and powerful, was primed for killing.

He'd heard it said many times that killing a man changes you. War changes you, and it had. He'd not buckled his Colt to his hip since he killed Russell, and he had no interest in doing so. He just wanted to farm the Oklahoma land he and his sister settled on. That was not to be.

On an uncomfortably hot summer afternoon, she and Wallace were sitting on their porch when a carriage pulled up. Two men got out and approached.

"Miss Darling? Miss Carrie-Mae Darling?"

"Darling, or McNeil, Carrie-Mae, or Kewanee. I answer to both, and this is my brother, Wallace."

"My name is Edward Byrd, and this is my partner James Givens, and I am here to make you rich."

"James, Edward, and you're here to make us rich. Well, how?"

"Oil, Miss Darling. We want you to lease your land to us, and then we will put oil wells on it. You've got 320 acres if I have that right," Edward said while his partner futilely mopped the sweat from his brow.

"Yes, 320 acres, that's right."

They walked up on the porch. "May we sit? It would be easier to talk if we may join you." She allowed it as she did not want Mr. Givens to die from the heat and have his spirit trapped on her land.

Mr. Byrd pulled out some papers. "We have the lease right here, ready for you to sign. You get money just for the lease and a lot more once we hit oil."

Carrie-Mae took the papers and thumbed through them disinterestedly. "I'll read these over."

"Oh, no need for that, Miss Darling! Just a lot of legalese; it's a formality. My apologies that it is so long, but you know how these lawyers get! Everything is, of course, in order."

"No, I'd rather read them over, thank you. Would you like to wait, or would you need to come back tomorrow?"

"We'll wait, and don't be too long. And, the people we work for don't take no for an answer, so you might as well sign those papers."

Wallace started to speak, but Carrie-Mae put her hand on his shoulder and shook her head, halting him. Neither of them had better die of the heat on her porch, as there was not enough sage in the whole county to smudge them out. She got them each a glass of cool tea and left them on her porch while she went inside to her library, Wallace following.

Since the Stonewall incident, Wallace had become sullen and particularly suspicious of strangers. He wrestled with the knowledge that he'd killed a man, and it haunted him and changed him. He struggled with the reality of living in the West, the need to be armed to protect himself and his sister, and the horror he lived with each day, knowing his actions took a husband and father from his family.

He placed his hand on his right hip, half expecting his Colt to be there. He didn't like being unarmed and having strangers here. Carrie-Mae tended to the contract. Wallace went to the closet in his bedroom and removed Murdoch's double gun belt hanging from a brass hook that he'd left Wallace. The belt was full of cartridges, and it felt satisfyingly heavy.

He opened the wooden case in the closet, removed and loaded the cartridges into the pair of pistols that his mother had given his father so long ago. He slid them into the holsters and buckled the matched pair around his waist.

An hour passed, then two. Mr. Byrd knocked on the front door.

"Miss Darling, did you forget about us here? Miss Darling?"

She emerged with papers in one hand and a pen in the other. Wallace remained just inside the door, listening. "I've made some changes in the contract. If you agree to these changes, I'll consider your offer."

"We don't make changes, Miss Carrie-Mae. Do you know the value of land? Do you want to make money? There's black gold underneath your feet!" Givens said.

"But, Mr. Givens, this payment structure and the species promised make little sense. I have restructured it with guaranteed minimum payments. Also, this appears to be written to give you total ownership of the land should you fail to find oil. I believe this contract falls short of mutual consideration. You might have a court issue if I sign this, gentlemen."

"You talk like a lawyer, Miss."

"I am."

Mr. Givens continued, not having listened to her response. "I don't believe I've made myself clear. We don't intend to leave here without a signed contract. You might even say it's an insurance policy of sorts. We protect the land and the buildings on that land when we sign an oil lease. We protect it from things like, oh, I don't know, an unfortunate fire or a well going sour. Do you understand?"

Wallace had exited the back door of the hacienda and moved quietly behind and within earshot of Givens and Byrd unnoticed.

Wallace spoke in a calm and clear voice, "I think you gentlemen have worn out your welcome."

Givens and Byrd turned and saw Wallace sporting his Colts. Givens moved to draw his own sidearm, but Byrd grabbed his wrist before the weapon left the holster, looked at him, and shook his head. "He's too fast."

Byrd turned pale, "McNeil......Wallace McNeil. You were at Stonewall just a short time back. You're the gun that Pels hired. Your father was Murdoch McNeil, correct? The rancher and freight owner over in Cimarron?"

"That's right. Let me tell you what's going to happen here, Byrd. If our ranch catches fire for any reason. Oh, I don't know, like a lightning strike, or maybe I just trip over a kerosene lamp and start a fire, or if our water goes sour because a cow pissed in it. I'm coming after you. Not Givens here, you. And you get to see how fast I can throw this Colt. So, you go back and tell whoever sent you here we're not signing any contract. Now get off our ranch."

They climbed into their wagon, let the reins fall onto the horses' back, and rode off without looking back. Carrie-Mae sat down on the porch. Wallace pulled one of the Colts from the holster and looked at it, as if he was staring at a rattlesnake. No fear clouded his expression. The fine engraving on the pistol did not change what the Colt was made for.

Wallace sat on the bench next to Carrie-Mae on the porch, the air leaving him in a mournful sigh, "Sis, I didn't want to put these back on. I never told you what happened at Stonewall."

Carrie-Mae put her finger to her lips. "You don't need to say anything, Wallace. Remember what Dad would say? He'd say, 'You spend the first half of your life getting something worth holding onto and the second half working to hold onto it.' It didn't work that way for him, but we can make it work for us. Maybe for the families that we'll both have someday."

She paused, looking thoughtful. "I think with the right combination of using the law we're saddled with and knowing that you can protect what's ours, we'll do alright. In fact, after talking with those two rascals, I wonder how many oil leases our Potawatomi brothers and sisters have signed under duress. I mean to find out. We'll use their own laws to keep what's ours and help others in the tribe do the same. You keep those .45s close, Wallace."

Wallace shifted uncomfortably. "Carrie, these guns on my hip, they've become heavier since I..." He looked away, a distant expression crossing his face. She recognized it—it was the same look she had seen on Murdoch's face that first night she arrived at the ranch. Wallace looked so much like his father.

Carrie gently placed her hand on his chin and turned his face toward her, "Since you shot Richard Russell at Stonewall? Yes, I know. How could I not know? I'm your sister. There's nothing I can say that will lessen the pain you must work through, but what if he shot and killed you? Where would that have left me? What if those oilmen come back and try and burn our home down? Wouldn't you unleash the fury of those Colts on them to save our home? To save my life? If you weren't here with me, do you think those oilmen would have left without their contract? Do you think what happened to me at the boarding school couldn't happen to me here?"

Wallace bit his lower lip and sipped the tea that had warmed to the outside temperature. "What do you think Dad would have thought of all this? Losing the ranch, me killing someone, William disappearing? What he'd say to us about how he got the ranch in the first place, and then Pels finds out it's land fraud, and it's taken away?"

Carrie-Mae was silent for some time, gazing out at her lush pastureland, the green landscape, and the red soil of the Oklahoma heartland where the Potawatomi reservation was located. It was so unlike the dry, harsh land of the New Mexico high desert, where scenic and colorful vistas tried in vain to make up for the lack of water. Here, she finally felt at home and nourished, though all Potawatomi held the Great Lakes—the area from which they were removed—in their hearts. For now, this was home, and she found it even more beautiful than all those acres in New Mexico that were never Murdoch's, never hers.

"Your dad was a brilliant attorney. He knew the law, and we had the law in common. If it were not for him, we'd not have this land, nor would I have my law degree, which has taught me how to keep this land. He knew the value of land. What it takes to acquire land. What he never understood were the rules. Lawyers survive on rules. We learn about an issue, what law applies to it, and what the conclusion is likely to be. But the rules about land out here kept changing."

Wallace plucked a long blade of grass growing between the wooden porch planks and began chewing on it, which released its earthy taste. He rotated it between his fingers. "He didn't play by the rules, though. He got the ranch through fraud."

"Even getting land that way had rules that included participation from not just our dad, but the surveyor general of New Mexico, the governor, the congress, even the President of the United States and certainly the Supreme Court. I think that surprised him, but not just him. It surprised everyone who settled on the Maxwell. All those angry settlers that you faced in Stonewall had to deal with fraud and their homes being taken away from them, just like the Native tribes on the Maxwell that were the first to lose their land.

Wallace, still thoughtful, said, "What about the treaty that gave us the land here? I've heard you say that the government has broken every treaty that they signed with every Indian nation. What if they want this land back?

"The sad fact is, Wallace; they're likely to get our land if they want if bad enough. What happened on Maxwell should tell you that. It's just the history that's being created for us. The government breaking treaties is nothing new. My great-great-grandmother, Archange Ouilmette, was forced from her reservation around Chicago in the 1820s, not by war but by the courts charging her and her husband with every made-up petty charge they could think of, then fining them huge amounts of money so that they had to sell their land to pay the fine. They would have been sent to prison if they didn't pay the fine. In the end, there was no alternative but to leave their home."

"Like the government giving your family this land when you agreed to citizenship and then taxing your land, so you had to sell it off to white settlers when your family couldn't pay the taxes."

"That's right. For now, we must be careful of the oilmen. I'll file a complaint with the sheriff in Shawnee tomorrow and start talking with other tribal members. We're safe for now."

Carrie-Mae sipped on her tea and mused, "I wonder where our people will be in a hundred years from now. I wonder if the Dutch will still own 1.7 million acres of land that should have never been given to them and if the arguments concerning the other land grants will still be in the courts."

Wallace added, "Or if New Mexico will ever be a state, and you still have to carry a Colt .45 to feel safe?"

Carrie-Mae had a far-away look in her eyes. "Maybe where we are sitting, they'll be a large Potawatomi city, with homes, stores, a hospital, a theater, and maybe even electric lights like the ones I saw in

Chicago while I was at law school."

Wallace shook his head. "A hundred years is a long time, Carrie-Mae."

Carrie-Mae smiled. "Not in Indian time. It's today, tomorrow, and yesterday. Come inside, and we'll find the cedar box. You're Potawatomi now. You need to learn how to build a prayer fire so that we can cleanse this place of the oilmen."

Chapter XXV: Henry

August 1, 1889
Darling Land Allotment
Oklahoma Territory

The land is sacred. These hills, these valleys, these rivers - they remember. Even when people forget, the earth keeps our stories safe. *N. Scott Momaday, "The Man Made of Words," 1997.*

Carrie-Mae was in the habit of dropping by the telegraph office in Shawnee during her occasional trips for supplies or to drop by the courthouse to file papers for her growing and successful, but mostly pro bono, law practice. She was surprised to receive a telegram from Thomas Hernandez. She shook her head and mused that it had been only a year since Wallace and Frank had moved with her to the reservation in Oklahoma.

Carrie-Mae had remained busy with her law practice and her farm, focused on protecting the rights of the Potawatomi through the U.S. legal system. She secured her place in the Potawatomi hierarchy, in which women were equal to men in their society and were also exceptional businesswomen. Getting telegrams was not unusual; usually someone needing her help.

> HENRY TOWNSEND DEAD FROM STROKE STOP URGENT WE MEET WITH YOU STOP ARRIVING SHAWNEE 15 AUGUST.

That was curious, she thought. Ada sent a letter that arrived just before the court hearing on the ranch last October, informing them that Henry had been having seizures again. She wrote that he had suffered a stroke that crippled him and left him unable to speak, so his death was not entirely unexpected. But Hernandez would not have anything to do with Henry's estate. Why would he travel all the way out here from Las Vegas, New Mexico, if there were just papers to sign, when he could have sent a post? And what did he mean by 'we?' Hernandez didn't make mistakes in his communications.

Carrie-Mae, Wallace, and Frank waited at the depot, where billows of black smoke from the coal-powered engine appeared on the horizon. Bystanders stopped and stared; many were just there for the newness of it all. The tracks bringing the train from Oklahoma City to Shawnee had been set down Kickapoo Street just that July Fourth. Mr. Hernandez was accompanied by another gentleman who stepped off the train that Carrie-Mae did not recognize, but whom Wallace seemed to faintly remember.

Mr. Hernandez set his briefcase and his small suitcase down on the wooden platform and enthusiastically extended his hand but then embraced her instead. "Carrie-Mae! It is so, so good to see you, my dear! I want to hear all about your law practice, and I, oh, I really don't know where to begin! We have so much to talk about! Oh, my! This must be Wallace! Tall like your father! You look so much like him! And Frank, you've gotten bigger too! How old are you now?"

Frank, still the quiet one, said, "I'm nine since May, Mr. Hernandez."

The other gentleman stood politely at the edge of the conversation, and Wallace recognized him, last seeing him at his father's funeral. "Mr. Frank Angel! This is a surprise! Don't tell me you came all the way from New York City! Now I am bursting with curiosity. I'm sure it must be about Grandfather."

Frank Angel smiled and enthusiastically shook Wallace's hand. "I can't believe it's been nine years since your mother passed. I think of her and your dad often. I'm saddened, of course, as we all are at your grandfather's passing. That's the reason I'm here. As you know, I was a good friend to both your mother and father, and I've known Mr. Townsend for quite a number of years. Mr. Townsend asked that I act as executor of his estate, and what we must discuss is too complicated to explain via correspondence or by telegram."

They headed for the carriage they would take to their farm on the reservation.

Carrie asked, "I understand the complexities of estate law and how that may require an in-person visit, and I'm delighted to see both of you. But I have to wonder, Mr. Hernandez, what could bring you out from New Mexico in tandem with Mr. Angel?"

Mr. Hernandez removed his coat in an attempt to find comfort in the summer Oklahoma heat and humidity, then seated himself in the carriage. "Rather than trying to explain this in small snippets of conversation, let's wait until we can all sit down together. We have documents to show you. Being an attorney yourself, Carrie-Mae, you'll be of great help to unravel all that we have to explain to you."

The group made small talk, but all were excited to hear the reason for their trip. When they arrived at the farm, Mr. Angel commented, "This is so green compared to the New Mexico ranch. Beautiful, but in a different way. Does it suit you here, Carrie-Mae?"

"Yes, it does. I love being surrounded by my people."

They settled in the great room, sipped on lemonade, and Carrie-Mae apologized that she did not have anything stronger. "I remember Dad commenting about you, Mr. Angel, and something to do with you making Manhattans."

"That was your father. He really enjoyed playing the bartender for Anne and me. I always teased him about how lousy he was, especially at making Manhattans. I miss them both."

Mr. Angel unbuckled the brass clasps on his soft leather case and pulled out some official-looking papers. He leafed through them, muttered, "I think this one first," and then handed the document to Carrie-Mae.

She took the paper. "Let's see what all the fuss is about. Hmm, bill of sale." She looked in shock at Mr. Angel. "Is this some kind of joke? It's an almost exact duplicate of the bill of sale that Dad forged, but it's signed by Henry Townsend and Lucien Maxwell, and it's dated 1869! The Maxwell signature isn't in Dad's handwriting. Is the other signature really Maxwell's? The legal description is the same. I couldn't forget that. Frank, what is this?"

Frank nodded. "We have to go back to 1877, Anne and Murdoch's 8th wedding anniversary, when Henry announced that Murdoch, Anne,

347

and the boys were to be relocated to the ranch in New Mexico."

Wallace leaned forward. "I remember that anniversary party. William and I were only about six years old then. You were there too, right, Frank?"

Frank looked surprised. "I'm taken aback that you remember that night, Wallace. Yes, I wouldn't miss one of their anniversary parties."

Wallace became more excited. "I remember it because of Mom and Dad's fight. It wasn't some little disagreement either. There was a lot of shouting from both of them. Grandmother tried to calm them down but couldn't. Do you know what they fought about, Frank?"

Frank sighed. "I thought I did until I found this bill of sale and a letter explaining everything. I thought they fought about moving to New Mexico, but it was about the land fraud Murdoch committed. Murdoch told Anne about it that day, thinking they had to move to hide it, and she hated the deception."

Carrie-Mae frowned. "But Granddad didn't know about the fraud, right?"

Frank shook his head. "That's what I thought. But Anne told her dad that Murdoch had falsified the bill of sale. Dr. Spencer was in on it, too, being the Surveyor General of New Mexico. But Henry actually found out about the fraud not long after Murdoch created it. Anne just confirmed what your Grandfather already knew."

Wallace leaned back, shaking his head. "Granddad wasn't the most forgiving man. What did he do when he found out?"

Frank smiled. "Henry was angry but didn't confront Murdoch. Instead, he contacted his old friend, Dick Wooton, who knew Lucien Maxwell, and then Henry bought land directly from Maxwell to protect the firm and his family. The purchase contract held the exact survey and description that your dad used when he forged his purchase. He kept it secret and made Murdoch live with the guilt."

Hernandez added, "Henry knew Maxwell's record-keeping was poor. Even though fifty-seven thousand acres seemed like a lot, it was a fraction of Maxwell's land. He asked Wooton to help buy the exact land Murdoch falsified."

Carrie-Mae's eyes lit up. "So, there are two bills of sale. Murdoch created the fraudulent one, but Henry bought the land for real. Henry owned the McNeil Ranch all this time!"

Hernandez nodded. "Yes, Henry kept the legitimate purchase from Murdoch. He planned to reveal it when the fraud was discovered. When Anne died, Henry let it drop, then he had a stroke and couldn't speak. The secret almost died with him."

Frank continued, "I found the bill of sale, confirmed it with Luce Maxwell, and verified the sale was legitimate. Henry transferred the ranch to Murdoch to protect the firm and the family."

Wallace looked exasperated. "Does this mean we should have never lost the ranch? What about the money?"

Hernandez stood. "Your grandfather bought the McNeil Ranch. As his heirs, Wallace and Frank were left the ranch. We just need to get it back into your name. Murdoch knew he needed to show that the money was spent for the land, so Murdoch invested the money that would have been used to buy the ranch. It turns out that he made a lot on the investments and put it back into the firm. Henry knew and just let it be."

Frank added, "Murdoch wanted to do right by everyone and live his father's dream. He would have preferred to stay in New York."

Carrie-Mae, ever the attorney, asked, "How did Spencer file the false claim once Henry legitimately bought the land?"

Hernandez smiled. "Spencer either ignored it to hide his fraud or it got lost in the shuffle. He died in 1872, and the new surveyor didn't know. Land transactions around the Maxwell Land Grant were often fraudulent."

"What will you do once this is through the courts, Carrie-Mae? Wallace?" Frank asked.

Carrie-Mae replied, "I have cases and clients here, but with Wallace's and Frank's help, we can manage the ranch from here. Consuela and Diego are still out there."

Wallace said, "We're farmers tied to the land, but Dad ran the ranch from New York. I'm eighteen now, and sometimes I miss that ranch. Maybe Frank will help manage it, too."

Hernandez laughed. "We'll spend the next few days making a plan that Pels won't like. I'd love to see his face when he explains to the Dutch how he lost fifty-seven thousand acres of what they thought was their land."

The three lawyers presented their case to the court of land claims later that year, which resulted in the McNeil Ranch being reinstated to the McNeil family. The agreement was hotly contested by Pels, and through the litigation the court found that Pels had a habit of trying to remove people from their land that they had legitimately purchased from Lucien Maxwell.

To Consuela and Diego, the McNeils' return as their Patron was a welcome change after working for the Maxwell Land and Railway Company. They declined the offer to move into the hacienda on the ranch. They told no one that at sunset when the light was just right, they'd see Anne and Murdoch sitting on the front porch.

Frank Angel, assigned to investigate the Lincoln and Colfax County Wars and land fraud on the Maxwell Land Grant, was suspicious of Murdoch's activities and sent a telegram to Luce Maxwell asking for confirmation of the land purchase. By then, Lucien Maxwell had died, and Luce Maxwell had never answered that telegram.

Had Frank Angel followed up on that telegram, perhaps both the fraudulent and legitimate claim would have come to light. Because of his close friendship with Murdoch and his love for Anne, he chose not to pursue his suspicions. Had he informed Henry Townsend of the scam, Henry would have revealed that he was the owner of the ranch, and the Maxwell company would have had no claim. As New York's Attorney General, he was particularly concerned about the telegram he had sent to Luce Maxwell and his lack of follow-up. If this were ever revealed, it could destroy his meticulously built career, which forced him to constantly watch his back.

***

June 12, 1919
McNeil Ranch
New Mexico Territory

Murdoch disassembled his new Schmelzers fly rod into the five pieces that fit nicely into the cloth cover, then into the wooden tube---a birthday present from his grandpa Wallace. He placed the cap on the tube, tied it to his horse, and swung his creel over the saddle horn. The sizable trout flopped in protest. He led his horse to the Cimarron River flowing lazily beneath the Palisades Sill to have a last drink of water before heading back to the McNeil Ranch.

Murdoch was thirsty too. He bent down to bring the sweet water to his lips, then stopped. Bright silver-colored metal shone from the bottom of the crystal-clear water—just a corner of whatever it was, brightly reflecting the light.

He reached into the water up to his elbow to free the metal. The water was deeper than it looked, but he didn't mind its cold sting. He wrenched the metal free, feeling the suction of the water give way. It was a belt buckle—probably silver—tarnished and crusted in brown, red, and hints of light blue. The only shining part was the corner of the buckle that had first caught his attention. The water must have kept it polished, he mused. He pushed the mud and dirt from the surface of the buckle, exposing two large letters: WM. It looked just like his grandpa's buckle.

Murdoch tied his horse to the rail in front of the McNeil Hacienda. His grandfather was sitting in one of the huge chairs on the McNeil porch, his chin to his chest signaling that he was napping. "Grandpa, take a look at what I found in the Cimarron!" he said, extending his hand with his find.

"That new fly rod work out for you, son?" His eyes snapped open and his back straightened---he stifled a yawn.

"Grandpa, take a look at this! It looks like your buckle, but all messed up from the river water---except for one corner, see? It has the same two initials as yours: WM, Wallace McNeil. But how could that be?"

The End

A Note on History

History is shaped as much by the people who lived it as by the ones who record it. *Land Shadows* is a work of historical fiction, built on a foundation of extensive research into the Maxwell Land Grant, the land struggles of the Gilded Age, and the lives of those caught in the sweeping changes of the American West. While the story itself is imagined, the backdrop is very real, and I have taken great care to weave historical accuracy into the narrative while allowing for the creative liberties necessary to bring the past to life.

Over the course of writing this novel, I consulted more than three hundred sources, including historical documents, academic works, firsthand accounts, and legal records. Many of the events depicted in *Land Shadows* are drawn from true stories, and where historical gaps existed, I filled them with informed speculation based on the realities of the time.

Rather than presenting a full bibliography here—which would likely test the patience of even the most dedicated reader—I have included a curated selection of sources for those interested in learning more. For a complete list, along with additional historical context, I invite you to visit www.landshadows.com. There, you will find a full bibliography, archival materials, and insights into the real histories that shaped this novel.

As an educator, I also recognize the **instructional possibilities** within historical fiction. While *Land Shadows* naturally lends itself to discussions on westward expansion, indigenous land rights, and economic power structures, its educational value extends beyond history. **The novel is rich with STEM connections**, from the mathematics of ocean navigation aboard the *H.M.S. Badger* and *Sara* in Chapters 2 and 3, to the engineering challenges of 19th-century land surveying, the chemistry of mining operations, and the environmental science of land use and resource management. To support educators, I have developed **lesson plans, discussion questions, and curriculum resources across multiple disciplines**, all available on www.landshadows.com. I encourage teachers and students alike to explore these materials and use the novel as a tool for deeper engagement in history, science, mathematics, and beyond.

As with all historical fiction, *Land Shadows* is an interpretation, one that seeks to honor the past while engaging the present. I hope it inspires further exploration into the lives, struggles, and triumphs of those who came before us.

— R.J. Striegel

Recommended Reading

In writing Land Shadows, I consulted over 300 sources—enough to challenge even the most patient reader. For those interested in exploring further, a full list of references can be found at www.landshadows.com. Below are selected readings and sources that may be of particular interest.

Burr, B. G. (2016). *Historic Ranches of Northeastern New Mexico* (1st ed.). Arcadia.

Cooper, B. C. (2005). *Riding the transcontinental rails: overland travel on the Pacific Railroad, 1865 - 1881.* Polyglot Press.

Crampton, M. (2016). *Human Cargo: stories & songs of emigration, slavery and transportation.* Muddler Books.

Custalow, L., & Daniel, A. L. (2007). *The true story of Pocahontas: the other side of history: from the sacred history of the Mattaponi Reservation people.* Fulcrum Publishing.

DiGirolamo, V. (2019). *Crying the news: a history of America's Newsboys.* Oxford University Press.

Jordan-Bychkov, T. G. (1993). *North-American cattle-ranching frontiers: origins, diffusions and differentiation* (1st ed). University of New Mexico Press.

Laderman, G. (1996). *The sacred remains: American attitudes toward death 1799-1883.* Yale university press.

Lamar, H. R. (2000). *The far Southwest, 1846 - 1912: a territorial history* (Rev. ed). Univ. of New Mexico Press.

Montoya, M. E. (2005). *Translating property: the Maxwell land grant and the conflict over land in the American West, 1840 - 1900* (New ed.). University Press of Kansas.

Moore, M. (1990). *Los remedios: traditional herbal remedies of the Southwest.* Red Crane Books.

Murphy, L. R. (1972). *Philmont* (1st ed.). University of New Mexico Press.

Richards, E. (2022). *Patrick Sellar and the Highland Clearances: Homicide, Eviction and the Price of Progress.* Edinburgh University

Press.

Sleeper-Smith, S. (2001). *Indian women and French men: rethinking cultural encounter in the western Great Lakes*. University of Massachusetts Press.

Staller, K. M. (2020). *New York's Newsboys: Charles Loring Brace and the founding of the Children's Aid Society*. Oxford University Press, Incorporated.

Uncle Dick Wootton (1st ed.). (1890). W.E. Dibble & Co.

Vučković, M. (2008). *Voices from Haskell: Indian students between two worlds, 1884-1928*. University Press of Kansas.

Wootton, D., & Conard, H. L. (1980). *"Uncle Dick" Wootton, the pioneer frontiersman of the Rocky Mountain region: an account of the adventures and thrilling experiences of the most noted American hunter, trapper, guide, scout, and Indian fighter now living*. Time-Life Books.

Zimmer, S. (1999). *For good or bad: people of the Cimarron country* (1st ed.). Sunstone Press.

For more information on sources and a complete reference list, as well as supplementary educational content, please visit http://www.landshadows.com.

This Page Intentionally Left Blank